Valter Dos Santos

Butterflies in the Garden

A story of how true love travels through time

J.Bento Publishing house

Butterflies in the Garden – a story of how true love travels through time © Valter Dos Santos

English edition published worldwide by J.Bento Publishing House.

ISBN 978-0-9573302-7-6

Editor; Nick Jones – Full Media Ltd

Art cover by; James Willis, Spiffing Cover Design.

Paperback edition November 2013

Printed by Create Space Ltd

About *Butterflies in the Garden*

My first romance, *The Truth Never Dies*, had been released for only a few weeks when I arrived in Miami for my holidays. I was still feeling extremely excited and happy for having been able to launch the book in Europe and in the USA. I experienced that sort of feeling of accomplishment which takes over and makes us feel like a small kid again.

I remember when I was on the line at the immigration border at Miami International Airport, waiting to be seen by an immigration officer, a man in front of me started to talk. Like me, he was coming from England. He told me he had a finance job and as a hobby he played guitar and composed songs. According to him, every time he needed some inspiration he went to Miami, which he regarded as a well of inspiration and creativity. Right there, standing in that line, feeling half asleep, I looked at that man and thought, "Maybe it's time to be inspired again and write my second novel."

On the following day I was sitting by the pool when friends back in England began to text my cell phone. They were sending me the news that *The Truth Never Dies* had reached number one on the Amazon US best sellers list. I could not believe it. I got hold of my tablet and checked on the internet. It was true. My first ever romance had been read by thousands of people in America. I immediately knelt down, closed my eyes and thanked God for that blessing. At the same time I said, "God, if it is your wish for me to write another novel then please help me with the inspiration."

Well, I couldn't have received a better and stronger answer from God. On that night while I was in bed I went back in time. More precisely, back to the fifteenth century. I saw two women riding horses. They were running away from something or someone. I could feel their apprehension. Soon I saw men riding horses, galloping through a field. It didn't take long before they captured the two women who were fleeing. I saw those men capture them and torture them in the same horrific way as I describe in this book.

When the vision faded away I was sitting on my bed. I had sweat running down my entire body. I felt those two women's despair and fear. I could smell the breeze of that night in the woods back in the fifteenth century. It was the inspiration I had earlier asked God for. During that holiday week in Miami I remember seeing horses everywhere. I saw horses in advertisement pictures in magazines. I saw horses as part of decorations in stores and in people's T-shirt prints. By the end of that week in Miami I had no doubt. I had to write about the story of those two ladies.

I DEDICATE THIS BOOK TO EVERYONE WHO HAS EXPERIENCED THE 'LOSS' OF A LOVED ONE.

BELIEVE AND KEEP THE FAITH THAT OUR LIVES DON'T END WITH THE DEATH OF THE PHYSICAL BODY. AS SPIRITS WE LIVE FOREVER.

THANKS TO:

Thanks to my father for being there for me and my sister Luciana when my mother passed away, and for going beyond his nervous and emotional limits in order to raise two small children. Dad, your unconditional love for us will live forever in my heart.

Thanks to my partner for all of the love and care. Thanks for supporting me and helping me to become a better human being.

Thanks to the butterflies sent by God down to me to help me through the darkest moments of my life: Marcia De Iasi, Fernada Lofiego, Marcelo Amaral. You three stood by me, saved me many times and brightened my way through those darkest moments, helping me to find many reasons to keep the faith. I will be eternally grateful to you.

Thanks to all the other beautiful and colourful butterflies who many times comforted my heart and my soul: Dona Madalena Nunes, Isabel Pereira Michelao, Erica Rodriguez, Jucelia, Luana Bin, Gisela Lorencao, Fernando and Joelma de Lucia, Iassana Mulrooney And Sandra Avila.

Thanks to all my beloved grandparents for giving me so much love and care: Francisca, Benedito, Dedeka, Dedeko, Joaquim and Geraldina.

Thanks to all those who inspired me and motivated me to continue with my dream of writing: Lucie Wood (this book is also dedicated to you), Bernard Sharp, Tracie Roberts, Amir Azadeoglu, Daniela Stoyanova, Liam Nolan, Ed Underhill, Steven Davies and Samira El Bakri, .

Thanks to three very special and beloved butterflies: Auntie Guiomar and my cousins Sandra and Leo.

And last but not least, thanks to my dearest sisters and the love of my life: Luciana and Mariane. Love you always.

BUTTERFLIES IN THE GARDEN

Prologue

The Kingdom of Navarre, the successor of the Kingdom of Pamplona, was a European medieval kingdom which occupied lands on either side of the Pyrenees, alongside the Atlantic Ocean between present-day Spain and France.

Navarre Kingdom. Winter, early years of the fifteenth century.

On a cold night, two women were riding horses. They were running away. Both ladies had long, dark hair and looked very similar apart from the noticeable age difference, as one appeared to be more mature than the other. Both were dressed in long gowns. They rode very fast, and were now a few miles away from the bridge that linked the village to France and headed towards the forest. The cold November night was very dark. Once they reached the interior of the forest, the young lady who was leading the way shouted to her horse.

"Go Asas, go!" she said, stroking the horse at the same time as urging him to go faster. Her hair was flying with the wind and her face was full of braveness and determination. She checked the other lady, who was not far behind, to ensure she was keeping up, and continued riding fast through the forest.

Suddenly noises of horses approaching could be heard. Far behind, torches could be seen amongst the trees. The young lady continued to stroke her horse and prayed in silence, hoping for a successful escape. She pulled the necklace of her gown and, getting hold of the pendant with the image of the Virgin Mary, she took it up to her lips and kissed it. *'Oh Virgin Mary, I don't care what happens to my life but please look after my mother. She doesn't deserve anything bad to happen to her. I beg for your protection,'* she prayed in silence. Suddenly her prayer was interrupted by the loud noise of men approaching on their horses.

"I can hear them getting close to us!" shouted the older lady. "They are going to catch us!" She made her horse stop and stayed still.

"What are you doing? They are coming! We need to go faster, otherwise they'll catch us!" said the young lady, stopping her own horse so that it faced her mother's. She made a sign with her head and said, "Come on Mama, let's run."

"No. I am not going anywhere. I can still save you. You go. Run, my daughter, run!"

"What are you saying? I'm not going anywhere without you, Mama. Come on, let's go."

"If I stay they will catch me and that will give you time to escape."

Suddenly the noise of horses and men approaching became louder. They were swearing loudly at the two women, saying things such as "You'll regret running away, you witches."

"We don't stand a chance, daughter. Their horses are much faster and they will end up catching us. I will stay and surrender. Go and get out of here. Go to France and find my sisters. There you will be safe," said the older lady with tears in her eyes. "Go, you are young and still have a chance to escape this curse. Don't worry about me."

But before Carmen could say anything they found themselves surrounded by the men, who were holding lances and torches. They all had long golden chains with crucifixes around their necks.

"We've got you," said one of the men. Pointing his spear at them, he ordered, "Get down off your horses now!"

Six other men approached the two ladies and dragged them down from their horses. Two of them took hold of the ladies and tied their hands with extreme force. They dragged them both away from their horses and laughed with bitter sarcasm. One of the men took his crucifix and kissed it before slapping the young lady in the face.

"We are not Jewish, neither are we witches. Please let us go," begged the young lady's mother, "Please!"

"There's no salvation for you two. You are both going to the stake!" replied the man.

"Now you two, watch what we are going to do with your horses," said the leader, who was still mounted on his own steed, pointing his spear at the ladies' horses with evil in his eyes.

Both the animals got agitated, as if they were feeling the evil energy directed at them. Four men moved closer to the horses and, holding their long swords, they waited for more instructions.

"Please don't do anything to our horses. Let them go," begged the young lady. "I beg you, leave the horses in peace."

The leader of the band replied, holding his crucifix, "They carry the same evil as you do. They are bewitched and we must kill them as we are going to kill you." He laughed loudly, lifted his spear up in the air and ordered, "Fellows, in the name of the father, the son and the holy ghost, I command you to kill the bewitched animals which have been serving Lucifer!"

The young lady tried to reach for the horses but she was immediately pushed away by one of the men, and fell on the grass. She was followed by her mother who had been pushed by the same man.

The four men lifted their long swords and, with extreme violence, they struck the legs of the mother's horse, who gave out a deafening shriek of pain and fell flat on the ground in agony. Both daughter and mother were horrified. The men smiled, watching the horse writhing in torment on the ground, and made a joke out of the young lady's horse, who had become agitated with panic.

"Don't worry, big boy, you'll soon be joining your friend in hell," said one of the men holding the swords.

The four men lifted their swords again, this time to hit the young lady's horse, Asas. She screamed while watching the men strike the animal's legs. Asas fell on top of the other horse and both of them cried, making horrifyingly loud noises which could be heard from miles away. The agonised creatures were squirming and hitting each other's heads while their blood formed a pool on the ground.

"Asas!" she shouted in horror. "My boy…Oh my boy!" she screamed, looking at the inquisitors with tears rolling down her face. "You are not human, you are monsters. You are not serving God but your corrupted church."

The men were positioning themselves to hit the animals in order to finally kill them but were stopped by their leader.

"No! Don't use your swords." He looked at both women and gave them a cynical smile. Using a very cold tone of voice he told the men, "We will burn them alive!"

The men went around collecting trunks and tree branches and surrounded the horses with piles of wood in order to create a bonfire. The ladies were crying loudly and the animals screeching in agony. Within minutes the men had put trunks and wood around the horses and set them on fire. The leader said, with pleasure in his voice, "Watch your animals burning and feel their pain and their agony. It's a very slow death and it's exactly the same death you two will soon face."

PART I

Chapter The long weekend trip

Asheville, North Carolina, USA.

Roy and Linda were going away to the Great Smoky Mountains for the weekend, and were leaving their five-year-old daughter Katie with Linda's parents, who had agreed to look after her. Roy was a very tall and handsome man, with dark hair and deep blue eyes. Ever since he became a teenager he had attracted the attention of many women because of his extremely good looks. He was originally from England and had moved to the US after the death of his parents when he was still young. He was brought to the US by some relatives who lived in America and, out of compassion for his early orphanage, decided to take care of him. Years later, when he graduated from High School, he moved to North Carolina to continue his studies at the University of North Carolina, where he met Linda. Roy graduated in finance and economics and found a job at a subsidiary of an international bank. Linda and Roy were married, and one year later their baby daughter Katie arrived. Very ambitious and efficient at his work, Roy reached a senior position within the bank at a very young age. Because of his responsibilities he worked long hours, and also had to travel outside North Carolina for business meetings, staying away from home most of the time.

 Linda was also a very beautiful woman, with honey blonde hair and blue eyes - a lighter shade of blue than Roy's. She had a small figure and a certain fragile and innocent way about her. Linda was a primary school teacher but had left work to be a full-time mother and look after their daughter. Since her marriage she had embraced the housewife role with great care and pride, and dedicated her entire life to looking after her daughter and husband.

"I'm so excited about this trip, my darling," said Linda to her husband.

Roy seemed to be very impatient, walking in circles around the living room. This was going to be the first time since his daughter Katie had been born five years ago that he and his wife were going away to spend time on their own.

"Mommy, mommy!" screamed Katie, who was running down the stairs to join her parents.

Linda knelt down on the living room floor and hugged her daughter. "Oh my little sunshine, this weekend grandpa Joey and grandma Elizabeth will be with you, as I explained before."

"But I want to go with you and daddy."

"What about grandpa and grandma? They are here to spend time with you. Are you going to leave them here by themselves?" asked Linda, looking into her daughter's eyes. "Don't you love them a lot?"

"Yes…but…"

"So, they will be sad if you say you don't want to stay with them. It's going to be fun." Linda fixed her daughter's hair and continued, "Grandma said she will bake cookies with you. Think; you two baking cookies and cakes just as you like to do with grandma." The conversation was interrupted by the sound of a car pulling up outside the house.

Roy went to the porch to welcome his in-laws. Linda and Katie went after him and each beamed a wide smile when they saw them in the car.

"Where's my little girl?" said Linda's mother Elizabeth as she left the car. She opened her arms to Katie and gave her a big smile.

Katie ran towards her and hugged her, saying excitedly, "Grandma! Mom said we'll bake cookies and cakes!"

Linda gave her mother a wink and Elizabeth replied to Katie, "Yes we will! And we'll play with the dolls and play all of our favourite games in the garden. We'll have lots of fun together."

Roy greeted his father-in-law Joey and helped him with their suitcases.

"Thanks for coming, Joey," said Roy, shaking Joey's hand. "I know this was a bit of a last minute call. We appreciate your help, looking after Katie while we're away."

Joey didn't reply to Roy. He simply nodded. Linda's parents had never got too close to Roy. They believed their daughter was too young to marry and that perhaps Roy was far too immature for Linda. Elizabeth held her granddaughter's hand and went inside with her. Linda was Elizabeth and Joey's only daughter and they were very caring and protective towards her. Katie was pretty much similar to her mother; she was blonde with bright big blue eyes and very kind and gentle.

"Hi Dad," said Linda in her usual kind and loving way. She kissed him on his cheek and said, "It's so nice to see you. Thanks for coming. Roy and I really needed this time together."

"Anything for you, my daughter. Anything for you, my angel," said Joey, smiling.

Roy looked at his watch and said, "Come on Linda, let's hurry. Get ready while I load the car. I want to avoid the traffic on the highway."

"I'm ready. Let me just kiss Katie goodbye and I'll be right back."

"Come on Linda, we're going to be back on Sunday afternoon. You make such a drama about everything. It looks like you'll never see her again. We're only going for three days; come on, chop chop!"

Linda went back inside and found her daughter in the kitchen with her mother. Elizabeth was going through the cupboards, finding ingredients for their baking, and Katie was next to her grandmother, talking non-stop. Linda watched them both for a moment, admiring her daughter, and then said, "Sweetheart, mom is going now."

Mother and daughter hugged each other. Katie kissed her mother all over her face, said "I love you mommy" several times and then finally asked, while holding her mother's hair, "Are you going to be late, mom?"

"There is no way I am going to be a minute late on Sunday afternoon. Mom and dad will be back just in time to tuck you into bed and read your favourite bedtime story. Now it's time for you to go and have some fun with your grandparents. Dad and I will be back very soon." She took hold of her daughter's hands and said, "Be nice to your grandparents. Don't make too much of a mess."

"I will be very good, mom, I promise."

"I know you will. You are my little princess, aren't you?"

They both smiled and hugged again.

"Linda, come on," said Roy, who had come into the kitchen to fetch her. He knelt down and kissed his daughter. "We'll be back very soon, honey," he said.

Linda hugged her daughter for the last time and, giving her a long kiss, she said, "Never forget that mom loves you. Always."

They both got in the car and waved goodbye to Elizabeth, Joey and their daughter, who were also waving from the porch. Suddenly Katie shouted, pointing at a yellow butterfly that was flying around the porch, "Mom, mom... Look, it's a butterfly!"

From inside the car Linda smiled at Katie and replied, "I can see, darling and it's a beautiful one. I sent her to be with you for the weekend. When you miss me, look at the butterflies and when you see one it will mean that I will be there with you. And when I see butterflies I will also think of you, and you will be there with me. Is that a deal?"

Katie replied "It's a deal. I love you, mom!"

When the car started to move, Linda shouted, "Love you always, sweetheart! When you miss me, just watch for the butterflies. Bye mom, bye father!" And they left. Linda looked backwards after a few moments and she realised her parents and daughter had gone back inside. She looked at the house and felt quite nostalgic as she watched the distance growing, making the house look smaller and smaller. She admired the neighbourhood with its gardens and tall, green trees, and a tear came to her eye.

"Why are you so emotional, Linda? We're only going for a long weekend," asked Roy, laughing and making fun of her.

"I don't know, Roy. I simply am." Linda switched the radio on and tried to find a station playing music that would snap her out of her mood.

"*Carolina in my mind* is on!" exclaimed Linda.

"Oh Linda, come on... James Taylor? Talk about being emotional," said Roy, laughing. "Soon you'll be feeling like cutting your wrists."

"Oh Roy, you know I'm a big fan."

Roy jokingly did an impression of James Taylor, saying some of his singles titles. "Oh my Sweet Baby James, I could be a One Man Dog and a Walking Man, perhaps a Gorilla and still know that you are James Taylor's biggest fan."

"See, you know all of his records' names! That means you're a big fan too," said Linda, laughing.

"I guess you didn't give me any choice."

They both laughed and continued their trip towards the Great Smoky Mountain Park with James Taylor's *Carolina in my mind* playing in the background. It was a warm and sunny day of early summer. Roy put the car roof down and let the wind blow. The road was clear and they were surrounded by the stunning nature of North Carolina.

Far away from there, at a spiritual colony called Lunas, there was a spirit named Geraldine, who had the appearance of a mature lady with brown hair and blue eyes. She was engrossed with gardening, and talked to the roses while preparing the soil to plant more seeds. It was a small garden, but filled with very colourful flowers. There were hummingbirds in the air drinking the nectar of the flowers, and many other birds and butterflies all around, attracted by a very pleasant smell in the air. Next to the lady were two puppies playing with each other and rolling all over the grass.

"Hey, you two, be careful with my roses!" said Geraldine to the two puppies. She blew a kiss to the roses and continued, "These beauties here are very delicate and sensitive, aren't you my darlings?"

"Geraldine, it's time," said a lady who appeared in the garden suddenly, catching Geraldine by surprise.

Geraldine fell backwards on the grass, dropping her gardening tools on the ground. "For God's sake, Teresa, you scared me, coming out of nowhere!" she said, smiling. She picked up her tools from the ground, stood up and cleaned her apron, shaking off the soil.

"It's time, my sister. Linda, Roy and Katie, they need us," said Teresa, who was looking concerned.

"Oh…I see…" Geraldine looked down and went pensive for a while. She seemed to be a little upset when she asked, "It's gone so fast…Are you sure it's…"

Teresa didn't let her finish her sentence and said, "Come on sister, keep the faith. We have a mission, remember? We will help them all to get through this." She lifted Geraldine's head gently with her right hand and said, "Life presents us with the obstacles so we can learn from them and progress."

Geraldine held her head up high and, taking a long breath, she said, "You are right. It is going to be very difficult indeed but… we will make it through this."

Teresa smiled at her sister and then told her the plans for the upcoming events on Earth.

Chapter The passage

Back on Earth, it was a beautiful summer night with no clouds in the sky and many stars enhancing the nocturnal beauty. Linda and Roy were lying down on the grass, side by side, watching the stars in the sky.

"It's been so nice to spend this time with you, Roy. We should do this more often," said Linda.

They were holding hands and feeling the fresh breeze of the night run through their bodies. Next to them there was a tent which they had brought to spend the weekend in, and not far away was a bonfire that Roy had built earlier that evening. The sound of crickets and owls in the background gave them company and helped to make the moment even more magical.

"Work has been so hectic in the past few years. It's not been easy to balance work and personal life. I'm sorry, only now I can see how distant from each other we've become. I'm never at home and these past two days have shown me again…" Roy paused for an instant. He stroked Linda's hair, kissed her on her lips and then continued, "These past two days have shown me again how much I love you!"

They gave each other a long and passionate kiss and made love under the stars.

****

The following morning Linda and Roy woke up embracing each other and feeling the fresh breeze of the morning. They watched the sun rising through the trees and in between the mountains, brightening the lagoon and bringing a new day. Carried away by that beautiful view, they kissed and made love.

During that weekend they experienced moments of love they hadn't known for a long time. Linda usually spent most of her time at home looking after Katie, and she missed her husband dearly. When Roy proposed that weekend camping trip in the mountains, she felt happy to know they were going to spend some time together after so many years of her husband focusing so hard on work.

They prepared some breakfast and, after eating, they swam in the lagoon and played in the water as if they were two teenagers who had just fallen in love for the first time and were just happy to have a lot of fun.

Later that day, after undoing the tent and packing all their belongings, Roy fixed the last bags at the back of the car and said to Linda, "We're all packed, darling. It's time to go back home." He pulled Linda close to him and, crossing his arms around her waist and embracing her tightly against his body, he asked, "Did you enjoy your weekend?"

" Hmm…Nope," said Linda, shaking her head and giggling.

Smiling, Roy asked her, "What? You didn't enjoy our time together?"

"I didn't just enjoy it…I loved it. I loved every second of it!"

Roy kissed her and squeezed her even more tightly against his body. They remained embraced for moments, enjoying the feeling of their bodies touching. Their moment was spoiled by a sudden strong wind which was bringing a smell of dust to the air, followed by a cold wind announcing a summer storm approaching. The sunny blue sky rapidly turned cloudy and was quickly filling with very dark clouds.

"We'd better head back before this storm reaches us," said Roy.

They got inside the car just in time as the first drops of rain started. Thunder could be heard. Even though Roy drove quickly, trying to escape the storm, it ended up reaching them when they were on the highway, and became very heavy within just a few minutes. Roy and Linda were very apprehensive. The only noise inside the car was the tape playing James Taylor. Outside, the lightning and thunder increased in intensity by the minute, making horrible sounds. Roy was focusing on the highway, paying extra attention to his driving. Linda suddenly felt shivers down her spine and was affected by a strange feeling. They both felt immense pressure on their chests, and enormous tension was in the air. Linda shed a tear which contained a mix of feelings. Her heart was beating even faster and cold sweat rolled down from her forehead. Roy grabbed Linda's hand with his right hand and squeezed tight. Lifting her hand, he pulled it next to his lips and kissed it.

The inside of the windscreen went blurry because of the torrential storm. Linda unfastened her seat belt so she could reach for a box of tissues to clean the windscreen, but at the same moment a deer ran on to the highway, forcing Roy to make a quick turn to avoid it. The car, moving at high speed, skidded out of control. Roy extended his right arm across Linda's body to try and protect her, but at the same time he completely lost control of the car, which rolled over several times, going off the highway and smashing against the trees. Linda's body was ejected through the windscreen, falling a short distance away. Roy remained inside the car, which finished upside down between two trees.

 Teresa, Geraldine and another three of their spiritual friends, who worked as rescuers, were there to assist the two souls involved in the accident. Five of them were surrounding the scene, forming a circle, and the energy generated an immense bright light which was invisible to human eyes but possible to see from very high up in the sky. The spirits were silent, praying for the two souls involved in the car accident. On one side was Roy, inside the car, unconscious and bleeding heavily, while on the other side was Linda's body, lying on the ground covered in mud and blood. She had suffered major injuries and was about to die. Teresa and Geraldine approached her body and stayed next to her. With hands held up and their palms facing down, they prayed for Linda. Within minutes the fluidic laces that bonded Linda's soul to her corporeal body were broken, setting her spirit free again. Feeling very confused, Linda looked around and saw Teresa, Geraldine and the other spirits staring at her. Linda looked at the car and, noticing that Roy was inside and that he was covered in blood, she screamed in horror, asking for help. She spoke to him and tried to wake him up but Roy was completely unconscious.

"Come on Roy, wake up please!" she begged in agony. At that point Linda turned around to search for help, and it was then that she saw her own body which was lying down on the grass, covered in mud and blood under the heavy storm that continued to pour down.

"What's happening?" she shouted, feeling horrified, and fell down on the ground unconscious. Teresa ran towards her and quickly picked her spirit up and held her in her arms delicately, as if she was holding a baby. She then carefully handed her to one of the other spiritual friends who took her in his arms. The spirit carrying Linda became illuminated by a very bright blue light that increased its intensity and brightened everything around until he left the Earth, taking Linda to a hospital for debilitated spirits in the spiritual world.

After their spiritual friend and Linda had gone, Teresa and Geraldine approached the car where Roy was stuck and managed to contact his soul. Roy's body had bad injuries and was severely bleeding. His soul had departed from his body but the fluid laces were still strong, bonding his soul and his physical form together. Looking at Geraldine and the other two friends, Teresa said, "We are going to have to take his soul to a spiritual hospital near the Earth to recover from its wounds. His corporeal body is very delicate at the moment and it's not able to host his soul. Our doctors at the hospital will be able to heal the wounds and prepare him for the difficult reality when his soul returns to his corporeal body."

The other two spirits took up Roy's soul very gently and carried him to a spiritual hospital near the Earth; a recovery hospital for souls which had had their corporeal bodies injured and needed spiritual assistance.

The storm was still heavy, with thunder booming and lightning striking in the area. Teresa and Geraldine looked at both bodies: Linda's, lying metres away from the car and Roy's, inside the vehicle. Before they left they needed to ensure Roy was found so his body could be taken to the hospital to receive treatment. They thought quickly of a plan to find someone who could come and rescue his body, and immediately they were inspired by enlightened spirits with the idea. Teresa picked up the information that there was a family inside a car parked not too far from the accident scene. The family were on their way back home, coming from the mountains, and had stopped to wait for the storm to subside. Teresa and Geraldine left the accident scene and arrived within the same instant where the car was. They saw the family inside the car and realised it was a man with his wife and three children. Teresa projected herself inside the car in between the man and his wife, and, getting close to the man, she sent him inspiring thoughts, guiding him to go back to the highway and continue the journey. Even though the man could neither see nor hear Teresa or Geraldine, he followed his intuition - which was nothing but his soul connecting with Teresa's thoughts - starting the car engine and returning to the highway.

"What are you doing, James?" asked his wife. "It's pouring down. I thought we'd decided to stay here until the storm got calmer."

The man seemed to be in a trance and didn't reply to his wife. His soul, following Teresa's guidance and inspiration, drove miles under the heavy storm. When he approached the accident scene he saw a brilliant light that obfuscated his vision. Geraldine, who had returned to the location where Roy and Linda's bodies were, was emanating a very bright light in order to get his attention. Her plan worked, and the man stopped his car to follow the light. Still in a sort of trance guided by Teresa, he left the car, following the light given out by Geraldine, and soon found Roy's car upside down.

"Roy will be fine now, Geraldine. This man will find a way to call the paramedics and Roy's body will be taken to a hospital where it will receive the assistance needed and be treated. Once his corporeal body recovers, his soul will then be able to return and his body will wake up from the coma."

"Yes, let's go and see our Katie now. She will need our support," replied Geraldine.

They held hands and disappeared into the air, reappearing in the same instant at Roy and Linda's house. They arrived in Katie's bedroom and found Katie with her grandmother Elizabeth, playing with her dolls. Teresa and Geraldine lifted their arms in the air, held their hands positioned in the direction of Elizabeth and Katie's heads and prayed for them, sending vibrations of encouragement.

The storm had reached Asheville and it was very heavy. Elizabeth was getting very apprehensive, feeling nausea and dizziness. She stood up and looked out of the window. *'They should have been here by now… I hope Roy has stopped the car and isn't driving in this weather,'* she thought, with her intuition telling her something was wrong.

"I feel for them, Teresa," said Geraldine, still with her hands held up in the air transmitting vibrations of encouragement. "They are about to receive such sad news."

"Don't tune your thoughts into negative and depressive thoughts, my sister. Keep on thinking positively so you can continue to transmit vibrations of love and encouragement to them. Focus on the love we feel for them all and our love will help them to get through this. Don't forget that love can heal any wound."

A few hours later they heard a knock on the door. Elizabeth left Katie playing in her bedroom with her dolls and went down to see who it was. When she was halfway down the stairs she saw Sheriff Russell standing at the door with her husband. The sheriff looked pale and very sad. He took his hat off and held it against his chest.

"Please come on in, Sheriff. What brought you here in the middle of this horrible storm?" asked Joey, pointing him towards the living room.

"Mr Cooper, Mrs Cooper... I'm sorry but I bring bad news." He paused for a few moments and after taking a long breath he continued. "It's about your daughter Linda and her husband Roy." He took another long breath and said, "I am so sorry to say this...They had a car crash... We still don't know what happened exactly and all we know for now is that the car rolled over..." - he cleared his throat - "it could be because of the storm...or..."

"I'm in agony, Sheriff. Please tell us what happened to our daughter," said Elizabeth, running fast down the stairs, looking desperate. She had both hands running through her hair.

He continued, still looking very awkward. "When we got to the scene we found the car upside down."

Elizabeth cried out loudly in horror and Joey embraced her tightly. Sheriff Russell continued, "Roy has been taken to the Saint Martin hospital. He is in a coma and...

and…" He looked down before he delivered the news. "Your daughter Linda was dead when we found them. I am so sorry."

"No!" screamed Elizabeth. "No! Not my daughter… my little daughter," she cried non-stop.

Teresa and Geraldine arrived in the living room and were joined by more of their spiritual friends. They all started to pray, creating an invisible bright light which brightened the entire house, aiming to comfort the hearts of the two parents. Sheriff Russell apologised again and explained that Roy was at the hospital in intensive care and he didn't have much chance of survival. He added that the doctors said he would only survive by a miracle, as his injuries were very bad. He offered all his help and support before leaving the house.

Elizabeth and Joey stayed there, immobile and speechless, each engaged with their own deep sorrow of losing their daughter Linda, who had gone at the early age of twenty-seven. Their silence was broken by Katie who had come to the top of the stairs searching for them.

"Have mom and dad arrived yet?" asked Katie, excitedly coming down the stairs and looking around the room.

Elizabeth couldn't reply. She had tears rolling down her face and could barely speak. She didn't want Katie to see her crying so she covered her face and went to the kitchen, being careful that Katie didn't notice anything.

Joey held back his tears and replied, "No, my dear." He held Katie's hand and, using an extra soft tone of voice, he said, "They won't come back today." He held her hand firmly. "Why don't you go back upstairs to your bedroom and wait for grandpa. I'll help you to build a tent for you to play with your dolls."

Katie ran back to her bedroom, excited about playing with her granddad and not aware that her life had just completely changed. Later in the evening, Joey went to the hospital to check on Roy, and Elizabeth tried her best not to cry in front of her granddaughter. When Joey came back late that evening, he found Katie already sleeping and Elizabeth sitting on a chair in the garden, crying and staring at the stars in the sky. Joey brought a chair next to his wife and hugged her. They both spent a long time embraced, crying, thinking of their daughter.

When they had both finally stopped crying, Elizabeth looked again at the stars and asked Joey with a broken voice, "Do you think she is somewhere up there?"

"Yes I do, my dear. I do believe she is there somewhere amongst the stars. Let's not lose our faith and remember what we believe: Our bodies die but our spirits live forever. One day we will reunite with her…and our faith will keep us stronger in our journey here."

"You're right. I try and try to think our daughter isn't dead but alive in a different world, but gosh I miss her…and I know I will always miss her deeply."

"We will…we will. But every time we think of her we need to remember our happy moments together and send her our love, and I'm sure she will feel our love wherever she might be." Joey waited a moment and then shared the news that Roy was in a coma and that the doctors were doing everything they could to bring him back to life. Together they decided not to say anything about Linda to Katie until they had more news on Roy's condition. Both continued staring at the sky as if trying to see their daughter's face in one of the stars above.

"Shall we go, Teresa? I want to see how they are doing," said Geraldine, with her eyes fixed on Elizabeth and Joey.

Teresa showed some sort of sadness when she replied, "Let's go. Linda should be asleep for a while - that's what usually happens - so let's go and visit Roy first."

They prayed one more time with their hands in the direction of Joey and Elizabeth, and left the Earth.

Chapter Waking up to a new reality

Three days later, Elizabeth and Joey were at the hospital when Roy came out of his coma. Both were looking visibly drained and tired. When Roy opened his eyes for the first time he saw Elizabeth and Joey next to him.

"Where am I…?" asked Roy, looking confused, with a fragile tone of voice.

"You're at the hospital, Roy," replied Elizabeth.

Roy put his hand on his forehead and a feeling of panic overcame him as flashback scenes of the accident started to appear in his mind. Suddenly everything became clear: the last kiss, the storm approaching, the lightning and thunder and heavy rain on the motorway; it all came back to him. Like watching a speeded-up movie going through his mind, he remembered Linda trying to reach out for the box of tissues, the deer jumping on to the motorway and finally the car rolling over.

"Oh my God!" exclaimed Roy in panic. "Linda!" He tried to get up from his bed but was stopped by Elizabeth.

"Calm down. You are badly hurt," said Elizabeth, putting her hand against his chest gently. "You suffered many injuries, Roy."

"How's Linda? Where is she?" asked Roy in panic.

Elizabeth and Joey went silent, unable to reply to him. Elizabeth shed a tear in front of Roy and left the room crying.

"Where is she, Joey? I need to see her…please tell me, where is she? She is okay, right?" begged Roy who was shaking and in panic.

Joey took a long breath and closed his eyes. After a few moments he replied, "Linda's dead, Roy. She didn't make it… Our Linda died there in the accident."

"No…no…Not Linda. It's not possible… Please don't say that." Roy couldn't stop crying. He closed his eyes and screamed out loud, swearing and asking, "Why, God? Why you didn't kill me instead of her?"

"Calm down, Roy. I know it's hard but you have to be strong for Katie," said Joey while drying the tears on his own face. Once he had stopped crying he looked again at Roy and said, "Katie doesn't know anything. Elizabeth and I couldn't find the courage to tell her. God knows how hard it's been for me and Elizabeth…we lost our daughter, we lost our everything, but we are trying to find strength so that we can support Katie."

"How long have I been in here for?"

"Three and a half days. The doctors had said that you were only going to survive by a miracle and when we thought you wouldn't make it you surprised everyone; on the second day you started to show signs of recovery. Elizabeth and I decided to wait for you so we could plan together how to talk to Katie and tell her what happened."

Roy was speechless, just gazing at the ceiling. Tears were running down his face non-stop.

"I'll go now and check on Elizabeth. She hasn't been well since the news and I'm worried about her. I guess you need some space too." Joey picked up Elizabeth's bag that she had left on the armchair next to Roy's bed and he said before leaving, "I'll be back later, Roy. I know it's difficult but we must plan how we are going to deliver the news to our little Katie."

In that hospital bed Roy went through in his mind his last moments with Linda over and over many times. Sometimes crying, at other times feeling anger against life and God. He imagined several different scenarios for the accident, and an immense feeling of guilt overcame him. Teresa and Geraldine and his parents, who had passed away a few years ago, were there next to him at the hospital. He couldn't see them but they were there, sending him thoughts of tranquillity and courage to face the new lessons that life was putting him through. They also transmitted thoughts with the image of Katie so he could think of his daughter, and focus and find again the motivation to live. He fell asleep as soon as Teresa and the other spiritual friends in the room started to pray for him.

****

Linda woke up after spending a few days asleep at the recovery hospital in a spiritual zone. She felt very light and very peaceful. She looked around and saw Teresa and Geraldine next to her. They were both smiling, excited at her return home.

Linda sat on the bed where she was lying and after giving a brief look around the room she asked, "Am I back, then?"

"Yes dear, you returned to the spiritual world which is now your home. You left Earth only a few days ago," replied Teresa.

Linda had been asleep at the hospital since the car crash, so that her spirit would heal properly. Her spirit had been put to sleep, as was the normal practice. The most common scenario is that all the pain and sadness felt by the family and friends of those who departed the Earth are transmitted to the spirits, affecting their recovery and adjustment to their new condition. In order to avoid the negative vibrations transmitted to the spirits who had just returned to the spiritual world from their loved ones on Earth upon the news of their corporeal death, most spirits are put to sleep for a while until the level of negative and depressive vibrations surrounding them decreases. However, this depends on the evolutionary level of the spirit; more enlightened and purified spirits don't need to go through this process and make an immediate transition from Earth to the spiritual world. Linda, who was an enlightened spirit, didn't stay asleep for too long since she already had a good knowledge of the spiritual life. She knew how to block the negative energy and depressive vibrations and filter them, transforming them and sending them back to the universe as vibrations of harmony and positivity.

Linda embraced Teresa and Geraldine, giving them a long and tender hug. She felt a strong pain as she could feel and even hear the cry of her mother coming from the Earth. The picture of her mother Elizabeth, crying in the kitchen, thinking of her, came into her head. Before that picture began to affect her, she focused within herself and sent her mother vibrations containing her love. After a long moment in silence she said to Teresa and Geraldine, "I missed you both. I missed you two so much. Thanks for all of your support." She looked through the window, watching the green fields covered by lavender flowers outside the hospital with some sadness in her eyes.

"Oh my dear… We can sense that you're sad. Everything will be fine. Don't forget our plans. We knew it would be like this," said Teresa, giving her another hug. "Continue to filter their sorrow and their sadness. Send it back to them as love and harmony."

Linda gave a shy smile. Geraldine gently touched her face and said, "The good news is that you are ready to leave the hospital. We can go to Lunas now."

Linda had an angelic face. Her honey blonde hair had a special shine and her material clothes, no longer needed in the spiritual world, were replaced by a white dress covered with floral prints, made from the same fluidic material as most things in the spiritual colony. She had a bright and sparkling light - which can be found in all the most elevated spirits - and she was looking as vivid and shiny as Teresa and Geraldine.

The three left the hospital and walked outside into the field. Linda took a long breath to inhale the pure air of the spiritual world. She knelt down to the ground and touched the lavender flowers, smelling the fresh fragrance coming from them. Closing her eyes, she thought of her mother, who was still in the kitchen, feeling very upset. "Please God, allow the wind of the universe to deliver this gorgeous fresh fragrance to my mother Elizabeth on Earth, so that the fresh smell of the lavender may bring her peace of mind and tranquillity. May this fresh smell of lavender remind her that our spirits live forever and that I am here thinking of her," she prayed. Immediately that fresh fragrance travelled the universe and reached the kitchen where Elizabeth was. As per Linda's wish, at the moment Elizabeth smelled the fragrance of lavender she thought of her daughter with happiness and felt comfort in her heart.

Once Linda realised her mother was feeling better and had stopped crying, she got up and held Teresa's hand. The three left the Hospital and travelled at the speed of light, heading to Lunas. They arrived within less than half a second inside Geraldine's house where Geraldine's two puppies were waiting for them. The pets got very excited when they saw the three of them come into the room. Geraldine had inhabited the same spiritual colony where Linda now lived before she reincarnated for her latest experience on Earth. This colony was named Lunas because of the three nearby moons which were permanently visible, from anywhere in the colony, to all its inhabitants. Linda and Teresa sat down on the sofa while Geraldine went inside the house to prepare a revitalising fluidic juice for Linda.

Linda was still feeling sad about her departure when she said to Teresa, "It's so difficult to leave just now. It feels so early. Katie's only a little kid and Roy…" She stopped for a moment and then continued, "I don't think Roy is ready for what's about to come. I don't think he's ready to give Katie all the care and love she needs as a child."

"He might not be ready, my dear, but that's life. He needs to face it as we all do," said Teresa with a certain authority in her tone, but still sounding serene. "Obstacles are evolution knocking at our door; they are like exams that we all have to face and pass in order to progress."

Geraldine walked back into the room holding a jar and a glass. The jar contained the revitalising fluidic juice prepared by her using a mixture of ingredients unknown on Earth but very popular in the spiritual colonies. She poured a full glass for Linda and kindly told her to drink in order to boost her energies. Linda took the glass and drank the full contents.

Teresa continued, "It's their time to go through this together and they will grow from this experience. This is part of their mission, remember? We have all done our part in this and now it's up to them." She held Linda's hand and said carefully, "Soon Roy will deliver the news to Katie. It won't be easy, Linda, but we thought you would like to be there with them when he tells her what happened, and perhaps you can help by transmitting vibrations of love and encouragement for both of them."

"I don't know if I can keep control of my emotions. I think I'll end up making them even more upset if I send out the sad vibration I have right now." Linda looked at both Geraldine and Teresa, and after a brief pause to think she continued, "Perhaps I'm being selfish. It's not time to think of my feelings, but to realise that they need me now. I've got to go there and be by their side to ensure they feel loved and know that they have to carry on."

Teresa and Geraldine smiled and said together, "We will be there with you at all times."

Chapter A little girl's broken heart

Back on Earth, Roy left the hospital one day before Linda's funeral. He had agreed with Elizabeth and Joey that he was the one to deliver the news to Katie, so they respected his wish and waited for him to leave the hospital and talk to her.

When Katie heard the noise of Joey's car approaching outside the house, bringing Roy back home, she ran happily to the car to meet with her father. "Dad, you're back!"

Roy got out of the car and went down on his knees. Face to face with Katie, he gave her a tight hug. He stroked her hair and even though he tried hard to hold his feelings he shed a tear which he quickly wiped away before Katie could notice.

"Where's mommy? You came back together, right?" asked Katie, looking over his shoulder as if looking for her mother inside the car. "I can't see her...Is she playing hide and seek?" Katie ran around the car searching for Linda, giggling while calling for her.

Roy gave a quick look to Elizabeth and Joey, searching for support. Taking Katie's hand, he said, "Sweetheart...let's go to the garden. Dad wants to talk to you."

Once they reached the garden, Roy asked her to sit on the bench next to the tree and he followed, sitting next to her. His hands were shaking; tears ran down his face. He was just about to deliver the most difficult news he had ever had to tell anyone in his life. Roy was well used to dealing with tough businessmen, but difficult negotiations were nothing compared to what he had to face at this moment. His daughter, not quite six years old, the most innocent creature he knew, was there, vulnerable and in need of care. His own heart was broken but now he was about to break the heart he wanted to protect the most.

"We've got to talk about mom, Katie." Roy was looking her squarely in the eyes to ensure she knew that she was going to be safe whatever happened.

The girl was silent, paying attention to her father. She had already been affected by a sad feeling, which began when she saw the tears running slowly down her father's face. Linda was there, kneeling down in front of the two of them, focusing hard on transmitting vibrations filled with love. Geraldine and Teresa were nearby with their eyes closed and completely focused on Roy's and Katie's thoughts, sending them positive vibrations.

"Mom and I had a car accident when we were coming back from the mountains. There was a big storm..." Roy was speaking very slowly as he was trying hard to hold in his emotions and not to cry even more. He didn't want to show Katie that he was also heartbroken and insecure about their future, as he knew he had to give assurance to her and make her feel that everything was going to be fine. "Mom and I suffered very bad injuries... and..."

"Is she at the hospital, dad? Are the doctors looking after my mom now?"

More tears streamed down his face and he felt as if the world was falling apart. He took a long breath and with his right hand he held her little face. "The injuries were very bad for mom, sweetheart... Mom passed away."

"I don't know what you mean, dad. When is she coming back? When is my mom coming back home?" Katie looked very vulnerable and scared.

"She isn't coming back, darling. When people pass away, they don't return... They can't come back home. She is gone forever..."

"Will I never see my mom again?" Katie had begun to cry, feeling completely lost.

"No, sweetheart, we are not going to see her again. Mom has left forever." Roy embraced Katie and held her head against his chest.

The little girl pushed away his arms and ran through the garden, crying desperately. She ran until she reached a green bush that she used to play in as if it were a house. The bush had a small passage and it was hollow inside. Katie ran in and sat down on the ground. She cried even more, to the point where she nearly lost her breath.

"Sweetheart," called Roy from outside the bush. "Sweetheart, I know you're hurt...I'm hurt too. We both lost her."

Roy knelt down and Katie could then see that he was crying too. She came out of the bush and gave him a tight hug. Father and daughter remained standing, hugging each other for a long time. Both were crying, thinking of the moments they had had with Linda. Katie was remembering every second of the last day she spent with her mother. Their conversations, their kisses…She recalled Linda's smile. After a while, Roy held Katie's hand and walked with her back to the same bench where they were sitting before she had run away. They couldn't see her, but at that moment Linda embraced Roy and Katie and surrounded them with her bright light. They all shed tears of sorrow. Teresa and Geraldine moved closer to them and with their arms opened high up in the air they prayed, asking for the family to find peace and comfort. Suddenly an immense light appeared in the air. The light turned into a rainbow of colours which were a result of the love vibrations created by Geraldine, Teresa and Linda. Although the light could not be seen by human eyes, the positive and comforting energy from it could be felt by everyone present.

Elizabeth came in to the garden, followed by Joey. They approached Roy and Katie and sat on the bench next to them. Katie was crying non-stop. She looked at her grandparents and with a broken voice she told them that her mother wasn't coming back home again.

"Oh my princess... I know it's sad. We're all very sad too," said Elizabeth before hugging her.

"I miss her, grandma," said Katie, crying. "I want my mother to come back home now."

"We all do, my dear, we all do. But you need to know that it isn't your mother's fault. She didn't choose to leave us. When death comes we can't say no, so please don't think that your mother chose to leave you, because she didn't. Her body was much too injured and she had been called into heaven," replied Elizabeth.

"Be strong. I am not dead; remember, we don't die, we never die. We evolve, we progress and we live forever," said Linda to Katie. She touched Katie's little face and continued, "I live and I am here looking after you all, but not in a human body any more. The separation we are facing today hurts, but one day we will reunite again, I promise."

Although they could neither hear what Linda was saying nor see her, they all began to remember the happy moments they had enjoyed with her. Linda took the opportunity to step back from the scene and, closing her eyes, she prayed and asked God for a butterfly. She imagined the butterfly and within seconds a radiant blue creature materialised and flew across the garden, landing on Katie's knee. The girl stopped crying. She looked first at Roy and then at her grandparents and said, "It's mommy! We promised each other...We promised we would send each other butterflies! Mom has sent me this butterfly, I know she did."

Roy, Elizabeth and Joey smiled at Katie. The butterfly took off again and landed on each member of the family before returning to Katie's knee. Katie imagined her mother was there next to her, watching for her, and thought, *'Please come back mom...I need you with me.'*

"I can't return, my darling. At least not as it was before, but I will always be here next to you. Any time you need me I will be here with you," Linda said to her before giving her a kiss on the cheek. She gently touched Katie's face before returning to Teresa and Geraldine.

"Let's return?" suggested Teresa. "We'll come back soon."

Linda nodded and blew a kiss to them before leaving, accompanied by Teresa and Geraldine.

Elizabeth, Joey and Roy remained in the garden next to Katie, watching the skies, each one with their own feelings of sorrow for missing their loved one who had departed.

Chapter Butterflies

A few weeks later at the spiritual colony Lunas, Linda was sitting on the grass facing the lake. She was staring at the sky, thinking of Katie and her loved ones on Earth. Although she missed them deeply she was comforted by the spiritual knowledge that those difficult times were necessary for their progress and their development. She suddenly shook the sorrow away and, looking around, she began to admire and appreciate Lunas.

Lunas was a beautiful place with many green and flowery gardens and fields everywhere. The colony was surrounded by green valleys around the crystal clear lake, which was long and crossed most of the colony. It was at the centre of the lake that most of the main buildings of the colony were located. All the spirits living in that colony were free of human material needs and human vices. They were all connected by unconditional love and by the desire to continue to purify their spirits, and also to assist other spirits to rise towards their purification. In Lunas all the inhabitants were spirits who had set themselves free of jealousy, possession, anger, envy, violence and evil feelings which only delay the purification of the spirit. They were engaged in charity, truly believing that there is no salvation for the spirits, or any being in the universe, without charity.

Linda was contemplating this stunning place, meditating to the sound of the birds that were flying high in the skies of the colony, when Geraldine approached her unexpectedly.

"I was looking for you." Geraldine had the two puppies with her. They ran around Linda, jumping on her, barking and very excited.

"You look sad, my dear. Are you okay?" asked Geraldine after sitting down on the grass alongside Linda.

"I'm fine, Geraldine. I do feel a bit melancholic, you know. I've been thinking about Katie and Roy a lot. I do hope they are alright," replied Linda while stroking the two puppies.

"It's been a few weeks now since your return and I guess it's time for you to occupy your mind. An empty mind is the devil's office. Keep it busy and the evil won't work on it." The two puppies barked when Geraldine finished her sentence. "Even these two agree," she joked.

Linda smiled and replied, "You are right. I need to go back to my routine. I feel I need to go back to work and get my mind occupied."

"Yes. Let's talk to Teresa and perhaps you can go and work in the chambers of the lost and suffering spirits."

"It sounds like a plan. To occupy my time with important things, that's what I need," said Linda, looking happier, "occupy myself assisting others."

"I know it's tough to think that they are on Earth now, putting into practice everything they have learnt so far. It's even harder to know that there's not much we can do to help other than pray and continue to encourage them. But let's not underestimate their strength and their capability. We must trust them; you have to believe that they will make it through. We all do at some stage, so they will," said Geraldine as she stood up. She gave her hand to Linda, inviting her to follow.

Geraldine and Linda walked alongside the lake, speaking about Linda's previous experience when incarnated on Earth. Together they reviewed and analysed the most difficult times Linda had to face during that period and what lessons she had learnt from it. They compared scenes lived during her most recent incarnation on Earth with her past experiences, as a learning exercise.

The sky in the colony was always bright and the climate there was always pleasantly warm. The valleys and the fields were covered by particularly vivid, tiny flowers, making the whole place very colourful. The flowers also gave a very special fragrance to the colony's air.

The spirits at Lunas were always in action, assisting other spirits in their missions and carrying out many other types of work. They pursued their studies, continuing to learn skills which could add to their knowledge and evolution, and they also engaged in hobbies such as arts. Geraldine worked at the colony's library, while Teresa was a manager at the chambers of the lost and suffering spirits located at the dark regions near the Earth. The chambers were a temporary rescue place for those spirits who were in the dark regions and were searching for assistance. All those who looked for help and care at the chambers of the lost and suffering spirits had completed their passage from Earth to the spiritual world, and after leaving Earth had continued to engage in evil behaviour or depressive and destructive thoughts. Some of the other spirits rescued by the volunteers at the chambers were those who, after their reincarnation, spent their time hunting and stalking spirits who were still incarnated on Earth, playing jokes and causing emotional and physical damage, mostly driven by revenge. Others were spirits who were suffering after their passage for being still very emotionally attached to the material traps and addictive behaviour they used to have while living on Earth, such as heavy consumption of alcohol, taking hallucinatory drugs, and self-destructive feelings like jealousy.

Geraldine and Linda walked by the lake and talked for a long time until they reached the residential area. They strode upwards towards a small hill, then walked down a street flanked by tall trees with large trunks and long branches filled with bright yellow leaves. The trees grew on both sides of the street, which was miles long, and they were so tall and wide that they created with their leaves a sort of yellow roof all along the street. When walking underneath the trees, all that one could see was a stunning bright yellow roof made out of leaves and flowers. The ground was different from the Earth's; it had tiny coloured flowers similar to the ones in the fields and valleys, and they formed a natural colourful carpet effect.

They soon reached Geraldine's house. When Geraldine and Linda arrived, Teresa was there waiting for them.

"Hi Teresa," greeted Linda, followed by Geraldine.

"Hello, you two. How nice to see you." She smiled.

"Should we go to the garden?" asked Geraldine.

The three went there, accompanied by Geraldine's puppies.

"So, my darling, I understand you would like to go to work at the chambers of the lost and suffering spirits?" asked Teresa, going straight to the point.

"Yes I do. It's time to occupy my mind. I need to put into practice everything I've been learning and I would also like to assist others who are in need," replied Linda.

"And I agree with her, Teresa. Linda has always been a great counsellor and it's time now to pass on her learning to help and enlighten others in need," said Geraldine, with her two puppies sleeping on her lap.

"It's fine with me. I am sure that everyone at the chambers will be delighted to meet you," said Teresa, looking very happy.

"I'm looking forward to meeting all of them too. By the way, I can start as soon as possible."

"Let's finish our conversation and then we can go there straight afterwards. What do you think?" said Teresa with a sparkle in her eyes.

"Tell me Linda, do you like the butterflies Katie has been sending to you?" asked Geraldine.

Teresa's question seemed to touch Linda's deepest emotions. She looked at the skies and took a breath, remembering Katie, and replied, "I love them and I always send one back too." At that moment Linda closed her eyes and imagined a bright yellow butterfly. Within a few seconds a butterfly exactly like the one she had imagined materialised in front of her. Linda focused and transmitted to the creature many vibrations of love, and once ready, she sent it to Earth. It disappeared in the air and appeared at the same instant on the Earth; more precisely, at the playground of the school where Katie was eating her lunch surrounded by her school friends. Katie saw the yellow butterfly and followed it with her eyes as it flew and landed next to her on the table. The butterfly had arrived just at a moment when Katie was feeling very down, missing her mother. The moment she saw it land on the table, she felt refreshed and touched with the positive vibes sent by Linda, and immediately thought of her mother, remembering the day she shouted from inside the car, *"Love you always sweetheart! When you miss me, just watch for the butterflies."*

After feeling that Katie had received the butterfly, Linda thanked God for the blessing and, after a few moments in silence, she said, "I'm concerned about Roy. He's been going out drinking after work every night and he's getting heavily drunk and losing his mind. Many times my father has had to go to the bar to collect him, and found him unconscious sleeping on the bar. Elizabeth and Joey are doing their best by looking after Katie, though she's very vulnerable and now misses not having her father next to her. She needs him."

Teresa and Geraldine looked at her with tenderness, paying a great deal of attention to what she was saying. Linda continued, "I have been going to Earth every night to watch over them. I pray and send them vibrations of harmony, and once Katie has fallen asleep I collect her soul and bring it here to the colony so she can spend some time here with me. I talk a lot with her and we both play in the field. Last night we rode the horses."

"Does she remember any of this?" asked Geraldine, to which Teresa replied, "No, my sister, for Katie, as for many of the humans on Earth, these moments when their souls leave their bodies when they are asleep are nothing more than a night's dream. Most spirits when incarnated don't remember that it's when the physical body is asleep that the fluidic laces are loosened and they become free to explore the spiritual universe."

"She thinks she dreamt it all," said Linda.

"Though her soul feeds from the love she receives when she is here with Linda while her body is resting on Earth."

"I don't intend to tell her anything about our stories," said Linda. "My intention is to spend some time with her and help to ensure her that I am here looking after her. On the following morning when she wakes up she'll believe it was all a dream, but she'll feel so excited and happy for having had a dream with me."

Chapter The chambers of the lost and suffering spirits

Teresa and Linda went to the chambers of the lost and suffering spirits. The dark regions where the chambers were located had a very dense and extremely negative atmosphere, due to the bad and evil vibrations carried by the habitants there. The sky colour alternated between purple and dark blue and the air had a very bad smell which was almost unbearable for those used to the enlightened spiritual colonies. The hundreds of streets were very narrow and formed the shape of a labyrinth, with houses that seemed to be made out of tin. It was a very disturbing place because of its looks and its low energetic vibration. Teresa and Linda approached one of the tin houses and Teresa indicated the way.

"This place is horrible. I feel shivers all over," said Linda, looking shocked and crossing her arms.

"Here you get only the worst of the energies. It's as if all the evil and dark thoughts and energy were accumulated in one place. The spirits who inhabit these regions carry inside evil and primitive emotions. The low and negative vibrations of the ones who inhabit these regions is what makes this place dark and creepy," said Teresa while gently uncrossing Linda's folded arms. "Unfortunately there are many spirits who choose to live this way. They close their eyes to all the beauty in life and instead they choose to live here surrounded by their evil and depressive thoughts. Lunas is the way it is only because those who live there have inner peace. They all have love in every action they take and in everything they do; the same as in the colony where I live and in all of the enlightened spiritual colonies. Because the spirits living there chose harmony and strive for their purification, they only receive the very best in the universe back to them."

Following Teresa's reasoning, Linda said, "It's the universal law of action and reaction -correct? You get back from the universe all the vibrations and actions you give out. If you think and behave with harmony and peace you will attract harmony and peace, and if you think and behave with violence and anger you will attract violence and anger."

"And so on for everything you do," concluded Teresa. "Your house is the mirror of your thoughts." She put her right hand on the broken handle of the tin door and the entire place became illuminated by a bright light. The door opened and they entered the small house made of tin, which was in fact the chambers of the lost and suffering spirits secretly disguised so as not to attract attention from tormenting spirits. Once they were inside, the whole place lit up, and to Linda's surprise it was completely different from its exterior look. The place had marble floors and white walls giving a soft and comfy feeling to it. Linda also felt the energy change completely, feeling much more pleasant and almost similar to the one in Lunas.

"Can you feel the difference?" asked Teresa.

Linda nodded and smiled after taking a long breath to feel the fresh air and clear herself from the energy felt outside.

"This is because those who are in here are being treated and are already looking for a positive change; they are already looking for peace and happiness," replied Teresa.

"Linda! What a pleasure to see you here."

Linda was greeted by one of the nurses. Realising that Linda didn't know her, the nurse redressed herself. "Apologies. My name is Rita and I am a long-time friend of your aunt Teresa. I accompanied Teresa on her visits to you while you were incarnated on Earth. Many times I was by your side transmitting thoughts and vibrations of encouragement to you."

"I remember you now, Rita. I remember our talks and your advice in my dreams at night," said Linda, smiling and recalling that while she was incarnated on Earth she had had many dreams at night with a mysterious woman who would talk to her and give her good advice.

Rita gave Linda an unexpected hug and then said, "I must say huge congratulations on your achievement. You have done so well on your latest experience in life. We are all very happy for you."

Looking very shy, Linda thanked Rita.

"Rita, Linda is going to join us here at the chambers and help our work," said Teresa very enthusiastically.

"It will be a pleasure to work with you, Linda."

"I have to go now on a mission and visit a friend who is incarnated. She is having a baby today and I would like to be present and work with my spiritual friends on the labour. Rita, could I kindly ask you to show Linda around and introduce her to our patients?"

"Of course, Teresa. I will take care of Linda."

When Teresa had left, Rita went around the different rooms introducing Linda to all the other workers and volunteers. They were all happy to meet her as most of them had heard of Linda before, and some others had met her by accompanying Teresa on her visits while Linda was incarnated on Earth.

After the introductions were complete, Rita showed Linda a corridor and asked her to follow. Once they were near the door at the end of the corridor, Rita warned her, "Now I am going to take you to the room where the wounded and suffering spirits are. Most of them are in pain and agony, and the noise of screams and the low energy coming from their depressive thoughts inside there can be quite disturbing."

"Do they feel actual physical pain?" asked Linda.

"Oh no. It's all in their minds. They create the pain in their own minds and they believe they are in actual physical pain. They are so obsessed about their previous experience on Earth, and they are so attached to the life they used to have while they were living there, that they refuse to believe that they are no longer imprisoned in a corporeal body. They refuse to accept their spiritual life, so they carry with them the wounds and suffering they once had on Earth."

When they entered the room Linda soon understood what Rita meant about disturbing. The beds, which were very similar to hospital beds on Earth, contained hundreds of suffering spirits. Some of them were crying out loud; some screamed and shouted aggressive swear words. There were enlightened spirits from different spiritual colonies there, working as nurses and counsellors offering assistance and support.

Linda looked around and saw that some of the enlightened spirits were talking and counselling, while others were medicating and performing first aid.

"What do I do now? Should I start talking to them?" said Linda, looking very overwhelmed.

"Yes, talk to them, let's get closer and offer them our support. It may be a good idea if you stay with me for now. We can do it together. What do you think?"

Linda nodded and asked, "And how do we heal them? Do we use any medicine or drugs?"

Rita smiled at Linda and both laughed. Rita then replied, "Love heals any wound. There's no medicine more powerful than unconditional love."

They both approached a spirit with the appearance of an old lady. She was lying down in bed, crying quietly at the same time as swearing someone's name. She was dirty, covered in what seemed to be mud. When she noticed Rita and Linda she got up, excited, and stopped to cry and swear, "Finally some help! Finally my God Almighty has sent someone to help me to have justice!"

"What justice do you need, Marie?" asked Rita.

"You know my name?" Smiling, the spirit put both hands in the air. "Thanks, Lord, for sending me two angels - and they even know my name! This is the proof you didn't forget about me, my Lord." Looking back at Rita and Linda, the old lady said, "I have been waiting in this place for a long time. They said here I could find help. They said here God would help to heal my soul."

"You are right, Marie. We are here to help," said Rita with kindness in her voice.

Marie lowered her voice so no-one else could hear what she was going to say. "You need to help me to destroy that evil woman. She is jealous of me, she is jealous of my beauty and has been trying to do everything to destroy me and my marriage." Thinking that Rita and Linda were feeling sorry for her, she believed she had finally found someone to help with her plans. She continued, "She doesn't love her husband. I am sure of it. I can tell she looks at my husband Rob with other intentions; she desires him. But not because she finds him attractive, oh no... no...it's only because she wants to live my life... She wants to be me."

Rita interrupted the lady. "Stop, Marie. Stop tormenting your sister. It has been over seventy years since you passed away and left Earth. Your sister Joanne also passed away many years ago and she lives now in a beautiful place where you could also be living if wasn't for your obsessive and evil thoughts."

"No!" shouted Marie. "What are you saying, you silly woman? She is jealous of me. She is the one who is obsessed, not me. She wants everything I have. She has always been like that; a twisted, evil woman. I need to find that evil woman."

"Stop lying to yourself, Marie. The jealousy you see in her is the jealousy that you have been nurturing inside yourself for all of your existence. The evil you see in others is the evil that you insist on keeping in your own heart. Wake up, Marie and realise that the time you have spent searching for ways to destroy Joanne was a precious time of your existence that you wasted. Instead of spending your time looking for ways to evolve and progress, you wasted it by focusing on other people's lives and wishing them misfortune. While you were consumed by all these perverse and evil feelings, the others around you were using the opportunities given to them to become better spirits. They all now live happily and in peace, while you are here stuck in time."

Marie sat down on the bed, crying. When she recovered her breath she asked, "How could God allow all of this to happen to me? I look old and ugly now. I lost all my jewellery and my money. I have no servants to serve me any more. This isn't the heaven I was promised in church."

"You spent most of your life going to church, and while your mouth pronounced memorised prayers, inside your spirit was closed to the beauties of life. You hid yourself behind saints and prayers while deep down you were wishing bad things to happen to the ones around you. You never appreciated the blessings you were given; not only the material ones such as your physical beauty and your wealth, but the blessings of being surrounded by loving and caring spirits like Joanne, your husband Rob and your brother-in-law William."

Marie covered her face with her hands. Rita gently removed them and continued, "They were all there next to you, willing to help you to get out of the darkness and see the light, but you never appreciated their help. Although they all knew of your weakness, they forgave you time after time and tried for a long time to teach you about the things that really mattered in life."

Marie turned to cover her face, feeling ashamed of the truth from which she could no longer hide. Rita continued, "You left Earth when you were at an old age. You spent all of your life hating your sister and you forgot to look around and appreciate all the opportunities that were given to you by God to become a better being." Rita again gently removed Marie's hands from her face and finished by saying, with even more kindness in her voice, "We have to go now, Marie, as there are many others in the same position as you are. The day you decide to change your life the whole universe will smile back to you and many doors leading to a happier life will open to you. We will be back to visit you shortly, and perhaps if you truly wish to unload your spirit from all this hate and jealousy we could then take you to a beautiful place where you can start again."

Rita and Linda walked away and approached a spirit with the appearance of a young lady who was crying quietly in a corner. She was sitting on the floor, barefoot, with a dress covered in blood.

"Hi Daniela. Why are you crying?" asked Rita.

"Because I love him... I love him so much. I've been trying to show him how happy we could have been if we were together but..."

"He chosen Veronica," said Rita affirmatively.

"Yes! How could he? After everything I did for him. I gave him all my love but he ignored my feelings."

There was a very dark and low energy surrounding her. She had deep dark circles around her eyes and looked extremely disturbed. Her hands were bloody and some marks of blood could be seen around her face too. She was sobbing and shaking. "The day I found out that they had got engaged was like I had lost the will to live. I stopped eating and started to get very drunk every day so I could forget my misery. The gin was my only friend." Making an even bigger scene, she screamed loudly, "I had to forget him!" The cry suddenly stopped and the girl seemed to quickly change her mood. Her eyes filled with violence and anger. She made a motion as if she was stabbing someone and said, "I told her I had to talk to her about something personal and she invited me to her house. She was beautiful and she was so damn good that I couldn't take it any more. I lied that I was having some problems at home with my parents and she was so supportive to me." She put a finger in her throat and said "Urgh! Such a lovely girl, whatever!" The lady looked more and more angry. "Once when I was at her house she offered to brew me a cup of tea and when she turned her back to me I pulled the knife from inside my dress and stabbed her. I stabbed her eighteen times. I counted them because I wanted to make sure she died. I had to do it; she had my man, she had the man I loved. I had to kill her…I had to kill her…"

"Veronica was your best friend, Daniela. She loved you and she always wished you well. You became obsessed with her boyfriend and never told her the truth. You didn't love James, that was obsession, and your obsession for James made you blind to what really mattered in life. Veronica trusted you and you were never truthful to her. You betrayed not only her but her family, who always welcomed you into their home as a family member."

Rita looked inside her eyes and said, "It's important for you to know that what you have done brought horrible consequences for many others. Veronica's mother fell into a depression and was never able to recover from her daughter's death. She passed away many years ago and until now we have been encouraging her spirit to learn to forgive you and to move close to Veronica where she can get some assistance. Veronica's father separated from his wife due to her deep depression; and he also spent the rest of his days on Earth extremely sad and was only able to recover from the murder of his daughter upon his passage to the spiritual world, after receiving immense support from his spiritual friends."

"Don't tell me about how much they suffered! I spent many years in prison. I paid for what I've done," said Daniela, pointing a finger at Rita with a lot of aggression in her voice.

"You did pay indeed, according the law of the men on Earth, but so far you failed to understand the severity of your acts. You haven't so far asked for their forgiveness. You still believe that what you did was right. Here in the spirit world we cannot hide our true feelings and thoughts; everyone can see through everyone and you cannot pretend you regretted taking her life and interrupting her experience on Earth with such a violent act."

"It's because I don't feel sorry. I don't regret what I did! She deserved it. She always had the beauty and all the attention from the teachers and all the boys. Everybody loved Veronica. Why her and not me? I hate her!" Daniela shouted, grabbing hold of her own hair and pulling it down angrily. She ran down the room, bumping into the beds, and went out, heading back to the dark regions.

"Her case is very similar to Marie, the lady we met before," said Rita to Linda. "They have both been consumed by hate and jealousy. Unfortunately neither of them is ready to accept their mistakes and move on. While all those whom they have hurt at some point have forgiven and are now carrying on with their lives, Marie and Daniela are delaying their progress and happiness by nurturing such dark feelings."

"Is this your job here at the chambers of the lost spirits, then? To give counselling to the ones who are in need?" asked Linda.

"I don't call what I do counselling because I don't give advice; I only remind them of the truth. I remind them of the facts that sometimes, for several different reasons, they don't see any more. Those who are ready to accept their new condition and to forgive their acts or forgive those who once hurt them can go to a colony. Others like Marie and Daniela, who are still lost, living blind in anger and hate, cannot go back. Not because we prevent them but because they themselves refuse to move on."

Chapter Two old spirits reunite

Weeks later, Linda was already mentoring and assisting the lost spirits on her own when Rita approached her after she had just seen another patient and said, "Linda, I would like you to see this lady. I have been instructed by elevated spirits that you should be the one to guide and mentor her." Rita showed Linda the bed where a spirit with the appearance of a young lady was lying down. "Her name is Rebecca and she arrived here at the chambers a few days ago. She has refused to speak to any of us, and we believe that because of your connections she might open up to you and begin to talk."

Linda walked towards the lady, and the closer she got the more she could feel her vibrations loaded with depressive thoughts. When she reached the bed where Rebecca was lying, she said hello but didn't get any reply. Rebecca had curly red hair and deep green eyes. She was tucked in bed covered by a white sheet. Linda stroked her hair and at that moment a vision showing the young lady's corporeal death came up in Linda's mind as if were a movie. Linda saw that young lady sitting in a living room surrounded by bottles of alcohol and boxes of medicinal tablets everywhere. The young lady was crying with a great deal of sorrow, and her body showed the marks of cuts which she had inflicted upon herself during the many self-harming incidents she had been through. The vision continued, showing two primitive and evil spirits surrounding the living room where the lady was. They tormented her even more, telling her to commit suicide. Looking very depressed, the lady picked up a box of barbiturate pills and swallowed dozens of them. Within a few seconds she fell completely unconscious to the floor and the two spirits began an onslaught of depressive remarks to her. The room filled with more evil spirits who were seeking other depressed spirits like her. Such spirits feed on the negativity and the misery of others. Like vampires, they suck the energy from the vulnerable, and can only be satisfied and happy when they see others suffering too. Watching the misery of others was the only way they had to feel better about their own existence. Slowly the lady's spirit left her corporeal body, which was unconscious, lying on the floor. Within hours the fluidic laces that linked her spirit to her corporeal body were broken and she passed away, returning to the spiritual world. Upon her passage the two evil spirits took hold of her. They were in ecstasy, laughing out loud, celebrating the fact that they had managed to induce another incarnated person to commit suicide. Once Rebecca returned to the spiritual world, imprisoned by the other two evil spirits, she found darkness and a lot more suffering. Many deformed spirits, who looked more like monsters and beasts, were wandering about, some moaning, others screaming in pain. It was her vision of hell. For many years those two spirits used her as a personal slave, forcing her to follow them everywhere and help them to torment others who were also suffering from depression. The picture showing Rebecca's recent experiences slowly faded away from Linda's vision.

"Rebecca... Rebecca, my darling. Talk to me," said Linda softly while stroking her hair.

Rebecca seemed to be extremely depressed as her eyes had a very sad look.

"You're fine now, my darling. This is a place of tranquillity and love. Try and forget everything you went through, as none of that will happen to you here."

Rebecca began to cry. When Linda leaned over toward her she embraced Linda and gave out a very deep and sorrowful cry. She didn't say anything; she just stayed there, hugging Linda and crying for a long time. Eventually she said, "I'm hungry, I'm lonely...and I'm very scared. I've been used as a servant by two horrible spirits and I ended up doing so many bad things to others because they threatened me. If I didn't torment others they would hurt me and make me suffer. How could God forget me and leave me in that horrible place?" she exclaimed, her grief now mixed with anger.

Linda stroked Rebecca's face and said, "God hasn't forgotten about you. You, on the other hand, have distanced yourself from Him."

"I wanted to get out of there…that place, it's horrible. I can't bear being around all those creatures and its darkness any more."

"Come with me. I'll take you to a place where you will be treated much better. There you'll have food and be able to have a shower and rest." Noticing that Rebecca was hesitating, Linda held her hand and asked, "Please trust me. I'll look after you."

Rebecca nodded and they both left the chambers of the suffering and lost spirits and travelled through the universe at the speed of light. They shortly arrived at a spiritual recovery colony called Magiar. They found themselves next to a high building which was all glazed and had dozens of floors. Inside the glass building, at its centre, was a very tall tree with a massively thick trunk and many branches. It was so tall that it reached the very top of the high building. They entered the building and Rebecca, looking all around, felt amazed by the beauty of the construction. Linda pointed to a seat. After they were comfortably sitting down, Rebecca began crying again. As she shed her tears she asked, "Why didn't I die? Why am I still alive? I wanted to end my life and instead I ended up going to that dark place with lots of strange creatures."

"You didn't die simply because we never die. You ended your life experience on Earth, that's all. That place you were in was the dark region and the strange creatures were nothing but spirits like you and me. The difference is that they chose to look like that, much as they chose to surround themselves with misery and evil. Their appearance is simply the reflection of their own thoughts."

Rebecca had the look of someone who was constantly scared. She couldn't face others and make eye contact owing to her lack of confidence, and for that reason she was always looking down. She touched the ends of her hair all the time. Gazing downwards, she said, "I thought that once I committed suicide I would be gone…from ashes to ashes as they say, but I see that it isn't like that. Even though I committed suicide I'm still here, alive."

"No it's not like that," replied Linda. "You thought you could get rid of your depression by committing suicide but actually, as our life is infinite, all you did was hand yourself over to those evil spirits who took advantage of your vulnerability. You opened up yourself for them to inflict pain and misery on you."

Sadness overcame Rebecca again and she shed tears of sorrow. Still looking down and remembering all the sad moments she went through when incarnated on Earth, she said to Linda, "I used to hate myself so much. I never found myself good-looking or exciting like the other girls. I only felt like cutting my skin and drinking because I wanted to punish myself." Tears were flooding down her face. Rebecca took a long breath and continued, "At one point I didn't want to live any more. All

I could think of was dying and finishing with my life. My parents tried a lot of things, but I didn't want to hear or see anyone. Every day in my life felt like a never-ending sadness."

Linda embraced her and said, "The more depressed you became, the more you attracted to your surroundings evil and depressed spirits. In the spiritual world, they become focused on tormenting you and driving you into an even deeper depression."

"Why did God allow such spirits to do this to me?"

"We all are given free will. Imagine your thoughts as a radio that you are capable of tuning into good and positive vibes, or into bad and negative ones. Depending on your choice, you will attract to your side similar spirits. If you focus on positive and happy thoughts you will attract towards you spirits who are positive and striving for happiness. What happened was that you attracted spirits who were at that moment similar to the quality of your thoughts and behaviour. Once you chose to see only the bad side of life, you then became depressed and attracted spirits who were in a similar vibe to you. It all becomes an addictive circle where everyone involved feeds each other with more bad and negative vibrations, generating even more badness and negativity."

Stroking her hair and clearing the tears off Rebecca's face, Linda continued, "Your low self-esteem and self-depreciation made you vulnerable to evil spirits. They fed your mind with even more depressive thoughts and drove you to commit suicide. After you passed away and returned to the spiritual world you became a slave of those two evil spirits for a long time, and only after a lot of suffering you remembered God, and then you finally begged for mercy. Immediately after you called for Him, you were rescued by the team of volunteers and taken to the nearest rescue point which was the chambers of the lost spirits. You have the help you need now, and you have a chance to re-start. Seize this opportunity and help yourself. You are beautiful, Rebecca, and you were created to be happy. Be strong and take the opportunity to be treated."

"Am I going to stay here in this place?" asked Rebecca, looking anxious and scared.

"Yes, you are. Here you will be looked after by our spiritual friends who will give you fraternal assistance. You will also be helped by doctors and therapists who are specialists in depression. They will give you all the support you need to self-discover and flourish and recover from your depression. But I want you to know that I will be visiting you every day and you can trust me that you are not alone. For now, you need food and a good rest."

A spirit with very bright light arrived next to Linda. He had blond hair and very soft features. He approached the two and introduced himself to Rebecca. "Hello Rebecca, my name is Nathaniel, and it's a pleasure to meet you. Please come with me and don't be afraid, because you won't be held here against your free will. You can come and check the place and what we can offer to support you, and if you don't like it you can simply leave as you wish. Your wishes will always be respected."

Rebecca nodded without saying anything, then, looking at Linda, she asked, "Do you promise that you'll come to visit me?"

Linda replied, "Yes. I am definitely coming back, I promise." Linda softly kissed her on her cheek and stood up, looking at Rebecca, assuring her that everything was going to be fine.

Nathaniel showed Rebecca the way and she accompanied him.

Chapter A broken man

When Linda returned to Lunas both Geraldine and Teresa were waiting for her.

"We are here, excited, waiting for you," said Geraldine, holding the two puppies which were asleep in her arms.

"Have you met Rebecca?" asked Teresa.

"Yes I did and I felt so sad for her. She is so involved with all of this sadness and sorrow and she doesn't want to get out of it...How sad."

"It is not a matter of wanting to get out of it," said Teresa. "Unfortunately she doesn't know any better."

"I'll go back to visit her every day and help to show her all the blissful and amazing things about the gift of life," said Linda.

"You definitely will. You two are connected, Linda," said Geraldine.

Looking intrigued, Linda asked, "What do you mean, we two are connected, Geraldine?

"Everything happens with a purpose, remember? Everyone we meet in our lives we meet for a reason, a divine purpose. You two are going to be very close and have at some point in your existence been connected."

Anyway, we are here because we have something else to tell you," said Teresa. She looked deep into Linda's eyes and continued, "It's Roy. He is still getting drunk every night after work. By the time he gets home late at night Elizabeth and Joey have already put Katie to bed. He has been attracting a lot of evil spirits."

"I need to go there and visit them," said Linda.

Teresa and Linda nodded, whereupon Linda closed her eyes and left Lunas. When she reopened her eyes she realised she had arrived in a bar back at Asheville in North Carolina. It was crammed with men drinking and semi-naked woman dancing among them. Linda saw that there were evil spirits about, and they were feeding their vices and addictions through the incarnated and sucking their energies. For each incarnated there were dozens of evil spirits consuming their energy, and the drunker the men got, the more they allowed the evil spirits to act on their souls. Linda moved around the bar, making herself invisible to both the incarnated and to the evil spirits, and after searching for quite while she finally saw Roy, completely drunk, sitting by the bar. Next to him there were many evil spirits who were enjoying seeing Roy's depression. As energy suckers they were feeding from the bad thoughts and depressive vibrations coming from him. They were laughing at him as if feeling happy about his misery. Linda moved close to Roy and made herself visible to the evil spirits. When she asked them to leave they all began to swear at her.

Linda could read Roy's thoughts when she approached him. *'What a shit life I have. I'm stuck in this world's end place living a damned life,'* Roy was thinking.

"You have a beautiful little daughter waiting for you at home. She needs her dad. You can comfort her broken heart, Roy, and once you do your heart will be comforted too."

His vibration was so low and negative owing to his depressive feelings that he couldn't capture Linda's encouraging thoughts. Roy ordered another beer and drank the whole glass in one go. *'What have I done to Linda? What have I done? I killed my wife!'* he thought, feeling very sorry for himself. *'What if I hadn't driven in that horrible weather? What if that deer hadn't got on to the highway?'*

"You were not responsible for the accident, Roy. It was my time to go. Stop blaming yourself my dear." Linda stayed there, watching Roy, but his thoughts were so negative that it wasn't long before even more evil spirits arrived to torment him. Linda moved even closer to him and said, "Your body has not been created to absorb alcohol and other chemical substances. By drinking this much alcohol you are slowly destroying your own body."

All of a sudden, a drunk man pushed his girlfriend aside and poked Roy in the hip, saying, "Hey you! I seen you looking at my girlfriend!"

Two of the many evil and lost spirits in the bar moved towards Roy and, ignoring Linda's presence, began to instil in him thoughts of violence and aggression. The two spirits had a female physiognomy and were having fun with the argument that they had just started.

"Get off my face," said Roy, pushing the guy backwards.

The man fell backwards over the pool table and everyone in the bar started to laugh loudly at him. The two evil spirits split, and while one was next to Roy telling him to confront the other guy and engage in a fight, the other spirit was next to the drunken man doing the same.

"Go on and hit him! He is making you look like a fool! Hit him hard, you coward!" said one of the inferior spirits in the ear of the drunkard.

Linda was praying while watching the whole scene, but she knew that there was nothing she could do as everyone in that bar was attuned to the very low and bad vibrations which made them vulnerable to that sort of behaviour. She made herself visible to the evil spirits and asked the two of them who had caused the argument to stop, but she was completely ignored. The two were laughing and taking a lot of joy from the confusion they had just created. Soon the bar was filled with hundreds more evil and primitive spirits, all laughing and feeding from the aggression and violence that was permeating the air.

By now, the man had Roy by his throat and was punching him in the stomach. Roy managed to grab hold of a glass bottle and hit the man on the head, making him fall to the floor. Roy looked at his shirt and realised it was completely covered in blood. He had never acted aggressively before and had certainly never been in a fight, so when he saw the man on the floor his instinct was to extend his hand out to him to offer him support, but as he moved closer to him he was grabbed by one of the man's friends and was thrown against the bar, smashing a glass panel. All the bottles which were displayed in the glass shelves behind the bar fell on him. The fight continued, with three more friends of the man joining in to beat Roy up.

In the invisible world the place was immersed in a bright light, announcing the arrival of several enlightened spirits who had arrived, answering Linda's prayers. The hundreds of evil spirits, feeling scared of the enlightened spirits, immediately vanished from the place and soon the sirens of the police cars could be heard arriving outside the bar.

Chapter You've got to move on

Katie was still looking asleep as she sat by the kitchen table where her grandmother had just served her favourite dish, a plate of fresh pancakes with lots of syrup and strawberries.

"I haven't seen my dad for a long time, grandma. Where has he been?" asked Katie, looking disheartened.

Elizabeth tried not to look at Katie when she replied, as she didn't want her granddaughter to realise she was annoyed with Roy. She said, "He has been working very hard and he comes home very late when you are already sleeping, my darling." Deep down she was also worried about Roy, who had spent most of the previous night in jail.

Elizabeth finished setting the table for breakfast and hurried Katie to get ready for school. It was past eleven o'clock when Roy came down to the kitchen for his breakfast. Katie had already gone to school and Elizabeth was waiting for him in the kitchen, looking very serious. Roy had black eyes and several scratches on his face.

"Good morning, Elizabeth," mumbled Roy, looking very embarrassed and smelling of alcohol.

"For God's sake, Roy, I can smell alcohol on you from miles away. What's going on? Is it not enough you getting very drunk every night? Now you've ended up in jail!"

"I went out after work last night because I needed some fresh air," responded Roy, looking embarrassed and avoiding looking Elizabeth in the eyes.

"What kind of lifestyle is this, Roy? You're getting drunk every night. People are making a fool of you in the streets. Before we were getting phone calls from random people asking us to go and collect you from the bar because you were too drunk to even stand up, and now we were called in the middle of the night from the police station asking us to go and pay your bail! What are you doing to your life?"

Roy didn't say a word, and Elizabeth continued, "Katie has been asking about you. You're never at home." Elizabeth sat down next to him. "She needs you, Roy. This little girl is missing her mother desperately, and unfortunately there's nothing we can do about that - but her father is here, alive, and she needs him."

"She has you two and that should be enough," Roy replied. "I've never been here very often anyway; before Linda passed away I was always travelling out of town for work and I'd rarely see the two of them anyway. The only difference is that now I'm not travelling as much as I used to before."

"Are you insane? Yes, Joey and I are now here but she needs you, Roy, she needs her father more than ever. You are her family; a big part of her world is gone and the other part that could help her to feel loved and to feel stronger and to feel safe isn't there for her..."

"I don't want you to tell me what to do and not to do. I appreciate your help looking after my daughter, though I don't want to impose any trouble on either you or Joey."

"She isn't a problem at all. She is the reason I still have strength to carry on with my life after my Linda passed away. What I don't want is to see you getting drunk every night, throwing your life away like this. And the worst thing is you are hurting your daughter by not showing her any affection whatsoever."

Roy remained quiet, looking awkward while Elizabeth talked.

"You'll end up losing your job. Every day you wake up feeling hungover, smelling of alcohol, and you're constantly late for work. They won't be patient with you for much longer."

Feeling very annoyed and speaking without thinking, Roy stood up and said sharply, "Why don't you leave us alone? You two never liked me anyway. You were against Linda and me getting engaged and later all you did was criticise me to Linda. Maybe the best thing you can do right now is to leave my home and leave us alone!" Roy stormed out of the kitchen and slammed the door before leaving the house. Elizabeth heard the car being driven away and went out to the garden for some fresh air.

'How can he be so ungrateful? I've been dedicating all my life to him and Katie and now I'm told to leave?' Elizabeth thought to herself as she began crying.

Linda, who was at Lunas, could hear Elizabeth's voice calling her name and crying. She went immediately to Earth to visit her mother, and when she arrived she found Elizabeth outside the house in the garden, feeling very upset. Linda came closer to her ear and said, "I'm here, mother. I haven't left you. Please calm down, mother, and don't let your thoughts be contaminated by negativity. Roy didn't mean what he said to you earlier. He is as vulnerable and sad as all of you are, and perhaps he is the least prepared among you all for the separation and the loss."

Elizabeth suddenly remembered her daughter's face and some of their special moments together. Thinking of Linda and those happy times, Elizabeth began to feel calmer. Looking at the sky, she then closed her eyes and asked, "Oh my daughter, you were our rock. What do I do now?"

Linda whispered in her ear, "Katie needs you, mother, and so does Roy. Please be patient with him. These sad times won't last forever, I promise. It's all a matter of time. You've got to move on with your lives."

Elizabeth opened her eyes and looked up. As if looking at Linda in the skies, she said, "I promise to you, my daughter, I will look after Katie, whatever happens. I promise you I will give her all my love and care."

****

Later on that day, Katie had come back from school and was playing on the swing in the back yard. Elizabeth was sitting in the conservatory reading a book and from time to time she stopped her reading to watch Katie playing. The girl was swinging and singing happily. Linda, Geraldine and Teresa arrived in the garden at that moment and went to speak to Elizabeth.

"How has she been?" Teresa asked Linda.

"She has been strong - well, as much as a child her age who's lost her mother can be. She became a little bit introverted, but nothing to worry about. Sometimes she gets melancholic but she always pulls herself together quite fast."

"Are you still taking her soul away to Lunas at night?" asked Geraldine.

"Yes, I am. I leave my work at the chambers of the suffering and lost spirits and come here to pick up her soul for our trips. She never recalls anything though. In the morning sometimes she remembers our moments together as a pleasant dream, but that's all."

"And that's how it's supposed to be anyway. This time is allowed for you two so her spirit can gain comfort and reassurance that everything is going to be fine," affirmed Teresa.

Linda noticed that Katie had stopped the swing and had gone quiet. Linda walked towards her and realised that Katie had begun to cry. Katie's soul had felt Linda's presence and a great many memories of her mother had come into her thoughts.

"Don't cry, my sweetheart. Mom is here, remember? I am always here with you." Linda stroked her face - which for Katie felt like a gentle breeze - and focusing on pleasant thoughts she transmitted her vibrations of love. Linda closed her eyes and imagined two yellow butterflies which suddenly materialised in front of her and began to fly around Katie in circles. The girl's face opened into a huge smile once she saw the butterflies, and she followed them around the garden, screaming in happiness. "Grandma! Grandma! Look, butterflies! I'm sure it was my mother who sent these butterflies."

Elizabeth left the book on the chair and went towards Katie, giving her a hug. "Come on, my darling, let's go inside and bake some cookies."

"No, grandma. Not now. I want to run after the butterfly my mother has sent to me."

"Alright, my darling." Elizabeth chased the butterflies with Katie for a while, laughing away with her, and when she grew tired she left Katie playing in the garden. "Katie, I'll go inside and make us some lemonade and bring some slices of cake for our afternoon tea."

Linda dropped a tear while watching her daughter running around the garden.

"Don't let yourself be taken by those sad feelings, Linda," said Teresa.

Linda smiled and replied, "I know...It's just that sometimes it's a bit difficult."

Geraldine held Linda's hand and smiled at her, saying, "We are all here with them. We will help them through this."

"Should we go now?" asked Teresa.

Linda nodded and the three left the garden and returned to Lunas.

Chapter Promises

Later that night Elizabeth tucked Katie into bed and she fell asleep after her grandmother had read her a few chapters of *Peter Pan*. Elizabeth went to the living room and joined her husband, who was sitting in an armchair, reading a book. She sat down on the sofa and Joey, noticing that she was looking worried, asked her what was going on. She told him about the discussion she had had with Roy earlier in the day at breakfast and confessed she was worried about him.

"His behaviour isn't healthy and I'm so concerned that he'll end up losing his job. Also, and not least, I'm worried about Katie, who now has to deal with the fact that her father isn't present at such an important time of her life," Elizabeth concluded.

"From everything that Linda used to tell us, we kind of knew that Roy was quite immature. We can only think that he isn't strong enough to get through this right now, and drinking is his way to escape and forget about his problems. We've got to continue to advise him and help."

"But he told us to leave," said Elizabeth.

"Is that what you want?" asked Joey, to which his wife replied no.

"In that case, let's wait until tomorrow morning when we see him at breakfast and wait for him to apologise. I'm sure he didn't mean to say what he said, but if he doesn't apologise it will mean that he really wants us to leave his house…" He paused for few seconds and then continued. "Well, in that case we would have to leave."

"We can't leave right now. Katie needs us and it's obvious that Roy isn't prepared to be a father," exclaimed Elizabeth, looking extremely upset.

"Let's wait until tomorrow and work from there. Let's not suffer for a problem that we don't even have yet."

Elizabeth finished her tea and stood up from the sofa, heading upstairs. "I'm going to bed. I don't want to take the chance of staying awake and have to see Roy coming home drunk tonight. I know I would argue with him." She kissed Joey on the cheek and said goodnight before leaving the room.

On the following day, the phone rang in the early hours of the morning, waking both of them. Joey answered the phone, and when he hung up he looked very worried. Elizabeth was facing him, waiting for him to say something. After he had recovered from the news, Joey said, "Darling, I have bad news. Roy is in the hospital. I don't know exactly what happened but it seems like he was driving while drunk and had a car accident."

When she heard her husband saying the words 'car accident', her heart accelerated. The recollection of the sheriff giving the news about her daughter's death came to her mind and she could feel her legs going shaky. Elizabeth went pale and automatically looked upstairs, thinking of Katie. At the same moment Katie, who had heard the news, ran down the stairs crying desperately.

"What happened to my dad?" screamed Katie, who was crying.

"Nothing, sweetheart…nothing!" said Elizabeth, bending down to hug Katie.

"I heard grandpa saying that my dad had a car accident!" Katie was crying non-stop.

"Your father is at the hospital and the doctors are looking after him," said Joey, who had gone down on his knees to talk to his granddaughter face to face.

"He's going to die like my mother died!" the girl cried.

Elizabeth hugged Katie tightly and said, "No, no, sweetheart, let's pray to our Lord to look after him and bring him back to us." Elizabeth dried the tears off Katie's face. "Let's go and get changed so we can go to the hospital and see him. Grandpa will take us there now - okay?"

Katie nodded and, holding her grandmother's hand, they both went to get changed.

They reached the hospital and once they entered the ward they found Roy being looked after by a nurse. Katie ran towards her father and, close to his face, she cried, "Please don't die, daddy, I need you."

Before Roy could answer his daughter, the nurse who was administering the medicine said, "Your daddy will be fine, little girl. He will be home very soon. The accident wasn't very serious." She then excused herself and left the room.

Roy looked embarrassed at Joey and Elizabeth. He had bruises on his face and arms. Katie was holding his hand and was still crying, scared.

"So what happened, Roy?" asked Joey. "We came as soon as we got the phone call from the hospital."

"I had a minor accident coming back home from work." Roy waved a hand in Katie's direction and continued, "Can we talk about this later?"

Elizabeth rolled her eyes and said impatiently, "Come on Katie. Dad's fine as you can see. He won't die and soon he'll be back at home. Let's go, darling; you'd better go to school now."

The girl looked down, and as she was leaving, Roy took hold of her arms and said, "Sweetheart, dad isn't going to leave you, I promise you," and a tear trickled down his face. "The doctors said I'll get better soon and will be able to go home today. Go to school and daddy will see you when you come home."

Surprised by her father's caring behaviour, Katie kissed him on the cheek and said, "I love you dad, more than anything in this world. Please don't die."

"Dad loves you too, my little princess, and I promise that I won't die." He gently touched her face. "And I promise as well that things will change from now on, we will see each other a lot more from now on," said Roy, holding her tiny hand.

Smiling, Katie asked, "You don't need to promise, dad. Grandpa and grandma tell me every day that you've been busy working hard to make lots of money and make our lives better. I love you very much."

More tears flowed down Roy's face. As they were leaving, Roy asked to have a word with Elizabeth. Joey agreed to come back to the hospital to pick Elizabeth up after he had dropped Katie at school.

"I'm sorry, Elizabeth. I didn't mean to say what I said yesterday."

Elizabeth took a long breath and, looking in his eyes with tenderness, she said, "I know. It's okay Roy…it's just that it pains me to see you throwing your life away like this and…"

He interrupted before she could continue. "Please don't say anything else. Believe me, I already feel very stupid. My heart sank when I saw Katie here earlier." Looking at the ceiling, tears streaming down his face, Roy closed his eyes and went quiet for a moment.

Elizabeth came closer and said, "Get it off your chest, Roy. Allow yourself to cry. Nobody taught you how to get over such big loss or even how to raise and support a little girl who has just lost her mother. It's okay to feel this way."

He thought of Linda and mentally asked her for some advice. At that moment Linda arrived in the room next to Elizabeth. Neither Elizabeth nor Roy could see her but they both instantly felt lighter, as if their sorrow was slowly fading away.

"Be strong, Roy. Don't forget that we all chose these challenges because we knew that they would help us with our progress. We knew it wouldn't be easy but only this way will you be able to repair what has happened in the past and move on," said Linda, who was surrounded by a bright and shiny blue light.

Roy stopped crying immediately and, looking into Elizabeth's eyes, he said, "I will try and change. I realise I can't run away from the situation any more. Katie needs me and I'll look after her, I promise."

"And Joey and I will always support you," Elizabeth continued, smiling, "But please, no more car crashes. Our hearts can't take any more news like that!"

"I promise no more car crashes from now on," smiled Roy.

"Hey you, watch out," replied Elizabeth.

Linda watched them both for a while longer before heading to the recovery hospital in Magiar where Rebecca was being treated.

Chapter Magiar

When Linda arrived she found Rebecca sitting on a bench. Rebecca looked younger and had a certain brightness around her.

"Hi, Rebecca. How are you?"

"Linda!" Rebecca's face opened into a wide smile. "It's nice to see you."

"Wow. You look so much happier now and you're even smiling," Linda said, sitting on the bench next to her.

"It's been great to be here. They are all very caring and they've been teaching me a lot. I like to spend time with the fraternal counsellors and with the therapists too."

"Tell me more about your time here."

"Slowly I've been remembering my past experiences on Earth, and every time I remember a new passage we discuss all the happenings and the lessons from it. We then analyse together every mistake that stopped me in my evolution, so that I can learn from them. Since the earliest moments of my life I can see that I've been engaging in depressive thoughts and self-destructive behaviour that only attracted even more dismal and negative consequences."

Linda was paying close attention to Rebecca, who looked so fragile and vulnerable. She then felt a warm and pleasant energy when realising the progress of the spirit next to her.

Rebecca continued, "One of the experiences I just remembered was lived centuries ago in England. I was born into a poor family, and I had an early age disease that left me crippled. I felt ashamed about my disability and hated myself. I felt ugly compared to the other girls in the village and I never saw any good in life. My parents were very caring and tried their best to educate me, but we were so poor that sometimes we hardly had anything to eat. I was only a teenager when my parents died, the victims of a fatal disease. Our house was repossessed by the landlord and I was thrown out into the streets without anywhere to go. I began to wander around London, sleeping every night in a different place. It didn't take long before I got myself into prostitution, and wandering around the streets I used to sell my body in order to survive. That was for me an easy way to make a living. Men would use my body in exchange for some rum and old bread, and the more I let strangers use my body the more I hated myself and who I was. Eventually, old age came and I couldn't find any men willing to pay me for sex any more. I found myself living on the streets, surrounded by rats and pests." Rebecca, looking down, paused for a while and made a huge effort to continue telling the facts of that past life experience without crying.

"Are you okay?" asked Linda.

Rebecca nodded and continued the story. "I contracted cholera and died alone in the streets. When I passed away my spirit went straight to the dark regions. That place was far away from being the heaven that I was promised by the church. It was dark, cold and terrorizing, just like the streets of London where I used to live. There were horrible creatures everywhere; some screaming in pain and some others seeming to enjoy the pain suffered by spirits like me. When I passed away, my spirit was still similar to the woman I was on Earth. I was still ugly and crippled, and I carried with me all of the bad feelings and depression I had when I was on Earth. That was my worst hell. If once I believed in what the church said - that when I died I was going to enter heaven and free myself from the ugly woman I was - reality showed me that all of that preaching from the priests was untrue. My heaven was actually a horrible, dark and cold hell."

"And you carried your personal hell with you until now," said Linda, gently touching her face. Linda raised Rebecca's head slowly and continued, "As you are learning, your depressive thoughts and lack of self-esteem only separated you from all the beauties in life. I'm not saying that your life back in the early 1800s in London was easy, not at all. You had many challenges to overcome, such as losing your parents at such a young age, the problem with your leg, which alone was a reason in those times for people to cast you aside and for you to be forgotten by society. Your life was filled with many challenges and you failed to pass those tests simply because you lost your faith. By hating yourself you hated God and you separated yourself from Him."

Rebecca covered her face with her hands. Noticing that Rebecca was embarrassed, Linda embraced her with a tight and warm hug.

"I'm not here to judge you - remember?" said Linda. "You thought that you were lonely and forgotten, when actually home was always here, waiting for your return."

"That place was horrible. I suffered more than I suffered on Earth. The bad smell; the never-ending cold nights…Where were the heavens when I needed them most?"

"That was the place you attracted to yourself in that moment of your existence. You were not ready for a recovery, nor ready to accept that you wanted a change. You had entrenched yourself in so much suffering and pain that within yourself you thought you didn't deserve anything better than to be punished. It was your own choice to keeping on punishing yourself. You created your own badness in your mind, and it grew bigger and bigger inside yourself."

At that moment a bluebird alighted next to Rebecca on the bench. The bird started to tweet, making a beautiful sound.

"See how beautiful life is," said Linda, pointing at the bird. "Look at this gorgeous creature that came here to sing for us. This is the mistake many make. They have all the beauty and blessings around them, they have all the good and the support to help them to evolve, but they insist on keeping their eyes closed to the wonderful universe we have, and instead they insist on focusing on the darkness."

"And that's what I have been doing…" said Rebecca, her sad face showing she was close to tears.

Linda nodded softly. "Yes. Your lack of faith and self-esteem only made you get more stuck in the darkness you created for yourself." The bluebird jumped on to Linda's leg. "But one of the many beauties of life is that we learn and we have chances to start over and over again and make it right. God isn't punishing His creatures when life shows them difficulties, but actually giving them a new chance to learn and evolve."

Linda touched the bird, which opened its wings and flew away. She then concluded, "A very enlightened spirit taught the humans when he was incarnated on Earth. He said the following: 'Though nobody can go back and make a new beginning, anyone can start over and make a new ending.' This saying was one of Chico Xavier's teachings, and it reveals one of the most amazing laws of the universe: the law of reincarnation, which always give us a new chance to get it right."

Linda smiled again to Rebecca and said, "Any time you feel that depressive thoughts might be approaching your mind, you have to think, 'There's a light inside of me, and it shines from within to outside. This light will protect me through any darkness and bring only joy and happiness to my life!' " When Linda said those words, a bright light radiated from her centre and shone all around her. She looked around, as if showing Rebecca what had just happened, and concluded, "Your will power and your faith are the key to the switch. Turn on the light inside you and brighten not only yourself but also all of those around you. You have the key."

They both stood up and Rebecca thanked Linda for her visit. Before leaving, Linda offered her an invitation. "We are having a soirée soon at Lunas, where I live. I would love you to come and join us."

Rebecca asked "Are you sure I could come? Would you have someone like me in your colony?"

"What do you mean, someone like you, Rebecca? You are beautiful, just like me and all the other creatures of God in the universe, and yes, I would love to introduce you to my friends and to the place I now call home."

Looking very excited, Rebecca smiled, still not believing she had just been invited to a social event.

"I'll ask your mentors at the recovery hospital; I don't think they'll say no." Before leaving, Linda said, "Don't forget you have the key to turn on the light inside of you and brighten the way through any darkness!"

Linda left, returning to the chambers where she had some patients awaiting her care. Rebecca had felt love for the first time in her whole existence so far.

Chapter Unconditional love

Linda had arrived at the chambers of the suffering and the lost spirits, back from her encounter with Rebecca at Magiar, and was telling Teresa about how happy she was feeling after noticing Rebecca's improvement. She described the past life experience Rebecca had had in London, and spoke of the many ideas she had to continue helping Rebecca to learn to love herself and life.

"Did you invite her to the soirée?"

"Yes, I did. It will be nice for her to come and visit us, especially at such a special event as our soirée," replied Linda. "I was feeling a bit down after I left the Earth and, you know…It's been very difficult watching Roy, Katie and everyone going through such a difficult time, but then I went to the recovery hospital where Rebecca is, and I felt so much happier and re-energized after spending time with her."

"What you are feeling is called love, unconditional love. You are feeling happy at seeing someone you love progressing."

"But how can I feel so happy myself just by seeing a stranger's happiness?" asked Linda, looking a bit confused.

"We are never completely strangers to one another, my dear. Somehow at some point our lives have crossed with one another. Soon you will remember where you know Rebecca from. It goes back to a life experience that links you all: Katie, Roy and the others."

"I've been thinking a lot but I can't figure out who Rebecca was back then. Of course, you know…I remember myself and Roy, Katie, Marta, but not Rebecca."

"Very soon you will remember, but for now enjoy these moments you are having with her and continue to introduce her to the wonders of life. It's so gratifying to see that she is now finally letting go all the sadness and opening herself to the blessings and new opportunities in her life."

"You are right, it is, and I can't wait to see Rebecca evolving and progressing even more!" said Linda, with a sparkle in her eyes.

"The more she progresses, the happier you will become. This is because those who inject others' lives with love are given back even more love by the universe. You receive multiple times back at you all the energy you give to others."

"You are right, Teresa. It's such a rewarding feeling to see her progress. To see how much she's improved fills my soul with happiness."

"Soon others will be needing you. I guess you have figured it out already?" said Teresa, who was now looking serious. "Roy and Katie's lives are about to change once again. Life will give them the next stage of their tests very soon, and you know what's going to happen."

Pensive, Linda asked, "Do you mean that…they are about to meet…"

"Yes, my dear. It's time for Marta and Roy's lives to cross once again. Difficult times are heading their way."

****

Katie's corporeal body was resting, sleeping in bed and her soul was next to its body when Linda arrived.

"Mom, mom! You're back!" said Katie, looking amazed at Linda. She ran towards her mother and gave her a strong hug. Daughter and mother remained embraced for a long time.

"I miss you so much, mom… why you don't come back to stay here with us?" asked Katie, looking down.

"Oh my sweetheart…I am here with you and will always be." Linda dried a tear that was falling down the little girl's face and continued to stroke her hair.

"I'm scared, mom. I feel so lonely sometimes. I look everywhere, looking for you. Sometimes I close my eyes and pretend it's all a bad dream and count to ten and think that when I open my eyes you'll come through the door and come back to us."

"I know my darling…I know. And every time you wish I was here with you I actually am. You can't see me but I am here looking after you at all times." Linda kissed her and said, "Believe me, you are never alone. Mom is here any time you need me, and I will always be."

Linda stood up and, extending her hand to Katie, she invited her to come travelling. Katie smiled excitedly, saying yes. They both sped around the universe at the speed of light and arrived at Lunas by the lake. Even though it was night in Asheville, at Lunas it was sunny and pleasantly warm. The sky was blue with no clouds and three moons could be seen clearly up high. Suddenly two horses arrived and approached Linda and Katie. Linda stroked the mane of one of them and said, "Look sweetheart, who's here? It's Asas!"

The horse stooped down completely, allowing Katie to mount. Once both Linda and Katie were seated on the horses they rode along the fields in Lunas. At one point the horses flew high up in the air and Katie's laughs could be heard from far away. Both Linda and Katie were way up in the skies on their horses, and Linda couldn't stop watching Katie's happy face.

"Come on Asas, faster…faster!" said Katie, giggling and looking very happy. She was clinging on to Asas very tightly and from time to time she kissed him.

Linda looked at her and felt content seeing Katie smiling and happy after she had gone through so much suffering. From up above they could see the lake in Lunas, and the colourful valleys covered by flowers.

"Look sweetheart, ahead," said Linda, pointing forwards.

"Wow, mom, it's a rainbow!" Katie looked amazed and urged Asas to go towards it.

Both horses flew all the way to the rainbow and passed through it, and for few moments it was like a shower of colours coming down over them. After a beautiful journey around the skies in Lunas, both mother and daughter landed back in the field. Katie was so happy in the spiritual world that her corporeal body back on Earth was laughing in bed while sleeping.

Teresa and Geraldine came in to pay them a visit before Linda took Katie's soul back. "Hello princess. How are you?" asked Teresa, smiling at Katie.

"I'm fine thanks, aunt Teresa. I'm always happy when I'm with my mother," answered Katie, giggling.

"I see..." responded Teresa.

"Were you two playing?" asked Geraldine.

Katie, still giggling, said, "No. We were riding our horses through the skies." She was gesticulating and performing movements showing how she had ridden the horse. She told them about the rainbow they had just seen. Katie then ran off into the field, asking Linda to run after her, and so Linda did.

Teresa and Geraldine watched mother and daughter running around the field and laughing like two children. Looking worried, Geraldine said to Teresa, "They are about to meet, Teresa. Roy and Marta, and I don't know if Marta is ready for this yet. From what I can see, so far in her life experience she is still making the same mistakes she made before."

"This time it's got to be different, my sister. She has to have learnt, with all the blood that once was shed," Teresa said with her hands together as if praying.

"We hope that that horror may never happen again, but you know how difficult it is for some to leave all the negative and evil thoughts of such violence and vengeance behind and let love in. I just have a feeling that she might not be ready yet. She had too much hate within her, and even before she reincarnated she was thinking evil things."

Linda returned to Teresa and Geraldine. She was holding Katie who was asleep in her arms. "It's time to take her back. I gave her lots of positive vibrations and love, and I feel that her soul is now recharged."

Geraldine and Teresa kissed Katie's forehead and both said at the same time, "Go in peace, my dear."

Linda closed her eyes and travelled to Earth, arriving in less than a second at Katie's bedroom, where the little girl's corporeal body was asleep in bed. Like all the incarnated spirits, her soul had fluidic laces that linked her soul to her body, and even though her soul could travel millions of miles away in the universe, the fluidic laces were always connecting body and soul. These fluidic links are only broken at the moment of the corporeal body's death. The breakage means that the soul is then free and returns to the spiritual world in its spirit form. Linda returned Katie's soul back to her corporeal body just in time for the sunrise on Earth, bringing a new day in Asheville. Soon Elizabeth came in to the room to wake up her granddaughter and, kissing her on her forehead, she said kindly, "Wake up, my little girl. A new day has arrived and it's time for school."

Katie slowly roused herself from the deep sleep and gently opened her eyes. When she had woken up completely she jumped on the bed, excited and happy, telling her grandmother she had had a dream with her mother where they had both ridden flying horses together.

"I can't remember much but she was beautiful, grandma…and she was bright, very bright."

"It sounds like a very nice dream, my darling. Now let's go and get dressed. You can tell me more about your dream at breakfast."

Katie was so excited that she couldn't stop talking about the dream. Although she didn't recall much, she remembered the hugs and kisses she received from her mother, and also the flying horses. She was talking non-stop as she dressed. Linda was there in the room watching the scene, and before leaving she prayed, asking for the home to be filled with love, harmony and happiness.

When they got to the kitchen, Roy was there, ready for work.

"Good morning, dad," exclaimed Katie, smiling.

"Good morning, my sweetheart. Good morning, Elizabeth."

Surprised by Roy being up and ready for work so early, Elizabeth asked, "Are you not joining us for breakfast?"

"I would love too, but I'm in a rush. It's very busy at the office and I'm planning to start early today." Roy kissed his daughter on her cheek and said, "I'll see you later, my darling. I promise I'll be home early from work so we can spend time together." He picked up a bunch of folders from the coffee table in the living room and left the house, fully focused on his work.

Roy had changed a lot since his car accident. He had stopped going to bars after work and getting drunk every night. He was more involved in Katie's life and even his relationship with Elizabeth and Joey had improved. Every night after tucking Katie into bed he spent hours talking to them about his day at work, and they all watched television together. Their relationship had become more loving and fraternal. Elizabeth and Joey were relieved to see the changes in Roy, and the more time they spent together, the more their feelings for Roy turned into love.

Chapter Destiny knocking at the door

At the spiritual colony of Lunas, the day of the soirée had arrived, and Linda had gone to pick up Rebecca in Magiar. Rebecca was waiting for Linda, feeling very excited at the thought of meeting her colony and attending the event. Rebecca looked different. She was more radiant, and instead of constantly gazing down as she used to, she was finally looking Linda in the eyes. Her facial expressions were softer and she looked happier.

When they arrived at the entry to Lunas, Rebecca was fascinated by the tall golden gates. She looked them up and down, admiring every crafted detail. Linda, noticing the shine in her eyes, told her, "We still have some time before the concert starts, so let me show you around and introduce you to our colony."

They walked past the tall gates and through the entrance. Rebecca could then see the magnitude of Lunas, with its miles and miles of fields and the valleys which were covered by a very colourful carpet made of flowers. She paused to admire the crystal clear lake and the white swans swimming on it, but what impressed Rebecca most was the enormous glazed building located at the centre of the lake. It was circular and very grand, with a huge dome covering its centre. The building was floating over the lake, as was a crystal clear bridge linking it to both sides of the water.

"That is our ministerial palace," said Linda, pointing to the glazed building floating on the lake. "It is where our representatives and ministers have their meetings and organize the society here in Lunas."

Rebecca was rendered speechless by such a beautiful place. They continued their walk, passing through the neighbourhood where all the houses were located. Linda took the opportunity to show Rebecca where she lived. A few yards after the residential area there were another three buildings constructed with the same design as the ministerial palace, but with three domes. They were surrounded by green and very tall trees. The three buildings were connected by small bridges. They were built with a see-through material, the technology for which did not yet exist on Earth.

"Wow, it looks so beautiful. I would say it looks as if the domes are made of bubbles next to each other… I mean…because the walls look so clear and so thin." She felt rather embarrassed, as if thinking she was being silly. "I mean, I've never seen structures like that before."

Linda smiled and said, "Don't worry. It's quite understandable that you don't know how to describe these buildings. They've been built with a completely new technology which hasn't been used on Earth yet." Pointing at the first structure, Linda explained, "There are three main buildings and they are all connected. That first one, the biggest of them all, is our temple. We go there for our prayers and for our spiritual meetings." Pointing to the dome next to it, she continued, "The next one is the reincarnation building. Spirits who are about to return for another incarnation experience spend their reclusion time preparing to reincarnate. The reason why the two buildings are so close is because, before the spirit goes to reclusion, we hold a party at the temple to celebrate and say our goodbyes to the spirit who is going. We all then perform our prayers to wish good fortune to the spirit going on the new journey. It's usually a beautiful ceremony."

"And the spirits who are leaving…I mean reincarnating… Do they get excited to leave?"

"Yes and no… For the spirit, the reincarnation is a trial which will give them a new chance to attain their purification. The majority of the spirits do feel happy and excited, mainly because reincarnation is always a new chance given to us to start over again. It's an opportunity to learn new things and especially a chance to repair a mistake committed in the past that is delaying their progress, although some spirits also feel the tension and fear of the unknown experience. It's like a traveller who is going on a perilous voyage without knowing if he is going to succeed or not."

"I imagine it can be quite a big conflict of emotions."

"Exactly," replied Linda. "It's usually a conflict between the excitement of the new chance to re-start and the fear of the obstacles that are about to come with the new corporeal existence."

The two continued exploring the unusual buildings while discussing more about reincarnation and its process.

"What I find strange is that even though the buildings are made of a clear material like glass, I'm not able to see inside them. The material looks transparent but I can't see through it."

"That is because you are in a different vibration from us here. One day you will not only be able to see it, but also you will live here. The more we progress, the purer we become, the more faculties we have and the more the universe opens all its doors to us. This is one of the many wonders of our existence. The more we purify our spirits, the more we get to know and experience the infinite universe."

Linda continued walking alongside Rebecca, showing her around and explaining more about Lunas, until they finally reached a large arena. A great many spirits were entering the building to watch the performance. Some were in small groups, others in couples or by themselves. There was a very peaceful and pleasant atmosphere in the whole place that felt to Rebecca very contagious.

"Here we are. This is our final destination."

"It's huge!" exclaimed Rebecca, looking up at the arena.

"Yes, this is our arena. Here we watch presentations of music, theatre, ballet and all sorts of arts. Tonight, as I explained earlier, Teresa and Geraldine, whom you met at the chambers of the suffering and lost spirits, will be performing with the orchestra."

"I'm so excited, Linda!"

"So am I. I haven't seen those two playing for a long time. The music here is pure and very touching, you'll see."

They both went inside and settled themselves on their seats, ready for the soirée to start.

****

Meanwhile on Earth, Roy, Katie, Elizabeth and Joey were sitting at the table having dinner. Katie was telling them how her day had been in school. Suddenly they heard someone knocking frenetically on the front door.

"Oh gosh. Who might that be, knocking so loudly?" Elizabeth was about to stand up when Roy volunteered to go and answer the door.

The hammering was non-stop and increasing in intensity. Roy opened the door and as soon he saw who was there he quickly stepped outside, closing the door so nobody could see the visitor. He said, almost whispering, scared that someone might hear him, "You?" He looked around and checked through the window to see if anybody was looking out, and then asked, "What are you doing here?"

The woman had long, dark, red hair and looked visibly agitated. She replied with a very strong New York accent, "I'm here to talk to you, Roy. I've been trying to speak to you for ages and you keep on ignoring my calls."

"Please leave. If my in-laws see you here they will ask me questions."

She raised her voice and said, "I won't leave until we talk. I got a proposal for you!"

Roy put a finger to his lips, urging her to speak more quietly, and said, "Okay okay… Go to my office tomorrow - Graham Palmer, Avenue 2566 - and meet me there."

"I do know where your office is, Roy!" she said, looking angry.

"Okay okay…please calm down. Meet me tomorrow."

"Roy, I'm telling you, if you don't see me tomorrow I will come back here and tell them everything about us, and then you'll have to listen to me, like it or not!"

"I promise…I promise. Now please go before somebody sees you here."

The woman moved closer and kissed Roy's lips before leaving, saying, "This is to remind you of what I mean to you."

Roy went back inside and joined the family at the table, looking pale and agitated. They were all anxious, waiting to find out who the visitor had been.

"So, Roy? Who was there? We could hear a female voice but not one we actually recognized," asked Elizabeth.

"Hmm... It was a..." He paused for a few seconds, trying to think of an answer. "She works in the office. She came in to say that she isn't going to be able to go to work tomorrow because of her daughter."

They all stared at him, not understanding why he was so nervous about the visit. Roy, still sweating, finished by saying, "Her daughter isn't feeling well and she asked me if she could have the day tomorrow as a vacation day or a sick day so she can stay at home and look after her daughter...that's it."

After a few moments Katie broke the awkward silence by saying, "Dad, grandma bought me a new book for our bedtime story. It's called *Alice in Wonderland*! Would you read it for me?"

"Of course, sweetheart. Let's look forward to bedtime, then. *'What does she want from me? It's been quite a while now. Why has she come back looking for me?'* Roy couldn't stop thinking of her. *'Does she know about Linda? Is that why she came all the way here to speak to me? Elizabeth and Roy must not find out about her - they would never forgive me.'*

****

Back at Lunas, the soirée had finished. There was a standing ovation from the public, and Teresa and Geraldine were at the centre of the stage among the other members of the orchestra, thanking everyone for their presence and support. Rebecca was enchanted with such a beautiful spectacle; she had been shedding emotional tears throughout the whole concert. When they left the arena Rebecca couldn't stop thanking Linda for the opportunity of visiting her colony and watching the spectacle.

"Please, Rebecca. You don't have to thank me. It has been a pleasure to spend time with you."

Rebecca smiled and Linda continued, "I'm so glad to see that you're now happier with yourself and enjoying life more."

"I am indeed, and I need to thank you for this."

Linda smiled and said, "No, don't thank me. I can only show you the way but it's down to you to walk it."

Rebecca had a sort of sadness in her eyes when she said, "I guess it's time to go back to Magiar."

"Don't say it like that. You are being looked after by very loving people there who want you to fully love yourself so you can grow stronger and go on with your journey."

"I know, I didn't mean that way. It's just that it still feels like being in a hospital."

"Make the most out of the present moment and of what you've got right now. The present time is what matters. We need to make the most of all of the opportunities given to us now in order to make a better future. You have to reap good things now in order to sow good things in the future." Linda smiled and continued, "Get to meet new friends at the Magiar and learn as much as you can. You are recovering very quickly, my dear, and I have a feeling that very soon you will be free to go to your new home, a spiritual colony where you'll be welcomed and get the support necessary to embark on your new test."

Rebecca smiled and agreed, "You're right. I need to be grateful for the blessings I have. They have been lovely to me there and it's been a very peaceful time. I've never known anything like it before. I've had time to learn things about myself I didn't know, and I'm actually getting to love myself as I am."

Rebecca held Linda's hand and together they left Luna, heading to Magiar.

Chapter A tempting lust

The following day arrived and Roy was walking around in circles in his office, feeling nervous and anxious. He could not think of anything else but the visit from the woman yesterday evening.

'What does she want with me? Why is she back?' He couldn't stop thinking of her. He had first met her on one of his business trips to New York City after a business dinner with some of the company's directors at a trendy Japanese restaurant in Manhattan. Her name was Penelope and she was alone at the table next to the one where he was sitting with his work colleagues. Penelope was tall, with long, dark, red hair and very big and fascinating blue eyes. She was a beautiful lady and was very aware of her own beauty. Although she was only twenty-two years old back then, she had already broken many men's hearts by getting them interested in her and leading them on. She enjoyed playing with other people's feelings and emotions as if it was all an amusing game for her. Her father was the owner of the restaurant and many others in Manhattan. A self-made multi-millionaire, he also owned many other businesses and properties around New York City.

'When Linda died I swore I would never see her again and now she's here after me,' Roy thought, moments before Penelope's arrival.

His thoughts were interrupted by a knock on his office door. It was his secretary announcing that Penelope was outside. His heart started to beat quickly. Feeling gripped by tension, he told his secretary to let her in.

Penelope entered the room with her usual confidence, running her hands through her hair. She looked straight into his eyes and immediately noticed his pupils were dilated, showing his attraction for her. *'Bingo, he's still crazy for me,'* she thought, and went straight to the point. "You've been ignoring my calls and haven't responded to any of my letters. I thought that you would have come to me after your wife's death. She was the only reason why we couldn't be together, correct?"

"How do you know about my wife's accident?" asked Roy.

"Come on, Roy. It wasn't difficult to find out. I contacted your offices several times, as you know, and once I realized you were avoiding me I started to ask people for information. Don't forget I have money, and money buys any information."

"Did you send a detective after me?"

"Don't be silly!" she laughed. "I would if I'd had to but it wasn't necessary. Your secretary isn't the smartest of women. Her brain's the size of a peanut and she ended up giving me all the stories over the phone after I kept her sweet by pretending to be her friend." Penelope moved very close to him and, putting her lips next to his, she said, "I know you still love me. I can see it in your eyes."

Roy stepped backwards and asked her to take a seat. He was shaky but trying very hard not to show his anxiety and his true feelings.

"What's happened?" asked Penelope as she sat down. "I want to know what's changed, since the only thing that stopped us being together was your marriage, and as far as I know we don't have that obstacle any more."

"Do you think it's easy for me? I have a daughter who needs me. I've been having the most difficult time trying to keep up with my job and being a dad. Plus I'm trying to deal with the loss of..."

"Give me a break, Roy. We were having great sex behind your wife's back for most of the time you were married, and now you're telling me you're dealing with the loss of your wife? Please!"

Roy faced her for the first time, looking furious. "I can't forgive myself for that. Linda didn't deserve it. It was wrong, we shouldn't...I mean, I shouldn't have..."

Penelope stood up quickly and, leaning over the desk, she grabbed him by his shoulders and pulled him towards her, finishing by kissing him on the lips.

"Now, look at me," she ordered, speaking with her lips next to his. "You love me and you know you do. I'm sorry for all of what happened but this is our time, Roy. Let's take this opportunity and get together. I know you like the idea of moving over and living the luxurious lifestyle I can offer you."

Roy moved away from her. "I can't. I don't think I can ever be with you again after what happened. I feel so guilty for the accident and…whenever I look at my daughter, Linda's face comes up in my mind, bringing all the guilt of my betrayal and the accident…"

"Stop, Roy! Stop being such a coward. It wasn't your fault. It was an accident! And you were about to go and tell her everything about us anyway, weren't you? You told me you were going to talk to her on that weekend and tell her it was all finished between you two."

You're making me sick, Penelope. Don't you have any sympathy for anyone? My daughter has just lost her mother and she is very vulnerable right now. She's only a little girl."

"Your daughter is very young, and in time she'll forget all about this and get used to the reality." Holding Roy's hand, Penelope changed her approach, Using a very soft tone of voice she said, "Your daughter needs a mother, and I can be a stronger influence in her life."

Realising she had managed to touch Roy's heart, Penelope filled up her eyes with crocodile tears, pretending to feel emotional, and then said, "I'm offering you a chance - a chance for both of us. I've inherited my father's assets. I don't know if you know, but my father passed away a few months ago and I feel so sad and lonely."

"Yes, I saw in the papers about your father's death. I'm very sorry for you."

"It's been very hard, you know. Dad meant everything to me since my mother died and now it's not easy taking all of the business decisions and going through life without him." She shed many tears. "I'm only twenty-five, Roy…I miss him loads."

Roy, feeling vulnerable, came closer to her and hugged her, kissing her softly on the cheek. Taking advantage of the situation, Penelope pretended to cry even more and she repeated time and time again how difficult her life had become after her father's death. It didn't take long for Roy to fall completely for her game.

'It's working. I need to keep up the sweet and vulnerable act and play the game,' she thought. Keeping her soft tone, she continued, "Roy...I know the pain of losing someone as important as a mother from your life, because I went through that pain just as your daughter did. I know that she will be able to relate to me." Still letting tears run down her face, Penelope continued, "Give us a chance and I promise you I will be a very loving mother for her."

"How do you expect me to go to my parents-in-law now and tell them that I was going behind their daughter's back all this time? That wouldn't only hurt them, but hurt my daughter Katie too."

"You don't have to mention our past. They don't need to know anything about it. Simply tell them that we've just met and they'll understand...they'll have to. You're young, Roy, and you have to get on with your life. They'll understand, you'll see. You are young and you met someone new and you want to be with this new person...simple as that."

Roy went quiet and pensive while Penelope described a complete plan. He felt a mixture of embarrassment and guilt for what he had done to Linda. Happy with the feelings she had created in Roy, Penelope took a business card out of her purse and put it on the desk top. She then gave him a kiss on the lips and said, before leaving, "This is my card with the address of the hotel where I'm staying. I'll be waiting for you tonight," and she left his office before Roy could say anything.

Roy stood there speechless, lost in his thoughts. *'Why does she get to me so much? What is it about this woman that makes me feel like this?'*

****

Later that evening Elizabeth noticed that Roy was different. They had their meal together as usual, but he was very quiet and introspective. Katie had tried to get him to play games with her after dinner, but he had said he wasn't feeling well and went to his bedroom. So that Katie wouldn't be upset, Elizabeth cuddled her and tucked her into bed, then read her the continuation of *Alice in Wonderland.* After Katie had fallen asleep, Elizabeth kissed her goodnight and went down to the living room to join her husband who was watching the evening news.

"Didn't you find his behaviour strange tonight?" asked Elizabeth.

"Yes I did. He was very quiet tonight and seemed very distant," replied Joey, looking at the television but deep down feeling worried about Roy. After a few moments he continued, "I just hope he isn't getting up to anything that he'll regret."

"What do you mean by that? Do you think he's gone back to drinking?" asked Elizabeth, standing up and getting agitated. "Oh Joey, I don't think I'd be able to go through all that again with him."

Joey thought twice before replying and then said, "Leave it. He might just be feeling under the weather. Let's not worry about what doesn't even exist. By the way, I wanted to talk to you, Beth."

Elizabeth knew what her husband was going to say. They had been living away from their home for quite a while, and even though they were going back to check on their house every weekend, she knew that at some point they would have to start thinking of going back to their own lives, leaving Roy and Katie.

"We've been away for quite a while now. Before we couldn't think of leaving Roy to look after Katie and we were waiting for him to stop behaving like a teenager." Joey took a long breath. "It seems like the time to go back home is getting closer..." Noticing that Elizabeth was upset, he leaned towards her and, with a soft tone, he continued, "I know it's tough. I'll miss her as well, but ..."

With a tear in her eye Elizabeth said, "Our little girl needs us more than ever. Linda isn't here to look after her and I feel that she's our responsibility now. I couldn't even think of leaving Katie now and... somehow I kind of feel responsible for Roy too."

"I know, my darling. I feel the same as you, but this is Roy's home and ..."

Very emotional, Elizabeth interrupted him. "Yes but it's our daughter's house too, and we have the right to be here for as long as we want and to look after our little girl."

"Don't cry, please. I'm only saying that I don't feel at home here and that I do miss having my own space and us having our life. But if this is the price we need to pay in order to stay closer to Katie then I don't mind. I was actually going to suggest that if we feel so strongly about being close to them, perhaps we should think of selling our house and buying one nearby, then perhaps we can still participate in Katie's life but have our own space at the same time."

Elizabeth smiled, feeling extremely excited with Joey's idea, and gave him a big hug. "Oh Joey, you're so special. That's exactly what I was thinking."

"I couldn't leave our Katie, and perhaps I do feel like caring for Roy too," said Joey. He smiled and finished by saying, "Tomorrow I'll go around some property agencies and see what's available."

Chapter The betrayal

On the following day Roy received a phone call from Penelope first thing in the morning. She had a very sensual tone to her voice as she said, "I was waiting for you last night, Roy."

"I'm sorry, I wasn't feeling well," Roy replied, feeling his heart racing.

"Perhaps we should meet for lunch?"

"When?

"I would say meet me at 1 p.m. at my hotel…otherwise…"

Roy's heart was going even faster and his hands were shaky. He paused for a moment, as he didn't want to show in his voice that he was feeling very excited and nervous at the same time. After a few seconds in silence he managed to recover and ask, "Otherwise what?"

Giggling, she replied, "I will go to your office completely naked and jump on you and kiss you in front of all of your staff. What do you think? Tempting?"

Roy found her answer funny and provocative. She had sounded so sexy, he couldn't resist. He broke out in laughter and played along. "Come on, you wouldn't dare."

"Don't tempt me! One o'clock at mine, otherwise, you know…I will be there completely nude." She finished by making a noisy kiss down the phone and hung up.

'How can she make me feel this way? I can't stop thinking of her,' thought Roy, still in a cold sweat and with his heart racing. He tried to concentrate on the pile of paperwork on his desk, but nothing could make him stop thinking of Penelope. Their nights of passion in New York City and the dates they had were forcing their way into his mind non-stop alongside recollections of Linda and the lies he had told her to hide his affair. His mind was divided between the desire to meet up with Penelope and the guilty thoughts about his betrayal of Linda.

He changed his mind several times during the morning and wasn't able to get any work done. At 1 p.m. there he was, outside her hotel room, knocking on the door. Seconds later it opened to reveal Penelope wearing provocative black lingerie. Before he could say anything she began to seduce him by putting her arms around his neck, and led him to bed straight away.

Two hours later Roy was getting dressed quickly as he had to rush back to work for a business meeting. Before leaving he stopped to watch and admire Penelope, who was sleeping naked on the bed. She was clutching a pillow, sleeping peacefully and looking very angelic, very different from the real Penelope, who was so assertive and loud, a woman he was never able to say no to. There she was in bed, looking so pure and beautiful, provoking a mixture of feelings inside him. He stroked her hair and gently kissed her lips, then whispered in her ear before leaving, "I'll see you later this evening."

****

Roy and Penelope met every evening that week, with Roy usually staying overnight with her at the hotel. On the few nights when he went back home, he avoided seeing Elizabeth and Joey, afraid they would ask questions. In the morning he would leave home before they woke up, again avoiding any possible questions about where he was going every night. On one of the few nights on which he came home after meeting Penelope, he found a note on the kitchen table saying:

Hi Roy,

We need to talk to you.

Elizabeth.

Afraid that his parents-in-law were going to ask him about where he had been staying at night, and that he would have to tell them about Penelope, he again made sure he woke up earlier than usual and left for work while they were still asleep.

"Where's daddy, grandma? He isn't in his bed or in the bathroom. I looked for him everywhere. I haven't seen daddy for days now," asked Katie, sitting at the table eating her breakfast.

"It seems like your daddy has gone to work earlier today, my sweetheart. Eat your pancakes and grandpa will take you to school," responded Elizabeth pensively, also wondering about Roy's absence.

When Katie went to the bathroom Elizabeth whispered to Joey, "It seems like Roy has gone back to his teenage days again. I bet he's going to the bar after work and getting drunk all over again."

"Calm down. Let's not draw any conclusions without giving him the benefit of the doubt. I'll call in at his office today and tell him we need to talk to him. We have to tell him about the house we found in Damien Avenue and then we can take the opportunity to ask him if everything's okay."

"It's alright then. Tell him I'll cook his favourite chicken tonight."

"Are you ready, grandpa?" shouted Katie from the front door, holding her school bag.

"I'm coming, Katie." Joey kissed his wife on the cheek and left with Katie. After dropping her at school he stopped by at Roy's office, without having mentioned that he was coming.

"What a surprise, Joey!" said Roy while shaking his hand. "Please, take a seat."

Roy's secretary served Joey a cup of coffee and left the two of them alone.

"What brings you here?" asked Roy.

"Oh Roy... I'll come straight to the point with you. Elizabeth and I are worried about you. Last time we saw you, you seemed a bit troubled. You know, a bit distant and pensive. Then for quite a few nights you've been getting home late, usually after midnight…and we noticed a few times you haven't come home at all." Trying not to come across as if he was aiming to control Roy's life, he changed his tone of voice. "Sorry, I don't mean to tell you what time you should be at home, you know…we were just worried about you after the accident and…"

"Please Joey, don't worry. I'm not thinking anything bad of you two for being concerned. I know you and Elizabeth really care about me and yes, I agree I might have given you some reason to think that there's something wrong lately."

"So? Is there any reason why we should be worried about you?"

Roy took a sip of his coffee and replied, with a timid smile, "No, no. You don't have any reason, I promise you. Actually I was going to talk to you two tonight. I have some news I would like to share with you. But I'm afraid that you'll have to wait until tonight, as I want to tell both of you and Katie all together."

Joey seemed surprised with Roy. He asked for some sort of clue about what Roy was going to say that evening, but Roy was giving nothing away. Instead he changed the subject by asking, "What about the note Elizabeth left on the kitchen table? Do you two also have something to say?"

Joey drank the rest of his coffee and, standing up, he replied, "Well…it's nothing too important, but let's keep it for tonight. Elizabeth asked me tell you that she's going to prepare the roast chicken you like."

"Okay then. I'm looking forward to it. I should be home at the usual time." Realising what he had just said, he smiled. "I mean, the usual time when I'm not coming home late…you know…"

"Alright then, I'll see you at seven, Roy," replied Joey at the door before leaving.

"See you later, Joey."

Immediately the phone rang and it was Penelope calling. She wanted to know if Roy had plucked up the courage to speak to his parents-in-law about their plans. She was euphoric when he told her that he had just received a visit from Joey and that he had told him about delivering the news later at dinner.

"Are you sure you don't want me to come with you? I would love to meet Katie," asked Penelope.

"No, it's more respectful if I talk to them first. It is a very sensitive subject,"

"So I won't see you tonight then?" she asked with a forced crying voice.

"No, I haven't spent any time with Katie this week and she's probably in need of some dad and daughter time. Soon we'll have all the time in the world to be together anyway."

"Okay darling, I'll let you get on with work. Kisses, baby," said Penelope, and hung up.

"Some dad and daughter time?" she repeated out loud to herself. "Barghh." She put her finger in her throat as if feeling sick. Feeling very irritated, she looked at herself in the mirror and brushed her hair while continuing to speak out loud to herself. "It's more respectful if he tells them first? Respectful? Is he kidding or what? He spent over three years going behind his wife's back with me and lying to everyone around him and now he wants to be respectful? Ha! What a joke."

She put on a fitted slim black dress, and just as she had finished getting ready the phone rang. It was her personal assistant Nigel.

"Hi Nigel, what now?" she asked in a very arrogant manner, very different from the soft tone she used when speaking to Roy.

"The shareholders are requesting a meeting and I need to know if you're planning to be back for the meeting next Thursday?"

"Yes I am. I can't bear spending much longer in this world's end full of rednecks everywhere. This place is a shithole and I'm just about to commit suicide."

Nigel laughed and said with irony, "I guessed so."

"I need you to arrange for the pilot to pick me up from the same airport I arrived at. Get the limo ready to pick me up from La Guardia and make sure there's plenty of champagne waiting for me in the limo."

"I will make sure the champagne is on hand to celebrate you returning to civilization," said Nigel.

"Back to the centre of the frigging universe more like! By the way, Roy and his little brat are coming to live with me. I want a room to be made up for a little girl. You know, get some fresh linen, towels and all of that."

"So you've decided then? You're bringing the rednecks with you?"

"I will have him as I said I would. I always get what I want, Nigel, don't ever forget that. I always get what I want."

Nigel tried to get more information out of her and asked for more details about the girl, so he could organize the decoration of the bedroom according to her age, but Penelope went back to her initial rude tone. "I guess it's five or six…something like that. To be honest I don't care. There's no need to worry too much about the room. Very simple…one bed for her to sleep in, sheets… you know, the essentials." Before hanging up she remembered something. "Aw… throw in some teddy bears and dolls or whatever around the bedroom so it looks like I've put some thought into it and it'll be fine. By the way, I want you to use that room near the staff area, the small room by the kitchen, far from the main areas. Very far from my bedroom."

She hung up and drank in one go a whole glass of champagne she had poured herself moments earlier. She put a long black fur coat on and said out loud, without noticing the housekeeper who had entered the room, "Now let's have a stroll around this shitty little town and have some fun watching the scruffy looking people." She suddenly bumped into the housekeeper and nearly fell to the floor. "For God's sake! What are you doing here sneaking into my room?" Penelope screamed at her.

The housekeeper was so scared she could hardly speak. The only words she managed to get out of her mouth were, "So sorry, ma'am."

"Get out of my way!" shouted Penelope, pushing the housekeeper to the side.

****

Later in the evening Elizabeth was preparing the table for dinner while talking to Katie, who had an kitchen apron on. She was telling her grandmother about her latest dream.

"I had another dream with my mother last night, grandma. She looked sooo beautiful," said Katie, smiling and making great gestures with her arms.

When Katie mentioned the dream about her mother, images of Linda flashed into Elizabeth's mind. Elizabeth remembered her smell, her smile and many happy memories of her daughter were popping up in her mind non-stop, as if in a movie. *'Oh God, I miss my daughter so much, my beautiful Linda,'* she thought, with tears in her eyes.

"Did you hear me, grandma?"

"Yes…yes I did." She quickly dried her tears before Katie could see. "How lovely, my dear. What was your dream like?" asked Elizabeth.

"It was like the other night." Still making big gestures, Katie continued, "We were in a very green place with a lake and lots and lots of big trees around. I can't remember much but I remember that we hugged all the time like we used to do. She says that she's always near me."

Elizabeth's eyes filled with more tears which again she quickly dried off so as not to upset Katie. Their conversation was interrupted by Roy and Joey, who had entered the kitchen together, jokingly saying that the food was taking too long.

"It's ready. Please take your seats at the dining table and I'll serve you now."

"Let me help, grandma, let me help, please!"

"Course, my darling. Boys, take a seat. Katie and I will serve the dinner now." Looking at Katie, Elizabeth pointed to a small bowl and asked, "Darling, please help me bring the bowl with the grits and place it on the table."

Once they were all seated and ready to start eating, Joey started to tell their news. "Well, the reason why we wanted to speak to you, Roy, it's that Elizabeth and I have been feeling like... although we do feel we are at home here at your house, and although we couldn't imagine not being close to Katie and you at this moment, we think that it's time to give you back your space..."

Joey was interrupted by Roy, who said "You two, don't be silly, please. It's been a pleasure to have you both here with us, helping me to look after Katie. But most importantly you have been giving us a sense of family. I couldn't imagine what our lives would have been like without you two."

"Thanks Roy, it means a lot to know that you do appreciate us being here. The thing is that Elizabeth and I decided to sell our house and perhaps buy one nearby so we can look after Katie during the daytime while you're working, and then we could go home at night, giving you two some space. We would be only a few blocks away, which means you know we could always be on hand for you two whenever you wanted or needed us."

Elizabeth, looking excited, said, "And the best thing is that we found a beautiful house in Damien Avenue which is for sale, and the owner seemed very keen to sell it to us."

"Yes, but we didn't want to do anything before speaking to you, Roy. We wanted to make sure you agree with the idea and, you know…make sure you are happy with having us so close to you."

Roy went very quiet. It was not as if he didn't like the idea of having Elizabeth and Joey living close. He had learnt to love them and he was very thankful for all their care and devotion to him and Katie since Linda's death. Even though it was painful, as he knew he was about to break their hearts, he took a long breath and broke his news before he lost the courage to do so.

"Erm… Joey, remember I told you earlier that I also had some news? I've got a transfer at work. I received a very good job offer and I decided to take it."

Elizabeth went pale. Something inside her was telling her that it wasn't going to be good news. She looked at Roy and asked, "A job offer? Where to, Roy?"

"New…" He paused and then replied slowly, "It's to…New…New York City."

"What?" exclaimed Elizabeth, accidentally dropping her wine glass on the table. The wine poured down the white tablecloth, reaching the floor. Joey tried to move his chair but was stopped by Elizabeth, who was panicking. "Are you moving to New York? Is that what you just said?"

"Where are you going, daddy?" asked Katie, looking confused.

"Sorry sweetheart, dad meant to explain to you better. We both are moving to New York City." Roy looked really sorry after Elizabeth's reaction. He tried to explain but was stopped by her.

"I'm sorry but I am shocked," said Elizabeth, shaking her head. "You are moving away and didn't even think of consulting us?"

"Are grandma and grandpa coming with us, dad?" asked Katie, nearly crying.

After a few moments of silence Roy replied, holding Katie's hand, "They are not," and noticing Katie had got upset and begun to cry, he stroked her head and kissed her, saying "But they will come to visit us and we will come back to visit them. We'll see them all the time."

Katie got up from her chair and ran to hug Elizabeth, who was also crying. Roy looked at Joey and said sorry for the way he had just broken the news.

"You should have spoken to us before breaking the news to Katie like this, Roy" said Joey, disappointed.

"I'm sure this is something to do with that woman who came here late that night!" said Elizabeth, getting up from her chair and offering her hand to Katie. "Let's go to the bedroom my darling, grandma will read *Alice in Wonderland* for you," said Elizabeth, still embracing Katie.

"I don't want to separate from you and grandpa… I don't!" said Katie, crying.

"It will be alright. Everything will be fine. Let's go now and leave dad and grandpa to talk. I am sure dad is thinking of the best for you."

When Elizabeth and Katie left the room, Roy broke down in tears.

"I'm sorry Joey…I'm really sorry. It isn't easy for me either. I know how much you two love her and I know she has become very attached to you since Linda passed away, but this opportunity came up and I decided I need a new life. I need some fresh air, a new start."

Roy didn't mention that evening anything about Penelope and his real plan, which was to move in with her in New York and work for her corporation. He thought it would be too much for them to take and he was afraid that it would scare Katie even more. Later that night, after Katie had fallen asleep, he spoke to Elizabeth and Joey again and assured them that Katie would always be well looked after. He planned to take Katie for a day out tomorrow and explain things better to her. Before going to bed he called Penelope to tell her about his experience of breaking the news earlier on.

"I've organized the pilot to pick me up on Monday morning. I have lots happening and I can't stay any longer. Let me know what day you'd like me to send my private jet to pick you two up and I'll organize everything," said Penelope in a very sweet voice.

"I reckon I can get everything done for the move in three or four weeks. I have one more week at work and then I need time to organize the house, and Katie is going on summer vacation in two weeks' time."

"Whatever time you need, my honey…but don't take too long." Adopting a sensual voice, she asked, "Are we still meeting tomorrow and Sunday?"

"I'll take Katie for a day out tomorrow and I'll meet you after at the hotel. I'm sorry but she's very upset and I think it's best if I spend some time with her."

"Whatever works for you, honey. I'll be waiting for you. Please don't take too long."

Once they had both hung up, Penelope exploded in anger. She got hold of a vase of flowers that was nearby and threw it at the wall, smashing the vase to pieces. "If he thinks that little girl will come before me when we're in New York he is badly wrong! I will make her life a misery if she crosses my path!"

Chapter Domus Deus

Three weeks later at the spiritual colony of Lunas, Linda was coming out of the temple, where she had gone to meditate and pray, when she heard the news that Rebecca had been discharged from the recovery hospital at Magiar and been sent to a spiritual colony near Earth. The colony was called Domus Deus, which meant 'home of God' in Latin.

In Domus Deus the spirits were still attached to human feelings and vices; they were on the lower rungs of the evolutionary ladder, studying to learn and develop their spiritual fraternity and compassionate skills. All of them stayed there for a very quick transitory period of time, preparing for their next reincarnation on Earth, where they would go through another human experience and put into practice all they had learned from their mentors in the colony.

Linda closed her eyes and, within less than a second, she travelled through the universe to Domus Deus, arriving outside a small house. She looked around and noted how busy the place was; immediately it looked and felt very different from Lunas. The construction of the buildings reminded her of those in Italy, with many sculptures and design details. There were many spirits everywhere, all carrying out different activities. A lot of joy could be felt everywhere in the colony.

 Linda made herself invisible to everyone, in order not to disturb the local energy and cause any disturbance by her presence. She walked down the street, observing the place. She passed their temple, in this case a Christian church as it was a colony where the majority of the inhabitants were Catholics. She saw a huge number of spirits inside the massive church, praying and meditating, asking for blessings for their loved ones who were still incarnated on Earth. She continued walking and soon approached the colony's library where she stopped, as her intuition was telling her that Rebecca was inside. She waited outside while admiring the new place and soon she saw Rebecca coming out.

"Linda, what a nice surprise. It's so good to see you," said Rebecca with a beaming smile.

"It's nice to see you too, Rebecca," replied Linda, feeling glad that Rebecca was looking happy and radiant.

"How did you find out that I was here?" asked Rebecca.

"Nathaniel communicated with me via thought when I was leaving the temple and he told me you had moved to here. I felt so happy to know you had left the hospital and I decided to come and visit you straight away."

"Come on, let's go for a wander. Let me show you the colony," invited Rebecca, who seemed very happy.

"What a beautiful name: Domus Deus," Linda said, and took her hand.

During their stroll, Rebecca pointed out all the joy and happiness she could see around them. The spirits were everywhere in groups, laughing and making the colony look like a huge street party with all the members of the community uniting just to enjoy each other's company. Linda and Rebecca walked until they found a square with a beautiful water fountain at the centre, and they sat on the grass to talk.

"How do you feel, Rebecca?" asked Linda.

"I feel happy. I learnt a lot at the recovery hospital in Magiar and I feel much better than I've ever felt in my whole existence."

"I know. I can see that. Your appearance has changed, you look very radiant and you have this bright aura around you now. Even the marks of your cuts have faded completely. I'm very happy for you Rebecca," said Linda, holding her hand and smiling. "Please tell me, what is the most important thing that you have learnt?"

"I have finally learnt to love myself and learnt to love life; I spent so much time hating myself and I ended up becoming bitter and miserable. Now I can clearly see how much I had closed myself to the beauties of life, as you said when we first met. When I reviewed my previous incarnation with the mentors at the recovery hospital, I realized that I could have done so much better. I could have evolved so much just by loving myself," replied Rebecca, still smiling.

"You're correct. Only by loving yourself could you have loved the others around you. Once we are engaged in negative and depressive thoughts, we attract more and more sorrow and darkness to ourselves, making our existence unbearable."

Rebecca looked at the sky and continued, "I only went as far as my life experience in London, England. They said I'm still to recover an important life experience back in Spain in the 1400s... or 1500s... I don't remember exactly. They said you are going to review that life experience with me."

"I will... I mean we'll do it together. There are important things happening at the moment that involve you and people whom you know. Soon you'll understand more," said Linda, looking more serious and a little upset.

Linda stood up and, smiling again, extended her hand out to Rebecca as if asking her to hold it. Rebecca took Linda's hand and stood up next to her. Linda then said, "I have an invite for you; a very special invite indeed. I would like you to meet my daughter, Katie. Remember I told you that sometimes I meet her when she is asleep on Earth and that I bring her soul to spend time with me while her corporeal body is asleep?"

Excited, Rebecca nodded.

"She's going through some difficult times and tonight I would like to bring her soul to Lunas so I can inspire her with energy of love. Would you like to come with me?"

"I'll be honoured to. You told me so much about her, and also I'm really interested to see how you bring her to the spiritual world."

They both agreed to meet again later and go to Earth once Katie had gone to bed and fallen asleep.

Chapter Learning to face problems as lessons

Linda looked at Rebecca and said, "I need to remind you of something. Now you are used to living here, you might feel the energy on Earth quite depressive and negative. There's a lot of negativity everywhere, so you'll have to keep a strong focus on your positive thoughts so as not to get dragged into the negative vibrations." Rebecca nodded, showing she understood, and Linda asked, "Ready?"

Even though Rebecca felt a little hesitant about going back to Earth after her previous bad experiences there, she said yes and they both departed from Domus Deus, arriving immediately on Earth, in Asheville, South Carolina; more precisely, in Katie's bedroom.

When they arrived they found the room filled with boxes everywhere. All Katie's belongings had been packed ready for their house move the next day. The only item which had not been packed was Katie's bed, in which she was now sleeping, holding her teddy bear tightly. Her soul was floating in the air above her human body, the fluidic laces linking them. Her soul was very bright and shiny, similar to those of Linda, Teresa and Geraldine. Rebecca considered hers and realized that she was less bright compared to them, but pretty similar to those who inhabited Domus Deus.

Katie seemed sad. She was looking down and crying. When she saw Linda she ran towards her and gave her a tight hug, not wanting to let her go. Linda showered her with kisses until she managed to make Katie stop crying. Linda introduced Rebecca, but Katie didn't seem to be herself. She didn't smile or say anything. The three held hands and departed, leaving Katie's bedroom behind. Travelling at the speed of light, they arrived almost instantly at the shore of the lake in Lunas.

Katie began their meeting as she always did, crying and telling Linda how much she was missing her. "I miss you, mom. Why are you not there with me? Every day I look around thinking you might come back and surprise us, as if was a lie that you died, but then you never come back…"

"Oh my sweetheart, I haven't died. I'm here, aren't I? Mom is always near you, don't ever forget. Sometimes you can't see me but I am always here."

Rebecca watched with tears in her eyes as Katie embraced Linda, crying and holding her tight. Linda was already used to it, and with a great deal of patience and care she explained time and time again to Katie that she had never left her.

"Have you not been seeing the beautiful butterflies mom's been sending down to you?" asked Linda, while kissing the top of Katie's head.

Katie replied that she had, but continued to cry deeply.

"You are my little star, aren't you? Mom will never leave you, darling. Our love lives forever, remember? I know it's been difficult but you have dad with you and also grandma and grandpa..."

Linda was abruptly interrupted by Katie, who broke free from her arms and, out of control, screamed, "I don't have my grandma and grandpa any more - dad is taking me away! I'll never see them again, just like I never see you!"

Linda was beginning to feel upset. Rebecca, noticing that Linda's vibration had begun to be affected by the negative energy transmitted by Katie, began to pray and send vibrations of love and harmony to them both. Once Linda began to feel calmer again, she lowered her voice even more and invited Katie to sit down on the grass with her, saying, "My daughter, you will always see grandpa and grandma. You might be apart from them for a while but our love is pure and all of us will always be connected by our love for each other. We will always be together. Even if we can't see each other we will still be present. The spirits who are connected by true love are never apart from each other." Realizing that Katie had also calmed down, Linda continued, "You have to be strong, my little angel. You have to believe that things will be alright."

Katie sat down on the grass, putting her head down on Linda's lap. She looked so vulnerable and fragile, in a way that Linda had never seen before. Katie then told Linda everything that was happening back at home: Roy revealing that he had met another woman; that they were leaving North Carolina for good; her grandparents getting upset and accusing him of cheating on her. She said that they had had a horrible argument with her dad and they had then left home. She talked non-stop until she broke down crying again. "Come back home, mommy, please. We need you…please!" She was becoming so upset that the sensation her soul was experiencing was that of a human's body with difficulty breathing. Although she found it difficult to speak, she said, "I feel so lonely, mommy. Come back, please"

Rebecca moved closer to them and began to pray again. Soon they were joined by Teresa and Geraldine, who arrived and joined Rebecca in praying for Linda and Katie. Immediately the area was illuminated by a very luminous blue - the same light that is generated when someone prays for serenity and peace. Linda started to sing nursery rhymes while gently stroking her daughter's hair, making Katie feel calmer.

"Everything's going to be alright, my little angel. Keep the faith," said Linda.

"Do you promise you are going to be with me, mom?" asked Katie, no longer crying. "I'm feeling scared. I'm going to meet dad's girlfriend tomorrow and he want us to live in the same house as her!"

"I promise. You might not see me with your eyes but you will feel me with your heart. Whenever you need me, close your eyes and think of me and you'll soon feel very strong and able to overcome any problem," said Linda, smiling and still stroking Katie's hair.

Feeling calmer and happier, Katie jumped up from the grass and joyfully shouted, "And we have the butterflies!"

Linda got up, also looking happier. She replied, "Yes we do. Mom will always send them to you whenever you need me. They will show you that I'm there next to you."

Katie ran off around the field, laughing and asking her mother to come and catch her. Linda ran after her, also laughing and feeling relieved to see that Katie was happy again.

"I feel so sorry for her. Poor little girl," said Rebecca to Teresa and Geraldine.

"We need to remember that difficult times are nothing more than lessons that we all have to go through to evolve. If God is allowing us to go through a challenge, a difficult moment, it's because he knows that we are already strong enough to pass that test and that we will evolve from surviving such difficulties. What seems to you to be a pitiful situation of a little girl who has lost her mother is actually part of a major divine plan from the universe to help many spirits to evolve and purify their spirits," said Teresa, with a very wise air about her.

"But she's just a little girl," said Rebecca.

This time it was Geraldine who replied. "Not really. She is a spirit like you and me who's been going through different incarnations for many, many centuries, seeking her purification. At this present moment in her life experience on Earth, her spirit is involved in a child's human body, but as her human body grows into a woman, her spirit will slowly regain its astral knowledge."

Teresa continued, as if taking over from Geraldine. "Yes. When spirits incarnate into human bodies to go through another trial, their astral memory is temporarily blocked by the divine veil so the spirit can have a new and fresh start without being influenced by the past. The spirits have many limitations when involved with any human body, especially a body in its infancy stage; that is the time when the spirit is most restricted and vulnerable."

Rebecca was listening carefully, paying a lot of attention and feeling very privileged to be around such kind and wise spirits as Geraldine and Teresa. They continued their conversations about basic knowledge of the universe and the spiritual life, and it wasn't until much later that they saw Linda and Katie finally returning from their walk.

"So does it mean that Katie's life will improve now that her father found someone new who could perhaps help him look after her?" asked Rebecca to both Geraldine and Teresa.

They both looked down and answered, "No." Teresa finished by saying, before Linda and Katie returned, "I'm afraid this is just the beginning of her and her father's difficulties. They are now about to face very challenging times."

"Did you have fun?" asked Geraldine to Katie, who returned with a flower in her hand.

"Oh yes! We ran very far and then mom took me to see our horses."

"How nice… did you ride him?" asked Geraldine.

"Not today, but mommy promised we'll ride them next time I'm here."

"Yes we will, my darling," said Linda, extending her hands to Katie and inviting her to go back. "It's time to return. Mom will take you home now."

Katie hugged Geraldine and Teresa, and after Linda asked she hugged Rebecca too. Her eyes were closing slowly and by the time Linda picked up her soul in her arms she was already asleep. Accompanied by Rebecca, Linda took Katie's soul back to Earth minutes before the sunrise. Linda and Rebecca waited for Roy to come into Katie's bedroom to wake her up. Linda watched Roy with tenderness and kindness in her eyes. She prayed for him, then left the room with Rebecca and returned to Domus Deus.

Chapter The Big Apple

The private jet Penelope sent to collect Roy and Katie arrived in New York City at the arranged time. Roy was holding hands with Katie when they arrived, and he was very excited about starting their new life at Penelope's luxurious penthouse in Manhattan. There was a limousine waiting at the airport to take them there. Penelope had told Roy only to bring absolute necessities, as she wanted them to buy new items. She pretended that the reason for this was that she wanted them both to have a fresh start, but the truth was that Penelope was only worried about maintaining her luxury standards in her penthouse. She wouldn't accept anything from their old house in North Carolina. Penelope was extremely materialistic, and keeping up appearances was non-negotiable for her. Her penthouse was in Central Park West, one of the most expensive locations in Manhattan, and had stunning views of Central Park. Her three-floor penthouse had been one of the many properties left by her father, and now it would be the new home for Roy and Katie.

While Roy was intrigued and looking forward to the new lifestyle, enjoying every single minute of that journey from the airport to the new home, Katie was looking at the tall buildings and the busy city through the limousine's window, feeling scared and not comfortable at all. Holding her teddy bear tightly against her chest, she could see the excitement in her father's eyes and she began to feel more and more lonely.

"Here we are, sir," said the driver, parking the limousine in front of the building.

They got out and stood up in front of the tall building. Both were looking up and feeling different emotions; Roy was even more excited and content about what he was seeing, while Katie, who had never been to New York City before, was completely overwhelmed and scared. They were greeted by the doorman, who promptly showed them the private elevator in which they then rode up to the penthouse. When they arrived on the twenty-fifth floor the elevator's door opened and their new home was revealed. Penelope was waiting for them with her arms wide open, accompanied by a housemaid.

"My darling, I'm so excited! Welcome home." She gave Roy a hug and skipped, looking happy and excited.

"Wow, this place is amazing," said Roy, looking around.

Penelope grabbed his hand and dragged him with her, eager to show him around. She completely ignored Katie and left her behind.

"Hey you, little Miss, it's nice to meet you. My name is Dolores. What's your name?" asked the housekeeper.

Katie was very scared and feeling vulnerable. Her little legs were shaking and her arms were crossed, holding her teddy bear very tightly against her chest.

"Come on, tell me your name... or do I have to guess it?" said Dolores, smiling and softly touching Katie's face.

Katie replied in a very low voice, almost whispering, "Katie. My name is Katie Grace Taylor."

"What a lovely name, Grace. Come on with me, Katie, I'll take you to your bedroom."

Penelope had chosen a bedroom for Katie on the first level of the penthouse near the staff area, far from the main areas on the second and third floor, and especially far from her and Roy's room. Katie's bedroom had a view of Central Park and it was filled with toys and dolls.

A boy who seemed to be around the same age as Katie was peeking out at her from behind the door. Katie looked at him warily. Noticing that the girl was nervous, Dolores said, "Oh, that's my son Ricky. He's six years old...don't be scared of him." Looking at Ricky, Dolores said in Spanish, "Son, come and say hello to little Katie."

The boy came out from behind the bedroom door and said hello to Katie, who quickly looked down to the floor, answering with a shy 'Hello.' Dolores went around the bedroom trying to make Katie feel comfortable and showing her how beautiful the room was. She explained how to operate the television. Katie stayed with her teddy bear held tightly against her chest, deeply wishing that that situation was nothing but a nightmare. She imagined that soon she and her father would be back in their house in North Carolina next to her grandparents.

Without paying any attention to what Dolores was saying, Katie looked around and wished she could simply go back to her old bedroom with the pictures of her mother and her grandparents in frames on the top of the bedside cabinets, and a view of the garden where she used to play with her grandmother. Timidly she put the teddy bear on the chair next to the bed and picked up her back bag. She opened it, taking out the blanket her grandmother had knitted for her. She spread the blanket wide open on top of the bed then quickly took hold of her teddy bear again and held it against her chest. Dolores and Ricky tried to start a conversation with Katie several times while fixing things around the room to make it more comfortable for her, but there was no interaction from Katie's side. She remained quiet, standing next to the window, looking down to Central Park and feeling very upset. The silence was broken by Penelope's loud laughter that could be heard from far away, announcing that she was coming. Hearing her, Ricky immediately ran back to the staff area.

"Hello Katie, my darling. I'm sorry I didn't say welcome properly to you. I was so excited with your father's arrival," she said loudly, with a very false tone, as she entered the bedroom followed by Roy. She grabbed Katie's cheek and asked, "How are you finding your new bedroom?" Penelope didn't wait for a reply and answered her own question. "It's very elegant and stunning, isn't? I knew you'd love it!"

"Wow, you have a view of Central Park - that's amazing, sweetheart!" said Roy to Katie. Noticing her sad face, Roy continued, "You'll love New York, Katie. This is the centre of the universe! The best of everything in the world is here: the best theatres, the best restaurants and the best toy shops. You're going to love your new home, you'll see."

All Katie wanted was to be alone. In her mind she was just asking that they would all leave so she could be alone and think of her mother and her grandparents. Penelope went around the bedroom, showing Roy every luxury feature. She proudly showed off the finest pieces of furniture she had bought to decorate Katie's room, and lied when she told him she had chosen everything, including all the toys, herself. She opened the closet and revealed all the new clothes she had bought Katie. Just as she was about to show the bed linen, she shouted in horror, "Oh my God! What is this horrible piece of whatever doing on your bed?" She was referring to the blanket Katie had put there moments earlier. "Dolores!" she shouted again. "What's this ghastly thing doing on the bed? Take this horrible looking thing from here and toss it in the trash right now."

"No! You won't toss it in the trash. This blanket's mine," said Katie, looking into Penelope's eyes with anger. "It's my blanket made by my grandmother, she knitted it herself and it took her a long time to do it for me."

Taken aback by Katie's angry reaction, Penelope smiled and, disguising her feelings, said "Oh you're right…I'm sorry. I see now how cute the blanket is. I love it…" Penelope didn't like anyone defying her authority. It took an enormous effort for her to hold back her feelings and instinct. Pretending she didn't mind Katie confronting her, she forced a smile and told Dolores that she needed to give her instructions for dinner in the kitchen. She excused herself and both she and Dolores left the bedroom. Alone with Katie, Roy came closer to her and sat on the bed, inviting her to sit down too.

"Why are you so upset, sweetheart? We need to face the changes now. Mom isn't here any more and we have to move on. I'm doing this for us; new city, new home, new start for everything. Look how stunning this place is. Here you'll live a very luxurious life. You'll go to the best school and meet very interesting people. Be happy."

"I didn't want a new home and a new life. I want to go back to our house with grandma and grandpa." Katie seemed to be begging as she spoke to Roy. Tears were rolling down her face. "Let's go back home, daddy, please…please. I don't like it here."

"Oh my love, we can't. Please enjoy this new life with me. We'll be happy here, I promise. Do you know how many people in the world would love to live here in New York City in front of Central Park? Besides, there are too many memories in that house and in that city, and here we both can have a fresh start."

Katie went quiet, thinking it was better to not say anything. She realised that her father wouldn't understand her. She also felt completely upset, thinking her father wanted to forget her mother and wipe out all of her memories. Katie was right; Roy was only interested in his own feelings at that moment, so fascinated was he by his new life of luxury.

After trying hard to cheer up his daughter, Roy left the bedroom and went back to explore the penthouse. Katie sat on the window ledge, looking down at Central Park. She stared at a family who seemed to be having fun, and at that moment she began to shed tears filled with sorrow. She could not understand why she had lost first her mother and now her grandparents. *'I'm lonely and I have no-one to look after me any more,'* she thought, as the tears rolled down her face. *'Oh mother, I wanted you to be here with me…holding me.'*

What she couldn't see was that right next to her was Linda, sitting by her side sending her thoughts of inspiration and courage to stay strong. Linda closed her eyes and prayed, asking God to allow a butterfly to materialise. At once it happened; a little yellow butterfly appeared outside the apartment and flew all the way to the outside of the window. Katie looked at the pretty creature and wished that it was her mother telling her she was there, watching over her. She put her hands on the window pane and stared at the butterfly, which was flitting about outside in small circles. Katie then began to remember all the happy moments she had enjoyed with her mother.

"Oh butterfly, I wish I was just like you. I would spread my wings and fly…far, far away from here."

Chapter Learning from the past

Kingdom of Navarre, fifteenth century

Several men, women and children were partying around the bonfire. The clear sky that night reinforced the beauty of the full moon which was brightening the woods. Among the crowd were three men strumming Spanish guitars while a young lady clicked castanets and danced to the rhythm of the music. There were children running around, people singing along and much joy in the air.

Like her mother, the young lady wore her long, curly, dark hair down, swaying freely as she moved her head in time to the music. She had a red flower in her hair and wore a long red dress. She danced beautifully to the music played by the guitarists, and was followed by the other men and women, all of them clapping and singing along. A young man, dressed differently from the others, was watching her closely. His bright brown eyes, totally fixed on her, had the shine of a man deeply in love; anyone could tell that from the way he was admiring every single one of her moves. He was dressed very smartly, with the appearance of someone from rich society. The people intensified their clapping, accompanying the lady's movements and the song, which had reached a frenetic rhythm. The faster they clapped, the faster she danced. Her sensuous moves showed great passion and her eyes were exuding love and lust.

'I have no doubt. She is the woman of my life. I don't care if she has wealth and gold or not; all I know is that I want to spend the rest of my life with her,' the young man thought while admiring his beloved lady dancing.

When she had finished, everyone applauded her performance and raised their cups filled with wine, wishing her good health and blessings.

"Happy birthday, my darling," said the young man, looking straight into her eyes.

"You came! I can't believe you're here," she said with great happiness.

"I wouldn't miss your celebration feast for anything in this world," he said, his eyes shining.

Her mother came in, interrupting their moment alone, and said excitedly, "Carmen, Carmen, my daughter, Justa has a gift for you."

A woman leading a white horse, accompanied by her husband, approached them. "Carmen, my dear…Your performance was beautiful. Ager and I couldn't stop admiring you."

"Thanks, Mrs Avila. I am so grateful to you for allowing me and my mother to invite our friends for my celebration here in your land."

"Don't be silly, Carmen. You and your mother are more than just staff members or friends; you are part of our family. I've known you since you were a new-born baby and it makes me so proud to see that you've now grown into such a beautiful woman." She handed the horse's lead rope to Carmen, saying, "This is your eighteenth birthday present."

Carmen took hold of the horse's lead rope and skipped, feeling very happy. She hugged Justa and said, "You didn't have to get me a present. You already do so much for me and my mother…"

Justa's husband Ager interrupted Carmen. "Please, just accept your present. You are the daughter we never had and we've been looking forward to giving you your gift this evening."

Carmen went closer to the horse and put her head against his, saying, "Asas. Your name will be Asas."

"Come on, go and show our guests what a stunning present you've just received from Justa and Ager," said her mother, who was also feeling very happy. "Go, my daughter."

Carmen held Alejandro's hand and, holding the horse lead with her other hand, she went back to the bonfire and proudly showed her present to all the guests.

The feast continued with much music, laughter and more dance performances. Carmen was extremely happy that night, as it was the first time she had introduced her boyfriend Alejandro to her mother and to her friends.

****

A few miles away from Justa's property where Carmen celebrated her birthday, Marta Cortez and her husband were in their castle, sitting at their long dining table having their dinner. Marta wore a dark blue dress with extremely pointed shoulder pads. Around her neck was a golden chain with a cross. Like all the other woman from the rich society, she wore a wig underneath her hat, and because of the lack of hygiene that was customary in those times, she stank badly.

"Enrique, we have been invited by the Avilas to their wedding anniversary celebration on the last Saturday of the month," said Marta while eating. As her husband remained silent, she continued. "We have to go. I can't miss this event for anything."

"It doesn't interest me a bit," replied Enrique laconically, keeping his eyes on his meal so as to avoid looking at his wife.

A female servant approached the table holding the wine decanter and filled Marta's glass. She was abruptly pushed to the side by Marta, who said, "We have to, Enrique. Apparently they are spending a lot of gold on the celebration. She has invited over one hundred people and she's planning a very luxurious banquet and entertainment."

"You don't like them, Marta. You don't like Justa or her husband. You keep on calling them a pair of peasants, so what's the point in going? You say that Justa and her husband are two bores and you always criticise them. Why do you want to go to this celebration if you're not going to celebrate their special day with them? Are you going just to make them to feel inferior to you, as you always do?"

"You're right. I don't want to go and celebrate anything, but I want to go because I know Justa won't be able to entertain so many people. I know for a fact that she'll mess it all up and I want to be there when that happens. I want to laugh at her. Who does that gypsy-blooded woman think she is? Only I can throw a festival, and I want to make sure I'm there to laugh at her when everything goes wrong." As if talking to herself, Marta went on, "I want to laugh at that pretentious cow. Who does she think she is? She'll always be a pleb, it doesn't matter how much gold she has."

Irritated by her husband's lack of attention, she screamed, "Enrique!" Banging the heavy silver spoon on the table, she screamed again, "We are going to this celebration and that's it! No discussion!"

Enrique remained silent as he knew it was pointless trying to discuss it with his wife. She would not accept no as an answer. Marta continued talking as if not bothered whether her husband was listening or not. Talking out loud to herself and making dramatic gestures with her hands, she made plans about the dress she was going to wear, and even imagined the words she was going to use at the celebration feast in order to put Justa down in front of the guests and make her feel bad. She closed her eyes. Picturing the scene, as if rehearsing a theatrical performance, she imagined the reaction of the hostess and their friends. She created in her mind ways to criticise Justa and make sarcastic jokes in front of everyone. Her plan was to make Justa look inferior in front of others, so as to show how much better and richer than Justa she was.

After dinner, Enrique left the dining area and headed to the studying room while Marta remained entertained with her own thoughts and fantasies of ways to humiliate Justa at her event.

Marta and Enrique had been married for eighteen years and were well known in the Kingdom of Navarre because of their vast wealth. Marta was the daughter of one of the richest men in the kingdom and her father was also very high up within the civil authorities. They had a daughter called Maria who was gifted with a stunning beauty that would have made many men feel attracted to her if hadn't been for her extremely haughty behaviour. Maria and her mother were into richness and luxury and were both very arrogant. They both despised those who were poorer than themselves, while treating those with similar or more wealth with a false respect, always wishing bad to anyone whom they regarded as any sort of competition. The only difference between mother and daughter was that, deep down, Maria lacked confidence and secretly didn't find herself attractive.

Enrique was a good man who had let ambition dominate his life from a young age. When Marta's father offered him gold and wealth in return for marrying her daughter, he didn't think twice, and left the woman he had loved since his teenage years. What Enrique didn't know was that by marring Marta he would become one of the many possessions of the Cortez family. At first his eyes were focused on the huge castle where Marta lived, and on the luxury lifestyle he would have: servants to do almost anything for him, the best wine and food in the whole continent, and of course the respect of the people in the kingdom. His dream of a rich and luxurious life didn't last long. Soon after the marriage, Enrique began to be treated as an asset by Marta and her father. From day one he had to listen to them giving him orders as if he were one of the staff, and frequently he was belittled by Marta. After a few years of marriage he lost both his shine and his interest in life. He was constantly scared of being near Marta, knowing that at any point she could lose her temper and humiliate him in front of others. Enrique spent most of his time dedicated to his work. During the few hours he spent at home each day, he avoided his wife's company as much as he could by locking himself in his library, reading books. He had tried early in their marriage to leave her, but he was threatened by Marta's father, who sent a few of his men to Enrique's old village to set his parents' house on fire. Having showed him what they were capable of doing, Marta and her father then blackmailed him in case he ever tried to leave again; Enrique never did. Since that moment, he lived his life depressed and submissive to Marta's wishes. Their daughter Maria was a beautiful child and gave him some happy moments when she was young, but once she reached her teenage years she became an exact replica of her mother, arrogant and insensitive to the feelings of anyone else, including her father.

****

The weeks leading up to the Avilas' wedding anniversary celebration went quickly, and their attempts to create perfect outfits kept Marta and her daughter Maria very busy. They had kept three of their staff members focused only on preparing the best dresses. Mother and daughter thought of nothing but the opportunity to show off their beautiful dresses and their wealth. Everything had been planned down to the last detail: their dresses, their jewellery; even the horses that were to draw the carriage had been exquisitely groomed. Everything had to be exactly as imagined by Marta in order to draw everyone's attention away from the event and show them she was better than Justa. Marta even spent a lot of time choosing Enrique's outfit.

Weeks went by, and on the morning of the big celebration Marta was looking desperate and afflicted. She knocked at the library where Enrique was making a great deal of noise until he finally opened the door.

"Enrique…I'm worried about our daughter. She has been very strange since she broke up with that Alejandro."

"I thought it was he who broke off the relationship with her, not the other way round," Enrique said, without taking his eyes off his book.

"It doesn't matter. If anyone in the kingdom asks, you must tell them that it was she who dumped him." Marta got hold of the book he was reading and roughly removed his hands from it. She threw the book across the room and said angrily, "Attention, Enrique! Attention! I am talking!" She walked in circles, impatiently making lots of gestures with her hands. "Our daughter looks sad, depressed. She is losing her beauty, Enrique. She doesn't even look like my daughter any more. I'm worried about my little girl. This man has done something really bad to my girl, Enrique."

"Marta, he was very respectful when he finished with her. He followed all the protocol that was expected of him, and explained to me and you in front of her that he didn't love her. So I think it was best this way. At least now she can find someone who really loves and cares about her."

Marta grabbed hold of her husband's collar with both hands and shook him. "No-one can say no to a Cortez, no-one! If my Maria wants him she will have him!" Marta let Enrique go and left the library, slamming the door.

Later that evening, Enrique, Marta and Maria were ready to leave their castle and go to the celebration at the Avilas' house. Maria had learnt that her ex-boyfriend Alejandro and his family had been invited, which for a while made her reluctant to attend, but finally she had reconsidered and decided to go. Before getting into the carriage, mother and daughter were laughing in good spirits, complimenting each other.

Marta put her hand very gently on her daughter's shoulder and, looking very excited, said, "I'm so glad you changed your mind, my little girl. I couldn't enjoy tonight if you had decided not to go." She adjusted her large wig and her hat and said, smiling, "It would have been so boring if it was just your father coming with me." She then looked at Enrique and, pulling a face, said, "Oh Enrique, it doesn't matter how expensive your vestments are, you still look like a peasant. You can't put an outfit together and look smart, can you?" She sighed. "Never mind dear, never mind. Just make sure you don't talk to people, otherwise you'll bore then to death as always."

Enrique bowed his head down and became upset. Even though he was a very handsome man, Marta always managed to drag his self-esteem down with a nasty comment.

When they reached the Avilas' property, they saw from inside the carriage that there were entertainers spitting fire and staff members with silver trays offering glasses of wine to the guests as they arrived. Once inside the house they found an impeccable decoration with a stunning bouquet of flowers, and exotic fruits all over the house.

"Look, they have these things everywhere. What are these funny-shaped things, my daughter?" asked Marta, pointing to the pineapples.

It was Enrique who replied, "These are very rare tropical fruits called pineapples, Marta. They can't be planted in our kingdom, or even in our continent. In fact only royalty and very wealthy people can get hold of these. They are a very expensive delicacy indeed."

Marta made a grimace at Enrique's answer. "If the Avilas can have them, so can we. We'll buy the whole lot…the whole lot!" Laughing loudly, she was caught by surprise when Justa approached the family.

"Hello Marta. Hello Enrique." Smiling at Maria, she said, "Hi Maria, you look gorgeous. How are you all?"

Marta replied, putting on her usual false tone of voice used when she was socialising with people from high society. Opening her arms and making a grand gesture, she raised her voice, sounding almost as if she were playing a character. "We are doing simply M A R V E L L O U S my dear, marvellous. By the way, what a beautiful decoration, Justa. We were just talking about your pineappollets."

Being careful not to correct her friend and come across as patronizing, Justa replied, "Do you like the pineapples? Thank you. To be honest I had never seen them before. It was Ager who got them from one of his voyages to the islands; apparently it's a very special fruit. He said that it's a tradition to welcome foreign guests with this fruit. If a pineapple is left at the entrance of a village then it means that the locals are welcoming you. I haven't tasted it yet; I'm waiting for the special occasion tonight."

"It is very special indeed," said Marta. She smiled at her daughter Maria, as if asking her to confirm her lie, and continued, "In fact we tried one of these pineapples weeks ago and the taste was quite…hmm…let's say it has an interesting taste. I wouldn't, you know, have one of them again." Marta always used lies and pretence when facing a situation where she felt insecure and inferior to someone.

They spoke briefly and Justa excused herself, saying she was going to look for her husband in order to start dinner. Marta and Maria went around socialising with the others, leaving Enrique behind.

Moments later the hosts invited everyone to join them at the table for the start of the banquet. They had vast quantities of food and wine for their guests, who were all looking very excited around the table. Marta was speaking loudly and making sarcastic remarks about the people and the place as usual, while Enrique, sitting next to her, was very quiet. Maria was next to Alejandro although he had told her that he was seeing another woman. All of a sudden a loud noise drew everyone's attention to one of the servants. She had just dropped a silver tray with a bottle of wine, splashing the red liquid everywhere. Immediately Marta jumped up and began to shout at the woman, who, for some reason, was trying to cover her face. Justa came in and apologised to Marta, helping to calm her down. Enrique stood up from his chair and picked up the tray from behind his seat. When he handed it to the servant he went pale as he saw her face. Enrique's heart began to beat rapidly and his legs started to shake. The woman, realising that he had recognised her, quickly pulled the tray from his hands and ran out of the room to avoid any more contact with him.

"Daughter, daughter, please go into the dining room and finish cleaning the mess I've made," gasped Sophia.

"Are you alright, mother? You look strange and drained. What's happening?" said Carmen, holding her mother's arms.

"I'm fine, don't worry about me. Now please go in there and clean up the mess. Go, go."

Enrique couldn't eat the rest of his food; his mind had travelled back in time. *'That was her… that was… Sophia,'* he thought. Next to him, Marta was complaining about the wine spilled earlier. She was moaning non-stop, disturbing his thoughts about Sophia. Moved by his instinct, he spoke his thoughts out loud and said, "Oh shut up, Marta!"

Immediately everyone in the room started to laugh at Marta. That was something that everyone in that room would probably like to have said to Marta at some point. Their laughter at her grew louder. Marta's face went red immediately, and she didn't make any effort to hide her anger. Before Marta could say anything, Justa and her husband asked for everyone's attention, as Ager was going to give his speech.

The rest of the dinner went according to plan, with no more trouble. Much to Enrique's despair, the staff member who had dropped the tray had not returned to the room. After dinner all the guests were invited to join the family in the ballroom for more drinks and a celebration of twenty years of Ager and Justa's union. Enrique avoided Marta and Maria for the rest of the night, and discreetly went around the property searching for Sophia.

"Mother, why are you behaving so strangely?" asked Carmen, holding a big bottle of red wine.

Sophia had sweat rolling down her face and looked very pale. She stood up from the chair and replied, irritated, "I told you, it's nothing. I'm just feeling tired, that's all. Now go back to serve the guests, otherwise Justa will tell you off. I'm going outside to get some fresh air; I'll be back to help you and the others shortly. And by the way, don't stay talking to Alejandro tonight. We're here to serve and work, not for you to be dating your boyfriend."

Carmen giggled and kissed her mother on the cheek, saying, "Yes mother," and returned to the main room to serve the guests.

'I can't believe he is here...here! I must get away from him, we can't meet again...we can't!' she thought.

Sophia ran as fast as she could down the corridor that connected the staff area to the back yard, desperate to escape from the situation. She couldn't bear the thought of meeting him again. When she reached the garden and breathed the fresh air of the greenery and the flowers she began to feel better. She could hear the guests socialising, laughing and joking a few yards away from her. Enrique's picture came into her mind again; her heart was beating fast. *'Was that rude and angry woman next to him his wife? He looked so well-dressed and well-groomed. He made it, then...He got the wealth he always wanted. Would he still remember me? He seemed surprised when he looked into my eyes, so perhaps, yes, he does.'* She couldn't stop thinking about their brief encounter earlier and questioned herself non-stop, wondering if he still remembered her.

Suddenly the voice of her daughter talking to someone could be heard among the guests. She walked towards the part of the back yard were all the guests were gathered and tried to listen more closely. Sophia was shocked when she saw her daughter and Enrique talking. "No God, no, please. They can't meet... Please God, don't allow this to happen!" she said out loud to herself in panic.

"Mother, mother!" shouted Carmen.

Sophia thought about running away. She wanted to escape from there as soon as possible, but her legs were paralysed. She was overcome by a feeling of utter panic that stopped her from moving.

Accompanied by Enrique, Carmen approached her mother and said, smiling, "This gentleman is looking for you, mother. His name is Cortez, Mr Enrique Cortez." Looking at both Sophia and Enrique, she asked, "Do you already know each other?"

"Go Carmen, go back to the service. You need to help serving the guests. I will talk to this gentleman on my own," said Sophia, looking serious. "I said go, daughter!"

Carmen found her mother's behaviour very strange but left without saying anything else. Enrique was speechless as he admired Sophia from head to toe. The two kept looking firmly into each other's eyes for a long time. It was Enrique who finally broke the silence by saying, "You look even more gorgeous than I remembered."

"What do you want? Isn't it enough, all the bad things you did to me in the past? I have nothing to talk to you about, Enrique. Just leave me alone," said Sophia, walking away.

Enrique held her by the arm and pulled her back gently. "Please Sophia, wait. I think of you every day of my life. There is not a day that goes by without me thinking of you and wishing you were alright and..."

"And? Perhaps you were wishing I wasn't doing too badly so you didn't have to feel guilty or feel sorry for leaving me bearing a child, and having to face everyone in the village as a mother without a husband, like you did just before our wedding. Or perhaps you haven't even thought about my feelings or my circumstances, but only thought about yourself and your own selfish feelings as usual?"

"I've been thinking of you because I missed you. I miss you and I realised back then how stupid I was by doing what I did." Suddenly he thought about what she had just said and, looking deeply into her eyes, he asked, "Did you say you were bearing a child when I left? I didn't know you were …"

Sophia blushed as she realised she had made a mistake in giving away these details about her past. Enrique continued, "Oh my God, you said you had to face everyone in the village as a mother without a husband, which means you…" Enrique went pale, staring at her, trying to make sense of things in his mind before concluding, "which means you had the baby? Our baby…"

Sophia immediately regretted what she had just said. She didn't know what to say. Even though she had managed to raise her daughter well, despite all the difficulties, deep down she always dreamt about the day she would see him again. And that day had now arrived, as he was there standing in front of her.

"Sophia, answer me, did you have our baby?"

Before Sophia replied, Carmen, smiling, shouted from a distance, "Mother, is everything alright? Are you two doing fine over there?"

Enrique looked at Carmen, this time with more attention, and realised that she had the same look that Sophia had when he had met her for the first time: long, dark, curly hair and big brown eyes. He looked back at Sophia and, astonished, he asked, "Is she? Is that young lady our daughter, Sophia? She is my daughter, isn't she? Tell me, Sophia, please."

Sophia felt like bursting into tears and telling him, *'Yes, she is your daughter, the one for whom I had to be brave enough to run away from our village, leaving behind our people in order to give birth to her and raise her with all of the difficulties only a single mother can understand. Yes, she is your daughter; she has the same smile as you, the same interest in books and riding horses as you have, and she is so similar to you that I can barely forget you, because every time I see her she reminds me of you.'* She wanted to jump into his arms and embrace him and feel safe as he held her once again, but before she could say a word, Marta approached them and pulled him by his arm.

"Enrique, what are you doing talking to servants?" Looking at Sophia from head to toe she asked, "Weren't you the stupid servant who dropped that tray and that bottle earlier? You're lucky the wine didn't spill over me, otherwise I would have asked my friend to dismiss you from your job." She pulled Enrique by the arm, saying, "Come on. Enough of talking to peasants. Let's get out of here."

And they walked away, leaving Sophia speechless as she watched Enrique leaving with his arrogant wife. Carmen came towards her and asked, "Who is he, mother? He knew your name and he was asking all the staff if they knew you and where he could find you. He seemed so eager to meet you."

Snapping out of her memories, Sophia looked at Carmen and said quickly, "He is just a friend, an old friend who I knew years ago and he remembered me when I dropped that silly tray on the dining room floor, that's all. Now let's go back to work, Carmen, come on."

Later that night, Sophia was lying down, thinking of Enrique and remembering their earlier conversation word by word, time and time again. *'So many years have gone by and he still looks very handsome,'* she thought at one point. Not far away, Enrique was in bed doing the same: running through every word of their conversation from earlier. *'I need to find a way to meet her again without Marta finding out. I have to see Sophia and find out more about the baby. She looks so gorgeous, it's as if time hasn't gone by at all for her.'* Enrique scratched his itchy nose and suddenly was surprised by Sophia's perfume which was on his hand. He then remembered that she smelled different from the other women in the kingdom. Unlike the others, Sophia didn't wear any wigs and always had her hair in a natural style with a simple flower. Going against the traditions of those times, she bathed with herbs and rose petals in the water of the lake or the river, which gave her a very special and pleasant smell. *'Her smell...she smells so different from Marta and the other ladies. The perfume...oh her perfume....'* Enrique fell asleep, still savouring the fragrance of Sophia left on his hands.

What neither of them knew was that their lives were going to cross again, this time amidst a major tragedy.

****

The picture faded away and Rebecca found herself back at the Past Memories room in the library. She felt connected to the story she had just seen and felt as if she had just experienced all those feelings from centuries ago once again. Leaving the building, she saw Linda, who was waiting for her at the entrance. Rebecca, feeling very emotional, opened her arms to Linda as if asking for a hug, and Linda embraced her very affectionately.

"Why are you upset? The past life you're reviewing happened long ago," asked Linda, drying Rebecca's tears and adding, "The reason why we are blessed with the opportunity to review our past lives from so long ago is to understand our mistakes, so we can improve the present and make a better future."

Rebecca nodded, still looking upset. After moments spent in silence she finally asked, "How did it end? I want to remember everything."

"You will soon remember. A horrible tragedy happened in that time and for this reason I'm going to accompany you to review that past life together with you. Once we've seen the whole experience you'll then understand a lot more about the current happenings." Linda held her hand gently and invited her, "Would you like to come with me and visit Katie on Earth?"

Rebecca smiled and seemed to appreciate the invitation. Linda gave her a sign, then both closed their eyes and disappeared into the air, arriving immediately at Penelope's penthouse in New York City.

Chapter Little girl

Six months had gone by since Roy and Katie had moved. Roy and Penelope had got married, with Penelope inviting all her friends and business partners to the ceremony. She paraded down the aisle wearing a very exclusive, high-end, designer wedding dress. She wanted a luxurious and expensive wedding and so that was exactly what she had: a lavish, extravagant ceremony, in keeping with her style. Every aspect of the wedding was over the top, from the flowers which decorated the rooms to the massive imported crystal chandeliers in the ceilings. Penelope didn't marry Roy for love; instead it was like signing a certificate to certify she had won the battle. The man who was once married and would not be with her was finally hers. Roy was so enchanted with all the luxury of the wedding, and so overwhelmed by being among people from the very highest society of New York, that he didn't even notice his daughter Katie's sadness.

A few days after the wedding, Roy had accepted a job as chief financial officer at the headquarters of Penelope's corporation, and had become completely immersed in his work. He was so fascinated with his new luxury lifestyle that he didn't realise how much Katie was suffering from Penelope's nastiness and controlling ways. When Roy was around, Penelope pretended to be nice and kind towards Katie, but behind his back she would treat the girl with great rigidity, showing her aggressive side. Katie had to dress exactly according to Penelope's directions, behave as told by Penelope and even had to follow a very strict list of daily tasks.

One day Penelope caught Katie crying in her bedroom because she was missing her mother. Penelope grabbed her roughly and told her to stop crying immediately. She said she didn't want Roy to see her like that because it would remind him of Linda. Katie couldn't stop her tears and Penelope, losing her patience, slapped her in her face, telling her that her mother was dead and she had to forget her and move on. She threatened Katie, saying she would send people to North Carolina and do bad things to her grandparents if she didn't stop crying. Katie, feeling very scared of her, held back her tears and promised not to mention her mother's name again. Katie had become very different from the way she was back in North Carolina. She always looked very quiet and scared. For Katie it seemed as if

Penelope was going to attack her at any time. Behind her shyness was a fearful girl who lived every day of her life scared of what was going to happen next.

Penelope was no longer faithful to Roy, and had gone back to having sex encounters with her personal assistant, Nigel. They had a long-lasting affair which could seem quite explicit to others, but Roy seemed not to realise any of it was happening. In order to spend time with Nigel, she created many international business trips outside New York on which Roy had to go and represent the company, leaving her free to do as she liked behind his back. Once Roy was away on business, Penelope would then have sex in her apartment, not only with Nigel but with many other men too.

One day, hearing screams coming from the upper level of the penthouse, Katie decided to go and investigate. The closer she got to Penelope's bedroom, the louder the noises became. It sounded to her as if Penelope was in pain and screaming for help. She crept closer and closer to the door, trying to hear more. Then, urged by her childish curious instinct, she opened the door and entered the bedroom. She screamed in horror as she saw Penelope and Nigel both naked in bed, then both jumping out of bed in the same instant, surprised by Katie's intrusion. Penelope quickly grabbed a sheet and covered herself up, then screamed at Katie to leave. Katie was shocked and confused by what she had just seen; even though she didn't know what sex was, she could feel that what Penelope was doing with Nigel was wrong, and a betrayal of her father. Penelope, still wrapped up in the bed linen, strode towards Katie, screaming for her to leave the room. She grasped the girl's arm and threw her out of the bedroom, locking the door afterwards.

"Damn girl! She is such a problem in my life!" shouted Penelope. "What am I going to do if she decides to tell her idiot of a father what she's just seen?"

"I'm sure he won't believe we were debriefing on the business naked in the bedroom," Nigel joked.

"This isn't time for your sarcasm, Nigel. If Roy finds out I'll be in trouble," said Penelope, putting her clothes back on.

Nigel tried to hug Penelope and comfort her, but she pushed him away. She finished dressing and told him to get his clothes on too. "I've lost the mood for this. Come on, go, go! Let me think of what I'm going to do to shut that damn girl up."

'I need to ensure that little brat keeps her mouth shut,' she thought. *'It's time to give her a little appetizer of what this mommy here can do to naughty little children like her.'*

After Nigel left, Penelope ran downstairs to the kitchen looking for Dolores.

"Dolores! Dolores!" she shouted. "Where are you?"

"Sorry madam, I didn't hear you calling. I was in the laundry room doing the washing. How can I help?"

"Whatever, Dolores. Are you going deaf? Pay more attention next time when I call. I want you to prepare something for me and Katie to eat. Make the salad I like and call Katie; I want her to join me. By the way, I want a lot of mushrooms, lots of mushrooms in her meal."

"I'm sorry, madam, but I'm pretty sure Katie doesn't like mushrooms. Should I perhaps only add them to yours and leave hers…"

Penelope abruptly interrupted her, saying, "No! I said lots of mushrooms in her meal. Now go and ask her to meet me at the dining table. I want to have some mother and daughter time alone with her. Now go, go."

Even though she felt very apprehensive, Katie went to the dining room and met Penelope, who was waiting for her to arrive before starting to eat. Katie entered the room and saw Penelope sitting by the table, smiling at her.

"Hello darling, sit down." Penelope sounded excessively fake. She gave a wide smile and again invited Katie to sit down.

Dolores came in straight after Katie arrived and served the food, feeling suspicious of why Penelope wanted to eat alone with the girl. She knew Penelope didn't like Katie and so far had only made her life miserable, so she was finding the whole scenario very bizarre. After serving the food she was told to leave them alone in the room.

"Shut the door when you leave, Dolores and no ears on the door. I know how nosy you are!"

Once Dolores had left the room, Penelope completely changed her facial expression. Looking serious she asked Katie, "How was school?"

"Good," answered Katie tersely.

"Why you are being rude to me?" asked Penelope, raising her voice. "Do you think I'm not interested in your studies? Do you think I don't care?"

Katie was already used to Penelope's behaviour and thought it was best not to reply. She kept her eyes focused on the food, not wanting to even look at Penelope's face in order to avoid making her more aggressive.

Penelope looked Katie up and down from head to toe and began to pick on her, saying, "You look like a mess. Why do you always look miserable? Is it because you're still thinking of your dead mother and all of that damn story?" Katie remained silent, to which Penelope continued to be provocative.

"You know your mother was a bit crazy, don't you? Yes, your father told me...crazy, crazy!" Laughing, she continued, "That's why she's dead now!"

Penelope knew that she could get under Katie's skin by talking about her mother. She noticed that the girl's eyes had filled up with tears, and that gave her more incentive to continue. "Oh come on, grow up. That crazy cow is dead now anyway. It's time for you to grow up and stop being such a miserable little girl."

"Stop talking about my mom! Stop!" shouted Katie, with tears in her eyes.

Penelope stood up from the chair and leaned across the table, putting her face right next to Katie's. Looking very angry and aggressive she shouted, "Did you shout at me? Did you just shout at me, you little brat?"

Katie, crying and desperate for Penelope to stop, said, "Don't talk about my mom, please...My mom is now an angel."

"Angel?" Penelope laughed again. "Who told you that lie? Perhaps that redneck grandmother of yours. I don't think your mother is an angel. She's seven feet under now, that crazy bitch."

"Stop, please!" said Katie, still crying. "Don't talk about my mom, please!"

"What did I say to you before? Do not be rude to me, do not be a naughty girl otherwise I will put you out on the streets and you'll be away from your daddy." Looking serious and with anger in her eyes, she went on, "Now let's talk serious here. Who told you to go upstairs earlier and enter my room without being invited?" Penelope lifted her right hand as if to punch Katie in the face, but didn't do it. "You're a nosy girl, aren't you?" Looking daggers at Katie, she continued, "You know how much your dad loves me, don't you? He loves me and all I have to do to get rid of you is to ask my car driver to drive you far, far away from here and dump you somewhere in the middle of nowhere, and guess what? No-one would ever find you. Well, nobody would even care about you anyway. Do you know why no-one will care?" Penelope continued, laughing, "Because you're an ugly little child, that's why no-one cares about you!"

Katie's legs were shaking and tears were streaming from her eyes. Penelope told her to stop crying because all this drama was annoying her. Looking at Katie's plate and noticing the mushrooms left aside, she remembered that Katie didn't like them.

"Eat all your food. There are people starving in the world. You've got to be grateful for what you have. You won't waste my food like this - eat it now!"

"I can't... I don't like mushrooms," replied Katie, feeling scared.

Penelope got hold of the fork and aggressively shoved the mushrooms inside Katie's mouth, forcing her to eat them one by one. Katie, in panic, tried to swallow but ended up choking, then threw up the food all over Rebecca's legs and on to her bright new red shoes.

"You're a disgusting little thing! Get out of here! Get out!" shouted Penelope. Pulling Katie by the hair, then pushing her away, she screamed, "You'll pay me for this! Now get out!"

Katie ran towards the door and flung it open. Running downstairs, she went to her bedroom and grabbed her teddy bear, holding it tightly against her chest. She was crying uncontrollably and her entire body was shaking. She closed her eyes, wishing her father was there to protect her. Shortly afterwards, Penelope came in. Very aggressively she grabbed hold of Katie's teddy bear and pulled it out of her hands, lifting it into the air.

"Please, please, don't do anything to him! He was a gift from my mom…please don't!" begged Katie.

Penelope looked furious. She walked towards the window and, facing Katie with anger in her eyes, she opened it. She held the teddy bear outside the window at arm's length, through the narrow space, threatening to throw it down.

"Say sorry. Say that you will never do it again. Say 'I won't be a naughty little brat ever again.' SAY IT!"

Katie couldn't stop crying. The teddy bear had been given to her by her mother, and was her only companion in life. She repeated the words Penelope asked her to say, adding "My teddy was a gift from my mother… I only have him. Please don't throw him down, please."

Penelope looked right into her eyes angrily and quickly opened her fingers, letting the bear fall. After watching it plummet all the way to the street, Penelope shut the window and stared straight at Katie, who sank to the floor, crying even harder.

"Now you know. Do not defy me. If you say anything about what you saw earlier in my bedroom you know what I will do? I will separate your father from you and you will be alone forever! It's bad to have lost your mother, isn't it? Now imagine losing your father and everyone else in your life." She knelt down and, grabbing hold of Katie's hair, she pulled up her head, saying, "Do you understand me?"

Penelope only let her go once Katie promised she wouldn't say anything to her father.

Linda and Rebecca watched Penelope leave the room. They had witnessed the whole scene, including the earlier incidents in the dining room. Katie was having a panic attack. She couldn't breathe properly and her heart was absolutely racing.

Linda sat down on the floor next to Katie. Embracing her, she transmitted vibrations of love and comfort. Meanwhile, Rebecca inspired Dolores to go into Katie's bedroom and show her some affection. When Dolores saw Katie lying on the floor she ran towards her and sat on the floor next to her. Gently lifting Katie on to her lap, she stroked her hair. Dolores could feel Katie's tears dripping down on to her own legs. Katie's little body was shaking. Dolores could feel all of her sorrow and pain, and she held Katie's body tighter against hers and kissed her head tenderly. With her eyes closed, she focused on love and peace. She then became connected to the same vibration as Linda, and could feel her energy. Linda spoke words in Dolores' ears, and even though Dolores couldn't see or hear her, following her intuition she repeated to Katie all the words inspired by Linda:

"Oh my little girl... You are not alone, I promise you that. Your mother is alive, just like you and me and your dad, but she's in a different place than us, and one day you two will reunite. Trust me when I say that she watches over you, because she truly does."

"Does she hear me when I cry at night, calling her name?" asked Katie in between sobs.

"Yes she does, my little girl. And she hears when you are laughing too. Your laughter makes her feel happy for you, but your crying makes her sad because she would like to be here with you but she can't be. And it's not her choice. It's just because in God's plan it was her time to move closer to Him."

At that moment Ricky walked into the bedroom. Dolores immediately looked at him silently and pointed at Katie who was still lying in her lap. Ricky tiptoed towards them, then sat down on the floor next to them. Ricky leaned his head over his mother's shoulder and started to stroke Katie's hair. Both mother and son stayed there with Katie, stroking her hair and giving her love. Linda and Rebecca remained in the bedroom, invisible to them all that time, and only leaving when Katie had finally calmed down and stopped sobbing.

Linda, moving closer to Dolores' ear, thanked her in a very soft tone. Even though the housekeeper couldn't hear her words, her soul felt the positive and loving energy sent by Linda. Dolores and Ricky kept holding Katie tight and praying for protection.

Chapter The honey bees and the black flies

At Lunas, Linda and Rebecca had just arrived back from Earth and were sitting on a bench by the lake, talking about the earlier events on Earth. Rebecca was visibly upset with all she had just seen and couldn't understand how such cruelty could be happening to such a young child without God intervening and helping. Teresa and Geraldine appeared in the air, arriving next to them. Rebecca started to tell them the story but was politely stopped by Geraldine, who said, "We saw the entire scene, my dear."

"We didn't see you two in there. Where were you?" asked Rebecca, looking confused.

"We were not exactly there, but we saw everything," replied Geraldine.

Teresa continued, "Spirits are like the sun's rays; we can reach anywhere and into many places at the same time. The more elevated we become, the closer to God we get, which also means we become lighter, with more attributes and gifts."

Rebecca looked even more confused, but before she could ask more questions Teresa read her thoughts and continued, "Now you can see your spirit has become free of all human needs, such as having to eat food in order to generate energy, or needing to shower or bathe to feel clean. Also you are now able to travel back and forth between Earth and the spiritual colony Domus Deus where you live, correct?"

Rebecca nodded, to which Teresa continued, "But you'll notice that some spirits who are still on a very low degree of evolution aren't able to do the things you can do, and perhaps you cannot do things that spirits like me and Geraldine can do, and so on... That's the evolution law: the more we evolve, the more connected to the divine creation we become, the closer to God we get." Noticing that Rebecca was paying close attention to her, Teresa continued, "Back to your question. We spirits can irradiate to different places at the same time, and the more evolved and the more enlightened we are, the further we can irradiate and reach. Just like the sun, which can reach so many different planets with its rays and so many different places at the same time, bringing its warmth and light to so many beings, even though it's physically a whole entity in one exact place."

"So you are saying that, depending on our evolutionary state, we can get to a point where we could be in many places at the same time?"

"Yes," replied Teresa. "Forget the human idea of a body made of matter and think instead of an ethereal body which becomes lighter and lighter as it reaches the higher levels of its purification. Each incarnation is like a filter that removes our impurities, so we become more connected to the divine energy of the universe."

"Rebecca was just telling me she doesn't understand how God can allow suffering - especially the suffering of such a little girl as Katie. Perhaps you could help me to explain this better," asked Linda to Geraldine and Teresa.

"All the sufferings are nothing more than lessons we receive to help us to progress. Our selfishness can see certain situations as suffering, although we should always look at the big picture and remember that God always has a master plan. Katie's challenges now are not only going to be beneficial for her at some point, but are also a tool to act on others who now need to go through a similar process." Geraldine then opened her arms and said, "Let me show you something."

Suddenly the space around them was taken up by a twist of colours which rapidly formed shapes until it showed the picture of a disabled child in front of them. The picture around them became more defined, and soon they could see that the child was a boy in a wheelchair. He seemed unable to speak or to move any of his muscles. Once the picture had become totally clear they could see the boy looked no more than ten years old. Linda and Rebecca were complete immersed in it, as if they had entered the house where the child lived. Suddenly they saw the boy's mother, who looked very dedicated. She was trying to move her son on to a bed, but was having great difficulty. The woman looked very fragile; she had a small figure and had to exert a lot of effort to be able to move her son from the wheelchair on to the bed. After finally succeeding, she removed his clothes with some difficulty, then bathed him with a wet sponge. She carefully towelled him dry and dressed him with fresh clothes. The apparently simple task of moving him from the chair to the bed, then bathing and dressing him again, took a very long time and also required a great effort from his mother. The picture faded away slowly, finally disappearing completely.

Once the picture had vanished and they saw themselves back in Lunas, Geraldine said, "What you have just seen is a very small fraction of the day of a family who are now incarnated on Earth, and whom I visit quite often to inspire them and transmit to them thoughts of encouragement and love." She gave a gentle smile and continued, "In that scene you met Yasmin and her son Peter. Yasmin and her husband Michael are very loving, caring and dedicated parents. They have been devoting all their love to their son for just over seven years now. Peter was born with severe congenital malformation of the brain and spine. He has never been able to talk or walk or move any muscle of his body. Although the doctors said when Peter was born that he wasn't going to live a long life, Yasmin and Michael have always treated him with immense love and care."

Rebecca looked extremely sad and sensitive to the story. Geraldine paused for a while and continued, "Don't look sad or feel pity for them. First of all, you have to put your faith in God above everything and believe He has a purpose for everything that is happening in life. Even a small leaf doesn't fall from a tree without God having a plan for it. You have to remember that God has a plan for all of us and His plans are always to help us to reach for our purification."

Linda, Rebecca and Teresa were all admiring how Geraldine was able to explain things in such a nice and natural way. Geraldine went on, "Yasmin and Michael are learning a very important lesson in this new incarnation on Earth. They are learning about the true meaning of love; the unselfish and unconditional love that makes you dedicate all of your strength, all of your energy to make the life of someone else better. They are learning that love unifies, love cures, love is what moves the universe. Before this current life experience, they behaved very selfishly, never minding others' wishes, hurting peoples' feelings and having evil behaviour towards others only in order to achieve their own pleasures. If earlier they were locked into their own material worlds where wealth was all that mattered, now they think and behave totally differently. Right now, all their money and vast wealth cannot cure their son, but they love him. Their love for their son is the only thing that can help him to have a better and less miserable life. What is now a time of suffering and hard work will turn out to be a divine lesson that will change their spirits forever. Peter, on the other hand, in a previous incarnation had a baby with his then wife. His son was born with the same illness that he himself suffers from today. Back then he rejected his son and abandoned him in a trash can in the street, and the baby died within a few hours. After many years, when he passed to the spiritual world, he realised the wrong he had caused, and, extremely regretful, he chose to return to Earth and incarnate with his corporeal body having the same illness as the baby that he once rejected."

Teresa followed on from Geraldine and concluded, "Suffering is nothing but lessons we go through to evolve our spirits towards purification. It's through lessons that we can discover important things we still have to learn. We usually choose our lessons according to what we think will be most beneficial for our progress, but sometimes such lessons are also imposed by God."

"Like a punishment?" asked Rebecca.

"No. God never punishes but teaches, just as a father should do. For example, if someone kills a person - causes someone's death - they will at some point go through the same thing in order to experience exactly the same feelings they once caused someone else, and hopefully learn they should never take another's life. Or, say, a person who once blinded someone deliberately, with the intention to harm and inflict pain, will have an incarnation as a blind person so they can understand, through the same pain they caused someone, how it feels to be blind and live one's whole life in darkness."

Linda said, "It's the same scenario with Katie in her current moment. God isn't punishing her or the others involved, but actually giving them all an opportunity to have another life experience together and learn together. Perhaps Katie, at some point in her existence, decided to return to Earth and incarnate and have this encounter with Penelope in order to help her to change her ways. Penelope has around her enlightened spirits, which are incarnated and have their lives connected to hers, so they can help her by giving her good examples and showing new ways to live her life. Now it's down to Penelope to change or to continue making the same old mistakes."

"It's difficult not to hate Penelope after seeing what she's just done; the cruelties she's been inflicting, not just on Katie but on so many other people. How can anyone stop her?" asked Rebecca.

Teresa replied, "We were all created ignorant and our aim is to seek the knowledge to evolve. Each one of us was created with the same means and it's up to each individual to decide which roads to take. Some of us decide to take the roads that lead to bliss and some others go the opposite way. At some point, even those who decided to take the road of evil will come back to God. It can take a long time or you could be a quick learner; it all depends on the individual."

"I like to use the honey bees and the black flies as an example of choices in life. While the honey bees chose to surround themselves with flowers and beauty, and to feed from the nectar of flowers, the black flies decided to surround themselves with dirt and all the ugly things in life, and so they feed on faeces. Like the honey bees, we can chose to surround ourselves with good and beauty, feed our intelligence by reading good books and consuming arts, or we could be like the black flies and surround ourselves with all the negative and bad things in life," said Geraldine.

Teresa continued, "Penelope has been making the same mistakes time and time again and delaying her progression. One day she will return to her purification process but unfortunately it seems as if this isn't happening just yet."

The four continued their conversation for a little longer and Rebecca seemed to take great interest in learning more about the spiritual world. She then realised how immense the universe is and how perfectly it works in order to provide all its inhabitants with the knowledge they need to reach for total purification.

Chapter The two sisters

Somewhere in the dark regions were two spirits with a female physiognomy, talking near a bonfire on a street corner. They were the same spirits that had been in the bar and created the argument that led to the fight between the drunkard and Roy. They looked deformed, with very thin hair and bald patches, and had exaggerated make-up on. They were extremely skinny and had some bones exposed through their clothes.

The blonde one, named Filomena, was saying to her companion, "I was in her apartment today. I had so much fun watching that bitch making that little brat suffer."

The other one, Fortunada, asked her to tell what she had seen. Filomena narrated all the events that had happened earlier on Earth between Penelope and Katie. She finished by saying, "Then suddenly, when I tried to approach the girl, I was thrown away by the enlightened ones."

"By who? The mother?"

"No, this time it wasn't her mother who sent me away, but proper angels did. Oh, I've got to say I don't mind the enlightened ones - I love laughing at them and winding them up, but with those angels I don't take the risk. I've only seen those angels three times in my whole life, but to be honest I'm scared of them," replied Filomena.

Filomena and Fortunada were typical evil spirits who inhabited the dark regions. They dedicated their existence to futile matters, spending most of their time focused on gossiping about others and wishing ill fortune on them. They enjoyed tormenting incarnated spirits on Earth, causing them suffering in order to absorb their energies. Taking advantage of the vices available to incarnated spirits on Earth, such as addiction to alcohol and drugs, the two spirits, alongside many others like them, fed their own addictions and vices by tormenting them. Motivated by extreme jealousy, they spent centuries tormenting Penelope, following every step of her life, taking pleasure from watching her misfortunes and bad behaviour.

Now Penelope was once again incarnated, the pair spent a lot of time close to her, always feeding her with dark thoughts and bad energy.

"I still can't believe that Rebecca has joined the enlightened ones. We spent such a long time tormenting and driving her to commit suicide, and when she finally died we couldn't even enjoy the pleasure of having her as our slave for long," said Fortunada, while trying to fix the heel of one of her shoes that had broken.

Filomena commented, "I know. If it wasn't for that Linda, she would still be here, serving us and meeting all of our wishes, but anyway, now we need to continue focusing on driving Penelope mad and ruining her life. I also like to see that little brat suffering, annoying little pest."

"But how can we be around the girl if her mother's always there, and now even the angels are there too?" asked Fortunada, getting angrier as she heavily twisted the heel into the shoe's sole. The heel finally snapped completely and Fortunada threw it against the tin wall. "I hate that woman!" screamed Fortunada, referring to Penelope. "How unfair is it? Once again she incarnates back on Earth and has all the best in life! Amazing cars, a private jet… nice shoes! We can't rest until we manage to destroy her life once again, my sister."

What they didn't realise was that Linda, Rebecca, Geraldine and Teresa were there, invisible to them, listening to everything. Rebecca was petrified of what she had just seen. To be back in the dark regions felt like torture for Rebecca. She had only agreed to accompany the other three because they had promised to be next to her at all times while they were there. Geraldine was close to Filomena and Fortunada, praying and transmitting them thoughts of love.

"It's so sad to see spirits like those two spending all of their existence focused on causing bad things to others," said Linda.

Teresa put her hand on Linda's shoulder and said, "If they only knew that they are just causing bad for themselves. All the ill fortune they wish upon others returns back at them multiple times. They still don't realise that no evil can get through those who work for God."

Rebecca was looking pale and shaking. She took hold of Linda's hand and held it tightly. She was close to fainting.

"Don't let their evil vibrations and negative thoughts affect you, my dear," said Teresa. "Elevate your thoughts, always seeking positivity and love." Teresa looked into Rebecca's eyes and told her, "Now focus your mind on peace and love, hold on to your faith. Imagine a beautiful place, think of all the beautiful things in the universe you have seen, focus on your love for yourself and for others, and suddenly love will surround you and brighten your way."

"Filomena, look at that corner near the bonfire," exclaimed Fortunada, pointing with her index finger, which looked to be made partly of flesh and partly of bone.

"What?"

"It seems like I've just seen that stupid Rebecca here watching us!"

Filomena walked towards the bonfire where Fortunada was pointing but could see nothing. "Oh shut up, you. You're demented, there's no-one there, you idiot!"

Slowly Rebecca recovered and the paleness faded away. She stood back up on her feet again and thanked Teresa for her help.

"You shouldn't seek happiness and goodness in the place where you are, or in the people around you. Instead you should search for it within yourself and yourself only. It doesn't matter how difficult the circumstances might be, or how negative and low the energy of the place you are in. You must always focus your thoughts on positivity and on the beauties of life, and you will be fine," said Teresa. "By lowering the quality of your thoughts you ended up getting yourself into the same vibration as those two. This is a lesson for you: it doesn't matter where you are or who you are with; keep your thoughts elevated at all times and you will be fine."

"Why did you bring me back here? Those two are the last ones I wanted to see right now. They only caused me pain and drove me to suicide, then once I disincarnated they used me as their servant."

Still holding Rebecca's hand, Linda said, with extra kindness in her voice, "Your own depressive and negative thoughts attracted them to your side. When you were incarnated and living on Earth, every time you harmed your corporeal body by using those chemical substances and by cutting your physical body with razor blades and knives, you were not only hurting your body but also hurting your soul too. At the same time you ended up attracting inferior and evil spirits like those two close to you. The more depressive your thoughts became, the more evil spirits you attracted towards you. The results were your deep depression, leading to you ending up committing suicide." Linda dried the tears from Rebecca's face and continued, "The reason why you are here is that we would like to show you how much you have progressed. Not long ago you were in the same vibration, indulging in the same sort of behaviour as those two, and now look at you! Look how much you have evolved just by learning to love yourself. But we are also here to talk to you about forgiveness. We cannot progress without helping those less fortunate, and the only way we can do that is by starting with forgiveness."

Teresa pointed to Filomena and Fortunada, who had just got into an argument and begun to fight. She then said to Rebecca, "They are spirits like you and me and all the others, with the difference that they are still very primitive. Let's say that they are still in the infantile stage of their evolutionary journey and have lots yet to learn. What you need to realise when you see the mistakes they make is that you, I and everyone else have probably made those same mistakes at some point in our existences, when our knowledge about life and the universe wasn't as it is today."

"Do you mean that at some point I was also as mean and evil as they are?"

"I wouldn't say evil and mean, but yes, you at some point could have made mistakes as bad as theirs, as could any other spirit. Remember that we are all evolving and we were all created the same. Nobody was created with more intelligence or knowledge than anyone else. That's how fair and just God is."

"Would you like me to get closer to them again?" asked Rebecca.

It was Teresa who replied, "No, no. Forgiveness in this case means don't hold any bad feeling inside you, because once you have hate inside, you will still be linked to them. Understand that they have only done to you the things they know in life. They believe this is the only way to live. They could not have offered you anything better, simply because they still don't know anything better than the evil they insist on nurturing inside themselves. To forgive isn't to make you feel like a victim and blame others, but instead to accept what happened as a learning process and move on." She gently touched Rebecca's face and finished by saying, "Wish them the best in life. Ask God to show them light and knowledge. Believe me when I say that, however long it takes, one day they will also evolve like everyone in the universe."

"It's time for us to visualise everything that happened in the life experience in Spain," said Linda.

Geraldine performed her final prayer for Filomena and Fortunada, then returned, staying close to Linda, Teresa and Rebecca. They all held hands and left the dark regions, heading to Lunas.

Chapter Maria's despair

Sitting on the grass by the lake in Lunas, Linda, Geraldine, Teresa and Rebecca were ready to review the scenes of the past. Suddenly their sight became blurry as a twist of different colours appeared in the air. The colours grew very intense and shortly the vision of a past life experience back in the Navarre Kingdom started to appear in front of them. It quickly took over, involving them all in the scenes of the tragedy.

Navarre Kingdom, fifteenth century

Carmen and Sophia were in the field with their horses, heading to the market. Sophia was quiet and pensive, coming across as very irritated since her encounter with Enrique the previous night.

"Mama, why did you look so strange last night when that man came to talk to you?"

"Carmen, my daughter, I told you to forget it. Leave me alone!" said Sophia abruptly. "He is just an old friend of mine… I mean, he is just someone I knew and who I wish I'd never seen again."

"That's not what he told me last night."

Sophia stopped and faced Carmen, looking surprised. "What did he say? Tell me everything you two spoke about!"

"Well, I will if you tell me first who he is and how you know him," said Carmen, giggling.

"Carmen! Tell me, daughter, what did he say to you?"

Carmen continued to giggle and, mounting her horse, she said, "Mama, now you have to ride and catch me, and once you do you will have to tell me first." As she finished speaking she spurred her horse to run across the field, shouting to her mother to catch her.

Sophia mounted her horse and galloped after Carmen, who was going very fast. Mother and daughter were suddenly playing in the field with their horses, engaged in a play chase. After much running about, laughing and joking, chasing one another, they stopped by the river and both lay down on the grass.

Sophia, looking at the clouds in the sky, took a long breath and then told her daughter her story about Enrique, starting from when they first met in the village where they were born, and how they had fallen in love with each other.

"Enrique was tall, with deep green eyes and dark hair. He was the most gorgeous man in the entire village. We met when we were only kids and we grew up together as friends. One day when we were teenagers we were alone by a waterfall. It was a summer night and we were laughing away as usual. I knew by then that I was completely in love with him but I hadn't said anything to him up to that point. I couldn't, because I was so scared of being rejected by him. We got lost in the woods and the darkness fell, so we decided to find a place to stay the night."

Carmen got up and sat closer to her mother, looking very interested. She teased her to hurry up and get to the part where they made love.

"Carmen!" She laughed along with her daughter. "Well, we decided to find a place to stay the night and...laughing with joy, underneath the stars on that gorgeous summer night, we kissed for the first time and we made love."

Those memories took Sophia back to a very happy moment of her life, and she closed her eyes as if trying to feel Enrique's kisses again. She recalled the smell in the air and the feel of his touch. She was happily daydreaming, remembering every detail about that night, when suddenly she was brought back to reality by Carmen, who was keen to hear the end of the story.

"Enrique and I began dating, and shortly afterwards we became engaged. Our families were very happy and they all planned our wedding celebrations as our people do, with a big and grand party. One day, Enrique was invited to do some work in Pamplona and he had to stay away from the village for a few weeks. Some time went by, and when he returned he seemed very different. Our relationship cooled down and he didn't seem interested in any of the arrangements for our wedding any more."

Carmen realised her mother had become upset with the sad memories, and she started to stroke her hair very gently. After moments in silence, Sophia took a long breath and continued, "Enrique ran away from our village the night before our wedding." With tears running down her face, she went on, "I loved him so much, my daughter… I then learnt he had married Marta Cortez, who was the daughter of the richest man in the kingdom." Sophia decided not to tell the part of the story where she found out she was expecting a baby, and that she had to leave the village in order to keep her child and face life as a single mother.

Not too far from there, in Pamplona, Enrique was also thinking of Sophia. At the same time as Sophia was narrating their story to Carmen, he remembered their happy times together and recalled the love he used to feel when by her side. A sad feeling took over his soul, reminding him of how he had left Sophia, diverted by the ambition of having a wealthy life. He left behind their plans of marriage and a life together, opting instead for luxury and the status of Marta's family.

'She still looks so gorgeous,' he thought. *'And her daughter looks such a beautiful and gracious lady, just like Sophia was when she was young.'*

His thoughts were interrupted by Marta, who had entered the room, smartly dressed and clearly about to go out.

"Where are you going, Marta?" he asked, looking interested.

"Justa has invited me to hers for some wine. You know, she probably wants to show off about her fest and how grand and great it was."

"Justa isn't shallow like that, Marta. I'm sure the reason she's invited you is to meet with you and friends and talk about things. She doesn't have any desire to show off."

"Whatever, Enrique. You keep living in this imaginary world where everyone is happy, as if living in happy land. People are mean and you need to wake up. Open your eyes, quickly, before someone comes and bursts you out of this imaginary happy world that you choose to live in! Anyway, my friends Filomena and Fortunada are waiting for me outside."

Enrique realised that this was a chance for him to see Sophia again. He couldn't bear spending time with his wife and her friends Fortunada and Filomena, and hated having to endure all those conversations which consisted mainly of nasty gossip and slagging off others. However, the desire of seeing Sophia again spoke more loudly, and he decided to grasp this great opportunity to see her again. Enrique also liked Justa and her husband Ager. He found their company very pleasurable. He didn't think twice; disguising his excitement, he casually told Marta he was going to join her and her friends. At first Marta hesitated, not understanding why her husband wanted to join them. After all, he had always said how he despised Fortunada and Filomena, and that they only engaged in futile conversations, so why would he want to come? However, she ended up agreeing in the end.

Moments later at Justa's home, Marta, Enrique and her friends were enjoying some wine offered by Justa and her husband Ager. Justa was pleasant and kind as usual; completely the opposite of Marta and her two friends, who were always making sarcastic remarks about other people. Enrique felt embarrassed at his wife's behaviour, always provoking intrigues and laughing at others without any sympathy for anyone's feelings, but deep down he was already used to her ways and didn't expect anything better from her. When next to her, Enrique was always very quiet and discreet, as deep down he didn't approve of any aspect of his wife's behaviour. At one point, when they were all engrossed in conversation, he stood up and excused himself, saying he needed to go and catch some fresh air. Of course, this was actually an excuse to walk around the property and try to find more information about Sophia. He went to the kitchen and to the servant's rooms in search of her, but couldn't find either Sophia or her daughter. Then, inspired by spiritual friends who were invisible to him, he was guided to go to the back yard. When he reached the back of the property he heard female laughter, gradually growing louder. Looking to see where the sound was coming from, he saw the two ladies riding horses, approaching the property. They were singing a jolly song and seemed to be very happy. His heart accelerated and the palms of his hands were sweating. The two ladies drew closer to where Enrique was standing, until Sophia noticed him and stopped. His and Sophia's eyes met and they both stared at each other from a distance.

Sophia's impulse was to run away from there and not talk to him, but Carmen, feeling that her mother was about to leave, held her hand and looked at her, nodding. Carmen's protective look showed that she was there to support her mother. Enrique's heart was also beating fast and he felt as if he had butterflies in his stomach. Both kept gazing into each other's eyes without speaking. It was Carmen who broke the silence.

"Senor Enrique! How nice to see you again." She dismounted from her horse. "We are coming over. Please wait there."

"Carmen!" Sophia snapped. Realising she had no way to escape, she whispered to Carmen, "I'm scared."

"Come on, Mama, he is here, you can't stop now. Let's see what life is bringing to us now and embrace this gift from destiny."

As they moved closer, Enrique and Sophia remained speechless. They both felt as if they had butterflies in their stomach, like a young teenage couple who had just fallen in love for the first time. Remembrance of their good times together came into their minds and the air was infused with a very pleasant smell. Life had brought them together once again. They couldn't see them, but Geraldine and Teresa were there next to them, smiling and happy at their re-encounter. Carmen was very gracious; understanding that they needed to be alone, she excused herself and went inside to the servants' room. From time to time she watched them from the corner of the window.

Enrique broke the silence. "I can't stop thinking of you, Sophia. I actually never did."

Sophia didn't reply. She remained quiet, and even though her heart was telling her how much she loved this man, she thought it better not to say anything.

Enrique continued, "There hasn't been a day or a night that has gone by in all these years when I haven't thought of you. I remember your smell, your touch and everything about you…"

"Then you shouldn't," said Sophia quickly. "You left us, remember?" She regretted saying 'us', as if she had definitely given away the truth about his being Carmen's father. She tried to correct herself by saying, "You left me, and now it's too late."

But even if was too late, Enrique understood at that point that his intuition was right about Carmen. His heart was telling him the truth: Sophia had been pregnant when he left. His thoughts went further, and he concluded that she had had the baby. "You just said 'You left us', so it's true then, you were bearing a baby when I left."

Sophia didn't reply and tried to walk away, but was held by Enrique. He looked deep into her eyes and asked, "Tell me, Sophia. I need to know the truth. You were bearing a baby, weren't you?" to which she nodded. "Why you didn't tell me? Why you didn't say you were expecting a baby at the time? I would have never left you and our baby if I'd known."

Sophia, losing all control, shouted at him, "Oh, you wouldn't have left, would you? But you did and you never came back. Do you think I would have gone after you to plead for you to love me, or do you think I should have begged for you to care for our daughter? You were blind, Enrique. Your ambition would never have let you stay where you were and be a village man, leading a simple life. Perhaps if I'd told you about our baby you could have stayed, but you would have been the unhappiest of men, always wondering how amazing your life could have been if you'd taken the opportunity to become a wealthy and powerful man. I decided to set you free to pursue your ambition." She looked deep in his eyes and finished by saying, "You can't force someone to love you. You either feel or you don't, and in this case I decided to face the fact that you didn't love me and move on with my life."

Very upset, looking down and with tears rolling down his face, Enrique had gone quiet listening to Sophia. He knew she was right. His ambition was so strong that his desire for wealth and status would have turned him into a bitter man if he had stayed in the village. Still staring at the ground, feeling embarrassed, he said, "What I learnt was that none of the gold in this world and not even the highest status could have replaced the happiness I felt when I was next to you." Before he could say anything else, Justa came outside, followed by Marta and her two friends.

"Is everything okay here, Sophia?" asked Justa, looking worried. Noticing that Sophia was crying, she went up to her and held her tenderly.

"Enrique, you are crying too. What's happening?" asked Filomena, with an evil glint in her eyes.

Before anyone could say anything else, Marta, looking furious, pushed Enrique away, screaming, "Enrique, what the hell are you doing here outside talking to the servant?"

Filomena and Fortunada laughed cruelly at what they were seeing, and Carmen, who had been watching the scene from the kitchen window, ran outside and joined them. Realising that neither her mother nor Enrique knew what to say, Carmen stepped forward and said, "Madame Justa, I am so sorry. My mother and I just received some bad news from one of our relatives in France, and I went inside to get my mother some water when this gentleman appeared and caught her crying desperately." Carmen had never lied before, but at that moment she couldn't even think about what she was saying. It was as if she had no control over the words that were coming out of her mouth; she knew she had to help her mother out of that situation. She explained that a relative who lived in France had been found dead in the woods, and told them how upset she and her mother were. Justa, very sympathetic, asked her guests to return inside. Thanking Enrique for giving support to Sophia and Carmen, she went back inside the house. Everyone followed apart from Marta, who stayed to confront Sophia.

"I don't know what you are playing at, you two rats, but you'd better stay away from my husband. There's something about you that I don't like and I'll warn my friend Justa about you. She's got to get rid of you two for the sake of our friendship."

"What a vile woman!" said Carmen after Marta had gone back inside. Looking at her mother and noticing that she seemed upset, Carmen asked, in a worried voice, "Are you alright mother?" then took her arm and helped her to sit down on a bench.

Sophia was shaking in panic. First the argument with Enrique and all those feelings from the past brought up all over again, and now his wife and the mean things she had just said. All this had been too much for her. *'I have to tell Carmen the truth. She needs to know that Enrique is her real father,'* she thought. When Carmen came back with a bowl of water, Sophia didn't hesitate and told her, "I have something to confess, my daughter. But before I do, I need to say that it wasn't my fault. I never meant to hide anything from you. He left us…it was he who left us…"

Carmen put the bowl of water aside, and gently touching her mother's face, she said softly, "I know, mama. I know what you are going to say. He is my father and I realised this when I first saw you two speaking. I felt in him something that I've never felt around anyone before. He is my father and you don't have to worry about anything, because I know how confused and scared you might be feeling right now with his return to your life."

Sophia was looking down and crying non-stop. She took Carmen's hands away from her face and kissed them. "Oh my sweetheart, I love you so much. I was so scared that his return could hurt you, just as he hurt me those many years ago. I don't want you to suffer as I once did because of him."

"You don't have to be scared, mama. I'm intrigued to know more about him, of course I am, but I also respect you and your relationship with him, and I know you two have a lot to talk about and go through first. But above all I want you to look after yourself without worrying about me. I'm fine. You have been my mother and my father at the same time for all these years, and with all the love you gave me through all this time I've never missed a father figure, simply because you loved me so much and so intensely."

Sophia replied, "But both of you deserve the truth, and have to get to know each other. He is your father and I cannot deny that. I will have to tell him the truth."

Justa came outside after her guests had left and approached them. Visibly anxious about Sophia, she asked, "What happened earlier, my friend? I'm so worried about you." She looked at both Carmen and Sophia and said, "And please don't repeat that thing about a relative being found dead, because I didn't believe any of that."

Justa and Sophia had been childhood friends born in the same village. Justa's parents moved away to another village when she was still young, but she came to meet Sophia again later in life, when Sophia, now pregnant, asked for a place to stay in exchange for her work. Justa and her husband, compassionate about Sophia's situation, invited her to come and stay until she had given birth. They owned land which was far away from their main property, so they asked Sophia to help look after it, and in exchange they offered her a small house. Justa and Ager had never seen Sophia as a servant, but more as a friend whom they loved and cared for.

Sophia told Justa everything that had happened in the past between her and Enrique, narrating the entire story from when she realised she was pregnant up to the recent events when she had met Enrique again at her party after all those years. Crying and hugging her daughter, she got everything off her chest, confessing to Justa and Carmen all her feelings for Enrique. Justa and Carmen listened to it all very closely.

When Sophia had finished, Justa gave a promise and a warning. "I promise you, my friends, that I will help you two to get closer to Enrique. I will try especially for you, Carmen, to be able to spend some daughter and father time. You need time to get to know each other and I will help you, but we must be very careful for Marta not to find out. I repeat, we must be very careful. There's something about Marta that scares me, I must say and I don't know what she might be capable of doing if she found out that Enrique is seeing you two. My intuition tells me that she is very dangerous."

****

Weeks went by and Justa did what she had promised; she welcomed Enrique into her property and her lands, and also covered for him so he could spend time with Sophia and Carmen. Her husband Ager also helped out by letting Enrique use his name to Marta as an excuse. Every afternoon Enrique told his wife he was meeting Ager to discuss some possible trade deal opportunities, but he was really meeting Sophia and Carmen back at their little house.

Although Enrique and Sophia were still in love with each other, they were both very respectful to his marriage to Marta. All the time they spent together was focused on his relationship with Carmen, so they could get to know more about each other, building their relationship and enjoying their daughter and father time. Their hours together were joyful. The afternoons with Sophia and Carmen were very different from being at home with Marta and his other daughter, Maria, where he spent most of his time listening to them either moaning about life or gossiping about others. The more time he spent with Carmen and Sophia, the more he grew to love them and appreciate their company.

****

Somewhere in Pamplona, Filomena and Fortunada were in their manor house, chatting. They had inherited the house from their parents and it had been in their family for many generations. The place was very messy, as if it had been abandoned for years, and it had an unpleasant smell. The interior and exterior both looked extremely dilapidated. Their house was the perfect mirror of their souls.

They were talking about their favourite subject: Marta. Their obsession for her occupied most of their time and used up most of their energy. They could spend literally hours in a single day discussing various aspects of Marta's life, sometimes gossiping about her and her family members, or on other occasions planning ways to cause her evil and ill fortune. They envied everything about Marta and her life. They wanted to be as beautiful as she was, dress like her and even behave like her. What they disguised as admiration and friendship was, deep down, pure hate and jealousy. They couldn't bear it when anything pleasant happened to Marta; it always brought them great irritation and frustration. Their smiles concealed a deep and perpetual wish for misery in her life. They celebrated every time something bad happened to Marta or to someone in her family, as if her misfortune was their triumph. The latest subject was her daughter Maria's depression over the breakup of her relationship with Alejandro. Fortunada and Filomena took great pleasure at Marta's despair over her daughter's troubled relationship.

"I knew it! I knew it wouldn't last," said Filomena, holding a cup of wine.

"Did you see the way she was after him at Justa's fest? And the way he avoided her all the time?" Fortunada laughed gleefully as she picked up the bottle of wine that was on the floor next to Filomena. She poured a full cup and continued, "Who does that girl think she is? She's as ugly as her mother and has that same horrible squeaky tone of voice; just like her mother." She drank half the cup in one go and finished by saying, "Arghhh! I despise the two of them!"

"Well sister, now we need to find out who the young and handsome Alejandro Vigar is dating…erm… because he has to be dating someone, right?"

"Correct. He must be engaged to someone else!" she laughed. "And we will find out and make sure the entire kingdom knows that Marta's daughter has been dumped and replaced by someone else!"

Suddenly they both screamed as they saw a massive rat in the corner of the room, and began an argument as to who was going to get rid of the rat infestation in the house.

****

One night, having made his usual excuse of visiting Justa's husband Ager to continue discussing their trading plans, Enrique managed to get out of the house and join Sophia, Carmen and their friends on a gathering fest, celebrating Carmen's engagement. Enrique hadn't yet met her fiancée and he was keen to meet the man who was making his daughter so happy.

The moonlight was shining all over the field and many people were arriving and gathering by the bonfire. Justa and her husband Ager were also there among the guests, enjoying the fun. Some young ladies started to dance around the bonfire while the men stood in a circle, drinking, talking and laughing. Sophia joined the young ladies in their dance. She had a sparkle in her eyes and looked more beautiful than ever. All the love she was feeling had made her look and feel ten years younger, and Enrique couldn't avoid staring at her. Enrique sat next to one of the guitarists, who let him have a go on his instrument and play a few chords. Justa and Ager had noticed how much Enrique had changed in the past few weeks. He was looking less stressed and was more talkative, even making jokes and joining everyone else having fun.

"The wonders of love, my sweetheart," said Ager to Justa, pointing at Enrique with his head. "Love brings out only the best in us."

Justa smiled in agreement and embraced her husband tenderly. Suddenly the crowd went quiet and everyone's attention turned to Carmen and Alejandro who were arriving on horseback. Carmen was riding her own steed, Asas, while Alejandro was on Sophia's horse. The guests all stood up and applauded. They all raised their cups and bowls to toast and welcome the couple. After a big cheer the fun continued with more music and dancing.

Carmen approached her father and introduced her fiancé. "Father, may I introduce you to the man who makes me the happiest woman in the continent. Papa, this is Alejandro."

Both Alejandro and Enrique went pale and looked visibly shocked. They both remained quite motionless, staring at each other without saying a word. Not understanding what was happening, Carmen asked them what the matter was. It was Alejandro who broke the silence, saying "Erm, Carmen...the lady who I was engaged to before you, that one I told you about, you know? She is..." He went quiet for a moment and, feeling very awkward, he finished his sentence quickly by blurting out, "She is his daughter, Maria."

"What?" she asked, still confused. "So the lady who is out of her mind and who is stalking you is actually my father's daughter?" Realising what she had just said, she blushed and kindly apologised to her father.

"Don't worry, my daughter. I know Maria isn't the easiest of people. She is not in a good place right now after the split." Looking at Alejandro, he said, "I'm just a bit surprised at this whole business. What a bizarre coincidence."

They were all feeling very awkward with the situation life was presenting to them at that moment. Alejandro approached Enrique and apologised, even though deep down he didn't even know what he was saying sorry for.

Enrique put his hand on Alejandro's shoulder and said, "I always liked you, Alejandro, and to be brutally honest I sort of felt that Maria didn't deserve you. As a father it pains me to say that about my own daughter, though I saw the way she treated you and spoke to you and that wasn't nice at all. Well... I confess I'm a bit speechless now, after learning that you're dating my other daughter... wow...I have no words."

Alejandro gave a shy smile as he said, "I am sorry, Senor Cortez. I didn't even know you had another daughter."

Carmen covered her mouth with both hands and broke into a nervous laugh, shaking her head and not knowing what to say. At the same time Enrique and Alejandro started to laugh as well. Enrique gave Alejandro a strong hug and explained to him his story with Sophia and how he had only recently found out about having another daughter. Enrique liked Alejandro a lot; he had met his parents and he knew he was a genuine, intelligent and kind guy, meaning he was perfect for Carmen. He kindly asked Alejandro if he would mind keeping quiet about the relationship, as he was not prepared yet to tell Marta and Maria about Sophia and Carmen.

"I do apologise if I come across as disrespectful towards your daughter Maria, but I truly don't have any intention to see her again. If, by any surprising coincidence of destiny, my path happens to cross hers, I promise I won't even think of mentioning anything." Pulling a pained face, he finished by saying, "Maria is already making my life very difficult. Imagine if she found out that I am engaged to her half-sister… It pains me even to think of it."

"You are a great young man, Alejandro, and I wish you and Carmen all the best in life," said Enrique, with admiration for Alejandro in his eyes.

A female friend of Carmen pulled her by the arm, inviting her to join the other couples who were dancing around the bonfire, so she went, taking Alejandro with her. Sophia, looking stunning in a dark red dress, approached Enrique and softly ran her fingers through her long and curly hair, moving it along with the breeze. As she drew closer to Enrique she realised he looked shocked. He told her about his discovery that Alejandro had been engaged to his other daughter, Maria. They both laughed at what they called a strange surprise of destiny.

A few hours later that evening, next to a tree and away from everyone else, Enrique and Sophia finally succumbed to their strong feelings for each other and kissed with passion for the first time since Enrique had departed from their old village and left her over eighteen years ago. The sky that night was clear and the full moon's light was brightening the fields, making the moment magic and special, just as the reunion of two spirits who deeply loved each other should be.

Back at the Cortezes' castle, Marta was concerned about her daughter, who had locked herself in her bedroom. She walked impatiently in circles around the living room, waiting for Enrique to return home. Maria had become depressed after her breakup with Alejandro and her state of mind was steadily getting worse. She spent every day crying, feeling extremely rejected and upset, nurturing obsessive thoughts about Alejandro. Nothing else mattered but to get him back - or so she thought. In the past few days she had lost a lot of weight and she now looked very ill, with deep dark circles around her eyes. *'He is mine…He is mine and I will make him realise that! He cannot leave me like that. I cannot believe he has another woman! Oh my misery…I hate you, God!'* she thought while holding a large knife against the skin of her chest area. Piercing her skin with the blade, she asked, *'Why am I so ugly?'* Another cut, this time a longer, deeper one, and she continued talking to herself. *'Maybe that's why he left me…yeah…I don't have the looks my mother has. I am ugly as hell! A terrible ugly beast that doesn't deserve to be loved.'* Tears were rolling down her face and many evil spirits were surrounding her at that point. They were encouraging her to continue slicing herself with the knife, telling her she was very ugly indeed and no-one would ever love her.

Her mother had knocked on her bedroom door several times, trying to talk, but Maria wasn't interested in conversation. When not locked in her bedroom crying and self-harming, Maria was on the streets, chasing Alejandro and begging him to come back to her. Earlier on that day, when leaving the church after the mass had finished, she saw Alejandro also leaving with his parents, and ran after him, begging him desperately to give the relationship another chance. She threw herself on the ground in front of hundreds of worshippers who were exiting the church and made a terrible scene. Like a toddler throwing a tantrum, she grabbed hold of his legs and screamed, telling him she would rather die than have to live her life without him. Alejandro managed to escape and, apologising to Marta, he left the scene quickly, accompanied by his parents. The onlookers had formed a semi-circle around her; some were laughing and others looked very sorry for her. Horribly embarrassed, Marta managed to grab Maria by her arm and dragged her away. The two sisters, Filomena and Fortunada, were among those watching the incident. They ran quickly to catch up with Marta and Maria, looking forward to telling them the news.

"Marta! Marta!" shouted Fortunada with her left arm lifted as if trying to reach for her. "Wait, ladies. We have some news for you."

Marta was too embarrassed to even look back, so she continued walking fast, pulling Maria by her arm. The two sisters ran faster, shouting their names until they finally managed to catch them.

Out of breath, Fortunada gasped, "Marta, Maria, wait. We have some news…"

"I'm not interested now, Fortunada. I just want to get home," said Marta, focused on getting Maria home as soon as possible, and not looking at the two sisters.

"It's about Alejandro!" shouted Filomena, knowing that by saying his name out loud she would make Maria stop and listen to what she had to say.

As Filomena predicted, Maria stopped dead in her tracks, then roughly pulled her mother's hand off her arm, almost causing Marta to fall. "Did you just say you have some news about Alejandro?"

"Yes, we do," said Fortunada, disguising the pleasure she was feeling.

"What do you know? Tell me."

'She looks really tormented. I can't wait to see her face when she hears this,' she thought, before finally saying sharply, while pretending to be sorry for her, "We know that he is engaged to someone else."

Fortunada, feeling secretly excited about the situation, said quickly, "We saw him holding hands with a beautiful lady not far from here."

Maria put her hands in her mouth and looked shocked. Without hesitating, Filomena and Fortunada exaggerated the situation. Gesticulating with grand gestures, they told how and what they had seen, and even lied, making up more stories about Alejandro and his new girlfriend.

After recovering from the shock, Maria dried the tears off her face and screamed, "Who is she? Who? Tell me!"

"We don't know yet. All we know is that she is a commoner. By the clothes she was wearing we could say that she is definitely not wealthy," said Filomena, making an apologetic face, still pretending to feel sorry for Maria.

"But she is very beautiful…gorgeous in fact," said Fortunada, also with feigned sympathy.

"Yes, I must agree with my sister. Although she is a peasant, she is very beautiful."

Maria screamed loudly, looking furious, and ran away as fast as she could. Fortunada and Filomena told Marta they hoped they hadn't upset Maria or caused any inconvenience, and promised not to rest until they had found out the identity of Alejandro's new lady. Marta didn't pay them much attention and left, running after her daughter, trying to catch her. Once she had disappeared, the two sisters laughed gleefully, taking great pleasure at Maria's misery.

Back in her bedroom, Maria locked the door and took out the knife she kept inside her dressing table drawer. She held the blade against her wrist…she pressed forcefully and…

"Stop! Stop playing this, please!" shouted Rebecca in distress.

The vision of the past life experience immediately faded away and Linda went over to Rebecca. She embraced her to try and calm her down. Rebecca was shaking, looking very disturbed.

"Stop!" Rebecca cried, out of breath and with panic in her voice. "I remember now what happened there… STOP showing this, please… I'm feeling a lot of pain!" she screamed. "I don't want to feel all that pain all over again. Stop!"

Chapter The trap

Back on Earth, Penelope and Roy had gone to the Hamptons to attend the house party of Patricia, a good friend of Penelope. Roy didn't say anything to Penelope, but inside he was feeling very anxious and intimidated, as Patricia was one of her multi-millionaire friends. Penelope's circle of friends was very different from Roy's, and he didn't know how to behave in the company of those with vast wealth.

'They must have so many different protocols, so much social etiquette, that I won't even know how to talk to them,' he was thinking. *'What if they find me boring or not good enough to be around them?'*

When they arrived at Patricia's luxurious mansion in the Hamptons, they were greeted by a semi-naked male waiter who had his whole body painted with leopard spots. His only piece of clothing was a very small item of Speedo underwear. Looking like a male model, he held a silver tray with champagne glasses on, and gave a flirty smile to Penelope which she returned. Standing at the door, they could hear loud laughter coming from inside the mansion. Once inside, Roy found a completely different world from the one he was expecting; around the luxurious entrance hall there were some guys and girls leaning on the wall, kissing in groups. Penelope and Roy walked down the hall and entered the living room, which seemed to be filled with more scantily-clad female and male models everywhere, not only serving the guests but also interacting with everyone.

"Pepe!" shouted Patricia, using a very exaggerated tone and wearing a mask in the shape of a cat. "Why did you come so late?" She gave Penelope two air kisses instead of properly making contact with her cheeks. "Hi, Roy. You look very handsome as usual!" Noticing that he didn't remember her, she joked, "Perhaps it would help if I removed my mask, right?" Patricia revealed her face and smiled at Roy. She called one of the male models, who brought a pair of masks, and handed them to Penelope and Roy, saying, "Penelope, you know the dress code. I'll ask Marcos to show you the changing room where you can leave your clothes." Then, eyeing up Roy, "And as for you, handsome boy, I'll call one of our leopards to show you your changing room." Patricia lifted her hand up in the air and clicked her fingers, at which a female semi-naked model approached them.

Roy then looked around properly and realised that everyone in the place was wearing different types of costumes, with some clad only in underwear or lingerie.

"Penelope, what's going on?" he whispered in her ear.

"Oh come on, Roy. Don't embarrass me, darling, with such a boring question. Go to the room and get changed."

"Do I need to strip completely?"

Patricia laughed and said, "No, no, silly. Well, you can if you want, but the idea is to feel comfy and wear whatever you fancy. You can follow this beautiful leopard girl here into the room and there you'll find a few options. Tonight the idea is that you can be whoever you want: a cowboy, a Roman gladiator…or a naked, handsome man. As you fancy, my darling."

Penelope had already left the room, holding hands with a male model called Marcos. Roy took his mask and, feeling completely out of place, followed the female model, who led him to one of the bedrooms in which Patricia had prepared a variety of male costumes.

He found a policeman's uniform and put it on, still feeling very strange about the whole situation. He had gone to the party imagining that it was going to be a very posh affair with a silver service dinner, but he had instead found a completely different scenario. On his way back to the main room he continued to be surprised by the exotic guests. Suddenly a completely naked woman, running and laughing, bumped into him. Taken by surprise, she kissed him on the lips and then left, scampering away towards the bedroom where he had just left his clothes.

"Gosh. What a crazy bunch!" he said, speaking his thoughts out loud.

In a bedroom nearby, Nigel was smothering Penelope in kisses and had his hands all over her body.

"Not here, Nigel. Roy might come in and catch us."

Nigel stopped kissing her straight away and with firmness in his voice said, "Roy, Roy. It's all about Roy lately. I still don't get why you're with that redneck."

Penelope put her mask back on and fixed her tight nurse dress, saying, "Come on, tiger, don't be jealous. I'm only having fun, as always. You know that my thing with Roy is an attraction that I can explain. I like him as I like any of my possessions. He looks good next to me." She kissed him and left the bedroom.

'Damn it! I thought this Roy would be another of the usual men that she uses until she gets tired of him and then leaves, but he's staying for longer than I thought. I need to find a plan to get rid of him as soon as possible,' Nigel thought as he left the bedroom and returned to the party.

The party raved on with music and eccentricity everywhere. Patricia was married to a Russian billionaire and her parties were known for their live show performances and wild themes, with vast amounts of heavy alcoholic drinks and drugs being consumed by all the guests. The incarnated couldn't see it, but the place had evil and addicted spirits everywhere, all circulating among the guests, sucking their energy and acting on their souls, and most of the time having fun causing various troubles and arguments between the incarnated.

Right in the centre of the garden stood a gigantic water fountain where many guests were gathering and taking drugs. Some were taking their clothes off and dancing frenetically, following rhythms and songs that were playing only in their own minds. The more drugs they took, the more they became vulnerable to the evil and addicted spirits who were surrounding them to act on their minds. All the drug users had dozens of evil spirits creeping over their souls, sucking their energy like leeches. On many occasions the spirits also took control of their minds and thoughts, influencing their every move.

Roy walked among the guests, searching for Penelope. Every minute he was surprised by more bizarre behaviour at the party. Suddenly a female voice could be heard singing, approaching him from behind. He looked round and saw Penelope with a bottle of champagne in one hand and a marijuana cigarette in the other. Her nurse's costume was covered in champagne and marks of lipstick, and she seemed happier than he had ever seen her.

"Wow, you look…" He looked her from head to toe. "…so happy, darling"

Penelope closed her eyes and continued singing, smiling at him and lifting the bottle of champagne in the air. Roy was feeling more and more uncomfortable and asked her about the reefer but she didn't reply. Then Penelope tripped on a small step and nearly fell flat on the floor. She was saved by Roy grabbing her dress and pulling her close to him, holding her against his chest.

"Slow down, darling. I think you need to take it easy. We haven't even been here for an hour yet and it seems like you're pretty high already." Taking the cigarette from her, he kissed her cheek and held her hand, leading her to a quieter area outside the house.

Roy didn't know, but she had already taken different drugs earlier with some of her friends, and at that moment Filomena and Fortunada were next to her, manipulating her thoughts. The two sisters, both invisible, were telling Penelope to push Roy away. Penelope, who was so vulnerable to their negative vibrations, immediately followed their request.

"Go away Roy. You're so boring! I'm having so much fun!" she mumbled incoherently. She tried to walk away but again nearly fell down.

With a lot of patience Roy tried to hold her up again. "I'm not trying to stop you having fun, darling, I just think that you need some fresh air now. You can barely keep still."

Pushing him again, she shouted, "Go away I said!"

"Yeah, scream at him! He doesn't want you to have fun. Scream!" said Fortunada, laughing.

Capturing Fortunada's thoughts, Penelope did as instructed and screamed loudly at Roy. Hearing her, a friend who was also high on drugs approached and also pushed him away, saying, "Let Penelope have some fun." Pulling Penelope's hand, she took her away inside the house.

Roy followed her but Penelope had vanished amongst the crowd. He searched everywhere but couldn't find her. There were just too many guests. Roy was then distracted by Nigel, who approached him, offering a cocktail.

"Have you seen Penelope anywhere?" he asked frantically, looking worried.

"Don't worry, man. Penelope is fine. This is her tribe." He invited Roy to go outside where they could talk without being interrupted. *'Why don't you just leave her life, you boring bastard!'* he thought while smiling at Roy, pretending to be sympathetic. "Why are you so worried about her anyway? Relax, man."

"I saw her a few minutes ago and she didn't seem to be well. I think she might have taken something very strong and I'm worried about her." He drank the cocktail and continued, "I'm not used to this world, Nigel. This is all new to me, you know?"

'Stupid fool,' thought Nigel, disguising his feelings with a smile. He tapped Roy's shoulder and said, "You'll have to get used to this because this is her life. Penelope likes to work hard and play hard. This is it, my friend, and you'd better get used to it" - *'He's got to be getting insecure by now'*- "Lots of drugs and partying hard; this is her idea of fun."

Roy put his hand to his forehead, feeling dizzy, and sat down on the grass, at the same time dropping his empty glass on the ground.

'Yes!' thought Nigel in celebration. Taking a tiny glass tube out of his pocket, he kissed it, thinking, *'This baby really works!'* He gave a sign to a lady who had been watching them nearby, and she approached.

"You know the plan." He kissed her and said, "Now go there, babe. Go and do what I explained to you earlier."

Nigel lifted Roy up and checked to make sure he was completely unconscious, then carried him to a gazebo in a quiet spot at the end of the back garden, leaving him there with the lady. Earlier, using all his charm, he had persuaded her to help him with a plan. Once alone with Roy, she undressed him completely and kissed him all over, leaving multiple lipstick marks on his body. Roy didn't realise what was happening; he was hallucinating from the substance that Nigel had poured in his drink earlier.

In the meantime, Nigel ran back inside the house to look for Penelope, and found her sprawled on a sofa surrounded by her friends. She was lying over two semi-naked male models, and was so high on drugs that she spoke very loudly, making no sense. Filomena and Fortunada, accompanied by other evil spirits, moved invisibly among Penelope and her friends, enjoying the drugs and the alcohol they were consuming. When Nigel approached her, Penelope stood up from the sofa and, crossing her legs, fell on Nigel. Laughing, she tried to stand up again, at which point he picked her up and kissed her on the lips.

'I want your money, you disgusting bitch,' he thought while saying, "Gorgeous…. You are so gorgeous and sexy. I can't resist you tonight."

"Oh Nigel…not here. Roy could catch us, I told you!"

"No he won't. I just saw him moments earlier getting it on with a blondie."

"What?" she screamed. She broke out laughing and, putting her finger in Nigel's face, she said, "I won't fall for that, Nigel. Roy is completely in love with me. He wouldn't do anything to me. Not boring frigging Roy."

"Well, I can take you where he is and show you that boring frigging Roy isn't as faithful as you think he is. He might be boring but he's definitely not faithful." Extending his hand, he grabbed her and took her to the gazebo.

"Roy! You pig! What you are doing?" she shouted, seeing the blonde lady naked on top of Roy, kissing him.

As per her plans with Nigel, the blonde lady quickly gathered up Roy's clothes and ran away through the back of the gazebo, avoiding any confrontation with Penelope, and leaving Roy to face her completely naked. Penelope, absolutely furious, strode towards him and slapped him several times. She was so high on drugs that she didn't even realise that Roy was unconscious. She carried on slapping and punching him until she was pulled away by Nigel, who dragged her away from the gazebo.

"He's not worth it. He's just a fool who isn't in the same league as you. Leave him!" Kissing her hands, he continued, "Only I love you as you deserve to be loved, nobody else does. I'm the only man for you." He embraced her tightly and began to kiss her.

Penelope tried to stop him, but in the end she let herself go and kissed him too. They were interrupted by a scream coming from near the pool. It sounded like a woman shrieking in horror. Suddenly all the guests were gathering around the pool and the noise grew louder and louder. Nigel and Penelope went over to find out what was happening and saw a naked body floating in the water. Someone had drowned in the pool.

"Oh my…it's Roy!" Penelope shouted.

One of the guests, a young man, jumped into the pool and swam until he reached Roy's body. Putting Roy's arm around his neck, he swam back to the edge. Other guests helped to pull Roy's body out of the pool.

"He's dead!" shouted a hysterical woman.

Penelope ran over to his body and went down on her knees, looking desperate.

"Roy…Roy…Wake up!"

Chapter The secret place

Roy was awakened by the sounds of the waves in the sea, feeling a gentle breeze through his body. He sat up on the bed where he had been lying and realised he was in a strange bedroom which he had never been in before. In front of him was a large window, half opened. He stood up, walked towards the window and opened it completely, letting the fresh breeze enter the room. The window had a stunning view of the sandy beach and the sea.

"Good morning," said Penelope, entering the bedroom holding a tray with fresh breakfast cooked for him.

As soon as the smell of the pancakes entered his nostrils he became nauseous. Penelope, noticing his colour had changed, quickly pointed him in the direction of the bathroom. Moments later Roy returned, looking a little better. Penelope placed the tray on a dressing table and handed him a glass filled with fresh orange juice, saying, "Drink it. It'll make you feel better."

Roy tried to say no, as he didn't want to throw up again, but Penelope insisted, saying he needed to replenish his energy. He sipped a little and then asked her, "What happened last night? All I remember was that I was talking to Nigel and then I don't remember anything else."

Penelope looked at him and replied, laughing, "It was one of Nigel's tricks. He spiked your drink."

"Nigel spiked my drink?"

"Yes, he did." She explained, laughing and finding the whole thing very funny. "I went mad when I saw you lying there with that naked girl all over you, but you didn't even give me enough time to get mad. You ran away like a crazy man and fell right into the pool!"

Roy covered his face with both hands and exclaimed, "Oh God, the shame!" then looked at Penelope, who was still laughing. "And you're laughing? I made a fool out of myself last night in front of all of those people and you laugh? Come on, Penelope, it isn't funny!"

Penelope went to him and kissed him. She then said, "Don't take life too seriously. It was fun, get over it." She took the tray and placed it on the bed in between her and Roy. She cut a small portion of pancake with the fork and fed him as if she were feeding a child. Both laughed like two kids and kissed each other.

"Where are we, by the way?" asked Roy in between the kisses. "Is this your friend's house?"

"No...no..." Penelope took a long breath and gave a look around the bedroom with a big smile on her face, then continued, "This is the place I run to any time I need to feel safe." She stood up and walked towards the window. Her eyes were focused on the sea but her mind had travelled back in time and her childhood memories came up.

Roy was looking at Penelope, admiring her standing by the window. He had never seen Penelope looking so vulnerable before. After a long time in silence she dropped a few tears which rolled down her face, and with a crying tone in her voice she said, "I used to spend my summer holidays here with my mother and my grandparents. In here I had the only happy moments I ever had in my entire life."

Roy stood up and walked towards her. "Don't cry babe," he said, hugging her from behind and putting his head next to hers.

She quickly snapped out of it and cleared the tears off her face. "Shall we go for a walk by the beach before we head back home? I requested a helicopter to come and fetch us. We should be back in New York City early this afternoon."

"Are you sure you don't want to talk more about these feelings?"

She shook her head, her hair moving along with the breeze, and replied, smiling, "No. All of those bad feelings are boxed up and kept inside a drawer hidden deep inside my mind. Now, let's go for a nice walk on the beach and then we can go home."

Chapter Sad tragedy

Embracing Rebecca, Linda said, in a very soft tone, "Rebecca my dear, please calm down. It's important for you to review that life experience back in the Kingdom of Navarre."

Rebecca had tears rolling down her face and her arms were crossed and held against her chest as if she could still feel the pain of that past life. "I don't want to see it… I remember what I did and I don't want to go through all that pain again," she said with difficulty.

It was Teresa who managed to convince her to continue watching the scenes of her past experience. "You are much more mature now and you know now that what you did was a desperate act driven by your low self-esteem. The acts you committed back then and in the other incarnation experiences were huge mistakes, and all because of your lack of faith in God and in yourself. It's all past now…it's gone. But the important reason for you to watch the happenings of that life experience is that you'll be able to see what also happened to everyone around you. You will learn how your actions, and the actions of those around you back then, generated consequences that you are all still dealing with today." She looked deep into Rebecca's eyes, showing how important her cooperation was, and finished by saying, "Even more horrible things happened in the Kingdom of Navarre. Once you have remembered the whole history you will then be able to understand the new mission on which you are about to embark shortly."

Geraldine wiped the tears from Rebecca's face. Rebecca then broke her silence to say she agreed to watch the continuation. The twist of lights with different colours formed in front of them again and the picture started to gain shape and form. Soon it had taken over the entire place.

Suddenly they were immersed in the picture and back at Marta and Enrique's house in the Kingdom of Navarre.

Inside her bedroom, sitting on the bed, Maria was holding the knife against her wrist. She was shaking nervously, with tears rolling down her face. *'Alejandro doesn't love me because I'm terribly ugly. No-one will ever love me,'* she thought. At the same time she slashed her right wrist violently. The cut quickly began to ooze blood. With equal violence and intensity she slashed her left wrist, dropping the knife afterwards. The blood ran down her forearms, dripping on to her thighs, then reaching the floor. The bedroom was surrounded by evil spirits and as more blood flowed from her body, more of them arrived. "I hate you, God for making me ugly like this…I hate you, God!" she cried while watching the pool of blood forming on the floor. She could hear her mother outside knocking on the door, and all she wished was that she could die before anyone came in. Her vision went blurry and she grew more dizzy and weaker every moment. After a few minutes the evil spirits suddenly became visible to her, appearing in different forms, meaning that her soul was about to leave her physical body. Her soul emerged completely from her body, although still linked by fluidic laces, and in horror she watched the hundreds of evil spirits approach her. They looked ghastly and horrendous. Together they made an unbearable screechy noise which grew louder and louder. Maria flew into a panic when she found herself totally surrounded by them with nowhere to escape. She tried to scream for help but no sound came out. She looked to her side and saw her physical body immobile on the bed. The pool of blood increased by the minute. She tried to return to her physical body by rubbing herself against it but without success. The evil spirits were laughing and still screeching loudly. Their sound seemed to pierce her and became unbearable. The scene was horrifying. It was many hours later that the fluidic laces finally broke, announcing the death of her physical body, and her spirit was arrested by the evil ones and taken away to the dark regions.

Later that evening, when Enrique finally arrived home, he found Marta looking desperate, waiting for him. She bombarded him with swearing and aggressive comments as usual, before finally explaining that she was very concerned about Maria. She told him what had happened earlier after the mass, and that she was now locked in her room, not answering her.

"You haven't been spending enough time at home to see what's happening. This isn't a simple melancholy thing. There's something wrong with our daughter and you being away from home every day isn't helping the situation. Today she caused me a lot of embarrassment in front of all of our friends and the people from the high society."

Marta dramatically stormed back upstairs, and with both hands she knocked again on Maria's bedroom door, but again she was ignored. "My daughter…please open the door!" Receiving no reply, she stormed back downstairs and, looking at her husband, she screamed, "Enrique! I tried to speak to her so many times but she isn't opening the door. She hasn't eaten or drunk anything for days. You've got to do something!"

When he heard her say those words he realised something was badly wrong with Maria. Marta wasn't the most caring of mothers, so for her to be so concerned meant there must be something very serious happening. He ran upstairs to Maria's room and knocked on the door, calling her name several times with no reply.

"Maria, we are worried about you. Open the door now, otherwise I'll have to break in!"

Enrique waited for a while and, noticing it was very quiet inside, he decided to break the door down. He walked backwards as far as he could, then ran quickly towards the door, ramming it with his shoulder. He repeated this until he managed to break through. Both Enrique and Maria shouted in horror at the same time when they saw Maria's body bleeding on her bed. They ran towards her, and Enrique examined her body. He saw the knife and concluded, "She slashed her wrists. Our daughter is…" He couldn't finish his sentence. The thought that his daughter had had committed suicide was too hurtful for him.

Marta cried "What happened? Tell me, Enrique. We need to take her to the doctor, quick, let's go!" Marta was in panic. She looked up in desperation and prayed to God to save her daughter's life.

"She is dead, Marta. Our little daughter is dead." Enrique broke down in tears.

Marta screamed and climbed on to the bed next to her daughter's body. Placing her hand under Maria's head, she lifted it up and pleaded, "Wake up, my little girl, wake up! Mama is here…Please wake up my daughter, mama is here…Everything will be fine. I will help you to get him back." She shook Maria's head and shouted at her, asking her to open her eyes.

Enrique watched Marta with immense sadness. He put his hand over Marta's, as they held and shook Maria's head, and gently gave her a sign that she had to stop.

Together they both rested Maria's head gently back on the bed and stroked her hair.

Marta was looking at her daughter's face, her tears running and falling down over Maria's hair. "Why did you do this, my angel? Why didn't you tell me how you were feeling?"

Marta carried on stroking her, sobbing over her head. After a while her cry turned into anger and fury. She screamed and swore revenge. Holding Maria's body in her arms, she promised to chase Alejandro and make his life hell. "I will have his blood on my hands, daughter, and I promise you he will pay for all the pain he has caused you."

Days later, after the funeral, Marta began to search for Alejandro, hungry for revenge. She sent the men who worked for her father all over the region looking for him, but with no success. Enrique, very worried about Alejandro's safety, had already warned Carmen and her fiancé to hide inside the house where she and her mother Sophia lived in Justa's land. He told Alejandro not to leave the house until the situation with Marta had calmed down. Marta was furious and obsessed about finding the young man to avenge her daughter's death at all costs. She spent every day imagining and planning how she was going to torture and kill Alejandro.

"It's not safe for Alejandro out there, Carmen. I'm telling you, Marta is very determined to kill him. I'm also concerned that she'll direct her anger towards you when she finds out that you two are together and have plans to get married."

"I am sorry for your loss, Señor Enrique. I can perhaps explain to Señora Cortez that I haven't done anything wrong with your daughter. I do feel terrible for what has happened, but the truth is that we only met a few times and once I realised we were not compatible I did everything proper and followed the protocol. I spoke to you and your wife and I also told Maria I didn't mean any harm, but unfortunately I didn't love her."

"Father, as Alejandro is saying, he didn't mean any harm. He didn't know Maria was going to end up doing what she did. It's very sad, but it's unfair to blame him."

Enrique's eyes welled up with tears. Even though he could see that Alejandro was not to blame for his daughter's suicide, he was missing her deeply, and deep down he also felt guilt about her death. Enrique sat down on the chair in the kitchen of Sophia and Carmen's house and let the tears out. Sobbing, he said, "My little daughter is now gone…forever…" He covered his face with the palms of his hands. "Why didn't I help her? Why didn't I do something to stop her thinking that way? At least I could have had more of a presence in her life, stood up to Marta and taken control of Maria's upbringing."

Alejandro quickly went to the sink and took hold of a bottle of blessed water. Every morning Sophia filled this bottle from the well and prayed, asking for God to bless the water. This was her daily ritual; every morning she would fill up the bottle with water and put it on the kitchen table. With both her arms lifted up in the air and her palms directed to the bottle, she would then say thanks to the Lord for all His blessings and ask him to turn the water into a healer to bring peace, tranquillity and good health for all those who drank it. Alejandro poured some of the blessed water into a cup.

Carmen knelt down next to him and embraced him tightly. Alejandro passed the cup of water to Carmen, who softly took her father's right hand and made him hold the cup. She then told him to drink the water.

"My father, you can't blame yourself for what she did. From what you have told me, your wife never gave you any space to approach and participate in Maria's life. Your wife has always been very controlling and kept your daughter away from you. I feel that it wasn't her fault that she stayed distant from you, but perhaps a consequence of such a domineering mother."

Enrique cried for a while longer. Once he had finished drinking the water, his soul was revitalised and he felt slightly calmer. Enrique composed himself and stood up, facing Alejandro. "Well…the fact is that Marta won't rest until she gets her hands on you, Alejandro. I guess it's okay for you to hide for a few more days here, but we should make a plan for you to escape from here and leave the kingdom very soon."

"You could go to my auntie's house in France. Marta will never find you there and you'll be safe. I'll go with you," said Carmen, looking determined.

"No, it's too risky. I'd prefer to go first and you can follow me after a few days."

"I agree with him, Carmen. You're best staying here with your mother until Alejandro has arrived there safe and sound."

"What about my parents, my relatives? I need to talk to them and explain where I'm going."

"Don't worry. I'll talk to them personally and explain it was the best idea we could think of to keep you safe," said Enrique.

Sophia arrived at the house and the three discussed with her the plans for Alejandro's escape. They decided that the best thing was for Alejandro to leave as soon as possible.

In the meantime, the sisters Filomena and Fortunada rushed in to pay Marta a visit and tell her what they had learnt. They were both holding long rosaries made of gold, and shouted Marta's name from the front door with urgency in their voices.

Dressed all in black, with a very bitter face, Marta said to them, "I'm not in the mood for talking. I can't think of anything else right now. All I can think of is that I have to kill that rat. What brought you here? Do you know where he is? Have you got any clue where he might be hiding?"

The two sisters looked petrified, and it was Fortunada who took the first step and said, "We came here for a different reason, Marta…"

Marta interrupted her. "I'm not interested. The world could be ending and I wouldn't be interested right now. I need to avenge my daughter and that's all I care about."

"It's your husband, Enrique…" Still shaking, scared of Marta, Fortunada carried on. "We saw your husband with another woman. We saw him kissing her."

Wary of a scandal at the front of her castle, Marta quickly asked them to come inside. Once they reached the dining area she asked, "Tell me now. What do you know?"

Noticing Marta's interest, Fortunada plucked up courage and said, "We followed him for the past few days to check if he was going to meet her again, and he did."

"He has been going behind your back all this time, and the worst thing is that you know the woman," said Filomena, disguising the feeling of joy she had at delivering the news. "She is that same servant we saw at Justa's property. Remember that servant who was in the back yard, crying?"

"Yes, yes…go on…tell me more," snapped Marta abruptly, feeling a terrible headache.

"Well, she has a small house with her daughter and the worst is…" She paused dramatically, holding her rosary up in the air as if feeling sorry for her friend. "The worst is that their house is located in our friend's land."

"What?" Marta screamed. "Friend? Which friend? Who would dare betray me like this?"

Both sisters smiled and said at the same time, "Justa."

"Justa has been helping that gypsy and your husband to go behind your back," added Filomena.

"I can't believe it!" she screamed loudly. "Enrique is a coward! He would never defy me…no…no, Enrique!" Marta punched the wooden table so hard that the noise seemed to fill the room. "Tell me everything you found out."

Fortunada took the lead and told how they had found it strange that Enrique was going around to Justa's property so often. This made them decide to follow him to find out the reason. It didn't take long until they saw him embracing the woman they had seen back at Justa's that day. The sisters investigated deeply, finding out Sophia and Carmen's names, then added a lot of extra lies, exaggerating everything to make the story more hurtful and to play even more with Marta's anger.

Marta was furious, swearing loudly. "I have so much going on in my life and now that man…that man decides to cause me trouble!" Looking at the ceiling, she screamed, "I crap on God! Enrique, that son of a pig!"

The two sisters looked at each other, and when Marta turned away for a few seconds they discreetly laughed at her desperation. Fortunada continued, "And they are in love with each other, Marta. They are all over each other, and even worse..." she said with increasing emphasis, "even worse is that Justa has been covering for her, the traitor."

"I can't believe it. Justa knows?" Answering her own question, she spat, "Of course she knows. They are meeting on her bloody piece of land, aren't they? How dare she!?"

"So what are you going to do now, our friend? You must do something. You can't let your husband go behind your back and make a joke out of you like this. Imagine what the people are going to say."

Enrique had returned home moments earlier, and quietly, not wanting to be seen, he stayed behind the door, listening to their conversation. He then took courage and entered the room and braved Marta. At the moment he came in, Marta went for his throat, shouting, "You! You pig, you are going to pay for what you've done!"

For the first time in his life Enrique confronted his wife. Getting hold of her hands, he shook them off his neck, and in a loud voice he ordered the two sisters to get out of the house. Filomena and Fortunada didn't hesitate, and left the castle feeling quite excited to know that they had caused what seemed to be turning into a fight between the couple. Once they had gone, Enrique sat Marta down on a chair and told her to be quiet. Marta, who had never seen Enrique so angry, went silent, perplexed by his reaction.

"Those liars! Those two snakes you insist on calling friends...They are exaggerating everything. Don't you realise that their presence is toxic? They only want to wish bad on you and our family. I don't know why you insist on hanging out with those two. I know you like the fact that they always seem so helpful and obedient to you, but they are not friends. This is not what friendship is all about." He took a long breath and continued. "Anyway, I haven't been having an affair with anyone. Sophia and I, we dated a long time ago. That was a long time before I met you. She was my first love but I left her in order to marry you, and I have never seen her since that night at Justa and Ager's celebration event. That night I met her again after all those years, and I then learnt for the first time that I have a daughter...A daughter who she raised on her own all this time without telling me."

Marta was avoiding looking at him. Her anger had now built up to a point where she could not speak. Enrique told her more about Sophia and Carmen and how he wanted to care for them and ensure they had a decent life, but Marta didn't hear any of it. All she could think of was that Enrique had made a fool of her, and she wouldn't let that continue.

"I won't let you, Enrique. I won't let you shame me and damage my name. I won't let that happen. They are dead, believe me they are dead. I will send my father's fellows to get them and they will soon be gone."

"It isn't necessary, Marta. They have relatives in France, so they can leave the kingdom and go and live with their family. Nobody will know about this story. I'll get them out of town." He changed his tone, and looked more as if he was begging for her to understand him. "Just give me a few days until I can sort out their trip. Please don't do anything to them. I will make sure they get out of here." Trying to get Marta to speak, he continued begging for her to wait a few days for them to leave Navarre.

'I'll take them by surprise,' she thought. *'It will be better that way. Right now, I need to save my energy to find the man who killed my daughter.'*

"Talk to me, Marta. Why have you gone quiet? What are you thinking? I can see your evil eyes planning something."

Marta got up from the chair and walked away, saying, "I give your peasant family one week to leave Navarre. One day longer and the two of them will be dead. I can't think of this right now, as I need to honour my Maria first and kill the man who killed her."

Next day, Marta woke up to hear the voices of the sisters coming from downstairs. They were begging the servants to wake her up, and they were making as much noise as they could in order to attract Marta. Within minutes Marta appeared at the top of the stairs.

"Marta, my dear, we found him. We found him!" said Fortunada.

Marta rushed down the stairs, asking, "Alejandro? You found Alejandro, that bastard?"

"Yesterday when we left we went straight to the house of the two women…You know, the gypsy ones."

Marta looked at them apprehensively, trying to understand what Alejandro had to do with the two women. "Come on, spill it out!"

"When we got there we stayed a few yards away, watching the house, and suddenly, once the sun had gone down, we saw a lot of movement around the small house. Then later in the night Alejandro left and escaped, riding away on a horse."

"What?"

"Yes, that's right. He was hiding inside the house of the gypsies all this time. He kissed the peasant's daughter on the lips and said goodbye. She cried and they stayed embraced and kissing for quite a while, making promises that soon she would go to France and be with him forever."

"Are you trying to say that that bastard has left my daughter to have a relationship with that peasant? My beautiful daughter Maria was left in exchange for a gypsy pig?"

Filomena held her rosary against her chest, trying to show Marta she was horrified and feeling sorry. She replied, "Yes…I'm afraid he did. They were dating all this time," hiding her real thoughts. *'Ha! You and your stupid daughter deserved that, you pretentious cow,'* she thought.

"Alejandro ran away in the middle of the night…I crap on God!" Marta was fuming. Her arms were up in the air as she gesticulated and swore loudly. "He's gone? He's gone and they helped him."

"What a terrible coincidence, isn't it?" Fortunada said, hiding her sarcasm. "Your husband's lover's daughter is actually the one who stole your daughter's fiancé's heart…"

Marta immediately jumped in, pointing her finger in Fortunada's face, and with fury in her eyes she told her to watch her mouth.

Deep inside, Fortunada was boiling, but held back her desire to slap Marta for pointing her finger and speaking to her like that. With much serenity, she spoke slowly, enjoying word by word what she had to say next. "And the worst thing is…your husband, Enrique, he was there. He got there just before Alejandro left and he helped him to escape. From what we saw, your husband planned his escape."

Marta screamed, punching the air with dramatic gestures. "I should have finished that gypsy lot last night…and I should have finished with that coward last night too! How could I be so stupid?" Marta was pulling her hair out. She then began to punch the pictures on the wall. Looking completely out of control, she said, "I'll get them…I'll get them right now!"

"You are right. You have to do something about this. He hasn't only betrayed you but betrayed your daughter too," Filomena said while smiling behind Marta's back. "You go and kill them before the whole town believes you are a complete fool."

"That would be terrible for your reputation, Marta," added Fortunada, enjoying watching her reaction.

"I will…I will kill them in honour of my daughter."

****

Marta arrived at Justa's and hammered at the door, making a cacophony of noise. When Justa opened the door, Marta rushed in, pushing Justa aside and insulting her. She walked towards the door that led to the back of the house, looking everywhere for Enrique and Sophia. Justa tried to stop her but she was again shoved away, this time with such strength that she fell backwards on to the floor. Marta stormed out of the house and strode quickly through the field towards the property where Sophia and Carmen lived. When she finally arrived at the small house, she found Enrique and Sophia packing clothes and some of the house belongings into sacks.

"Are you two planning to go somewhere?" asked Marta, pulling a knife from inside her dress and pointing it at them. "You thought you would make a fool of me for much longer?" Then, looking at Sophia, "Perhaps you thought you could run away with my husband, taking along your peasant daughter and the man who killed my daughter…but it seems you were wrong. You cannot fool a Cortez."

Enrique put his arms around Sophia to protect her, and begged Marta to put the knife down. Suddenly Marta was distracted by a noise. Carmen, who had gone out hours earlier, was approaching, riding her horse. Marta heard the hoofbeats and, realising that Carmen was coming, hid behind the front door. Although Enrique and Sophia shouted for Carmen to go away, she entered the house and was immediately caught by Marta who, completely out of her mind, put the knife around her neck and pulled it against her throat.

"Stop Marta, please!" begged Enrique. "Your problem is with me, isn't it? So let her go."

"Leave my daughter alone! I beg you…Don't harm my daughter!" cried Sophia.

"I will kill you all one by one, starting with this one here. You lot thought you could trick me, didn't you? Hiding that Alejandro in this house!" Shouting even more loudly, she went on."He killed my daughter!" She pressed the knife harder against Carmen's throat. "And as far as I can see he killed her because of this one. I lost my daughter because of your daughter, and now you will learn how it feels to lose someone you love as I did!"

At that moment Justa's husband, Ager, appeared behind Marta without her noticing. He managed to grab her from behind, pulling down her arm and making her drop the knife on the floor. Ager held Marta tightly, and Carmen managed to wriggle free from her arms and run to her parents.

"It's too late, Ager!" screamed Marta, trying to escape from his arms. "You can hold me but I've sent my friends to go and meet my father. They will tell my father and the inquisitors who are in town that these two have been practising witchcraft in our village. They are being accused now of being non-converted Jews and adoring Lucifer." She was kicking Ager's legs and shaking her body frantically, trying to escape from him. "They won't let two Jewish witches escape from the stake. The inquisitors should be here at any minute!" Laughing, out of control, she screamed, "You two will burn in hell, you peasants!"

"Come on, Sophia you two must go. Go, Carmen, go! You must mount your horses and get out of here now."

"What about you, Enrique?" asked Sophia.

"I'll stay behind with Ager and stop the inquisitors. If it's true that she is accusing you two of being Jewish non-converted and practising witchcraft, you'll be in big trouble. You two had better jump on your horses and get out of here now. Go, go!" Enrique kissed them both and they left.

"Run, you peasants! Run as fast you can and enjoy every breath of air you can, because soon, I will be watching you two burn at the stake!"

Sophia and Carmen mounted their horses and left, riding very fast through the fields while Marta screamed, shaking herself against Ager to escape from his arms. Moments later, ten men arrived, mounted on horses. They announced that they were inquisitors sent to investigate the accusation that two Jewish witches lived there.

"What's happening here? Señora Cortez, why are these two men holding you?" asked their leader.

Marta escaped from Ager's arm and said, crying, "These two men let the witches escape. They are holding me here so the Jewish witches could escape."

"Where did they go to, Señora Cortez?" asked the leader.

"They are riding horses." Pointing in the direction Carmen and Sophia had taken, she said, "They went towards France through the forest. Ride fast and you should catch them not too far from here."

The leader told three of his men to stay and arrest Ager and Enrique for obstruction of justice and for helping two suspects escape. The leader and the other six men then rode off to capture Sophia and Carmen.

****

The sun had gone down and mother and daughter were still riding fast. They were a few miles away from the bridge that connected Navarre to France. It was a cold November night and it was very dark. Once they reached the interior of the forest, Carmen, who was leading the way, shouted to her horse.

"Go Asas, go!" she said, stroking the horse at the same time as urging him to go faster. Her hair was flying with the wind and her face was full of braveness and determination. She checked the other lady, who was not far behind, to ensure she was keeping up, and continued riding fast through the forest.

Suddenly noises of horses approaching could be heard. Far behind, torches could be seen amongst the trees. The young lady continued to stroke her horse and prayed in silence, hoping for a successful escape. She pulled the necklace of her gown and, getting hold of the pendant with the image of the Virgin Mary, she took it up to her lips and kissed it. *'Oh Virgin Mary, I don't care what happens to my life but please look after my mother. She doesn't deserve anything bad to happen to her. I beg for your protection,'* she prayed in silence. Suddenly her prayer was interrupted by the loud noise of men approaching on their horses.

"I can hear them getting close to us!" shouted the older lady. "They are going to catch us!" She made her horse stop and stayed still.

"What are you doing? They are coming! We need to go faster, otherwise they'll catch us!" said the young lady, stopping her own horse so that it faced her mother's. She made a sign with her head and said, "Come on Mama, let's run."

"No. I am not going anywhere. I can still save you. You go. Run, my daughter, run!"

"What are you saying? I'm not going anywhere without you, Mama. Come on, let's go."

"If I stay they will catch me and that will give you time to escape."

Suddenly the noise of horses and men approaching became louder. They were swearing loudly at the two women, saying things such as "You'll regret running away, you witches."

"We don't stand a chance, daughter. Their horses are much faster and they will end up catching us. I will stay and surrender. Go and get out of here. Go to France and find my sisters. There you will be safe," said the older lady with tears in her eyes. "Go, you are young and still have a chance to escape this curse. Don't worry about me."

But before Carmen could say anything they found themselves surrounded by the men, who were holding lances and torches. They all had long golden chains with crucifixes around their necks.

"We've got you," said one of the men. Pointing his spear at them he ordered, "Get down off your horses now!"

Six other men approached the two ladies and dragged them down from their horses. Two of them took hold of the ladies and tied their hands with extreme force. They dragged them both away from their horses and laughed with bitter sarcasm. One of the men took his crucifix and kissed it before slapping the young lady in the face.

"We are not Jewish, neither are we witches. Please let us go," begged the young lady's mother, "Please!"

"There's no salvation for you two. You are both going to the stake!" replied the man.

"Now you two, watch what we are going to do with your horses," said the leader, who was still mounted on his own steed, pointing his spear at the ladies' horses with evil in his eyes.

Both the animals got agitated, as if they were feeling the evil energy directed at them. Four men moved closer to the horses and, holding their long swords, they waited for more instructions.

"Please don't do anything to our horses. Let them go," begged the young lady. "I beg you, leave the horses in peace."

The leader of the band replied, holding his crucifix, "They carry the same evil as you do. They are bewitched and we must kill them as we are going to kill you." He laughed loudly, lifted his spear up in the air and ordered, "Fellows, in the name of the father, the son and the holy ghost, I command you to kill the bewitched animals which have been serving Lucifer!"

The young lady tried to reach for the horses but she was immediately pushed away by one of the men, and fell on the grass. She was followed by her mother who had been pushed by the same man.

The four men lifted their long swords and, with extreme violence, they struck the legs of the mother's horse, who gave out a deafening shriek of pain and fell flat on the ground in agony. Both daughter and mother were horrified. The men smiled, watching the horse writhing in torment on the ground, and made a joke out of the young lady's horse, who had become agitated with panic.

"Don't worry, big boy, you'll soon be joining your friend in hell," said one of the men holding the swords.

The four men lifted their swords again, this time to hit the young lady's horse, Asas. She screamed while watching the men strike the animal's legs. Asas fell on top of the other horse and both of them cried, making horrifyingly loud noises which could be heard from miles away. The agonised creatures were squirming and hitting each other's heads while their blood formed a pool on the ground.

"Asas!" she shouted in horror. "My boy...Oh my boy!" she screamed, looking at the inquisitors with tears rolling down her face. "You are not human, you are monsters. You are not serving God but your corrupted church."

The men were positioning themselves to hit the animals in order to finally kill them but were stopped by their leader.

"No! Don't use your swords." He looked at both women and gave them a cynical smile. Using a very cold tone of voice he told the men, "We will burn them alive!"

The men went around collecting trunks and tree branches and surrounded the horses with piles of wood in order to create a bonfire. The ladies were crying loudly and the animals screeching in agony. Within minutes the men had put trunks and wood around the horses and set them on fire. The leader said, with pleasure in his voice, "Watch your animals burning and feel their pain and their agony. It's a very slow death and it's exactly the same death you two will soon face."

****

Sophia and Carmen were taken to the city of Logrono, on the northern region of the Kingdom of Navarre, where they joined Enrique, Justa and Ager. They were all kept in a dirty and cold cell where they were left without food and water. After many days of physical and psychological torture they were finally sent for trial. Enrique, Justa and Ager were charged with obstruction of justice, while Sophia and Carmen were accused of being non-converted Jews and also practising witchcraft. Marta's father, who was the wealthiest man in Pamplona and was also very senior within the civil authorities group, had made sure their trial wasn't fair and that none of them had the opportunity of defence. They had been so badly tortured in the days leading up to the trial that they could hardly stand up. They barely had the strength to speak, so weak were they. Enrique, Ager, Justa, Carmen and Sophia were forced to confess to being guilty of a crime they had never committed. Once the trial was finished, the civil authorities arranged a massive auto-da-fé and invited all the people of the Kingdom of Navarre to watch the sentencing.

When the day arrived, hundreds of people turned up to watch the auto-da-fé in the public square of Logrono. The people were very boisterous, all feeling excited in anticipation of watching what the church called in those times the 'combat to the heresy'; the punishment for those Jews who were living in the kingdom pretending to be followers of the Catholic Church. Before the ceremony started, there was a mass which started with a procession of the five prisoners: Justa and her husband Ager came in first, held by guards. They were followed by Enrique, then Sophia and Carmen. The crowd prayed while watching the exposition of the five prisoners lined up side by side in front of the inquisitors, who were the ecclesiastical and civil authorities of the Kingdom of Navarre, including Marta's father. Marta was in a private balcony nearby, watching everything with extreme pleasure which she couldn't hide and which could be seen in her eyes. Finally she was getting her revenge, both for her daughter's murder - which was how she regarded Maria's suicide - and at the same time for Enrique's betrayal.

The mass finished and was followed by a fanfare of trumpets that announced the beginning of the sentencing ceremony. The crowd cheered for several minutes, celebrating the forthcoming punishment of those who had committed heresies, then gradually went quiet to listen to the sentences being announced.

Marta's father stepped forward and called Justa and her husband Ager first. "Ager and Justa Avila, we declare you two guilty of betrayal of the sacred Catholic Church. As a punishment for your crime of helping to cover up for the Jews who were secretly living amongst our people, we sentence you two both to spend the rest of your lives in prison."

The crowd cheered again, and some even threw objects at Justa and Ager while they were taken away by the guards. Everyone then suddenly went quiet, as Marta's father told Enrique to step up to hear his sentence.

"With the power given to me by the Catholic Church and by the Pope, I declare you, Enrique Perez, guilty of bigamy and also guilty of betrayal of the sacred Catholic Church. I sentence you to life imprisonment."

Enrique wasn't paying proper attention; his mind and heart were worried about Sophia and Carmen's upcoming sentences, which he knew were going to be very severe.

The mob again cheered and celebrated his sentence. While the guards were taking him away, Enrique was looking back, trying to see Sophia and Carmen. When her father was about to read out their sentence, Marta called to him and said, "I want Enrique to watch their sentence. Keep him here, father."

Her father told the guards who were taking Enrique away to do as Marta had asked. He then read out loud, with more emphasis than the previous two sentences, "Sophia and Carmen Navarrete, you are accused of witchcraft, heresy and living amongst our people as false Christians. With the power given to me by the Catholic Church and by the Pope, I declare you both guilty and …" He lifted up in the air a crucifix made of gold and said, "I sentence you both to death." Then, with great emphasis, playing to the crowd, he finished by saying, "You will die burned alive at the stake."

"No…No… we are Christians, we believe in the sacred church!" screamed Sophia in panic. "Please, no…no!"

Carmen, pointing to Marta, shouted, "It was her, that woman over there, Marta Cortez! She accused my mother and me only for revenge. She fabricated all of these accusations about us. We are not Jewish, neither are we witches!" She knelt down on the ground. "We were baptised. Please don't do this to us…"

"Shut up!" Marta's father shouted, interrupting her. "You are in front of God and the ecclesiasts. Your heresy has been discovered and we will burn you two at the stake along with all the evil you carry inside you."

Enrique, tears running down his face, tried to run towards them but he was pushed back by the guards who were holding him. The crowd was in ecstasy, cheering and celebrating the sentences. Marta moved closer to her father and this time requested that he order the guards to place Enrique in front of the stakes, so he could watch the two burning to death. She then went down to where Sophia and Carmen were and said, "You should never have crossed my path!"

Carmen spat in her face and shouted, "You are the devil! You will burn in hell!"

 Marta cleaned her face and laughed out loud at Carmen. "Big mistake, you peasant. I will go to heaven, and you…you will burn alive!"

The ecclesiasts left the square, leaving Marta's father and all the other civil authorities there to proceed with the slaughter. The guards holding Sophia and Carmen took them to the stakes and tied them up. Mother and daughter were positioned on stakes in front of the crowd facing the stage. Marta looked into Sophia's eyes and laughed, feeling finally avenged. The branches of wood positioned underneath the women were set alight and the fire became intense very quickly. Enrique watched in horror the flames burning the loves of his life, Sophia and his daughter Carmen. Both were screaming in pain while the fire consumed their bodies.

Chapter Analysing the past

The vision went blurry, then suddenly faded away completely. Rebecca and Linda were holding each other tightly and both had many tears of sadness rolling down their faces. The four went quiet for a long period after the vision of that past life in the Kingdom of Navarre had come to an end; each one of them had her own remembrance and thoughts to analyse.

After the lengthy silence, Linda dried her tears and asked Rebecca, "How do you feel after remembering our past experience?"

Rebecca took a long breath and, still feeling a lot of sorrow, replied, "I feel very sad. Even though I committed suicide and wasn't physically present, now I remember that once my corporeal body died, I continued there on Earth, torturing my mother by instilling thoughts of revenge and anger in her all that time." Rebecca began to cry nervously and continued, "I remember now so clearly. When I disincarnated I learnt that Alejandro had got engaged to Carmen, and I blamed her for our break up. I went mad and became obsessed with the idea of vengeance. I didn't let my mother rest until I managed to get her to find Carmen and avenge me."

Teresa interrupted her and said, "We know, my dear. We were there, remember? Geraldine and I were there, trying to make you realise you had to stop those feelings."

Geraldine stood up, wiped Rebecca's tears from her face and gave her a tender hug followed by a kiss on her forehead. She then said, "We know what you are feeling now; you feel ashamed. But please don't feel that way. Remember, that past life experience happened hundreds of years ago. We have been given the opportunity to remember those moments now for a very important and elevating reason rather than to make you feel ashamed and upset."

Teresa continued, "Geraldine is right. God only allowed us to see those scenes again for a learning experience that will help us and others to evolve and progress. Let's analyse that experience together and learn from it, shall we?"

Rebecca, feeling more relieved, nodded. She had a great many questions about what she had just remembered. She started by asking what happened to every single person involved after their death, to which Teresa reminded her that there is no death, but a passage.

Teresa went on, "Enrique passed away after he had spent many years in prison. Once his spirit was free from his physical body he began to torment Marta, sending her negative vibrations until her passage. Marta, suffering the consequences of her acts, was afflicted by leprosy which affected her nerves, her organs and - worst of all for her - her skin. For Marta, who was extremely vain and materialistic, that disease was devastating. People in the streets began to laugh at her, and sometimes she had people throwing stones and other objects at her. By the time she passed away she was lonely and very depressed."

Geraldine took over the narrative. "Once back in the spiritual world she joined Filomena and Fortunada, the sisters in the dark region, and together they began a search for Carmen, Sophia and Enrique. In the meantime they tortured many disincarnated and incarnated spirits, causing bad things to many people and vulnerable spirits."

"Did they find them?" asked Rebecca, curious.

"No," replied Teresa, "Sophia and Carmen, after passing away in such a horrible way, having their bodies burned alive, were collected by me, Geraldine and many other spiritual friends. They were brought to a recovery hospital here in the colony. Enrique spent many, many years tormenting Marta while she was still incarnated, but one day, after many attempts, we finally managed to convince him to go to a colony where he could study and leave behind all of his feelings of anger and revenge."

"Marta never saw them simply because she never had access to them," clarified Geraldine.

"I see…" said Rebecca, "It's because they were all in different evolutionary and energy degrees? Sophia and Carmen were more enlightened, so Marta and the sisters couldn't get to them?"

"More or less like that. As you know, the purer you are, the closer to God you become, therefore Marta, being so full of anger and hate and so many other evil and retrograde feelings, got stuck in the dark regions for many centuries, refusing to evolve."

"Sophia, Carmen and I tried so many times to reach out to her, but she has been blinded by the evilness she carries. She could never see the light and reach out for help," said Linda.

"What about the stake and all the terrible things that happened to everyone? Why did God let you all go through so much pain and suffering?"

"God doesn't punish but instead he teaches, therefore we only go through difficulties that can teach us and help us to progress. Carmen and the rest of us in that life experience went through what we did because, at some point in our existence, we have also inflicted the same pain on other beings. We always receive back the good and also the bad that we do to others, and in that incarnation experience it was our time to learn those things," Linda replied.

"My astral memory is fully recovered now. I remember I suffered a lot in the dark regions, always being obsessed about my looks and thinking that life was a never-ending misery. After a long time suffering there, I was taken temporarily to a colony by a spirit from a rescue group. I was then sent to reincarnate, and that's when I was born in London, England. Again in that life experience I didn't see the beauty and the good things of life and continued attracting misery and depression. In this recent life I took the decision to commit suicide, once again not valuing the gift of life." Rebecca looked at the other three with a smile and said, feeling thankful, "And I remember that all of you have always been there for me. I remember clearly now the many times you three, plus Sophia who now lives as Dolores, and Carmen who is now living as Katie, have looked after me and tried to show me how wonderful life is." She touched each one of their hands and thanked them for all the love and care they had always given her.

They all smiled and gave Rebecca an embrace loaded with tenderness and love. Teresa looked at her, saying, "You are now ready for your next experience, my dear."

Rebecca lifted her head up high and said, "I am. I feel ready to put into practice all I have learnt so far."

"You know it won't be easy, though? After so many years rejecting the blessings of life, self-destroying your physical bodies, this time you will reincarnate in a very fragile body, and this will be the most challenging part of your next reincarnation. Your spirit will be very limited as it will be involved in a body and mind full of illness. Hopefully, despite these limitations in your physical body, and especially your brain, you will be able to overcome all the difficulties and remain positive and thankful for the blessing of life," said Geraldine.

"I'm determined to make it through. I know that having my spirit involved in a physical body with such limitations will be a way for my spirit to put in practice everything I've learnt so far about faith and appreciation for the gift given to us by God: the gift of life."

Linda held Rebecca's hand and, feeling emotional, said, "Do you know that you are going to reincarnate as Roy's and Penelope's daughter, which means you will once again have Marta and Enrique as your parents?"

Rebecca nodded, and Linda continued, "Your arrival will be a gift from God to brighten up their lives. We all hope that your incarnation brings peace and happiness to their family and also helps Penelope and Roy to realise all the mistakes they have been making."

"Your reincarnation will be difficult, very tough at times, but it will also be very rewarding, because it will help to fortify not only your own spirit but the spirits of those who love you too," said Teresa.

Chapter Sophia

Months later, back on Earth, Katie had become very close to Dolores and her son Ricky. Dolores had taken Katie under her wing, giving her love and care and ensuring she could be above all a friend to her, a friend whom she could count on however difficult times were. Katie was so happy with Dolores and her son Ricky that she began to smile again and have fun, as any other happy child would. Ricky had become her best friend and they spent a lot of time together, studying and playing games. He was a very creative and energetic kid, always messing around and making fun to try and make Katie laugh and forget about her sad moments. It didn't take long before Katie was speaking fluent Spanish, which helped to create an even more special bond between her, Dolores and Ricky. Although she missed her father, who was still almost totally absent from her upbringing, and especially missed her grandparents, she found in Dolores and Ricky a lot of love and care.

Dolores was a beautiful young woman. She was originally from Colombia in South America and had moved to the US a few years before her son had been born. Some months after arriving in the US, she met a man from Puerto Rico with whom she fell in love, but who left her after finding out she was expecting a baby. Alone and pregnant in New York City, she had a tough time struggling to find a job. One day, when her money had nearly run out completely, she bumped into a smartly-dressed man in the street who was in a hurry and ended up accidentally pushing her to the ground. The man, very worried about what he had done, helped her up and took her to a safe place inside a nearby restaurant which he owned. Once he had introduced himself to her, she learnt that he was one of the richest men in New York City. His name was Bobby Green, and he was Penelope's father. After a long talk, Bobby, feeling sorry about her desperate situation, offered her a job as housekeeper at his daughter's house. Dolores didn't hesitate to accept, and ever since then she had always been very thankful to Mr Green for his help. She had always found her work difficult because of Penelope's unpleasant temperament, although Mr Green paid her a good salary and had agreed to pay for Ricky's education until he had finished university. He kept his word, leaving a fund to Dolores in his will to help Ricky's studies. The insults and rude behaviour from Penelope increased when her father passed away, but just as Dolores was about to leave her job, Roy arrived with Katie. Dolores made such a strong connection with Katie that she decided to stay so she could be close to her and help her through the bad times.

Every morning the first thing Dolores did was to pray, thanking God for another day of life. She also asked God to bless Ricky, Katie and all those who were in need of help. She used to fill a bottle with water and ask God to bless it, asking that those who drank the water should enjoy peace, tranquillity and good health. After praying she would switch on the radio and listen to salsa music, which always helped to bring joy into her life. Soon the entire kitchen would be filled with exuberance and happiness. She would then wake up the kids, get them ready for school and serve them breakfast, during which they would always sing along to the happy salsa songs on the radio. Dolores, a very religious woman, had become a follower of the Spiritism doctrine after the passing away of her mother, and she studied the *Gospel according to the Spiritism* every night before going to bed. She taught Ricky and Katie to pray first thing every morning, thanking God for all the blessings that He had given, and also for all those still to come. She spent extra time with Katie, teaching her that the upsetting moments in life which seemed to be so difficult and unfair were all temporary passages of life, and one day everything would be fine. She taught Katie many valuable lessons: always to keep the faith and believe that better times would come; to continue to nurture love within herself; and to love everyone around her. Many times Dolores was inspired by Linda, who used her as a medium to send Katie messages of encouragement, to reassure her that she wasn't alone and that the difficult times were going to end one day, bringing happiness and joy in the future.

****

A few months before Rebecca's reincarnation, she began to visit Penelope, Roy and Katie more often, in order to study more closely the dynamic of the family she was about to join. This would allow her to understand what her mission was going to be like.

On one of Rebecca's visits to Dolores and Ricky, she was accompanied by an enlightened spirit named Peter, who was in charge of guiding her. He said, "The young man who, in that life experience, lived as Alejandro is now incarnated as Ricky."

"Wow! Do you mean that the man I was once obsessed by, Alejandro, now lives as little Ricky?"

"Yes, correct." They both watched Ricky sitting at the kitchen table next to Katie and Dolores. Peter continued explaining. "Dolores, as you know, was Sophia, Carmen's mother. When we all learnt that Marta was going to reincarnate, she agreed to return to Earth incarnated as Dolores and to be around Marta in order to try and contribute to her bid to evolve."

Looking amused, Rebecca said, "Destiny has put Sophia, Carmen, Enrique, Alejandro and Marta all together again!"

"Yes, my dear. No-one in life crosses our path without God having a master divine plan. All encounters happen for a reason. And now it's time for all of you to reunite again."

They were both watching Dolores reading out loud in Spanish the *Gospel according to the Spiritism* to Katie and Ricky. She was reading 'Blessed are the afflicted' (Matthew, 5:5, 6 & 10). Ricky was like any normal young kid with lots of energy and was easily distracted. On the other hand, Katie always paid close attention and asked several questions, because learning about the Spiritism was a way for her to understand that her mother hadn't died and vanished forever, but actually had only returned to the spiritual world. One day they would reunite.

When Dolores had finished the explanation, she set the kids free to go and play. Peter moved close to Dolores, who was still sitting by the kitchen table. He prayed, transmitting positive and beneficial vibrations to her.

"Please continue sharing with Katie your love and care. Katie has now built the strength to carry on with her life. Soon, Roy and Penelope will also benefit from your love and your kindness," said Peter to Dolores.

Peter then invited Rebecca to come with him to the study room, where Roy was reading a book. Peter pointed at Roy and began to explain to Rebecca, "Enrique came to have this experience as Roy for many reasons; first, to stop putting the material above the spiritual. In this life experience he once again wants a life of luxury, so until now he has kept his eyes closed to the important things in life, such as caring for his daughter, who needs his love so desperately. Because of his ambition for wealth and luxury he betrayed his wife, Linda, by his affair with Penelope."

"He keeps on making the same mistakes as in the past..." said Rebecca to herself, as if thinking out loud.

"Exactly!" exclaimed Peter, "Which happens quite often. This is one of the reasons why we all have our spiritual memory wiped out when we reincarnate to have a new life experience. It's simply because this is like an exam which we set ourselves in order to see if we have actually learnt the lessons we thought we had learnt from our past mistakes."

"I get it!" smiled Rebecca. "So far Enrique, now living as Roy, hasn't overcome his past errors. He's once again succumbed to the idea of wealth and a luxurious life, forgetting to care about the things that really matter."

They continued observing Roy for a while longer. They could both read his thoughts. At that moment Roy was thinking of Linda and comparing the life he had had with her to the one he was having now with Penelope. Linda had always been loving and caring, and even though they lived a simple life with no luxury, he'd had only happy and joyful moments with her. With Penelope it was the opposite; she was no longer the intriguing and sensual woman he had once known. She was aggressive at times, sarcastic and bitter, never showing respect to others. Penelope's mood swings were beginning to make domestic life hell, and Roy was beginning to ask himself if he had done the right thing when he decided to leave North Carolina for a life with her. Tears rolled down his face when he thought of Linda's gentle smile, and again the remorse for his betrayal came to torment his soul.

"Come on Roy, don't let depressive thoughts play in your mind. You have a gracious and kind daughter who needs your love and care, and you should focus on making yourself and her happy. Money, fancy cars and this big apartment don't really matter if you are not happy. No material things matter if you don't have love within yourself. Unconditional love has to be the main focus of our existence," said Peter to Roy.

Immediately after Peter had finished speaking, Roy's mind captured Peter's thoughts, and he changed. He started to think of Katie, and suddenly his mood lifted. He stood up from the chair and walked towards the stairs, looking for Katie. At the top of the stairs he could hear her and Ricky's voices coming from the kitchen below. He went down and to his surprise he found Katie and Ricky conversing in Spanish. He watched her, amused, thinking, *'Where have I been so that I didn't realise my daughter is speaking fluent Spanish?'*

"Daddy!" exclaimed Katie, surprised to see her dad. She ran to him and gave him a hug.

"Katie…Were you speaking Spanish just now?"

Katie went quiet and timid. She felt a bit embarrassed and nodded her head, to which Roy said with a big smile, "Wow, that's amazing, sweetheart! How did you learn…I mean who…taught you?" He was confused, and the words didn't seem to come out of his mouth easily.

"I've been learning with Dolores and Ricky. I asked them to teach me. They began to only speak to me in Spanish, so I now talk to them in Spanish too. I never found it difficult to learn, dad. It's awesome actually, because at school sometimes when I don't want the others to know what I'm saying I speak in Spanish," she giggled excitedly.

Roy smiled and hugged his daughter once again. For the first time he realised how much of his daughter's growing up he was missing. Holding her, he felt a very warm and strong energy of love he hadn't felt for quite a while. Peter and Rebecca smiled at the scene and left the apartment, returning to Rebecca's spiritual colony, Domus Deus.

"I'm still a bit concerned about how Penelope is going to accept me. Of all of them, she is the only one who seems not to have learnt much yet."

"You should now focus on your individual mission. Your main objective is to love yourself and to love the blessing of life, despite all the obstacles and difficulties that your new incarnation will bring. You must always keep your faith in God and don't let the difficult times depress you. One day Penelope will learn one of Jesus' most beautiful and important lessons to humanity: Love one another. Until then, it is down to all of us to continue helping to show her the way back to God."

Chapter Butterfly – a chance for a new start

Months later… The day for Rebecca's reclusion had arrived. It was another beautiful day at the spiritual colony Domus Deus. Linda, Teresa and Geraldine, plus some of Rebecca's new spiritual friends, were present outside the temple to wish her all the best in her new incarnation and give words of encouragement and motivation.

Linda was feeling emotional about Rebecca's departure. Looking at her, she remembered some of the moments they had spent together. She embraced Rebecca happily and said, "I'm so happy for you, my dear friend. I'll always be sending you love and vibrations of encouragement for you to succeed in your new mission. Promise me you'll be strong and that you will always look for the beautiful things in life. Promise you won't succumb when facing any difficult situation, and you won't let negative thoughts enter your mind?" asked Linda.

"I promise," Rebecca replied. She was shedding tears, and even though she wanted to tell Linda how grateful she was for all the time she had spent mentoring her and teaching her about the beauty of life, her emotions took over, and she only managed to say thanks before breaking down and crying.

Linda tightened her hug and stroked Rebecca's hair. She then said, "Always remember, you have the power to decide what goes on inside your mind. Good or bad, happy or sad thoughts - it's up to you to decide. Choose the positive. Choose happiness, my dear."

Geraldine came closer and joked, "By the time you finish saying your goodbyes it will be time for you to return back here." Smiling, she said, "You will be fine, sweetheart, go there and show the world what a beautiful being you are!"

Rebecca stopped crying and laughed along with everyone else. Before entering the reincarnation temple she approached Teresa and held her hands, saying, "You always have so many wise words and you're always so motivational…I'm scared of what's going to happen to me once I enter the temple."

Teresa replied, "You shouldn't be." She lifted her hands in the air and turned around with her palms facing up. She closed her eyes and brought to mind the image of a small egg. Immediately it appeared, seemingly resting in between her hands. Soon the egg broke open, giving life to a caterpillar. It was hairy and green and moved around with some difficulty. Then it grew quickly until it became completely encased by a tough cocoon.

Everyone around, particularly Rebecca, was paying close attention to Teresa, who continued with the projection. The cocoon changed from a green colour to a darker shade until it broke and a gracious orange butterfly emerged from it and flew beautifully around Rebecca. It then fluttered away, flying all around the colony. Rebecca was amused by what she had just seen, while her spiritual friends were smiling at Teresa.

"Now my dear, imagine the process you are about to go through as being the same as that of a caterpillar. Even knowing that it's about to experience unknown changes, the caterpillar faces these moments of transformation with faith and bravery because it knows that at the end of this challenging period a new life opportunity filled with renovation and opportunities waits for it."

Rebecca thanked Teresa and wanted to give her a hug, but hesitated, feeling shy. Teresa pulled her close and embraced her warmly. Everyone else said their goodbyes and Rebecca entered the reincarnation temple at last.

Once inside, Rebecca was taken to the chamber of reincarnation, where other spirits who were about to go back for another reincarnation experience waited as part of the process. The chamber had individual rooms for each spirit, and in each one there was a bed, similar to one in a hospital, where the spirit rested while waiting for the process of reincarnation to be completed. The invisible fluidic laces that connected the corporeal body and the spirit were slowly formed throughout the mother's gestation, and then were finally linked to the baby at the moment of birth. The cry of the baby upon his birth announced the end of this long process, and the spirit was then once again reincarnated on Earth for another experience.

PART II

Chapter A very special baby

Seven months later Rebecca reincarnated on Earth; more precisely, in New York City as Penelope and Roy's baby daughter.

The baby had been born prematurely as a result of Penelope's having to be rushed to the hospital after fainting suddenly. When she arrived at the hospital she was still unconscious. At the time of the baby's birth Penelope suffered an anaphylactic shock; her blood pressure dropped to a very low level and she went immediately into a coma. The doctors made frantic efforts to save her life, but her condition was critical. In the spiritual world, the evil spirits celebrated with excitement Penelope's dangerous state, wishing that her corporeal body would die.

In the meantime, back at the maternity waiting room, Roy was impatiently walking around in circles waiting for some news. Penelope had been gone for hours and nobody had come back to tell him what was happening. Katie, who had gone to accompany her father, had fallen asleep on the sofa. After hours with no news, a doctor arrived and approached Roy.

"Are you Mrs Green's husband?"

"Yes I am…How is she? How's the baby?"

"I'm sorry to have taken so long to come and give you some news. We performed a caesarean as the baby was at risk. It has been a very difficult labour. Your wife had some complications when delivering the baby and we've been working all this time to try and bring her back."

"Oh my God! Bring her back? What's happening, doctor? How is she?"

"She came out of a coma just over an hour ago and she is still heavily sedated." Noticing that Katie had woken up and was listening to the conversation, the doctor called a nurse to look after her, and took Roy to a nearby office.

"I have some more news concerning your wife and your baby." The doctor asked Roy to sit down and continued. "Your wife had severe bleeding, and an anaphylactic shock led to the rupture of an aneurism. Everything seems to be under control and okay now, but at the moment we cannot predict what injuries the aneurism has caused, and whether she is going to suffer from any after-effects. I'm afraid we'll have to wait until we know the results of the medical tests."

"What about our baby?"

"I really should wait for your paediatrician to speak to you, but I think it will be better if you're told this before your wife knows."

Roy had cold sweat dripping down his forehead. It sounded as if there was more bad news to come.

"All the features in your baby are consistent with trisomy 21. We also carried out some tests and…" He grasped Roy's right shoulder before saying, "I'm afraid your baby has Down's syndrome, Mr Green."

"What?" asked Roy, looking shocked and surprised. "Penelope did all the medical tests necessary during the pregnancy…how come..? Are you…"

"I'm afraid it's definite. We have carried out tests and it's confirmed; your baby has Down's syndrome." The doctor smiled at him, trying to give him encouragement to think positively. He finished by saying, "By the way, she is a beautiful baby girl, Mr Green."

"Taylor, my name is Roy Taylor. Penelope and I are married but she kept her surname…I don't even know why I'm saying this. It's totally irrelevant, isn't it?"

He felt as if he had been punched in the stomach, feeling totally confused and without knowing how to react to the news.

"Sorry, Mr Taylor. I know it's very difficult news. It's a shock at the beginning when you first find out, but I guarantee that once you meet your baby and see her angelic face you'll understand she is just as perfect as any other child." The doctor walked towards the door and suggested Roy should go and see the baby. "I would now like to concentrate on your wife's recovery. By the way, I've already contacted your paediatrician, Doctor Kapoor, and she will come and see you shortly. She'll explain more about trisomy 21 and the special care your daughter will require."

The doctor excused himself and left the room as he had to go back to check on Penelope. The metal clicking noise as the door closed sounded very loud in Roy's head, and at that moment he felt as if he was the loneliest and most lost man on the entire planet.

Later that evening, after a long meeting with Doctor Kapoor who explained all the details about a baby with Down's syndrome, Roy went to the nursery to see his new baby daughter for the first time. She was very tiny and was asleep, which made her seem even more vulnerable. The doctor's words from earlier on came back into his mind: *"I guarantee that once you meet your baby and see her angelic face you'll understand she is just as perfect as any other child."* And the doctor was right. Once Roy looked at her face for the first time his heart accelerated and he was consumed by an immense energy called unconditional love. He had a rush of adrenaline running through his body. Finally, Roy let out all the emotions that had been building up inside him and burst out crying. They were not tears of sorrow, but a mix of a scary feeling of not being able to offer his new baby girl all the love and care she needed, and a lot of joy and love for that small and gracious newly-born creature.

Next to him, in the spiritual world, Linda smiled, feeling content as she noticed how the reincarnation of Rebecca had already touched Roy's heart and brought pure and divine feelings to him. Linda moved close to him and, with both her hands near his head, she prayed and sent him vibrations of love and comfort. Roy captured her vibrations and felt immediately all the love Linda was sending to him.

He then put his hands on the top of the incubator containing the little baby and, sobbing, he said to her, "Welcome to the world, my little girl. Welcome! You are beautiful and I promise I will love you and look after you…always."

Minutes later, the nurse who was looking after Katie entered the room, holding Katie's hand. She took her up to the incubator and introduced her to her new baby sister. Roy held Katie's hand and together they both admired the new baby.

Looking amused and smiling at her sister, Katie said, "She is so beautiful, dad, isn't she?"

Roy kissed Katie on her forehead and said, "Yes, she is, darling. She is simply gorgeous."

Chapter Penelope's lesson

Penelope stayed in hospital for many weeks, recovering. The left side of her face was paralysed. Even though she had been seen by some of the most skilled professionals in the world, who were specialists in her condition, they couldn't find any treatment that could help her to regain the movements of the facial muscles on her left side. From her left eye down to below the neck, her muscles had lost all their firmness and had become saggy. Her left eyelid had dropped permanently over the eye and she also had a lot of difficulty moving her lips, which affected her speech too. The stroke had also impaired the sight in her left eye, leaving her partially sighted.

Penelope became bitter and angry. At the hospital she was forever showing aggressive behaviour towards the nurses and the hospital staff, and the way she treated Roy was even worse. Roy, very patiently, had tried many times to speak to her and to make her change her ways, but there was no conversation. Her attitude worsened from the day she found out her baby had Down's syndrome, and she refused to see or even have any contact with her baby. She didn't make any secret about her feelings that the baby's birth was responsible for what had happened to her. Penelope ordered Roy to keep the baby away from her at all times and made it clear she didn't want anything to do with the 'little beast', as she called her. "She is an abomination! She is a little beast that came into this world to ruin my life. Look what that thing did to me!" she screamed at Roy.

Respecting her wishes, Roy arranged for the baby's bedroom to be on the same floor as Katie's bedroom, near the staff area in the penthouse's ground floor, so Penelope didn't have to see her when she returned home.

****

On the day that Penelope returned home she went straight to her bedroom, continuing to avoid everyone else, even her baby. Patiently, Roy looked after her and complied with every single one of her wishes, trying to please her and help her to emerge from the depression he believed she was suffering from. Roy thought she was experiencing bad post-natal depression and felt sympathy for her. But he believed she would soon snap out of it and regain her passion for life.

Penelope was feeling ugly and disgusted with her own appearance. She kept a small mirror next to her bed and checked it every now and then to see if her face had gone back to the way it used to look before she had suffered the aneurism. Every time, after the mirror had shown there were no changes to her appearance, she would fly into a fury, throwing objects against the wall and screaming obscenities. For someone so materialistic and superficial, losing her beauty was like losing everything she had in life.

On the other hand, Roy became a very dedicated father to Katie and his new baby, whom he named Victoria. Initially, until he found a reliable babysitter, he decreased his working hours to be able to spend more time at home looking after Katie and Victoria. He was extremely patient with Penelope, hoping she was just going through a bad phase and that she would soon get used to her new condition and stop behaving as she was. He cared for Victoria and did his best to ensure she had the best upbringing possible and always felt loved. He and Dolores shared the care of Victoria until the day he finally managed to find a suitable babysitter.

Katie was also extremely dedicated and loving towards her new baby sister. Although she didn't understand much about her syndrome, she knew that she was a special baby. According to Katie, this meant that Victoria, in her words, "was special because she needed to receive lots of love." Every day when Katie returned from school she would run to Victoria's room to be with her, and once she had finished her homework she would help the babysitter, Lauren, to look after her.

One afternoon Katie, looking at Victoria asleep in Roy's arms, said, "She is so beautiful, dad." Smiling at Victoria, she added, "Such tiny little hands and fingers…"

"Do you love her?" asked Roy.

"A lot," replied Katie, kissing Victoria's forehead.

"She is veeeeeery beautiful, Mr Taylor," said Ricky trying to reach for Victoria, who slept peacefully in Roy's arms.

"Thanks Ricky. She is a beautiful little baby, Ricky, I know." Roy put her back in her cot and put a finger to his lips, warning the kids to be quiet so the baby didn't wake up.

Invisible to them, Linda, Teresa and Geraldine were in the room, watching the scene and feeling extremely happy.

"Look at Roy; he's becoming such a loving and caring father. It seems like he has finally learnt that wealth, money and all of those things aren't important," said Linda.

Geraldine replied, "Yes he is. He unconditionally loves her." Moving closer to Roy, she put her hands on his and sent him positive vibrations.

The three spirits left Earth, leaving behind many inspirational and positive vibrations which took over the entire bedroom, boosting the souls of Roy, Katie, Ricky and Victoria with harmony and encouragement to continue on their individual missions and journeys.

Chapter Dangerous mind

The curtains were drawn in Penelope's bedroom, obstructing the sunlight and keeping the room permanently dark. Many evil spirits from the dark regions surrounded Penelope, feeding her spirit with even more thoughts of misery and unhappiness. Unaware of these spirits and their harmful vibrations, she became more bitter and negative, which in turn made it easier for them to pollute her mind. Days went by, and she became so tormented that she even thought of suffocating the baby during her sleep, in order to set herself free from having to live under the same roof as her. The two spirits, Fortunada and Filomena, were always around Penelope. They gleefully enjoyed seeing her succumb to deeper and deeper insanity, and ordered the other spirits to intensify their depressive and evil thoughts.

Linda and the other spirits of light prayed and tried to transmit to Penelope as many vibrations of tranquillity and love as they could, but they were finding it more and more difficult to reach her; the quality of her thoughts had plunged so low that she was almost beyond help.

One day, when Roy was at work and the babysitter was out, Penelope went to Victoria's bedroom and finally saw the baby for the first time. She dragged herself so slowly and painfully across the bedroom that it was as if she was going to meet something from another planet. Slowly she crept closer to the cot where the baby was sleeping, and when she saw Victoria for the first time a mixture of feelings took her over. The baby was sleeping peacefully in her cot and she looked graciously cute in her pink layette. She had her arms up in the air and looked extremely fragile. Penelope moved closer to her and stared at her, watching her tiny baby features. For the first time since she had had given birth, Penelope opened a timid smile and, with a tear coming to her eye, she admired Victoria sleeping. *'My baby...she is my little baby...'* she thought, watching Victoria moving her hands as she slept.

The evil spirits surrounding her were laughing at the baby, and sarcastically began to turn Penelope against her. "Look at this little creature. She is as ugly as you, Penelope. Don't forget what she has done to you! She made you lose your beauty…your youth. You are now horrible and it's all her fault!" the evil spirits told her.

Engaged with those evil spirits' vibrations and attuned to their thoughts, Penelope stopped smiling and immediately changed her feelings. She let the anger and frustration take over her mind once again. "I hate you. Look what you've done to me. You destroyed my beauty and my life. I will always hate you!" She extended her arm towards Victoria's face and placed her hand over the baby's mouth and nose.

Victoria immediately woke up and Penelope stared at her, coldly looking straight into her eyes as she tried to suffocate her. Victoria's face blushed and soon her entire head went red. Suddenly the bedroom's door handle made a noise and the door opened. It was Dolores, who had walked in to check on the baby. Penelope quickly removed her hand from the baby's face. Victoria recovered her breath and started to cry loudly.

"Oh my God, Mrs Green, you scared me. I didn't expect to find you here." Without knowing what to say, Dolores began to mumble some words. Seeing the baby, Dolores rushed to the cot. "Oh my dear…what's happening with you? You look so red!" Dolores picked Victoria up and, holding her very carefully, she kissed her, asking her to calm down.

"She's fine… I guess it's just a tantrum. Anyway, I heard the baby crying and came in to check on her," said Penelope, walking back towards the bedroom door. Before she left she asked abruptly, "Where's that incompetent babysitter? Shouldn't she be here at this time of the day to stop this baby crying? Tell her I don't want to hear this baby crying any more!" She left the bedroom before Dolores could say anything.

Feeling the low energy in the air and the presence of spirits with negative energy, Dolores began to pray in silence, asking for protection for the baby. Smothering Victoria with kisses, she told her in Spanish how much she was loved by everyone and how beautiful she was. As soon as Dolores began to pray, all the evil spirits left the bedroom and returned to Penelope's room.

Soon after Penelope had left, Katie and Ricky ran into the room, excited and giggling, bringing with them a lot of joy and happiness. Linda, who was there, watching the scene, smiled. "Thanks, Lord, for this blessing. The love bond between these souls has definitely been created and it is getting stronger and stronger." She thanked God in her prayer as she was very happy to see that the plan was already working. Katie was going to assist Rebecca - now living as Victoria - and teach her a sense of self-respect and self-esteem, and most importantly, teach her to love and appreciate her life.

Influenced by Linda's presence in the room, happy memories of time with her mother came into Katie's mind, and she said to Victoria, "It's a shame my mother hasn't met you…and it's a shame you won't meet my mother, Vicky. She was a beautiful woman, very kind and she would have been the best mom for you. I miss her, you know, but Dolores taught me that she is alive in heaven and one day I'll see her again. So for now I need to be a nice, kind girl, then God will reunite us one day. Maybe one day you'll meet her as well." Katie kissed Victoria's tiny hand and finished by saying, "I will always look after you, my sister, always!"

Tears rolled down Linda's face when she heard Katie's words. Scared of transmitting any kind of sad vibration that could perhaps be absorbed by Katie, she left the bedroom and went straight back to Lunas.

****

Linda arrived by the lake and, looking up, she asked God for courage to continue to be strong in her mission. Immediately Teresa and Geraldine arrived nearby and walked towards her.

"Don't be sad. You have been so strong," said Geraldine, to which Teresa added, "Victoria has now brought happiness and hope to Katie's life. Let's hold on to our faith and continue to transmit them vibrations of love."

"I don't know why, but it's getting a bit difficult to hold the feelings when I'm there now. All the bad things I've seen Penelope doing, and the sad moments I've seen Katie going through... and she's still just a little girl... it's hurting, and I don't seem to be as strong as I was before."

Geraldine looked at both of them. "There is a reason why it is getting harder to keep up the positive thoughts. Penelope is getting more and more tormented, which is attracting even more evil spirits to her side and to those around her." Geraldine looked worried and pensive. "Before, there was only Filomena and Fortunada tormenting Penelope and feeding her with bad thoughts; now there are dozens of evil spirits surrounding her." Geraldine paused for a while and then continued. "Unfortunately, Penelope isn't coming out of the darkness, but instead she is attracting even more darkness to her side. Her mind has now affected her soul and she is very close to becoming dangerously mentally ill."

"Earlier today, before you got there, Linda, she tried to suffocate her daughter, but she was stopped by our spiritual friends who inspired Dolores to go to the baby's bedroom."

"So Penelope is so mentally disturbed that she can get to the point of killing someone at any time?" asked Linda, visibly worried.

"I'm afraid so, yes. We are all trying to work on the spirits who are tormenting her soul, trying to persuade them to give in and go to a recovery colony where they can get treatment and get out of the darkness, but so far we haven't achieved any success."

"What can we do now?" asked Linda.

"Well…we don't know right now what God's plan is. What we can do is continue to pray and send them vibrations of peace, harmony and love. A lot of our spiritual friends are there, trying to work on Penelope and on the spirits who are tormenting her, so all we can do for now is to pray those spirits leave her and go to a recovery hospital."

Chapter The evil plan

Somewhere in the dark regions, Fortunada and Filomena were among a group of other evil spirits. They had all just been in Penelope's apartment to send her more bad and depressive vibrations, and were disappointed with the failure of their plans. There were six in total, including the sisters. Three of the others had the appearance of shadows and one looked very tall, with a half human and half skeleton appearance. He named himself Dynamite. He engaged in a great deal of anger and violence, spending all his time tormenting other incarnated spirits.

He had had a life experience on Earth back in the fifteenth century in Spain, at the same time that Penelope was living as Marta. Dynamite, then named Juan Martinez, had fallen under Marta's spell and become her lover. Together they had many sexual encounters behind Enrique's back. Every time Marta wanted to get rid of someone she didn't like, she conspired with Juan to kill them. Juan, who was deeply in love with her, carried out several murders and cruel punishments of many people, all at Marta's request. Becoming even more passionate and obsessive, he started to pressure Marta to leave Enrique and be with him. However, Marta had no feelings for him. She only used him to satisfy her sexual desire and for his criminal favours. She started to become annoyed with his talk about love and passion, and when Juan threatened to tell the truth to Enrique, she didn't think twice and decided to murder him. She sent some of her father's colleagues, who caught Juan in a trap and killed him, stabbing him in the back.

Once disincarnated and back in the spiritual world, Juan found out about her betrayal. Some time later, united with the sisters and other spirits who also wished revenge on Marta, he began to follow her everywhere, trying to make her existence a miserable hell.

Looking at Filomena, Dynamite said with anger in his voice, "We've got to intensify the attack. We've got to see blood and lots of it. Let's take advantage of Penelope losing her mind and torment her even more."

"If only we didn't have that bloody Dolores in the apartment. She stops us achieving our results. Every time we have a plan she's the one who stops us. She prays every morning and the apartment gets surrounded by the enlightened ones who spoil all of our plans," said Filomena.

Fortunada, who was sitting on a barrel next to Filomena, remained quiet while her sister continued to fix the few hairs on her head. "She's got to go! We've got to get rid of her," Filomena said to Dynamite.

"Hey you, incompetent! Did you do the research I asked you to do?" asked Dynamite to one of the shadowy spirits.

"Yes sir, I did," he answered. "The substance is called Arsenic. It's fatal to humans and I know where we can get hold of some. That incarnated one, Nigel, Penelope's PA, he knows a drug dealer who can get it." The evil spirit, named Petro, noticing the air of satisfaction in Dynamite's eyes, continued. "I was thinking of the following plan. We can inspire thoughts of obsession and jealousy in Penelope's mind and drive her to become very jealous of Dolores. Then we can make Penelope think that Dolores and Roy are having an affair and…" He paused.

"Go on, creature. I quite like what I'm hearing so far," said Dynamite. "Go on!"

"So…we can drive Marta, I mean Penelope, to feel extremely jealous of Dolores. She will feel so jealous that she reaches the point of feeling like she has to kill her." With a sarcastic smile, he finished by saying, "We transmit to her the idea of poisoning Dolores. A few drops of the Arsenic and BOOM! No more of the 'chica Latina' in our way."

Dynamite laughed for a long time and finally said, "I love your plan. Actually, you're not a complete incompetent, as I thought. Well done you. But I only have one thing to say: We need to be very careful. I don't want Penelope to get arrested…not yet. I have other plans for her. I want her to suffer so much, but in different ways."

"Yes," said Filomena, very excited. "We've got to torment her even more while she is incarnated. Let's continue until we drive her to complete insanity. And then, once she has gone completely mad, we finish with her life."

"We'll need to pick a time when the babysitter isn't around to cause the murder of that Dolores. Enough of her in our way! It's time to show those enlightened ones what we can do," said Dynamite, with a croaky sound in his voice.

"I can't wait to put this plan into action," said Filomena very eagerly. She looked at the corner where Fortunada was staring at the skies, and found it strange that she had been so quiet and not participating in such exciting plans.

Fortunada was very upset and nostalgic, thinking of the spirits who had once been her parents back in Spain. She loved them dearly, though she made herself very distant from them because of her refusal to evolve and to search for purification. Her parents had gone through many other experiences incarnated on Earth, and as a result they had elevated themselves to a high degree of spiritual evolution and were living in a colony among other enlightened spirits with the same degree of purification. Now and then they visited her and Filomena, trying to show them the way towards God, but every time they started to speak about God and love they were immediately stopped by the two sisters. Fortunada that night was missing them more than ever before, and for the first time she began to wonder how life would be if she accepted the invitation to go to a recovery colony and leave all of her anger and bad behaviour behind. She thought, *'How many years am I wasting focusing on Marta and being jealous of her? So many centuries have gone by and...'* Tears were rolling down her face when she was snapped out of her thoughts by Filomena shouting at her.

"Fortunada! What's happening? We are here discussing an amazing plan to destroy Marta and have some fun, and you're just sitting there, quiet, staring at nothing. What's the matter with you, you silly cow?"

"Sorry," replied Fortunada, drying her tears.

Several evil spirits arrived, following Dynamite's request. Dynamite asked everyone to gather around and he then told them the plan to poison Dolores.

Chapter The Gospel according to the Spiritism

Roy entered the kitchen and found Dolores, Katie and Ricky all sitting at the table. Dolores was reading from the *Gospel according to the Spiritism.*

"What are you doing?" asked Roy, looking intrigued.

Dolores looked a little embarrassed and, expecting to be told off by Roy, she explained, "Sorry, Mr Taylor. I usually read some passages of the Gospel to these two, and teach them about the lessons Jesus taught us."

Very angry, Roy threw up his arms and told Dolores, "Stop everything! What's this about you converting my daughter to your Santeria stuff?" Looking at Katie, he said firmly, "Sweetheart, please go and play in your bedroom." Katie hesitated, but Roy looked sternly into her eyes and said, "Go to your bedroom now, please!"

"Come on Ricky, come with me please," asked Katie, feeling scared.

Terrified, Ricky ran away from the kitchen, going straight to Katie's bedroom.

Alone in the kitchen with Dolores, Roy looked at her. She seemed to be very upset and he apologised. "I'm sorry for speaking to you like that. I didn't mean to treat you so badly." Dolores remained silent and Roy continued, "I am not religious, as you know, and I don't want my daughter into any of this …you know…this spiritual stuff."

"I'm sorry Mr Taylor, I should have asked your permission before teaching Katie. I confess I thought you wouldn't approve of me teaching her things you're not familiar with. I ended up by taking the decision to do so. I think it's very important for Katie, after losing her mother, to learn that we don't die but we are actually infinite. But above all I think it's very important that Katie has faith."

"First of all, please don't call me Mr Taylor. You can call me Roy, Dolores. Second of all, yes, I am very angry for you to be teaching my daughter, who is so young, about a religion… which isn't something I believe in. I stopped believing in God when my wife died and since then I don't like to hear anything about religious stuff. Anyway, who knows what sort of crazy ideas you might have been putting into Katie's mind."

"Excuse me?!"

"I didn't mean to say crazy ideas…I meant…"

Dolores' face went red and she said, with firmness in her voice, "Have some respect, Mr Taylor. Katie has been left abandoned in this house by you and by your wife, Mrs Green. No- one seems to care about her. Your wife has…" She stopped there as she thought it was better not to make any accusations about Penelope. She was scared of losing her job and not being able to continue participating in Katie's life.

"My wife what?"

"Nothing. I just meant you and your wife abandoned this little girl and all I have been trying to do is look after her and show her through my faith that it's all going to be fine." Dolores was shouting at this point. Roy tried to speak but she didn't allow him to. She said over him, "This girl is going through a horrible grieving. She lost her mother and you separated her from her grandparents. When she came here to this house she didn't even speak and she cried herself to sleep every night. You were so excited about the luxury world you'd just discovered that you didn't even notice how upset your daughter was feeling. Now you are telling me you know what the best way to educate Katie is?" Dolores didn't believe she had just said what she had, but deep down she was glad she had got everything off her chest. She knew that it was time for Roy to hear the truth. She began to cry, as if her body was also expelling all those feelings and frustrations she had been holding inside for so long.

Roy, moving closer, tried to calm Dolores down. "I know I made a lot of mistakes. Victoria's birth taught me a lot. I actually now understand many things I couldn't see before." He was now so close to Dolores that their bodies were almost touching. In a very low voice he said "Please forgive me for what I said. All I'm trying to do is to look after her."

At this point Roy and Dolores were very close, body next to body, and instinctively Roy hugged her. What they didn't notice was that Penelope, who had heard Dolores shouting, had come down to the kitchen to find out what was happening, and was now right there looking through the semi-open door. She had seen Roy with his arms round her. Furious, she stormed back to her room without either of them having noticed her.

Roy, stroking Dolores' hair, said, "I'm sorry for upsetting you. I can't deny that I haven't always been there for Katie in her upbringing." Feeling very sad, he took some deep breaths and continued, "I can see why you would have taken the liberty to do the gospel classes or whatever you call it."

When both realised they were actually hugging each other they immediately stepped back and looked the other way.

" I left Katie aside all this time and you've been the only one looking after her, so …you did what you thought you should do," he said, regretting his angry reaction from earlier.

Dolores was about to speak, but Roy began to cry and continued, "I'm now regretting lots of things, but most of all I regret having neglected my daughter. The other day when I found out that she speaks fluent Spanish I felt so proud, but at the same time I felt so bad." More and more tears were flowing down his face. Linda arrived at that moment and was also listening to their conversation. "I feel bad for being such a terrible father. I neglected her when what she needed most was love and care."

"We all make mistakes, but we can all learn from them and make things better. There's still time for you to look after our daughter and make her feel supported and loved. And now you have another daughter who needs your love and dedication too, Roy. Learn from the past and change the present now, so you can make a better future, a happier future," said Linda to him.

Roy couldn't hear Linda, though deep down in his soul he felt her words and soon he calmed himself down. He sat down on the chair while Dolores opened the fridge and got hold of a jar containing the water she had asked God to bless that morning. She poured a glass for Roy and handed it to him, saying, "Every morning I fill this jar with fresh water and I pray and ask God to bless the water, so those who drink it can find harmony, tranquillity, good health and love. Please drink some and you'll soon feel better."

Roy put the glass on the table, still looking upset. Dolores went down on her knees and hugged him. She then reached out for the glass and offered it to him again. Roy drank the water and soon was overwhelmed by a strange feeling.

"What happened?" asked Dolores.

"I feel a strange feeling. It's like I've been through this scene before."

"What scene?"

"I'm sitting at the kitchen table receiving this hug and drinking this blessed water. It's like a 'déjà vu'. It feels like I've dreamt about a similar scene before…I can't explain."

Roy was right. Deep down he was recalling his experience in the Kingdom of Navarre when he, as Enrique, was crying, sitting on a chair in the kitchen, and received a glass of blessed water from his daughter Carmen, followed by a tender embrace.

"You're possibly right. Sometimes when we have moments which we call 'déjà vu' we are actually remembering moments we have already had in a past life experience."

"I don't understand. Do you mean what just happened has already happened?"

"Not exactly. I mean that perhaps you could have already gone through a similar experience in the past. We are all spirits who have been living for thousands, millions of years. We are all in a continuous evolution process and we incarnate in different life experiences in order to learn and evolve."

Roy went quiet and Dolores carried on. "It's high time that you stopped making the material stuff a priority, and lived a life focused on love and the search for your spiritual evolution. Focus on positive things, Roy, and especially right now focus on the most important thing you have, which is the love of your two daughters."

"I'm sorry, but I simply cannot believe that my deceased wife is alive, or that all the dead ones are living somewhere, as you believe…it's just all so much nonsense to me. The dead are dead and that's it." Roy stood up and apologised, intending to leave the kitchen.

Dolores took one of the books which was on the table and handed it to him, saying, "I know it's all too different for you, but please give it a chance and read this. This book is called *The Spirits Book*; it's written by Allan Kardec. This book explains a lot about what we are and where we come from. It will explain a lot about the studies Allan Kardec did back in the 1800s, and perhaps show you that you are wrong. Your wife isn't dead but alive, simply because we never die, Roy, we are infinite."

Roy hesitated but ended up taking the book and headed for the door. When he was just about to leave the room, Dolores invited him to join her in one of her weekly visits to the spiritual centre. The next meeting was the following Monday.

"I'll think about it," he replied. "Can I ask you to stop your teaching sessions - or, as you call the spiritual stuff, meetings - with my daughter for now? I don't want to be mean but this is just until I can research more about it and be able to understand all of this...erm...you know..."

Noticing Roy was trying to be polite about the subject, Dolores didn't take offence and replied, "I totally understand. Don't worry, I'll respect your decision, but please consider my invitation to come with me next Monday. Invite Mrs Green too; it would do her a lot of good."

Dolores had such an angelic and gracious manner that he couldn't say no to her. He said in a soft tone before leaving, "Well I'm definitely not sure about Penelope going, but from my side I promise to consider your invitation."

****

After seeing Roy embracing Dolores, Penelope had run back upstairs to her bedroom, slamming and locking the door. She was feeling very angry and tormented about what she had just witnessed. She repeated to herself many times, "This can't be happening. No, no, this isn't possible. She's just a servant. Roy wouldn't betray me."

Filomena was right next to Penelope, tormenting her and laughing in her ears. "You are too ugly now. Roy doesn't love you any more. Nobody does and nobody will!"

Penelope ran to the en suite bathroom and, with her hands shaking, slapped a large dollop of moisturizing cream on to her face. She followed this by applying full make-up. Staring into the mirror very closely, frantically she lifted the left side of her face, desperate to make it look as it used to before the aneurism. She pulled the skin and lifted, while the evil spirits surrounding her were laughing and insulting her. Penelope became more and more frustrated, and was rapidly overcome by immense anger.

"I can't let Roy betray me like that. I can't let that happen. What's going to happen to me? What are people going to say? I lost my looks and now I'm going to get dumped?" She picked up the glass jar of moisturizing cream and threw it across the bathroom. The jar smashed into pieces. Penelope sat down on the floor, surrounded by the fragments of glass and, sobbing, she began to pull her hair out with her hands.

Filomena knelt down next to her and whispered in her ear, "Get rid of Dolores…Get rid of Dolores. You have to kill her. It's the only way to stop Roy from leaving you!"

Chapter Love flourishes

In Lunas, a happy Linda met Teresa and Geraldine. She told them what had happened earlier between Roy and Dolores: their argument and how their love for each other flourished again. Teresa and Geraldine were both silent, staring at her admiringly. Linda asked, smiling, "What is it?"

"We are so happy for you, Linda. You just told us all about Roy and Dolores. It seems as if they are perhaps falling in love with each other again, and you are happy for him. There is not a part of you which is feeling jealous, and that's so admirable and elevated of you, my dear."

"Oh no, I wouldn't even contemplate the thought of getting jealous. I always knew that this was the purpose of our current experience on Earth. I was only an instrument from God to help Sophia, Enrique, Carmen and Marta. I'm very happy to see the two of them finally reunited."

The three held hands and walked around the field, talking about the recent events.

****

Roy became even more focused on looking after Katie and Victoria. He had become a very caring and loving father. He came home early from work every day so that Lauren, the babysitter he had employed, could leave, and he could then spend time with his daughters. Every night, with the help of Dolores, Roy looked after Victoria and helped Katie with her homework. He even found time to play with Katie and Ricky. The joy he felt from spending time with them boosted his soul with an immense energy which strengthened his being even more.

As Roy involved himself more in his daughters' lives, he automatically also became closer to Dolores, who was always involved in caring for Katie and Victoria. He and Dolores helped Victoria to take her first steps, and together witnessed her walking for the first time. They spent much time together, nurturing her with their love and helping to make her feel very supported and cared for. In time, Roy stopped having his dinner alone in the dining room - since Penelope didn't like to leave her bedroom and always ate on her own - and he started to join Dolores, Ricky, Katie and Victoria in the kitchen and eat with them.

At weekends they would all go for a picnic in Central Park, where Roy would play games with the kids. At first, Roy didn't know what was happening inside him; he couldn't stop paying attention to Dolores, admiring her soft and gentle ways with the children. She was always positive and smiling, as if nothing in the world could bother her. Many times he caught her by surprise and found her singing and dancing in the kitchen, looking really happy and excited. Dolores' love and passion for life were contagious, and as he spent more time with her, his positivity and enthusiasm for life grew. More days went by, and Roy realised he was falling in love with her. At night, when trying to read a book, he couldn't concentrate on anything else but Dolores and her beautiful features. *'She is so different from Penelope,'* he thought.

Every night after the kids had gone to bed he settled himself in his armchair in the library and read pages of *The Spirits Book* that Dolores had given him. Next to him, enlightened spirits inspired his thoughts, guiding him to read pages which could relate to questions he was asking himself, and which showed him signs that life didn't end with corporeal death.

Chapter The spiritual home

Weeks went by, and Roy finally decided to go with Dolores and find out more about the spiritual home she had invited him to. His decision was partly because he wanted to know more about the doctrine, but mainly because he was keen to spend more time with Dolores and get to know her better.

When they arrived at the spiritual centre, which was located in Queens, Dolores said, "This spiritual home is named after a spirit called Andre Luiz." She opened the small gate and made a sign for Roy to enter. They walked together through the garden, heading towards the front door, and she continued, "Andre Luiz was a doctor in the early twentieth century. When he passed away, he started a beautiful work as a messenger from the spiritual world, writing novels and books though his medium, a Brazilian man called Chico Xavier. His books are always full of motivational and inspirational words."

"Wait a minute. Did you just say he writes books even though he's…dead?"

"Roy!" Dolores corrected him, smiling. "We don't die, remember? Our corporeal body dies and sets our spirits free. We are infinite." She gave him another smile and, standing by the front door, she quickly continued her explanation before knocking. "Yes, Andre Luiz, since his corporeal body died, communicates with his medium on Earth, the Brazilian Francisco Candido Xavier, popularly known as Chico. Chico Xavier, alongside the spirit of Andre Luiz, writes books and shares with us knowledge about life in the spiritual world."

"So they…I mean, Andre Luiz and the Brazilian guy, Chico..." Roy looked a little confused. "They write books?"

"Yes, many books, just like the one you are reading now, except that it was written by Allan Kardec in the eighteenth century, but Allan Kardec was also a medium and his books were narrated to him by enlightened spirits. Their most recent work is called *Nosso Lar*, which in English means 'Our Home', and it was published not long ago. In this book, Andre Luiz shares with the readers his experience as a spirit from the moment of his corporeal body's death and his spirit leaving the Earth, through to the time when he enters the spiritual world, and what his life is like there. The book also narrates his first years back in the spiritual colony called Nosso Lar - Our home."

"It sounds interesting."

A very jolly lady named Amelie opened the door. She greeted Dolores with a warm hug and welcomed Roy. Roy was surprised by the simplicity of the house. Inside it was a pretty normal family home. The first room they entered was the living room, which seemed to have been converted to hold the spiritual meetings. It had simple furniture with very few ornaments. It looked very clean and felt comfortable. A long wooden table occupied the middle of the room, with seats all round it. A small blue light bulb fixed in the ceiling caught Roy's attention. Dolores introduced Roy to the other attendees, everyone took their seats around the table and Amelie began proceedings. With a soft French accent she welcomed everyone, especially the newcomer. The session started with a prayer. Amelie asked everyone to hold hands, making a chain, and then requested that they all join her in saying out loud the Lord's Prayer:

Our Father in heaven,
hallowed be your name.
Your kingdom come,
your will be done,
on Earth, as it is in heaven.
Give us this day our daily bread,
and forgive us our debts,
as we also have forgiven our debtors.
And lead us not into temptation,
but deliver us from evil.

Amen

Amelie closed her eyes and asked the enlightened spirits there to guide the meeting for protection; to assist all those present, the incarnated and the disincarnated, and everyone who was in need of vibrations of peace and comfort. "Lord Almighty, please allow us to have a peaceful meeting. May this meeting be a fountain of knowledge and love. May we all learn and benefit from this meeting in order to bring to our day-to-day lives love, peace, harmony and comfort. Please, Lord Almighty, allow our friends in the spiritual world to assist this meeting and allow them to guide us."

Several spirits were there, invisible to everyone: Linda, Teresa, Geraldine, Peter (who was Amelie's spiritual mentor) and two other enlightened spirits who were assisting the session. Peter was next to Amelia and Dolores, guiding them in their prayers and passing messages to the incarnated who were there.

These messages were always directed to each individual present at every meeting. They contained encouragement and inspiration. Most of them were to comfort those who were feeling afflicted, with a troubled mind. Linda and the others were around the room, sending vibrations and thoughts of love to each attendee according to each one's needs. Outside the house, in the spiritual world invisible to those on Earth, many enlightened spirits were lined up next to each other in front of the house, guarding the building against evil spirits and also receiving disincarnated spirits for counselling and help. Every time a spiritual meeting took place in the house, the enlightened spirits attended so as to help the spirits who were wandering lost on Earth. Many lost spirits were waiting in a long queue for the services to begin, the first one in line being a beautiful young lady. She approached one of the spirits who was part of the rescue group and said, "Excuse me, sir, my name is Gabrielle, and strange things have been happening to me. My parents and I were in this car crash and I remember that I was badly injured. When I woke up I was in a hospital but my parents weren't there. I had a really severe headache and there were some people around me, all trying to calm me down, but I went mad. I didn't want to stay in that hospital. All I wanted was to get out of that place and see my parents. I left that hospital and I ran and ran, far away, desperate to find my parents but I couldn't." She lowered her voice, as if feeling ashamed about what she was going to say, and said, almost whispering, "I think they died and now I can hear them. I can hear my mother crying and calling my name. She sounds so upset and her cry makes me very sad. I end up crying, feeling so frustrated for not being able to see or find her. I told a woman about my situation and she recommended this place. She said that this is like a spiritual place and I could perhaps talk to my parents, so I was hoping I could communicate with the dead and perhaps she could tell me what happened to them."

Marcos, the spirit she was speaking to, looked at her with kindness, and with a very gentle tone of voice explained, "Gabrielle, my dear. I am afraid to say that you have been wandering on Earth for many years trying to deny yourself the truth. Deep down you know what really happened to you on that day in that car accident. Your parents survived the accident but your corporeal body didn't. You passed away a few minutes after the crash." He looked deep into her eyes and, noticing she was about to cry, he said, "Please don't feel upset. There's nothing wrong with your current condition; you are not dead, Gabrielle. You live as you have always lived since your creation. Accept that you have to leave the Earth and come with me to a spiritual colony. There you will be able to see your grandparents and many other friends you haven't seen for a while. Don't hide from the truth because this will only delay your progression and cause you more suffering."

Gabrielle cried desperately and asked, "Why does my mother cry so much, calling my name? I feel so sorry for her."

"Your mother cries because she is not able to accept what has happened to you, just as you can't accept it either. She cries because she misses you and unfortunately she denies the truth; she refuses to believe that there's a continuation to life after the death of the corporeal body. Come to the colony with me and there you will receive the right support in order to help yourself, and then, once you feel stronger, you will be able to help your mother."

"I'm scared I'll be arrested once I'm there, and lose my freedom…and won't be able to return."

"It will be your home, not a prison. We are all free, and you will be able to come back if you wish, but I guarantee you will find yourself surrounded by so much peace and harmony and an immense fulfilling feeling of love that you won't want to leave until you feel completely renovated and ready."

Marcos looked straight into her eyes with a lot of kindness and offered his hand to her. Gabrielle hesitated for a moment; she felt completely drained, as if she had no energy left to continue living. Still feeling scared, she took his hand and nodded. Marcos closed his eyes and left the Earth, taking Gabrielle away to a spiritual colony where she would meet her grandparents and receive assistance.

The other enlightened spirits continued serving the spirits in the line one by one. When the session was nearing its end, a spirit who had been living in the dark regions approached one of the enlightened spirits named Nathaniel. She looked very disturbed and was covered in wounds. She spluttered, in an agitated voice, "I am not evil...I am not evil, mister, I promise you."

"Please calm yourself down." Nathaniel gently put his hands on her head and asked, "Please tell me what is troubling you, Fortunada?"

She was breathless. Still looking disturbed, with both hands holding her head and shaking it non-stop, she repeatedly said, "I'm scared of them. I'm very scared of them but I decided I can't live this life any more."

"I will help you. Please calm yourself down and be clearer about what is bothering you."

"They are planning to kill Dolores. They are going to kill her for no special reason, but only to be able to continue to play jokes on Marta, because they are jealous of her. Dolores is an innocent woman. It's wrong, it's wrong!" She was shaking desperately. With a great effort, she managed to explain more. "I used to be the same way, you know. I devoted my entire life to making Marta suffer. I enjoyed playing jokes on her and I took pleasure in her misfortunes, but I'm tired. I don't want to live like this any more. I look back and I see that I've achieved nothing. All I've done is to live obsessed with Marta's life." She knelt down and begged, "Please take me away from here. I don't want to be around them any longer. Please take me away."

"I can't take you away now, but I promise to give you assistance and help you make your way out of this situation you have put yourself in."

"You're denying me help? Why can't you take me now?"

"I am not denying you help, Fortunada. I am telling you that I will assist you and work with you to find a way out of this situation. Your actions have created the universe you now live in. You need to modify within yourself the way you think and the way you treat others, and then the doors to a better life will open for you. Continue praying with all of your energy and you will then light your way out of the darkness you created. I will be there with you, and although I will be invisible you'll be able to feel my presence. Together we now have to help Dolores and those who could also be victims of the other evil spirits. Please tell me more about their plans."

"I'm scared," she said, walking backwards as if preparing to run away.

"I know you are, but talk to God, ask him for mercy. Pray and ask for protection for Dolores and the other innocents who are about to become victims of the perverse spirits."

"I have to go," she said.

"Pray, my friend, and soon the light will brighten the way out of the darkness," said Nathaniel, before Fortunada vanished completely.

When the session was about to finish, Nathaniel went inside the house, to the room where the spiritual session was taking place, and told Linda what he had just learnt. Linda then asked for permission from her superiors to communicate the upcoming danger to Roy and Dolores, but permission was denied.

Amelie said, "Before we end our session tonight I would like to invite you all to pray with me and thank all of our friends who are in the spiritual world, assisting us in another session." After prayers, Amelie closed the session and invited all the attendees to stay for an extra few minutes for a cup of tea and a chat. Everyone was served herbal tea with biscuits, and they gathered together, talking about what they had learned that evening. Dolores took Roy's hand and led him to meet Amelie.

"Nice to meet you, Roy. I was expecting you here tonight. I'm glad you came."

"You were expecting me?" replied Roy, looking surprised. "Did Dolores tell you I was coming?"

Amelie smiled and replied, "No. My spiritual mentor told me you were coming." Noticing his expression, Amelie said, "Don't worry. It's all too new for you, and I know it's too much for you to believe."

Amelie pointed at the sofa in a corner and invited them to take a seat as she needed to talk to them. She followed them to the sofa, bringing a stool, and once they were all seated she continued. "I have something to say. Right at the end of the session, my mentor, Peter, asked me to give you a message. He said 'Difficult times are approaching. It doesn't matter how difficult things become, you must keep the faith in our Lord Almighty's divine knowledge. God will never leave you.' "

Dolores went quiet and became apprehensive because she knew that if she had been granted such a direct message from the spiritual world it was because something very important was about to happen. Next to her, Roy was intrigued by the message and tried to ask for more information. However, Amelie explained that not everything can be known to us, as it is part of our mission to face the difficulties of life as they happen. If our spiritual friends were to intervene or warn us it could be harmful.

They changed the subject and spoke about Roy's interest in learning more about the Spiritism doctrine. He asked Amelie several questions, learning about her life story and the reasons why she started the spiritual home.

"I have studied the works of Allan Kardec since I was a teenager, still living in the south of France. I then met my beloved John, the man who became my husband a few years later. John was American, and some years after our wedding we decided to move back to his home city, New York. We then had a beautiful son whom we named Philip. We had the perfect family life. John worked downtown as a porter and I used to earn some extra money for the house expenses by giving private classes in French. We weren't rich but we had love, and that was enough. One day John had gone with Philip to watch the Yankees play. Philip had just turned eight years old and that was our birthday present for him: tickets to watch his team play. On their way back home, a man who was intoxicated with drugs and completely out of control robbed them, and stabbed them several times. Philip's corporeal body died right there at the scene and John was rushed to the hospital but also died a few hours later. This was twenty five years ago. My whole world fell apart, and even though I believed in life after death and knew so much about the spiritual world through the studies of the doctrine, back then I couldn't cope with the pain of losing the two people I loved the most. Suddenly the two loves of my life had both gone. Philip was only eight when he did the 'passage' and John was only thirty years old." Amelie dried the tears that were rolling down her face and, after taking a long breath, she concluded, "It took me a few years but I got myself together and enrolled at a course at the university, and put all my energy into my studies. I graduated and got a job downtown as a bilingual law secretary. That was my job during the day and then I used to occupy the rest of my time doing charity work. Suddenly the emptiness I felt from not having John and Philip in my life was filled by a huge feeling of love. The more I gave and shared with those who were in need, the more I felt fulfilled with love. I went back to studying the Spiritism doctrine and regained my passion for life. One day I had a message from my son Philip, telling me how happy he was to see me continuing with my life, and how pleased he was with my charitable work. He inspired me to start the spiritual sessions here at the house and share with others the comfort I found by knowing that this life experience on Earth is just a very small moment of our infinite existence."

The three carried on talking and Roy was extremely fascinated by Amelie's story.

In the spiritual world, Linda was asking Peter why she had not been given authorization to deliver such an important message to Roy and Dolores, knowing that Dolores was in danger.

"Whatever may happen in their lives is because it was in the plans of our Lord for them to go through it. Don't let your emotions speak louder than your knowledge, Linda. The only messages from the spiritual world allowed to reach them are those that won't take them away from their missions, and in this case this message would."

Linda looked apprehensive, but deep down she knew it was destined for them all to go through difficulties and challenges in that current life experience.

The spirit Peter continued, "All we can do is to keep on sending them vibrations of love and encouraging them to remain strong in their faith in God. We can do this by transmitting to them our prayers and our vibrations of love." Peter held her hand and took her back to **Lunas**.

Later that night Roy was sitting in his favourite leather armchair, thinking about everything that he had learnt. He picked up *The Spirits Book* and opened the page where reincarnation was explained. He then discovered that the process of reincarnation was a divine law granted by God to all spirits. It was a chance to elevate and purify their spirits towards perfection by going through the new challenges of a life incarnated in a physical body. The main purpose of reincarnation is for the spirits, through the experiences of many lives, to learn to abandon any behaviour, feelings or actions that may take them away from the purification which leads towards God. God created all of his creatures the same. He created all of them ignorant and at the same level. We were all given the free will to choose which way to follow. That is why some spirits reach the purification more quickly than others. The evolutionary process through the experiences of many lives explains the disasters and misery on Earth, and why so many go through so much suffering every day. To some, this could seem like a punishment from God, but the Spiritism explains that the difficulties and challenges in life are nothing but a learning process that we all go through, depending on our level of evolution. While some are still very delayed in their individual learning and therefore still have many 'lessons to study', others are more advanced in their 'studies' and have reached higher levels on the evolutionary ladder that leads to purification.

Roy fell asleep reading the book. While his corporeal body was resting on the leather chair, his soul was taken by an enlightened spirit friend of his to a spiritual colony not far from Earth where he could continue learning more about the subject he had just read. When his soul returned to Earth and his physical body woke up in the early hours of the morning, Roy remembered nothing at all about his spiritual trip. However, the peace and the learning acquired while his soul was in the spiritual colony registered in his sub-conscious mind, and would have a very beneficial impact on his life.

Chapter Tormented

Back in Penelope's apartment, the two sisters and the other evil spirits following Dynamite had intensified their tormenting of Penelope. With the exception of Fortunada, they were all surrounding her, shouting things like "Do you really believe they went to a spiritual church? It's late in the evening and now they're screwing each other behind your back. Look at yourself in the mirror; see how ugly you've become. Do you think any man would fancy you with your deformed face? Roy is there now with Dolores, laughing at you and your ugliness. Dolores is slim and gorgeous; she has beautiful olive skin and you can't compete with her." They laughed loudly and continued to insult and torment her with thoughts of Roy and Dolores having sex. Penelope went to the bathroom and, facing the mirror, she shouted at her reflection, "I need to get rid of Dolores! She has to go."

"Yes," the evil spirits said. "You've got to get rid of her. She is taking over your life slowly. She started with the kids and now she is taking your man."

"I will kill that Latina," Penelope was thinking out loud, looking completely out of her mind. She applied her make-up with a lot of difficulty; the left side of her body had become stiff, making it hard to move her arm. She was crying in anger. Her hand was shaking as she applied bright red lipstick, and with a slip of her hand she ended up smudging it on to her chin. Shouting and crying at the same time, Penelope's thoughts became filled with even more anger. She could only think of murdering Dolores. *'I've got to kill her…kill that woman who is making a fool of me.'*

"Nigel…Ask Nigel to help. He will know of someone who could provide you with poison," the evil spirits told her. They inspired her to wait until the babysitter had gone away, so she would be alone in the house before putting her plan into action.

Days went by. Roy became gradually closer to Dolores and more affectionate towards Victoria and Katie, making Penelope even more jealous. For weeks the evil spirits continued tormenting her with thoughts of murder. One night, locked in her bedroom as usual and surrounded by darkness, Penelope had a dream in which someone dressed all in black told her to switch on the television. She dreamt of this person every time she slept, and he always told her things about Dolores and Roy which she became convinced were really happening. That night she woke up and, after remembering his words telling her to watch the news, she took the remote control and switched on the television. The news featured the case of a Mexican actress whose meals, along with those of her family, had been poisoned by her personal assistant. The whole family ended up in hospital with severe stomach burns which nearly killed them. When the police investigated, they found out that her personal assistant was adding Arsenic to the family's meals. She was arrested and confessed to poisoning the actress and her family, motivated by hate and jealousy. The evil spirits around Penelope told her that she should copy the plan, and she should call Nigel and tell him to help her. Nigel could get her the Arsenic as he knew many drug dealers in town, and together they could poison Dolores. Penelope didn't hesitate; she called Nigel straight away, asking him to come to see her in the morning after Roy had gone to work.

****

A few days later, Nigel arrived at Penelope's penthouse in the morning. As usual he was very careful as he entered the building, trying to be discreet. Penelope was waiting for him by the entry door, and once he arrived she quickly whisked him upstairs to her bedroom. After locking the door she demanded the Arsenic and tried to grab the small packet that he was holding.

"Hey, hold on…not so fast." Nigel held the packet tight, then hid it away from her in the inside pocket of his jacket. "Before I give you the stuff, you have to give me the money."

Penelope opened a drawer in her dressing table and took out an envelope packed with notes. She thrust it towards him and asked in panic for the packet.

'*Oh my...It seems like she's getting crazier every day. Look the state of her! How can someone deteriorate so fast?*' he thought. With a very cool air Nigel opened the envelope and counted the money inside. Satisfied, he handed over the small packet wrapped in brown paper. Penelope kissed the packet and then unwrapped it, finding a few small glass tubes inside.

Nigel moved closer to her and kissed the bottom of her neck. Whispering in her ear, he enquired, "May I ask what you're going to do with this?" - '*I hope you swallow all of it and die, your cow!*' he thought while kissing her lips.

"I decided to kill her! I will kill that Latina who's trying to take over my life!" Her eyes were focused intensely on the packet. "All I want is to destroy her!"

Not taking her seriously, Nigel asked her sarcastically, "And how are you going to do this? Are you thinking of forcing it down her throat?"

"Don't be stupid. Nobody will know it was me!" With madness in her eyes she whispered, "I know she has a bottle of water in the fridge which she drinks from during the day. It looks like she does some prayers and then she drinks it, as if it was a kind of healing water or something like that. The plan is that I will poison the water from that bottle myself."

"And how do you expect to do this without people finding out you were the one who poisoned her?"

"I've thought of everything. First of all you arrange a business trip for Roy, somewhere far away. Once Roy's gone, I'll then poison her healing bullshit." She continued to tell Nigel her plans and he made out that he was interested.

After Penelope had finished, Nigel smiled at her, pretending to have appreciated her plan. "You can count on me. I'll organize a board meeting in our San Francisco offices with all the directors. Roy will have to go and represent you now that you're away from the business."

"Perfect. Now you'd better go and organize this meeting for me. My sleeping tablets are kicking in and I feel like I need to rest." Penelope locked the packet with the tubes inside the safe, which was hidden behind a portrait. Sitting on the bed, she said, "Go, and keep me updated," before lying down, now feeling very sleepy.

Nigel was about to open the door to leave, but stopped and took some papers from his inside jacket pocket. He unfolded them, saying, "Oops, I forgot to ask you to sign these." He took a pen from his pocket and handed it to Penelope as she lay in bed.

Barely able to speak, she asked him, "What's these?"

"These are the papers of renewal of one of the leases. You know, one of those old houses your father left in New Jersey. The usual headache."

Penelope signed weakly and mumbled, before the tablets finally sent her to sleep, "I remember signing some papers when you came in last time..."

"Oh no, no...this is another property." Nigel raised his middle finger at her once he realised she had fallen asleep. *'You cow! The signature looks a little shaky but it'll do,'* he thought as he left.

In the spiritual world, the evil spirits celebrated their success. They reunited with Dynamite later in the dark region to tell him the news that Nigel had given the poison to Penelope and that soon she was going to execute the murder. Dynamite told them to pay full attention to every detail as nothing must go wrong. Filomena was in ecstasy; she lived her life in order to cause unhappiness to Marta, who now lived as Penelope, and every evil plan to inflict more pain and unhappiness on her was a reason to celebrate. Dynamite ordered the evil spirits to split up; the two sisters would stay with Penelope one hundred per cent of the time, tormenting her thoughts, while the others were told to afflict Nigel and ensure he followed the other part of the plan.

Chapter The poisoning

Everything was going according to plan. As Penelope had requested, Nigel organized a meeting of the board in San Francisco, California, with Roy representing Penelope for the company. Roy was reluctant to leave Dolores and the children, and asked more than once if someone else could go in his place, but Penelope insisted. She said it was going to be a very important meeting and she would like to attend herself, but considering her current physical limitations she would prefer him to go and represent her. So, even though it was against his wishes to be away from home, he had no choice but to go to San Francisco and attend the meeting.

On the day Roy left, Penelope prepared everything carefully. She rose early, put gloves on to handle the tubes containing the poison, and watched as Dolores filled the nearly empty bottle in the fridge with filtered water, singing a gospel song in Spanish as she did so. Once the bottle was full, Dolores put the top on and placed the bottle on the kitchen table. Penelope watched the whole scene with disgust, especially when Dolores held the bottle with both hands, closed her eyes and prayed to the Lord, asking Him to bless the water with vitality, good health and harmony for all those who drank it.

'Let's see what good health God will bring to you once you drink this poisoned water,' Penelope thought, being careful not to be spotted as she spied through a crack in the doorway. She waited for Dolores to start preparing the kids' breakfast. The doorbell sounded, and Dolores left the kitchen to go and let in Lauren, the babysitter. Penelope seized her opportunity, quickly entering the kitchen and putting a few drops of the Arsenic into the bottle of blessed water.

"More...more..." whispered Filomena to her. "You need more of it to kill her and the girl!"

Penelope checked to ensure Dolores wasn't returning to the kitchen yet, and repeated what she had just done, this time adding much more poison to the bottle. In a nervous panic, and rushing so as not to get caught, she spilt half the contents of one tube on Dolores' kitchen apron, which was draped over the table. She then dashed out of the kitchen before Dolores returned. Completely possessed by anger and evil thoughts, she didn't stop at any time to think of what she was doing. She returned to her bedroom and stayed there, waiting for Dolores to leave the apartment and take Katie and Ricky to school. Dynamite had gathered more evil spirits to torment her, and at this point there were hundreds of them surrounding her and feeding from her negative thoughts and energy.

Dolores served breakfast to the kids and got them ready for school. Before leaving the house, Katie and Ricky ran to Victoria's bedroom to kiss her goodbye. As usual, Dolores and the children left the apartment singing loudly and in high spirits. Once they were safely out of the building, Penelope went into Dolores' bedroom and hid the empty tubes amongst her belongings.

****

Later that day in the dark regions, Dynamite was furious. He strode about, swearing loudly, holding one of his followers in the air. His eyes were red and he looked very nervous as well as angry. He violently shook the spirit and screamed at him, "How could you let this happen? I sent you to watch her and ensure she drank from the bottle!"

"I'm sorry, sir… Our plan was leaked and the enlightened ones found out everything. They were there waiting for me. There were so many of them and they didn't let me get close to the kitchen. All I could see was that the bottle smashed on the floor and the contents were lost."

The dark spirit, petrified of Dynamite, repeated, "All I saw was that the bottle smashed on the floor …so sorry, my boss."

"You incompetent! You ruined my plans!"

At that exact moment the two sisters arrived. Filomena was looking excited and happy, and she told Dynamite the news. "It worked! It worked!" She had a wide smile, celebrating Penelope's misery. "Well, the bottle smashed on the floor, but before that happened, the babysitter had poured some of the water into the baby's bottle." Filomena, giggling and shaking her arms with excitement, continued, saying, "The babysitter gave the water to the baby, who drank it. The baby has now been taken to hospital. She's in a bad state; I doubt she'll last more than a few hours."

"Perfect!" smiled Dynamite, his mood totally changed. "At least I know I can count on you two!" He grabbed a golden stick from the floor and lifted it high up in the air. "It's a shame Dolores didn't drink it, though at least we managed to harm the baby." He shouted gleefully, "The baby is dying!"

Filomena, looking triumphant, said, "I guided Penelope with my thoughts to hide the empty tubes amongst Dolores' belongings, and even drove her to spill some drops on her apron, so now there is enough evidence to incriminate Dolores. I thought of this as a back-up plan in case something went wrong and Dolores didn't drink the poison. At least now she could be arrested, then she'll be out of our way. All we need now is for the police to find the evidence and she'll be sent to jail."

The evil spirits were all very exuberant, enjoying and celebrating the news. Dynamite went up to the evil spirit he had just thrown to the ground and pointed his golden stick at him, saying, "Now, you incompetent: I'll give you a chance to redeem yourself. Go back there now and ensure the police officers find the evidence left by Penelope in the housekeeper's room." Looking at the sisters, he said, "Come on, let's go to the hospital where the baby is. I want to recharge my energies by watching the baby suffering in pain until its death."

Chapter Afflicted hearts

Penelope was at the hospital, speaking to the doctors. She was very worried about the baby's condition. It was the first time she had left home since she returned from the hospital after the birth of Victoria and her aneurism. She had a scarf around her head, covering most of her face, and wore sunglasses to help hide her deformities. Tears were streaming down her face as she couldn't stop thinking of the moment the babysitter knocked at her bedroom door, screaming in horror...

Lauren was holding baby Victoria unconscious in her arms. Victoria's body was stiff and she had a very high temperature. Lauren looked very distressed and said to Penelope, "There's something really wrong happening to her, Mrs Green." At that same moment Victoria had a fit. Penelope was shocked, realising with horror that her baby could have drunk the poisoned water. Dolores soon arrived home and, inspired by her spiritual guide who was telling her that there was something wrong, went upstairs to Penelope's bedroom. She found both the babysitter and Penelope panicking over Victoria's little body.

Suddenly a doctor approached Penelope and she was jolted out of her thoughts of earlier events and back to the present. The doctor asked her to go to with him to a private room. He then said, "Mrs Green, I am so sorry, but we've carried out many tests, and they show that your baby has been intoxicated with a high amount of Arsenic. We are doing all we can to save your baby, but I'm afraid there isn't much hope. We need a miracle."

The police had been notified, and an officer entered the room. He approached Penelope and, feeling extremely sorry for her, asked her to tell him if she suspected anyone who could have done this. She replied that she couldn't imagine why anyone would have done such a wicked thing to such a little baby. Dynamite was in the room, invisible to everyone, watching the whole scene with extreme pleasure. He approached the policeman and told him, "The housekeeper is the murderer. Check the apartment and you'll find all the evidence you need." He repeated this several times until the policeman had assimilated his vibration and thoughts.

"Who is at your apartment now?" asked the policeman, to which Penelope responded, "My stepdaughter." She sounded very nervous. "Our housekeeper Dolores is there now with her son and my stepdaughter Katie."

"Where is your husband? Why is he not here with you?" asked the officer.

"He's in San Francisco on business. He's gone to represent me in a business meeting of my company."

The policeman left the room and immediately telephoned the police station, informing his colleagues of the crime and requesting a search of the apartment. Lauren was taken to the police station for questioning, while other officers went to Penelope's penthouse to search for evidence that could lead to the identification of the poisoner. It didn't take long for them to find the evidence left by Penelope among Dolores' belongings. Surprised at the accusation, Dolores tried to tell them how much the kids meant to her, but she was arrested and later charged with attempted murder. She was taken to the police station and locked in a cell.

"I haven't done anything. I would never do such a monstrosity against such a small baby. You have to believe me. The person responsible for this is free and might do it again to someone else." Locked in a the cell with a stranger, Dolores tried to convince the police to believe her, but after they found the small tubes containing traces of the poison they regarded the case as almost resolved. Holding on to the prison bars, Dolores cried, feeling absolutely desperate.

****

As soon as he was notified by the hospital staff, Roy caught the first plane back to New York, arriving very late in the evening. He went straight to the hospital to see

Victoria. He arrived in the intensive care unit and saw Victoria surrounded by tubes. He felt helpless and distressed when he saw his little baby girl fighting to survive. Victoria was breathing only with a lot of difficulty and needed help from a respirator. After speaking to the doctors, Roy felt desolate, knowing his baby daughter was about to die at any minute. He sat down on the floor and sobbed. He regretted ignoring his intuition that had told him not to go to San Francisco, and began to blame himself. Moments later a policeman approached him.

"Are you Mr Taylor?" he asked.

Roy looked up and didn't respond. The officer introduced himself and explained that he was in charge of Victoria's case. Roy stood up and followed him to a quieter spot. The policeman told him about the findings and finished by telling him about Dolores' arrest. At first, Roy's reaction was not to believe anything he was being told, but after learning about the evidence found among Dolores' belongings, including residues of the poison on her apron, he couldn't argue. He immediately went pale and dizzy.

"Dolores!" exclaimed Roy, looking pained. "I can't believe it."

"Are you okay, Mr Taylor? Would you like me to bring you some water?" asked the policeman, looking around to see if he could find a nurse nearby.

"No, no…I'm fine," Roy replied. He stood up and took hold of his jacket, which he had left on the desk, and grabbed his suitcase. "I've got to go home and have a shower. I need to check on my other daughter and make sure she's fine."

"Are you sure you are okay, Mr Taylor? I can drive you home."

"Yes I'm fine, don't worry. Thanks for the offer, but I need some time on my own. I need to ensure I'm strong now so I can help my daughter somehow." He took a business card from his wallet and scribbled on it the contact numbers in case the officer needed to get hold of him urgently. Then he excused himself and left the hospital.

'How could I have been so naïve? She was planning this all along and I didn't realise,' he thought in the back of the taxi on his way home. *'And I was so in love*

with her…How could she have done such an evil thing to Victoria? Why? How could she be so perverse and evil?'

When Roy came home, Penelope began to cry desperately and make a huge scene. The thought of Victoria dying had touched her deep inside, and the evil spirits took advantage of her vulnerability to torment her even more.

"Our baby…our baby is dead and that Latina killed her!"

"Victoria isn't dead, Penelope. She's fighting bravely to survive and I have faith that she will fight that poison out of her system," he said, walking towards Katie's bedroom.

"Hold on…Where do you think you're going? We need to talk about this…"

"I'm going to see my daughter and no, we don't have to talk about this, Penelope. You never cared about our baby and I don't see why I should waste my time here with you when my two daughters need me. I'm going to check Katie is okay and then go back to the hospital to wait for Victoria to recover, because I don't care what the doctors say, I believe she can survive this." Roy left the room and went straight to Katie's bedroom. Penelope shouted his name but Roy ignored her.

"Katie, sweetheart…" said Roy. He found Katie lying down in bed. "Are you okay, darling?"

When Katie heard her father's voice she stood up and opened her arms to hug him. They embraced each other tightly for a long time without either of them saying anything. Both cried, and at that moment father and daughter were bonded together again with the same pain and sorrow they once endured when Linda had gone through the passage. At that moment they both feared losing someone they loved once again. After a long time crying, Roy asked, "Do you want to come to the hospital with me and wait for Victoria to recover? If you want, I can take you with me now. It will mean spending the whole night in the hospital, though." Katie nodded. Roy kissed her forehead and said, "I'll have a quick shower to shake the day away. I'll be back in ten minutes to pick you up, okay?"

Katie looked sadly at him, and then told him that a strange woman had come to the apartment that afternoon, accompanied by policemen, and had taken Ricky with her. Katie said she was worried about him.

Roy put his hand around her face and explained, "The woman you saw taking Ricky away works for the social services. They will look after him until they find him a family that can take care of him. I know it's very sad, darling, but please let's focus on our Victoria now, okay? I promise that tomorrow morning I'll speak to the police officer and get more information about Ricky, and find out how he is."

Chapter Fighting for survival

Later that evening at the hospital, Victoria was still very weak and having difficulty breathing. Linda, Geraldine, Teresa and other spiritual friends of Rebecca - now Victoria -were there next to her little body, praying for her recovery.

"Is she going to survive, Teresa?" asked Linda, unable to take her eyes away from Victoria.

"I don't know my dear…I don't know. As you know, most spirits who committed suicide in their previous incarnation and stopped their life experience abruptly usually have a very fragile physical body when re-born in a new life experience on Earth. In most cases they do tend to pass away in infancy."

"So she could pass away within the next few hours?"

Teresa nodded and asked Linda to continue praying. Roy and Katie arrived at that same instant and went to look at Victoria. Katie cried as soon as she saw her baby sister lying there with tubes and wires all over her tiny body.

'Mother, please look after my little sister Victoria. Don't let her die. Please. She is everything I have and I promise I will always look after her, but please, please, please don't let her die. I beg you,' asked Katie in her thoughts.

Linda was right next to her, feeling very sorry, but made a great effort not to transmit any bad vibration to her. She put her arm around Katie and sent her thoughts of encouragement. "I am here with you, sweetheart. There are lots of people who love you and your sister, and we are all here hoping for her recovery. Let's pray with all our hearts and our love will help to heal her body." Inspired by Linda's thoughts, Katie looked at her father and said, "Let's pray, dad. Let's pray and ask God to cure our Vicky and he will, I'm sure he will." Roy wasn't sure about that, but thinking of Katie he held her hand and prayed with her.

Hours later, Roy and Katie had fallen asleep together on a sofa in the waiting room. Their souls were taken to Lunas by Linda, who had received authorization to spend time with them in the spiritual world.

The sky in Lunas was blue, there were birds tweeting and flying over the lake, and as always the atmosphere felt refreshing and comforting. As soon as Roy saw Linda he ran towards her saying, "Linda! Linda my love, you're alive!"

"I am, Roy," replied Linda, holding Katie's hand. She went down on her knees and said to her daughter, "Katie knows that I'm alive, don't you, sweetheart?"

"I do, mom." Looking at her father, she said, "Mom and I always meet here, dad. Sometimes she even takes me to ride my horse but when I wake up I forget everything."

Teresa and Geraldine arrived and invited Katie for a walk so her parents could talk. Once the others had left, Roy said to Linda, "I feel so ashamed of what I've done to you. I'm sorry. I don't deserve you to be nice to me."

"It's okay, Roy, I forgive you. I forgave you long ago. I knew about Penelope and I'm not here to make you feel bad about anything you did in the past, Roy. I'm here to talk about Dolores. She's innocent and you have to believe her. You need to help her; she isn't guilty."

"I would love to believe it, but they found everything in her bedroom, everything. They found small tubes with traces of the poison and even her kitchen apron had some of the poison on it too. I wish I could believe she isn't guilty, but I can't."

"I am telling you Roy, she isn't."

"Who did this to my Victoria, then? Who would be so evil as to harm and possibly kill a small baby?"

"Unfortunately, someone lost with an ill mind. Someone who has been intoxicated by her own evil thoughts," she replied.

"What about my little baby? Is she going to be okay?"

"Pray for her Roy, pray. She committed suicide in her past life experiences, which meant she reincarnated with a very fragile physical body. You need to give her a lot of love and help her to feel safe and cared for. Tell her how much you love her. Tell her how much you wanted her to be born. She needs all the love and support you can give." Linda felt it was time for Roy to return to Earth. She moved closer and told him, "You will wake up from this encounter and I want you to remember this phrase: 'Dolores isn't guilty…Dolores isn't guilty'…"

"Dolores isn't guilty," said Roy out loud as he suddenly woke up in the middle of the night. He looked around feeling scared, and then remembered he was at the hospital. He looked at Katie, who was lying curled up on a chair, and he moved her to a more comfortable position on a bigger sofa. He looked admiringly at her sleeping for a while, then walked towards the window. He looked out, down to the streets and thought of Dolores. *'Was I dreaming with Linda? Why did I wake up saying Dolores isn't guilty?'* he asked himself. *'They found the tubes with the poison in her drawers and also found some of the poison on her kitchen apron. Who else could have done it? Penelope is very depressed but she wouldn't try to kill her own baby. No…no…Penelope wouldn't do such a monstrous thing.'*

Chapter Action and reaction

On the following day at the apartment, Nigel paid a surprise visit to Penelope, who was not happy to see him.

"Well, well, I hear that you failed in your plan and you ended up poisoning your own damn baby…"

Penelope interrupted. "Shush! Someone might come in and hear what you're saying."

Nigel had a mischievous look and played back to Penelope her 'Shush'. "Shush? Why are you shushing me? Are you scared now? Didn't you think of what could have happened once you poisoned a bottle of water from which the entire family drinks, you silly cow? You're lucky you didn't kill everyone else."

Penelope was still worried about someone hearing their conversation and begged Nigel to shut up, but he was having none of it. He had a folder in his hands and he smiled widely. He rubbed the folder on her face before throwing it on her bed.

"What is this?" she asked, taking the folder and examining its contents. She leafed through the papers quickly, and in panic asked, "Nigel, explain to me. What is this?" She felt a shiver down her spine.

Nigel smiled cruelly as he watched Penelope being overcome by panic. She climbed out of bed and went for his neck with both her hands, but he pushed her away strongly and she fell flat on the floor by the bed.

"It's all mine. All you have, it's all mine now. I stole everything you have. Well, I haven't stolen it. You actually signed everything over to me."

"You're a pig, Nigel! Stop this joke!" She grabbed hold of the folder again and started to tear off the pages. "Stop this joke now!"

Laughing at her, Nigel knelt down and grabbed her by her hair, putting his face very close to hers. "It's not a joke, my beloved. You signed everything you have over to me. Your properties, your companies, I mean the whole lot!" Nigel removed the folder from her hands and threw it at her face. "You can tear it all up if you want. These are photocopies of the real documents. Do you think I'm crazy enough to hand you the original ones? I'm not stupid like you, Penelope."

"How? How did you do this?" she asked, shaking.

"Easy…it was very easy. First of all I had to be careful as I knew you could catch me, so I gradually began to give you a few documents for you to sign over to my name. You were so obsessed about Roy that you didn't notice anything. But that was only a few shitty properties you had out of New York. It was nothing too special. But then, after the beautiful baby Victoria was born…" Nigel laughed sarcastically and opened his arms widely. "Oh, the baby Victoria. I love that baby! Do you know why?"

Penelope, still sitting on the bedroom floor, tried to kick him but she didn't reach him. Nigel then grabbed her face violently, and holding tight he continued. "I love that damn baby. Do you know why? I love that damn baby because since she was born you destroyed yourself without me having to do anything. You were so consumed by your own misery, too busy feeling sorry for yourself. Every time I saw you, you were off your face on medication and sleeping pills so I gave you more documents to sign and you did. It became so easy."

"I wasn't expecting this," said Fortunada to Filomena as they watched invisibly.

"Dynamite arrived in the room, surrounded by his many evil spirit followers. Amid loud laughter he said, "This is a little surprise I've been working on. I inspired this idiot Nigel with all of these ideas and I must hand it to him, he did follow the plan well."

"You took everything from me?" Penelope said desperately.

"Oh no…not yet." He walked across the bedroom and got hold of a picture frame which was on the bedside cabinet. It contained a photo of Penelope and Roy together. He threw it to the floor and stamped on it, smashing the glass. "I still need to finish your family and then…then I will have taken everything from you."

"Nigel, please…" She dragged herself towards him, knelt down and embraced his legs, begging, "Please Nigel, don't do this. Is it me you want? You want to marry me, don't you? You want me to break up with Roy? I'll do it! I'll break up with Roy and be with you."

"Oh please, Penelope." He pushed her arms away from his legs. "Do you really think I want to be with you? Look at you! You lost your looks, you look horrendous. I would even say you look like a beast. I never liked you. I actually always felt you were a disgusting woman. I just wanted your money. And yes, I used to think that marrying you would be a way to get hold of it, but you actually made things so easy for me…well, that baby made my plans easy. I now have everything and I don't have to be married to you!"

Nigel walked towards the bedroom door and said, before leaving, "You are a beast, Penelope, a horrible-looking beast. And now you're a *poor* horrible-looking beast too!"

"Where are you going?"

"I've got lots of things to do…including finishing off ruining your marriage and destroying your life. But for now I want you to stay here, suffering and wondering what I'm going to do next." He slammed the door and left the penthouse feeling victorious.

Chapter Accepting the truth

Roy had decided to agree to Dolores' request for him to visit her in prison. He hoped to get some sort of answer and perhaps understand why she had done such a terrible thing to Victoria. When the prison guard brought Dolores out to the visitors' area, Roy looked at her and for a few seconds felt sorry for her. Dolores had dark circles around her eyes and looked as if she hadn't had a shower for days. Roy stared into her eyes and could see sorrow and sadness.

"Why did you do this? Why did you betray all of us?" asked Roy. "How could you try and kill a baby? My little baby…"

Dolores was looking pale and tired as she hadn't slept for days. In silence she felt terrible, seeing that even Roy was thinking she could be guilty, and had tried to kill an innocent baby. Tears rolled down her face and she felt so sad that the only words she could find were "How is she?"

"What do you care?" Roy snarled, getting agitated. "How dare you ask how she is! I only came here after you asked to see me because I thought I might find out the reason why you did this to Victoria. Why would you try and kill a baby? My little baby…" he cried deeply. "My little baby." Roy dropped his head against the table, crying non-stop and thinking of Victoria, who was back at the hospital about to die at any minute.

"I am as sad and worried about Victoria as you are, Roy. I didn't do this to her," she said with tears rolling down her face. "How dare you believe I could have done such a thing to her? I thought you would trust me and perhaps try and find who really did this to Victoria."

Roy, having fallen in love with Dolores, wanted to believe her but couldn't. All the evidence showed that it had been her. "They found all of those tubes in your belongings and even your apron had the substance on it," he said, looking her right in the eyes. "Who else could have done this? Are you trying to say that the babysitter, young Lauren, could have done it?"

"No, not Lauren. Lauren poured the water into Victoria's bottle and gave to her, but I'm sure it wasn't intentional. I'm almost sure it was your wife…your wife. I don't have any proof, but she was the only one apart from me and the kids in the apartment. No-one else was there. There is no-one else but your wife, Roy. She is very jealous, thinking I could be taking you away from her. I believe that water was prepared for me and not for Victoria. You've got to believe me. You and Katie are also in danger, because if she did that to Victoria she'll do it to you two as well."

Roy stood up rapidly and, about to leave, snapped, "Enough! You can't blame Penelope. She is a mother, and a mother would never try to kill her own baby."

"You've got to believe me, Roy. I would never do such a horrible thing in my life. I'm worried about my son, Ricky. I don't know where he is or who is looking after him. Do you honestly think I would try to kill a young and innocent baby? Victoria, who I learnt to love and care for? I love her and Katie as if they were my own kids."

Roy remained quiet and pensive as Dolores continued, "Since you arrived, Penelope has been treating little Katie very badly. Many times I caught Katie crying after being horribly spoken to by Penelope."

"Penelope is young. She just doesn't know how to educate a child."

"Do you really believe that?" Dolores tried to move closer to Roy, but he raised a hand, showing that she should stay where she was. She continued, "Have you never asked yourself why Katie is petrified of Penelope? Why she avoids being around her at any cost? Have you ever seen Penelope being nice and caring towards Katie?"

Roy abruptly interrupted her. "Enough…enough." The picture of Victoria in hospital, fighting to live, came back into his mind and his paternal instinct spoke loudly. "I hope you die in this prison to pay for what you have done to my baby," he said, and left the room without looking back.

Dolores closed her eyes. Before the prison guard returned to collect her and take her back to her cell, she prayed to God, asking for help. Her spiritual friend Peter had been by her side, in the spiritual world, throughout most of her time in prison, and he was with her at that moment. He prayed and sent her thoughts and vibrations of encouragement. By the time the guard came she was more serene and ready to face another night in the cold cell.

****

Later that night at home, after returning from the hospital, Roy entered Katie's bedroom and found her sleeping, holding tightly on to Victoria's blanket. Watching that scene made something click in his mind, and finally he realised he had made a huge mistake by marrying Penelope. At that moment he began to think and ask himself questions, like: where was Penelope when he most needed her? Where was she when her baby daughter most needed her? He went upstairs to the second level, stopping by the door when he reached their bedroom. Just the thought of seeing Penelope made him feel nauseous. He remained standing still by the door, holding the handle, then decided not to go in. Instead, he went to the library and sat down on his old leather chair and thought of Dolores. She had been everything he expected from a partner and a mother for his children. He thought of the happiness she had brought into Katie's life, making her feel cared for and loved again. Dolores had also showed so much affection and care towards Victoria, which Penelope had never done.

"Yes Roy, you are right. She has been very dedicated and caring towards your kids and towards you too. Leave behind the hate and anger you are feeling now and go and search for the truth. Perhaps it's very clear and there for you to see," said Linda to him via her thoughts.

Unable to see or hear Linda, Roy continued to remember all Penelope's awful behaviour and the lack of respect he had seen during the whole time he had known her. Dolores' words from earlier came back to his mind, and he realised she was right. The closer he became to Katie, the more he realised how scared of Penelope she was. Just the mention of Penelope's name could make Katie completely change her behaviour and become quiet and apprehensive. Roy recalled how indifferent Penelope had always been towards her, and remembered that he had never seen Penelope showing the slightest interest in her wellbeing. Suddenly Dolores' words in the prison visitors' room began to echo in his head. Word by word, they returned to his mind and repeated themselves:

"Your wife...Your wife. I don't have any proof but she was the only one apart from me and the kids in the apartment. No-one else was there..."

His heart was beating faster and faster, the more he remembered Dolores' words:

"There is no-one else but your wife, Roy... You've got to believe me...You and Katie are also in danger, because if she did that to Victoria she'll do it to you two as well."

Linda continued to tell him Dolores was innocent, and to urge him to search for the truth. As his soul slowly absorbed her thoughts and vibrations, Dolores' words repeated over and over in his mind, making even more sense.

"Your wife...Your wife. I don't have any proof but she was the only one apart from me and the kids in the apartment. No-one else was there...There is no-one else but your wife, Roy. You've got to believe me...You and Katie are also in danger, because if she did that to Victoria she'll do it to you two as well."

He thought, *'Oh my, what if she's right? What if Dolores is innocent?'* Sweat rolled down his face. *'Penelope wouldn't try to take her own baby's life...would she? No, no...she couldn't. A mother would never be able to do such a thing. Maybe she poisoned the water for Dolores, and by a tragic mistake Victoria ended up drinking it.'* Driven by his paternal instinct, he went back downstairs to Katie's room and checked that she was sleeping okay. While watching her sleep, his heart was still beating quickly, and a horrible feeling of loss took over him. *'What if Dolores is innocent and Penelope really has lost her mind? Katie is now in danger. She'll try to kill her too.'*

Roy remembered Dolores' spiritual sessions reading the gospel in the kitchen, and how much faith she had in God. He also recalled the night he had gone to the spiritual centre, and how he had spontaneously closed his eyes and spoken to God for the first time. The memory prompted him to say, "God, please give me a sign. Show me the answer. Show me who did this to my daughter." Before he could finish his prayer he heard Penelope's voice coming from the bedroom, calling his name. Immediately he got goose bumps and a cold feeling all down his spine. *'Maybe this is the sign I'm asking for. Was it her? Was it Penelope who did this to little Victoria?'* he asked God mentally, and immediately Penelope called him again:

"Roy, are you home? Come up," she said from the top of the stairs.

Again he felt nausea after hearing her voice. The thought of being next to her made him feel like throwing up. He became desperately worried. *'God, please help me. Help me by showing me the way. I can't let anything bad to happen to Katie. Help me, please.'*

That night Roy came to one conclusion: he decided to separate from Penelope. He wanted to look after his kids and start a new life. It didn't matter if it was a simpler life with no luxury. All he wanted was for Victoria to recover, and that he and his two daughters should live happily together. He resolved to speak to Penelope the next day, and move out with his daughters as soon as Victoria had left the hospital. Taking a duvet and some blankets from one of the guest rooms, he improvised a bed in Katie's bedroom, and there he slept that night.

Chapter The first steps towards freedom

On the following day, Roy was awakened by Katie who was saying goodbye.

"Lauren is taking me to school, dad. Are you sure I can't go to the hospital with you today?"

"Sorry darling, but you already missed a whole week of school. I'll pop into work first thing in the morning and then I'll go to visit our Vicky."

"Would you tell her I love her very much and tell her that I miss her?"

"Of course, darling." Roy kissed her forehead and held her hand, taking her to the living room where Lauren was waiting.

"Good morning, Mr Taylor," said Lauren, extending her hand out to Katie.

"Good morning, Lauren. Please take care of my little treasure," said Roy, kissing Katie on her right cheek.

Once Lauren and Katie had left, Roy looked across the living room in the direction of the stairs, deciding it was time to face Penelope. After much thought he had decided to separate from her. He knew Penelope wouldn't make it easy, but he was determined to start a new life with Katie and Victoria, away from that apartment. After a shower and a quick glass of milk Roy went to the bedroom where Penelope was sleeping.

"Roy?" she said, still feeling dizzy from the sleeping pills she had taken. "Where have you been?"

Choosing his words very carefully, Roy spelt out his desire for a change in his life, and that he wanted to try a separation. He explained how he knew that Katie wasn't happy and he wanted to give her a better life.

Penelope couldn't believe what she was hearing. She opened her eyes wide and, feeling furious, she threw herself across the bed towards Roy and punched his chest. "Who do you think you are to say this to me? You are no-one without me, Roy, no-one!"

Roy pulled himself away from her, causing her to lose her balance and fall to the floor. He tried to pick her up but she pushed him away, accusing him of being violent towards her. Roy was scared by her behaviour and for the first time he finally saw what Penelope was truly like. He stepped back towards the door, but when he tried to leave, Penelope, still on the floor, grabbed his leg.

"Let me go, Penelope. You seem to be very aggressive, so perhaps this isn't a good time for this conversation."

"You're not leaving me, Roy. I made you who you are now, and you won't survive without me. You are no-one without me," she said with a mixture of sorrow and anger in her voice.

Roy tried to leave again, but when he moved his leg Penelope grabbed him again. "Leave me," he said. "I'm going to the hospital to visit Victoria. Perhaps we can continue this conversation later when I come back. Now please let me go. This is too much now, Penelope." He pulled his leg away and walked out of the room, leaving Penelope on the floor.

Penelope erupted in fury and punched the floor non-stop, shouting, "That idiot! Who does he think he is, threatening to leave me? He can't leave me... He can't!"

She stood up, took a picture off the wall and smashed it against the furniture. "Katie isn't happy! And since when has he cared about that little redneck girl!" She stopped for a moment and thought, *'So Nigel hasn't spoken to him yet? Nigel hasn't done anything. Was he bluffing?'*

****

Roy rushed down the stairs and grabbed his coat from the living room. Feeling extremely nervous after the argument with Penelope, he left the apartment in search of some fresh air. He was sweating and feeling physically sick. As he entered the elevator he felt like vomiting. Invisible to him, Linda was telling him, "Dolores didn't do anything. Dolores is innocent. She is telling the truth. Our Katie is in danger, Roy. Penelope is very tormented and obsessed. She will try to harm Katie at any time soon."

The elevator reached the ground floor. Roy strode quickly out on to the streets, hailed a taxi and headed to the company's headquarters. He had to sign off some very important documents and he thought he may as well do that before going to the hospital.

When he arrived on the 58th floor where the directors' offices were, the receptionist gave him a strangely different look from her usual cheerful one. He said hello but she didn't reply and avoided looking at him. He walked down the long corridor, noticing that everyone was staring at him through the glazed windows of their offices. Some even came out, apparently just to watch him walk down the corridor. When he opened the door of his office he had a surprise. He found Nigel sitting on his chair, facing backwards and looking out of the massive window.

"What's this, Nigel? Why you are sitting on my chair?" he asked, noticing two boxes which were on top of his desk, filled with his possessions. "Why is my stuff all packed in boxes? Is this is a kind of joke or what?" He looked around the office and noticed that none of his belongings were there any more; everything had been packed into those boxes.

Nigel looked at him and smiled, saying snidely, "Take a good look around, Roy, before you say goodbye to what used to be your office!"

"Stop the joke, Nigel. I haven't even called the hospital yet to find out the news about my baby, and I'm not in the mood for your stupid jokes today." Roy lifted the receiver of the telephone on the desk, but as he was dialling the hospital's number, Nigel put his finger on the phone's cradle and stopped the call.

"I'm afraid it's not one of my jokes, my friend. It's reality!" Nigel pressed the intercom button and told his secretary to ask the company's lawyer, Mr Dawson, to come to the room. While waiting for him to arrive, Nigel took of a bunch of papers and put them on the desk in front of Roy. Pointing at the papers he said, "Read it."

Roy went through the pages one by one, not believing what he was seeing. Penelope had signed everything - the companies, the properties and every single asset - over to Nigel's name. "This is not possible," Roy said in disbelief. "You cannot legally do this."

Mr Dawson, who had collaborated with Nigel in tricking Penelope, entered the office and carefully shut the door. Having checked that nobody was about, he lied, "Oh yes, Roy. I was the witness for everything. As you can see, all the contracts have also been signed by me. I witnessed Penelope signing the papers and being very willing to hand everything she possessed over to Nigel."

"I can't believe this. Penelope would never have done this. I don't even believe you witnessed anything."

"Well, you are right, technically I didn't witness it but…who cares, hey?"

Roy was in shock, looking at Nigel and Mr Dawson lined up side by side in front of him. It was clear that the pair had tricked Penelope, taking advantage of her vulnerability. He tried to argue but he was surprised by two security guards who burst in and grabbed him by his arms.

"I'm sorry, but it's time for you to leave us to get on with business. As you know, we have a lot to do here, a lot of money to administrate and a lot more money to be made, so if you'll excuse me, I don't have any more time to waste."

Still held by the two guards, Roy said, "You're a pig, Nigel. I always knew you didn't have any good intentions towards Penelope. All of that obsession for her, always being around offering your friendship, your advice and services. You never fooled me, Nigel."

Nigel walked towards Roy and said, with a wide smile on his face, "Oh, but I did fool you. Many times, if you want to know. I was shagging Penelope behind your back all of the time you two have been together. Something you should learn about Penelope: she doesn't have any respect for anyone, and that includes you!"

"That's not true. Penelope wouldn't do this to me!"

"Oh really?" Nigel giggled and said, "Ask your daughter Katie. She saw us having sex in your bed. I bet she'll never forget that scene."

Roy spat in Nigel's face. "You son of a..."

Before Roy could finish speaking, Nigel punched him in the stomach and said, "I hate you and your redneck daughter. Now get out of here. Go and live on the streets where you belong, or even better why don't you just eff off back to the shithole you came from?" Nigel gave a sign with his hands to the two security guards, telling them to take Roy away. Before they left, Nigel said, "I'll ask someone to toss these boxes with your junk in a trash can. I don't want any of your trash here, and by the way I want the penthouse emptied by tomorrow morning. Otherwise you will all be removed by my security men and be thrown on to the streets."

The guards dragged Roy out of the office and to the elevator.

"You can let me go now. I don't care about this company any more. All I want to do is to get out of here as soon as possible," said Roy, feeling like vomiting. The guards let his arms go, but got inside the elevator with him. Following instructions from Nigel, they escorted Roy until he was outside the building and watched to ensure he didn't return.

Feeling horribly sick, Roy ran along the street and turned the corner. He stopped and, unable to control himself any longer, he threw up into a trash can. His heart was beating fast and a sickly sensation took over his body. He looked to both sides of the street and felt lost, not knowing what to do. Linda, who was at his side, transmitted vibrations of harmony and encouragement to him, telling him to calm down and trust God.

"A leaf doesn't fall from the tree unless it has been previously planned by God. Everything in life happens for a reason and serves God's masterplan for our evolution. Everything will be fine, Roy. Now you need to calm down so you can help Katie and Victoria, as both are at risk," she said while transmitting more positive vibrations.

At that moment his soul captured Linda's vibration and he recovered, feeling a bit calmer. *'I need to be strong. I need to find a way out of this mess, not only for me but for my daughter's future too,'* he thought while trying to regain his composure.

Linda transmitted him thoughts guiding him to go and see someone whom could he could count on at difficult times. Instinctively he got a taxi and directed the driver to Queens.

Chapter The kidnapping

The phone in her bedroom was ringing. Penelope answered and it was Nigel. Laughing at her, he told her what had happened earlier in the office; how he had humiliated Roy and even told him the truth about their long-term affair. To create even more panic in her mind, Nigel said that he was going to make an anonymous phone call to the police station and tell them she had been the one responsible for trying to kill her baby. He then hung up, leaving Penelope close to a complete breakdown.

"It's the end of the line, Penelope. You will be arrested and die in prison where you belong," whispered Filomena to her.

The other evil spirits in the room began to circle her, inciting her to do the most horrible things. They all sent many evil vibrations and violent thoughts to her, and soon she was driven to lose her mind completely and became insane. Filomena, looking even more deteriorated than usual, moved very close to Penelope and told her to take Katie and run away from that place as soon as possible.

"I'll get out of here before they find me. I've got to get out of here," she thought, picking up her bag. She went to the bathroom to apply some make-up, which ended up looking dreadful because of her shaky hands. She had lost her mind completely and was talking nonsense to herself non-stop. Penelope went around the room collecting all her jewellery and precious belongings and tossed everything into a bag. She took all her cash out of the safe, along with a gold-plated revolver, and put them in the same bag. The evil spirits were telling her to get Katie and do away with her. They directed her towards a horrible plan. Penelope, completely engaged with their vibration, followed every single step of their instructions.

She ran down the stairs and flung open Katie's bedroom door, banging it violently against the wall. Katie, who had been doing her homework, jumped up from the chair, feeling terrified. Penelope walked towards Katie, who tried to escape, but

Penelope managed to grab her arm. Holding her very tightly, she dragged the frightened child out of the bedroom.

"You're hurting me…let me go!"

"Shut up! We're going to the hospital to see your little sister. By the way, she's dead!"

"What? What happened to Vicky? Where's my father?"

Penelope had gone completely insane. She laughed and repeated non-stop, "Dead, dead…dead dead dead dead…"

"Stop it!" cried Katie. "Where's my father?"

"Come on, let's go to the hospital," said Penelope dragging her by the arm through the penthouse until they reached the elevator. They got inside and Penelope pressed the garage button. She looked completely out of her mind; her head was shaking and she couldn't stop talking out loud to herself. When they reached the garage, Penelope pulled Katie to the car and threw her inside, slamming the door. Once Penelope was in the driving seat, Katie asked her, crying, "Are we really going to the hospital? Is my father there waiting for us?"

"No, he's dead. Victoria is dead. Everyone is dead. Your mother is dead. All dead!"

Katie called her crazy and told her to stop, but Penelope's response was to slap her face violently. Katie began to cry more loudly and Penelope slapped her again, telling her to keep quiet otherwise she would hit her even harder. She then started the car and drove away fast.

Chapter A father's fight

Amelie answered the door and found Roy on her doorstep. He looked pale and desperate.

"Hi, Amelie…I don't know if you remember me, but I was here a few weeks ago with Dolores."

"Of course I remember you, Roy."

"I'm sorry for not telling you I was coming. Is this a good time to speak to you?"

"Don't you worry. It's a perfect time; please come inside."

She invited him to take a seat and they both sat down on the same sofa where, a few weeks earlier, they had enjoyed a conversation together with Dolores.

"You are here because of Dolores, right?"

Roy explained everything that had happened. As he did so, Amelie's spiritual mentor, Peter, approached her and inspired her to say to Roy, "She is innocent. Dolores is innocent and your children are at risk. You have to return back home immediately, Roy."

Roy felt shivers down his spine; the same sensation he had had on the previous day in the library when thinking of Penelope. "May I use your phone? I need to call the hospital to find out how my baby is doing. I left home early this morning with the idea of quickly going into the office to sign some papers, but here I am…To cut a long story short, I haven't been to the hospital yet."

"Of course, Roy." Amelie pointed out the telephone on a side table in the corner of the living room. "Please feel free to call whoever you need to."

She went to the kitchen to make a cup of tea for Roy. When she returned a few minutes later she found him on the phone, looking very agitated. He gave her a worried look; cold sweat was rolling down his forehead. "My baby…My baby," he said in shock.

"What's happening? You look like you're going to faint. Who are you calling?"

"I'm calling home but no-one's answering." Roy was shaking. He hung up and tried phoning again but there was still no answer. Almost out of breath, he told Amelie that he had rung the hospital and was told that Victoria had gone missing. Penelope had visited her an hour earlier, and when the nurses returned, the baby had disappeared. Roy was now trying to ring home to speak to Penelope and find out what was happening, but nobody was answering the phone. Roy had both hands clasped around the back of his head, looking as if he was going to have a nervous breakdown. "I have to go. I've got to go back home and find out what's going on…"

"You can't go on your own while you're in such a state. You look terrible, as if you're just about to faint. I'll go with you; give me one minute. I need to switch off the hob where I left the water boiling for the tea and then get my coat. Please wait for me."

Once they reached the street they tried to find a taxi but without success. Amelie looked at her watch and said, "The traffic's very bad at this time of day. It'll be quicker on the train."

****

When Roy and Amelie arrived at the penthouse in Manhattan they were alarmed to see several police cars outside. Roy dashed into the elevator, and when he reached the penthouse he found the front door wide open and a policeman standing guard, stopping anyone from entering. Inside, Roy could see more officers, who seemed to be searching the place.

"What's happening? Where are my daughters?"

"Are you Mr Green?" asked the policeman on the door.

"Taylor, Roy Taylor. I'm Penelope's husband. What's going on? Where are my daughters?" Roy tried to go inside but the officer stopped him. He then explained that they had received an anonymous phone call accusing Penelope of being the person who really poisoned the water, and that her intention was actually to kill the housekeeper. The officer also said that just as they were about to start investigating these accusations, they received another phone call, this time from the hospital, reporting that the baby had gone missing after Penelope had been to visit.

Lauren approached them nervously. Crying in desperation, she said, "I'm so sorry, Mr Taylor…I'm so sorry. I left Katie in the bedroom studying, while I went to the kitchen to make us a sandwich, and when I returned she was gone. I checked everywhere and then I noticed that Mrs Green had left too."

"Why you didn't call me?"

"I called your office but they said you didn't work there any more. I found it strange, but I thought maybe Mrs Green had taken Katie for a walk…I was stupid, I know," she said, sobbing. "I'm so sorry."

"Do you have any idea of where your wife could have gone to, sir?" asked the policeman, taking out a pen and a notepad.

Roy was in shock. He didn't say anything to the officer, just stayed absolutely still, staring at him. In his mind it was all confirmed: Penelope had tried to kill Victoria, and now she had run away, taking both Katie and Victoria with her. Panic took over Roy's body as he wondered in terror what Penelope might do to his daughters.

"Sir?" prompted the policeman.

"I'm sorry... I'm just in shock with all of this."

"Your help is very important to us. First of all we need to make a list of all of the possible places your wife could have gone to." He handed Roy his notepad and pen, saying, "Please remember that every minute's delay could represent huge danger to your children."

Roy tried to think of all the possible places she could have gone to, and made a list of them for the officer, who phoned the information through to the police station, suggesting where they should search. Roy's list included La Guardia airport, where Penelope's private jet was kept. The policeman and his colleagues then left to join in the search for Penelope.

Roy went to the bedroom, looking for clues. He found boxes of sleeping pills on the floor and empty bottles of whisky. In the en suite bathroom he saw the smashed mirror and pieces of glass in the sink and all over the floor. Returning to the bedroom, he noticed drops of blood by the bed and also on the carpet. "The safe's been opened," he said out loud to himself. "She's taken all of her jewellery and the money with her." He ran downstairs to Katie's bedroom, but it was in perfect condition with no evidence that could lead to a clue.

Roy sat on Katie's bed and broke down in tears, sick with worry about his daughters' safety. *'How could Penelope try to kill her own daughter? What is she going to do with Katie and Victoria now?'* he thought desperately.

Amelie, who had been looking for him all over the penthouse, came into Katie's bedroom and found Roy in tears. She sat next to him on the bed and in a very kind tone asked him to calm down and think carefully of where Penelope could have gone. She told him to close his eyes and ask God for the answer, which Roy did.

"God Almighty, please be merciful to us. I need your help. Please show me where Penelope has taken my children to. Guide me, my Lord."

Inspired by Peter, Teresa and Geraldine, Roy suddenly remembered the day after the pool party incident, when he had woken up in Penelope's beach house in the Hamptons, At the same moment his heart began to beat quickly. He felt his face getting very warm as the memories of that morning in the Hamptons flooded into his mind with great intensity. The spiritual friends present in the bedroom inspired him to continue remembering, and he then recalled Penelope saying to him that morning:

"This is the place I run to any time I need to feel safe."

Immediately he stood up and said to Amelie, "The Hamptons! She might have taken Katie and Victoria to her house in the Hamptons. It's a kind of a sacred place for her where she always goes whenever she's upset or needs some time on her own." He jotted down the directions to the house on a piece of paper and handed it to Amelie, saying, "Here, please let the police know the address and tell them to go to the house as soon as possible. I'll drive there now before it's too late."

Chapter Reviving a fifteenth century tragedy

Katie was asleep on the bed in the master bedroom of the house in the Hamptons. Penelope had drugged her with a sleeping pill to stop her making any more noise. She was tied to the wooden bed and had smears of blood on her body and clothes; blood that had been left by the cuts on Penelope's hands. On the same bed where Katie slept, Penelope sat holding Victoria in her arms. She looked totally out of her mind. Her hands were smothered with blood from when she had smashed the mirror in the bathroom earlier. She was holding Victoria's body extremely tightly against her chest.

"You have no way out, Penelope. You are going to jail," whispered Filomena in her ear. "The police are searching for you. They will blame you for kidnapping the children and, worse, they will jail you for trying to kill your baby."

Immediately Penelope's soul captured Filomena's vibration, and she felt even more tormented.

"Mom would never try to kill you. You know that, don't you?" she said, pressing Victoria even more tightly against her chest. "Mom was a bit upset with you for what happened, but I forgive you. I forgive you for making mom look ugly." Tears ran down her face.

Victoria was very sensitive to all the bad energy around her, which had been brought by the many evil spirits surrounding Penelope. She started to cry loudly, at which Penelope quickly put her down on the bed and stood up, looking extremely disturbed.

"No! No noise. Mom can't do with noise now." Penelope rifled through one of her bags looking for the tube of sleeping pills, but couldn't find it. She put her hands over her ears and left the bedroom.

Filomena followed her downstairs, hissing hurtful remarks to her non-stop to increase her agony. Filomena was taking a lot of pleasure from her behaviour, while Fortunada remained quiet and apprehensive.

"You lost everything. You lost your properties, you lost your fancy cars, your companies, your private jet and …" Filomena shouted even more loudly, "You lost your beauty! It's all gone, Marta!"

Penelope screamed as she ran down the stairs. She had such a throbbing headache that she started to hallucinate. She was suddenly surrounded by a multitude of horrible creatures; some looked like beasts, some like dark shadows and others resembled walking skeletons. Her vision went blurry and all at once the spiritual world became totally visible to her. All the evil spirits who were surrounding her and tormenting her all that time were there, right in front of her, and for the first time she could see them all. Scared witless by what she was seeing, she threw her arms in the air as if trying to fend off the creatures, but they wouldn't be put off. Filomena, who was enjoying the whole scene, appeared in front of her and celebrated the fact that she was finally visible to Penelope.

"Finally we reunite, Marta," said Filomena.

"Go away! Go away!"

"How does it feel to have lost everything you had, even your looks?" asked Filomena, laughing at her.

"What do you want from me? Where is my house? Where did you take me to?"

"You are still in your house, you silly…well, now its Nigel's house, since you lost everything!" replied Filomena.

The other evil spirits came closer and closer to Penelope, which freaked her out completely. She staggered backwards in the living room, trying to escape from them. Once she reached the wall she felt the warmth of the fireplace, which gave her an idea. Quickly she reached out for one of the vintage wooden weapons displayed on the wall by the fireplace as part of the decoration. She began to slash it through the air, trying to strike the spirits, but this had no effect; the evil spirits continued to close in and attack her. Some of them were old enemies of hers who had passed away many years ago, and now joined the sisters in tormenting her. Others were attracted by her behaviour and addictions to drugs and alcohol. They were all shouting different things; some clamoured for revenge, while others were urging her to drink or take drugs so they could feed from her addiction. In panic,

Penelope shoved the wooden weapon in the fireplace until it caught alight, then again she waved it through the air, trying to hit the spirits with the fire to drive them away.

Upstairs in the bedroom, Katie woke up feeling very dizzy and confused. She saw Victoria's little body laid next to her, crying and wriggling non-stop. She could hear Penelope's shouting in the lower level of the house, screaming names and swearing very loudly. Using all her strength, Katie tried to break loose from the sheets which Penelope had used to tie her to the bed, but the knots were too tight. She looked again at Victoria and noticed that she had gone red. She moved her face to the side in the direction of her sister and, with a lot of effort, she managed to get her forehead to touch Victoria's face.

"You're so hot, Vicky…You're not well!" she cried in panic, and then screamed out, "Help! Please, help!"

At the same moment, Victoria started to cry even more loudly. Penelope, still in the living room brandishing the burning wooden weapon, came out of her trance as soon as she heard the screaming. Her focus changed back to reality and the images of the evil spirits vanished. Dropping the wooden spear on the floor, she ran up the stairs towards the bedroom.

"What are you up to?" she shouted angrily at Katie as she stormed into the room.

"Nothing," said Katie, nearly crying. "Vicky isn't well. There's something wrong with her. She's burning!"

"Oh shut up, you little brat!" Penelope shouted, tightening the knots made with the bed sheets.

"Why are you hurting me? Why have you brought us here?"

"Shut up, I said!" Penelope screamed, then slapped Katie's face. "You drive me mad with your voice, you spoilt kid!" Putting her face very close to Katie's, she glared into her eyes and growled, "Do you want to know why I'm hurting you?"

Katie closed her eyes so she didn't have to look at her. Penelope continued, with anger in her voice, "It's because I hate you! I can't stand you. You remind me of your mother. She was a redneck and you're a redneck too. You smell like a redneck, you look like a redneck and that's why I hate you!"

With her eyes still closed, Katie thought of her mother and asked her for protection. *'Please mommy, please help me...help me....'*

Penelope shook the girl's head, telling her to open her eyes and face her. "I want you to look at me. Remember how beautiful I was? Every man desired me; every woman envied my beauty. My friends were jealous of me. They all wanted to be me, and now...now this is what your..." Looking furiously at Victoria, she continued, "your monster sister did to me. She came into this world as a beast and destroyed me."

 Penelope went across the bedroom to her suitcase and opened it. She took out handfuls of jewellery: necklaces, watches, diamond rings and bracelets. She removed all the items of jewellery from the suitcase and put them on one by one. She adorned her arms with the many watches and bracelets, then frenetically put every one of the diamond rings on her fingers. Katie opened her eyes and couldn't believe what she was seeing. Very scared, she stared at Penelope who was now putting dozens of necklaces around her neck. Finally she put a tiara made of diamonds and other precious stones on her head. At that moment Katie closed her eyes again, and crying quietly, she prayed, asking for help. Once Penelope had finished decorating herself, she then took the last item from the suitcase: the gold-plated revolver. She pointed it at Katie's face and said firmly, "Open your eyes and face me!"

Terrified, Katie did as she was told and saw the golden revolver pointed at her, just inches from her face. Her entire body went cold and she was convulsed by panic.

"I am going to kill you!" Penelope counted down from three to one and pulled the trigger.

A click sounded from the revolver and Penelope broke into manic laughter, saying, "Scary, isn't it? There are no bullets, your silly brat!" Still laughing, she continued, "I won't kill you quickly like this...I want you to suffer, little Katie."

Linda was in the bedroom alongside Katie, together with the dozens of evil spirits who were still there, tormenting Penelope. Linda made a barrier in front of Katie to protect her from the evil spirits who kept swearing and laughing at her, telling her how powerless she was. Filomena laughed cruelly at Linda, telling her, "It seems like we'll drive Marta to kill Carmen once again. We did it once and now we're going to do it again. This is so you will know our power, you silly one. You, Justa, always thought you were so superior to us, but look what happened to you. Back in Spain we managed to get you and your husband Ager sentenced to a lifetime in prison, and now here we are again, just about to kill three people all in one go. Where is your God now?"

"You don't hold any power, only God does," Linda replied calmly. "If God permitted that to happen it was because it was in his plans, not because you made it happen. Stop spending your time focusing on Marta's life. Only in that way will you evolve and progress."

While Fortunada kept herself quiet in a corner, watching the whole scene, Filomena kept on insulting Linda, who didn't lose her temper but continued, with the same kind and soft tone to her voice, "Have you not realised that while you've been focusing on other's lives, trying to cause misery to Marta and many others, you only managed to get yourselves stuck in time, and you only attracted more and more misery to your existence? All the bad you've done to others has been returned, much worse, to you." Looking at Katie and Victoria on the bed, Linda asked Filomena, "What do you gain from trying to make others suffer? All of those you tried to hurt are evolving and moving on, while you two are here, depriving your spirits of progress and evolution."

"Marta doesn't. She is ours. She is as evil as we are, and we won't allow her to join you," said Filomena, very close to Linda.

"You are not evil. You were not created to be evil. You choose to live your life in misery but that's not what you were created for. Marta hasn't progressed, it's true - though not because of your actions against her, but only as a result of her own bad choices. Once she decides to leave all her rage and bad actions behind, she will progress like any other spirit, independent of your actions, Filomena. Don't ignore the universal law of action and reaction: every evil and bad vibration you send to someone returns back to you multiple times. Stop right now and come home, come to a spiritual colony where you'll find support and assistance. Here, on the side where we are, life is only happiness and bliss."

Penelope was pulling her hair out with both hands, suffering from a terrible headache. She sat down on a chair next to the window, facing the bed where Victoria and Katie were. Her mind had become even more confused and disturbed.

"It's time…You are ugly now, Penelope. Nobody wants you and nobody ever will. Kill the little brat and the beast in the shape of a baby, and then kill yourself! It's the best you can do," said Filomena.

Suddenly Fortunada fell to the floor, sobbing. She curled herself up and cried with deep sorrow. At the same time a very tall guardian angel from the rescue spirit group arrived in the bedroom, brightening the whole place with an immense light. On his arrival, immediately all the evil spirits quickly retreated to a corner of the room and huddled together, scared of the towering angel.

"Oh angel Gabriel, to whom I have always been devoted... Please…" Fortunada dropped her head, still crying. "Please, I beg for mercy. I can't live this life any more. So many centuries I've wasted. So many opportunities of happiness left behind. I don't want to have to spend all my time chasing Marta any more. I'm sorry for all I have done. Please, God, forgive me."

 The angel spread his enormous wings across the whole room and his light increased its intensity, making the bedroom even brighter. He picked Fortunada up and lifted her, holding her against his chest. He then enfolded her with his enormous wings, and seconds later they had both vanished. The angel was taking Fortunada to a spiritual colony where she could be given assistance and support.

"She is gone…" said Filomena, looking lost. "You…" she said, pointing her finger at Linda, "You have taken my sister away from me. How dare you!"

"She has gone to a recovery colony where she can learn about all the mistakes she committed and receive support to start her life again. She's gone to the same place you should go, so as to escape this life of misery and sorrow."

"Oh shut up, you. I ain't going anywhere."

Suddenly they were interrupted by the sound of a scream. It was Roy who had arrived downstairs and shouted Penelope's name.

"Penelope? Where are you? Where are my kids?"

One of the living room windows shattered into pieces seconds after Roy's scream. The burning wooden spear Penelope had dropped earlier had set the living room alight, and much of the ground floor of the house was now on fire.

"What have you done? The house is on fire!" he shouted desperately. Realising he couldn't get in through the entrance door as the entire living room was ablaze, Roy frantically raced around the house until he reached the back yard, then barged down one of the back doors, gaining entry to the kitchen, which had a clear passage to the interior of the house.

He shouted desperately, "Where are my daughters? Penelope, answer me, where are you?"

"Get out, Roy, Get out of here or you'll die too!" shouted Penelope from the bedroom.

"We're here in the bedroom, dad! Penelope has gone crazy. Run!" shouted Katie.

Roy stared for a moment at the flames, which were now close to the foot of the stairs, then ran past them and up to the next floor.

"What have you done?" he screamed, bursting into the bedroom. "The house is on fire! Were you planning to kill yourself and my daughters?" Roy quickly undid the knots in the sheets that tied Katie to the bed.

Penelope, holding Victoria in her arms, walked backwards towards the bedroom window, saying "Go away…Go away, Roy, or I will hurt her!"

Roy quickly checked that the fire hadn't yet spread to the stairs and told Katie to leave. "Go, sweetheart, go. Go downstairs and get out of the house through the back where there's no fire. Go, quickly! I'll follow you as soon as I get Victoria."

Katie hesitated, feeling scared, but Roy didn't want to waste another second, afraid that the fire could engulf the stairs at any moment and make their escape impossible. "Go Katie, go!"

He turned back to Penelope and said, "I know everything, Penelope. I know about your disgusting affair with Nigel and, worse, I know about your murder attempt! How could you have done such a monstrous act against your own baby?"

Penelope was shaking badly and tears were coming down her face.

"You've gone completely insane!" Roy shouted. "How could I not have seen this before? I was totally blind!" He threw himself towards her, trying to get hold of the baby. "Come on, give me Victoria. We've got to get out of here before this whole place burns down!"

Penelope pressed the baby even tighter against her own body, refusing to let him take Victoria.

"I didn't try to kill her. I would never try to kill my baby!"

"This isn't time for your lies, Penelope. Give me Victoria, we've got to go." Roy tried again to take the baby from her arms but again Penelope pulled her away from him.

"I'm not lying. I poisoned the water…yes I did. But I wanted to kill that Latina. I wanted to get her out of our lives. Not my baby. I could see that Latina was trying to take you away from me. She started first with the kids by being nice to them and playing the good mommy, but her plan was to take you away from me. She wanted to be me!"

"We haven't got time for this now, Penelope. We'll die here if we don't get out right now! Give me Victoria and let's go!"

Suddenly car sirens could be heard, announcing the arrival of the police outside the house. Penelope walked quickly towards the chair by the window and picked up the golden revolver. She pointed it at Victoria's body and said, "They won't catch me, Roy. I refuse to lose everything I have. I'll die and I will take my baby with me."

The black smoke from the fire had reached the top of the stairs and was now rapidly filling the bedroom.

"I never tried to kill her. Believe me, Roy!"

"It's not time for this now. We have to get out!"

Penelope's whole body was shaking. Next to her, Filomena was telling her not to hand over the baby. "I wanted to hate her...hate her for what she's done to me, but I couldn't. Every day when nobody was around I sneaked into her bedroom and watched her. Sometimes I even played with her." Tears were rolling down her face and dripping on the baby. "She is so beautiful, isn't she? Sometimes I see her as a beast, a beast that destroyed my life, but sometimes I don't. I feel so confused, Roy."

"Come on! Let's go!" Roy was growing more impatient. He knew the fire was getting worse and they probably had only moments before the bedroom was in flames. The police outside were shouting through a megaphone for her to leave the house.

"Do you believe me, Roy? Do you believe I never tried to kill my baby?"

The black smoke was becoming more intense, while on the ground floor the flames had now reached the foot of the stairs. Roy was terrified she would pull the trigger of the revolver. "I believe you, Penelope, I believe you! Now let's go!"

"Dad!" Katie had come back into the bedroom. "There's no bullet. She told me before that there's no bullet in the gun. She's lying."

That was all Roy needed in order to take action. He immediately flung himself towards Penelope and elbowed her. She dropped the revolver and Roy managed to grab Victoria with his other arm. Once he was holding her safely in his arms, Roy kissed her forehead, gasping in relief, "You're safe now, dear," before running to the bedroom door, shouting, "Come on Katie! Come on Penelope, let's get out of here."

Roy walked swiftly but carefully down the stairs, holding Victoria in his arms. *'Hold on, my darling. Be strong. Dad loves you. I want you more dearly than anything in this world... please be strong,'* he thought, keeping her close to his face and kissing her. Katie walked just behind him with both arms around his waist. There were flames all around them as they descended. When they reached the ground floor, Penelope suddenly pulled Katie away from Roy. Katie screamed but Roy, distracted by the smoke and flames, didn't hear. Roy lowered his body and ran through the back of the house, carefully threading a path through the flames. The smoke was now affecting his lungs and he started to cough, losing his breath. With great determination he continued stumbling awkwardly through the house, carrying Victoria, until they managed to escape into the open air.

Once outside, Roy found the back garden packed with policemen and fire-fighters. A paramedic took hold of Victoria, while another approached Roy. At that moment, Roy was shocked to notice that Katie was missing. Realising that she must still be in the house, he ran back inside, pushing aside the paramedic who tried unsuccessfully to stop him. Roy knew he had to rescue Katie.

Inside the house, the smoke was now very intense and it was stiflingly hot. Roy, still coughing and having great difficulty breathing, couldn't see anything as the whole house was filled with black smoke.

"Katie? Penelope? Where are you? You must get out of here now!"

Katie couldn't cope with the heat and fainted, falling on the floor near Penelope, who laughed "We will die together!" Hearing her voice, Roy was able to tell where they were.

"Stop this, Penelope! Let's get out of here!" Roy tried to approach her, but just then a large piece of burning wood crashed down next to Penelope, the deafening noise scaring her. Taking advantage of her distraction, Roy pushed her away and managed to grab Katie from the floor. Penelope fell backwards. Another length of flaming wood, much bigger than the first, smashed to the floor in between them. The whole ground floor was now totally engulfed by fire, and the dense black smoke was everywhere, making it almost impossible to see or breathe. Holding Katie in his arms, Roy bent down slightly to shield his face, then walked quickly through the corridor to the kitchen. Almost completely exhausted, he somehow managed to draw on his last reserves of strength and drag himself and Katie to the outside of the house. Once across the patio, he lost consciousness and collapsed. The paramedics immediately rushed to him and Katie, carrying them both safely away from the smoke.

Inside the house, the entire ceiling of the living room and the hallway collapsed, making a colossal noise. Trapped by the concrete and wood that had fallen,

Penelope had no way to escape. She was about to be burned alive. She screamed in pain as she felt her flesh being consumed by the flames. As the fluidic laces became loose, her spirit stepped back from her corporeal body and she then witnessed in horror and agony her own body burning. Filomena, Dynamite and the other evil spirits were there, watching with pleasure the death of her corporeal body. They surrounded her in a wide circle, then moved nearer and nearer, closing the circle around her until they all reached her at the same time. Penelope was screaming, partly because of the excruciating pain, but also because of the horror of watching all those terrible creatures surrounding her. The death of her corporeal body, leading to the freedom of her spirit, took hours; long hours of pure agony, pain and horror for Penelope. Once her corporeal body had died and her spirit was finally set free, Dynamite, Filomena and the other spirits got hold of her and took her to the dark regions.

Outside the house, several firemen had hoses trained on the building, trying to extinguish the fire. The paramedics performed first aid on Roy, Katie and Victoria before taking them in an ambulance to the local hospital where they could be treated. Minutes after they arrived at the hospital, Roy suffered a cardiac arrest and his heart stopped.

Chapter Roy meets Linda

Roy opened his eyes. He could hear a very gentle female voice calling his name.

"Roy…Wake up…Wake up, Roy"

Slowly he recovered consciousness and his vision became clearer, revealing the woman next to him. It was Linda.

"Roy?" she said.

Speaking with difficulty, Roy asked, "Linda, is that you?"

Linda nodded and smiled.

Feeling confused, he asked her, "Have I died?"

"Your corporeal body and your spirit suffered major injuries in the fire. It was a huge trauma for you. Our doctors have refuelled your soul with vital fluids, and you've now been granted by our Lord more time on Earth to continue your experience."

Roy felt scared. The fire was still very vivid in his memory. He was stricken by panic. Linda, noticing his agitation, said softly, "It's all alright now. Katie and Victoria had some minor injuries, but they are well now and are being cared for."

"Who's looking after them?"

"Days ago, I began to inspire Elizabeth and Joey to pay Katie a surprise visit, and it worked very well. Guided by my thoughts and inspiration, they arrived in New York City on the day when Penelope kidnapped the children. Elizabeth and Joey were shortly told by the police and Amelie about what was happening. They are now at the hospital with Victoria and our Katie. Everything is going to be okay." She put her right hand softly around Roy's face and continued, "I'm so happy for you. You made it. You finally learnt unconditional and true love. You set yourself free from your addiction to human material things. You put your spiritual needs above the material, and this is the beginning of your way back to God."

"I'm sorry, Linda. I'm sorry for what I've done to you. I should never have got involved with Penelope. I feel so ashamed now."

"Don't worry about me, Roy. I never had to forgive you simply because I understood that you weren't ready at that time to truly love someone. I couldn't expect from you something you didn't have to give. It was part of your journey, part of your own development to meet Penelope and experience what you have just been through. It seems as if you've learnt that God lives where the unconditional love exists. The unconditional love is to love everyone and everything in this world as you love God."

She kissed his forehead and finished by saying, "Go back, my dear friend. Go back there and be very happy. Your wife and children are waiting for you to return home. We will meet again one day."

"I'm confused - did you say wife?"

"You'll soon understand what I mean. Bye for now, Roy."

Immediately after hearing Linda's words, Roy returned to life as the defibrillator resuscitated his body.

Chapter The Forgiveness

Days later, Roy had recovered sufficiently to be removed from intensive care and taken to a room where he could receive visitors. When he entered, on a wheelchair pushed by a nurse, he found the room filled with flowers and balloons. The first person he saw there was Katie, skipping with delight, overjoyed to see him. She came up to his wheelchair and gave him a kiss.

"Be careful, Katie. Dad is still very hurt. You mustn't touch him because of his burns," said Elizabeth, who was holding Victoria in her arms.

Next to Elizabeth was Joey, who greeted Roy with a big smile. "Welcome back to life, Roy. The doctors said you nearly died."

Roy was very surprised to see Elizabeth and Joey there in the hospital. They seemed happy to see him, which he found strange, considering the way he had left North Carolina and how upset they had been when they found out about his affair with Penelope. Roy smiled back at them, and before he could say anything, Ricky dashed into the room, giggling and waving a bouquet of flowers in the air.

"Mr Roy! Mr Roy, I got this for you. Look!"

Elizabeth, concerned that he might hit Roy with the flowers, gently stopped Ricky and said, "They're gorgeous. Aren't they, Roy? Give them to me, Ricky, and I'll ask a nurse to bring a vase."

"Yes, they are gorgeous. Thanks Ricky," said Roy, looking surprised to see Ricky there too.

"It's alright. My mom bought it just now. We went down to the flower shop near the hospital and…"

Ricky continued talking non-stop, but at that point Roy looked at the doorway and saw Dolores standing there. His heart thumped. He noticed that her long, dark hair looked even wavier than before, and also her natural skin glow had returned. Roy and Dolores stared at each other for a few seconds that felt to them like minutes. Dolores gave him a shy smile and, rearranging her hair, said, "Hi, Roy. We only came in to give you these flowers and say that we're really happy that you've recovered and are doing well."

Roy looked down as he remembered the things he had said to her while she was in prison. Feeling embarrassed, he replied by simply saying thanks.

"Dad, dad!" said Katie excitedly. "Ricky's now back living with his mother. Isn't it great that they're both together again! I told him that when you leave the hospital they can go back to living with us like they used to."

"But not with Mrs Green, right?" Ricky asked Katie.

Everyone fell into an awkward silence, then Ricky guiltily said, "Oh mom, I'm sorry. I know you told me not to say anything about Mrs Taylor being dead."

"Ricky! Come here now!" exclaimed Dolores, beckoning him. She looked at Elizabeth and Joey and said, "I'm sorry, perhaps we'd better leave you all alone. I know you have a lot to talk about."

Roy had his head bowed down, while Katie asked Dolores not to leave. Joey stepped forward and said, "Katie, why don't you go with Dolores and Ricky while grandma and I have a word with your dad?"

"Okay, grandpa!"

"Dolores, maybe we could go out for a coffee, what do you think? Elizabeth and I just need to have a quick word with Roy first. I'm sure he needs to rest, so perhaps we can join you and the kids in ten or fifteen minutes at that coffee shop on the corner?"

"That sounds great, Mr Cooper," said Dolores, and she looked at Roy, but he avoided eye contact with her.

Elizabeth handed Victoria over to Dolores, who left the room carrying her, with Ricky and Katie following.

Once there were just the three of them left in the room, Elizabeth said, "It seems like we're predestined to fetch you from hospitals, Roy. This must be the third time we've visited you in a hospital!"

"I promise you this time it wasn't my fault!" he laughed, but quickly stopped when he realised that she hadn't found it funny.

"Well…I wouldn't say this isn't your fault."

Joey gave her a disapproving look and said, "Elizabeth! That's not why we are here, remember?"

Roy thought for a moment about her words, then said, "You're right, Elizabeth. I put myself in this situation didn't I? I chose to be with Penelope. I was blind and obsessed about that lifestyle and the riches I could suddenly surround myself with…and I guess this is the result of my obsession."

"Roy, we're not here to talk about the past. We all know what happened. The only useful thing about the past is that we can actually learn from it and don't repeat the same mistakes again. Let's move on," Joey said with a sort of softness in his eyes.

"I thought you two were angry at me for... you know…for what I did to Linda."

"Yes we are." Elizabeth looked at her husband and corrected herself. "I mean, we were. We were indeed very, very angry at you." Tears ran down her face as she remembered her daughter, and she continued, "It did hurt, Roy, because it didn't just feel like you betrayed our daughter, but it was like you had betrayed us two as well. We know we had our differences when you two got married, but in the end we got so close to you that it was as if you were a son to us."

Roy had tears in his eyes too. He looked up at Elizabeth and lifted his right hand to her. She took it and held it carefully.

Elizabeth went on, "When Linda passed away, you and Katie became the most important people in our lives. We learnt to love you, Roy, as if you were a son. When you two went away, when you moved to New York, we missed you so much."

"I can imagine how much you've missed Katie. She loves you two a lot…"

Elizabeth interrupted Roy by saying, "We also missed you, Roy. We felt so angry with you, so disappointed for what you had done to our daughter and to your family, but with time we realised that our anger was working against us. We were distancing ourselves from you and Katie and so we became very unhappy. We carried so much anger and sorrow, and those feelings were like a poison that took the best of us away and filled our souls with sadness and misery."

Joey took over from Elizabeth. "The disappointment and the anger we felt for what you'd done vanished, and all of those bad feelings were substituted by our love for you and Katie. Love healed the wounds and it took the suffering away." He dried his tears and continued. "Months ago, Dolores found our telephone number and called us - it seems Katie asked her to - and so we got in contact with our Katie again. We began to talk quite often on the phone, not just with Katie but also with Dolores."

"So you two have made a relationship with Dolores all along?"

"Yes," replied Joey, "knowing that Dolores was the one closest to our Katie, we knew it was important to get to know her better, and we built up this relationship over the phone. Dolores used to call and keep us updated on how Katie was doing, and we also used to telephone her to ask about Katie. It was a few weeks ago, when Dolores said how worried she was about Penelope's strange behaviour, that we sensed something bad was about to happen."

Elizabeth continued the story. "We bought flight tickets, booked a hotel room for the week and decided to come and pay a surprise visit to you all. We thought we were going to visit you at home and try and get our relationship sorted out. The day we arrived in New York City, we went straight to the address of your apartment that Dolores had given us. When we got there we met this lady called Amelie, and she told us everything that had happened. We actually arrived at your apartment minutes after you left for the Hamptons," said Elizabeth, still holding Roy's hand. "God, we felt so scared. We didn't know what was happening. We learnt that Dolores was in jail and that Katie and Victoria had gone missing all at the same time. It was awful!"

Not wanting to bring such horrible memories back to Roy, Joey looked at Elizabeth and gave her a sign to drop the subject. He said, "Well, it's all fine now. You're all safe now."

"The fire!" shouted Roy suddenly. The memory of that evening in the burning house in the Hamptons shot back into his mind. Shivers went up Roy's spine and his heart accelerated. He remembered what Ricky had said moments earlier about Penelope, and looking in horror at Joey, he asked, "Has she..."

Joey and Elizabeth looked at each other, and it was Joey who replied, "Yes, Roy. The fire-fighters tried to get inside the house but the ceilings had collapsed completely, and..."

"She burned to death," said Roy, inadvertently speaking his thoughts out loud in shock.

"The funeral was yesterday," said Elizabeth. "Dolores looked after the kids while Joey and I went to the funeral. We were the only people there. It was very sad. Let's pray for her soul to find light and forgiveness. It's the best thing to do."

Tears rolled down Roy's face. Deep down, he knew Elizabeth was right; the best thing to do was to forgive what she had done and wish peace to her soul.

"How ironic. She always called you rednecks, and in the end you were the only ones to pay the final respects to her at her funeral," Roy said.

"Well, let's not think about that. As I said, let's pray for her to find light and mercy from God."

"By the way, did you say that Dolores stayed looking after the kids?" Roy asked.

"Yes, she did. She is such a kind and caring woman, Roy. You are very lucky she came along into your life."

"Darling, Dolores is waiting for us, remember? I guess Roy needs some time to rest." Joey pointed toward the door with his head.

"You're right. Let's go." Looking at Roy with tenderness in her eyes, she said, "We rented an apartment here, Roy. You, Katie and Victoria can stay there until you manage to sort everything out and decide what you're going to do."

"Do you also know that I lost everything I had?" said Roy. He explained about the papers Penelope had signed, transferring all the properties over to Nigel. "I'm without a penny to my name."

Elizabeth replied, "The day we arrived at your apartment, while we were talking to Amelie, a man told us that he needed the place to be cleared out by the morning. He didn't seem very friendly, and he explained that you'd all been thrown out of the apartment. We sort of figured out that something had gone wrong, but let's not talk about this now. We're here to support you in whatever you might need." Elizabeth kissed his hand once more, and just as she was just about to leave she said, "I forgot to say that Dolores is leaving the USA for good. She and Ricky are going to live with some relatives in Colombia." She nodded and said, "Fight for her love, Roy."

Chapter A love reunion

Dolores looked around, hoping to see Roy and the kids. In her mind it would happen like the movies, where the guy arrives at the last minute and stops the lady from leaving. Romantic music plays in the background and the film finishes with a happy ending. She looked around one more time, and after realising Roy wasn't there she handed a small black bag to Rick and said, "Son, help mom with this bag, please."

She pushed the trolley across the airport, followed by Ricky, who was also feeling upset about leaving. They walked towards the airline check-in area, both feeling nostalgic and unsure about their departure.

"How is Medellin, mom? Is it close to the beach?" asked Ricky, looking unimpressed.

"No son, it's a beautiful city but it's not by the sea." Noticing that Ricky looked sad, Dolores stopped and went down on her knees facing Ricky. "I promise you that you'll love Colombia. The people there are very nice and you'll see your aunt Lucie and your cousins."

"I don't even know who they are, mom."

'He's right,' she thought. *'My sister has never bothered telephoning or writing to me since I left Colombia.'* She tried to disguise the sadness she was feeling about

leaving, and smiled, saying, "Come on…We're together, aren't we? We're a team, aren't we?"

"Yes," Ricky said in a very quiet voice.

"What? I didn't hear you, son. We're a team, right?" She tickled him on his side and Ricky began to giggle.

"YES!" he shouted, laughing and giving her a high five.

"Much better now."

****

In the east village in New York, at the rented apartment, Elizabeth, Joey, Roy and the kids were also ready to leave New York City. Roy had accepted Elizabeth and Joey's invitation to return to North Carolina. He had also contacted his previous boss and managed to get his old job back. Joey bought a second-hand car for the journey back home and they had spent the whole of the previous day packing and preparing for their trip.

That morning Roy helped Joey load the car with the final bits and pieces, but his heart was sad as he thought of Dolores. He had learnt from Elizabeth that Dolores was supposed to fly to Colombia that day, and fond memories of the moments they spent together were coming up non-stop in his mind. He watched everyone getting into the car, still pensive and nostalgic, staring at the street, thinking of Dolores. He was even missing Ricky's laughter and joy and his questioning of everything. Roy remembered a moment with Ricky:

They were both at Central Park playing football while Dolores was sitting on the grass with Katie and Victoria. Ricky had stopped playing to ask Roy why the grass felt so soft and why it always looked green. Roy then grabbed Ricky's cap, dragged him closer and said, smiling, "Do you know what? I will call you Little Mr Why."

"Why you are going to call me that, Mr Taylor?" asked Ricky with his usual confused look.

"That's why, Little Mr Why...Because you always ask Why!" he giggled. Roy then picked Ricky up in the air, and holding him, he ran towards the spot where Dolores was sitting with the kids. Dolores looked at them both and smiled. It was the most beautiful smile Roy had ever seen...

"Go after them, Roy. They need you as much as you need them," whispered Linda softly in his ear.

The memory faded away and he was brought back to reality by Joey calling him and asking him to get in the car. Roy sat on the passenger's seat and said, "Can you take me to J.F. Kennedy airport, Joey? Please?"

Realising at once what Roy's intentions were, Joey replied, "She's flying in two hours, Roy. I don't think we'll make it...unless by some miracle her flight gets delayed."

"Let's try!" exclaimed Roy.

****

"Mom, we've been waiting here for ages...It feels like a whole day."

"I know, son. The lady said the flight's delayed. They'll soon call us."

"It feels like ages...and I'm very hungry."

Dolores opened her hand luggage, grabbed a sandwich she had made before leaving the house and handed it to Ricky.

"Mmm… Ham and cheese!" he said, looking happy when he saw the sandwich. He unwrapped the cling film and bit into it eagerly.

"Mom…?" he asked while chewing.

"What now, son?"

"Why is our flight delayed? Is it because they have to fill it with gasoline?"

"I don't know son, but they should call us soon."

Suddenly an announcement boomed out, informing everyone that the flight to Bogota was going to depart in forty five minutes. All passengers were to make their way to the security check quickly and go to the gate.

Dolores stood up, picked up the bags from the floor and urged Ricky to hurry. "Here we go. Come on, keep the rest of your sandwich in your bag and let's get inside. We'll be flying shortly now."

They approached the queue for the first security check and an airport staff member took their tickets to check their boarding passes.

"Lady, why do you need to check this? Is it because …"

Dolores looked at Ricky and said, "Come on Ricky, not now son!"

"Dolores!" shouted Roy, running across the airport. "Dolores, wait!"

Dolores couldn't believe what she was seeing. Roy was running across the terminal, bumping into people, jumping over luggage on the ground and waving at her. Behind him was Katie, also running. She could see Elizabeth, holding baby Victoria, and Joey following behind too.

"Mom, look! It's Mr Taylor and Katie! Wow, look, Katie's parents are here too with Vicky!"

Roy was shouting loudly. "Wait! Don't leave…Please!"

The people behind Dolores and Ricky in the queue were all staring at the scene, and they were all smiling. When Roy finally reached Dolores and Ricky he was out of breath and the words would hardly come out of his mouth. He said, "I love you…" He took a long, deep breath so he could speak again and continued, "I never felt like this before in my life. It's all brand new and I don't want to stay apart from you for another minute."

Dolores' heart was beating fast. She looked deeply into Roy's eyes and moved forward towards him. He didn't think twice; he embraced her tightly and they both kissed passionately.

A few people in the queue behind them began to clap, and soon everyone around joined in the applause and cheered the loving couple.

Katie arrived and hugged Ricky. Soon they were joined by Elizabeth, Victoria and Joey. Dolores grabbed Ricky's hand and they freed the way for the others in the queue to go through.

Roy knelt down, looking at Ricky and said, "And I love you too, Little Mr Why."

Ricky smiled, feeling very happy, and they all embraced one another.

"Dolores, come to North Carolina with us. Let's start a new life together as a family," said Roy with a tearful eye.

Dolores looked at Roy and remained quiet. She glanced at her tickets and heard the airport announcement:

"Last call for the passengers of flight 2581 from Fly South airlines with destination Bogota. We ask the passengers for this flight to make their way to the boarding gate. This is the final call."

"So, mom… We're staying with Mr Taylor and Katie, right?" asked Ricky, begging with his eyes.

Dolores looked at Ricky and Katie, who were holding hands, and then at Roy. Her heart was racing and she knew that what she felt for Roy was true love. She beamed a smile and said, "Yes, son. We're going to North Carolina."

Roy kissed her again, and Joey, Elizabeth and the kids celebrated the start of a new life for their family.

Linda was there with them, accompanied by Teresa and Geraldine. The three of them were happily witnessing the joy of their loved ones and continued to watch as Roy, Dolores, Joey, Elizabeth and the kids, holding hands, left the airport, heading to their new life in North Carolina.

"God bless you, my loved ones," said Linda with a smile on her face. She imagined a beautiful yellow butterfly and it materialised outside the airport, right in front of Katie. The butterfly flew around every one of them, as if bringing them all a kiss from Linda, and then flew away across the sky.

Teresa and Geraldine reached out their hands to Linda. Teresa said, "They will be fine now, my dear. They are now at peace."

Linda gently took hold of Teresa's and Geraldine's hands and nodded, smiling.

Chapter Butterflies in the Garden

North Carolina, USA, ten years later

Dolores ran down the stairs quickly as she was behind schedule. She looked at the clock on the wall, worried they would be late if they didn't rush. She wore a beautiful red dress and had her curly dark hair tied up with small white flowers as ensembles. When she reached the bottom of the stairs she stopped and looked at Victoria, who was waiting impatiently by the door. Dolores stood still, staring at Victoria for several seconds. She couldn't help but admire her. She was now ten years and eleven months old, and was wearing a beautiful yellow dress.

"Why are you looking at me like that, mom?" asked Victoria, looking confused.

"I'm just admiring you, my princess." She walked over to Victoria, smiled and said, "You look gorgeous." Dolores kissed her forehead. In her head a movie played, reminding her of all the beautiful moments she had had with Victoria since she was a little baby.

"Why are you crying, mom? Are you feeling sad?"

Dolores cleared the tears from her face and replied, "No, my sweetheart. These are not tears of sorrow, but of joy."

Roy was watching the blissful scene as he came down the stairs. He touched Victoria's face gently and smiled, also with tears of joy in his eyes. At that moment Ricky came in from outside the house. He was now a teenager and had grown nearly as tall as Roy, but still had the same boyish face as he'd had when he was a child. Ricky opened his arms and urged the others to hurry.

"Come on dad, come on mom! Why are you two crying? Katie won't forgive us if we miss her speech. Let's hurry!"

"You're right. Let's go, we're already running late," said Roy, grabbing the car keys from his pocket and heading for the door.

The whole family got into the car and headed to Katie's school. When they arrived they saw a big sign written in blue capital letters which said:

<u>CONGRATULATIONS CLASS OF 1987</u>

Elizabeth and Joey were sitting in the front row of the audience. Next to them there were four empty seats they had reserved for Roy, Dolores, Victoria and Ricky. The family sat down just in time, as the high school principal was about to introduce Katie. She had been chosen by her class colleagues and the principal to be the one to perform the graduation speech. After the principal introduced her, Katie stood up and went to the centre of the stage. It was a lovely summer day. The sun was shining brightly and a fresh breeze blew on her face like a kiss blown by her mother. Katie adjusted the microphone stand to her height. She looked at her family and saw them sitting proudly in the first row. Katie gave them a smile and then began to deliver her speech.

"Here I stand. At my very first day at school I remember being very scared of going in and separating from my mother. I was most of all scared of the unknown. What would that new world be like for me? My mother was my whole world and I felt extremely insecure about the new world I was about to discover. My mom then told me: if you feel lonely or if you ever feel scared, think of me and I will be there with you in my thoughts. A small butterfly flew past us then, and my mom said, 'Watch for the butterflies, and every time you see one it's because I have sent it to look after you.'"

Katie paused for a moment as if she was about to cry, but she cleared her throat and continued. "My mother passed away a few months after I started school. I was only five years old. The entire world seemed to have collapsed on top of me. Everything changed, and life suddenly became a dark and scary place to be in. I felt lonely, I felt lost and I felt extremely fragile."

Roy had many tears streaming down his face at that moment. Elizabeth, next to him, held his hand tightly and rested her head on his shoulder. She was also in tears.

"I remember that when I was a child I used to look out for the butterflies in the garden, look for the butterflies in the streets, look for them everywhere. Every time I saw a butterfly I used to think that my mother had sent it down from heaven to show me that she was watching over me and looking after me. There were times when dark and difficult moments kept visiting me. Life became sad and scary, but I never felt lonely. I never lost the faith, simply because every time I saw a butterfly I used to pick myself up and renew my faith. I knew she was there watching over me."

Victoria and Ricky watched their sister with admiration in their eyes. Katie stopped for a moment to clear her throat again and continued:

"Now I look back at the difficult times and I know for a fact that my mom and God had never stopped looking after me. They sent many butterflies throughout my whole life to show me that everything was going to be okay. Those butterflies are here today. They are in fact all sitting in the front row of this audience. The butterflies can also be called family and friends. In the darkest moments God sent me dear friends who later became family, and whom I like to think of as butterflies that came to shine my way through the darkness towards a bright future." She blew a kiss towards her family members in the front row and carried on. "We are all here today finishing a moment of our lives. We are all very excited and ready to embark on a new journey. Some will go to a university here in North Carolina, some will change state and others will even change country. We all have different challenges ahead of us, but we are all about to face a common path; we are all going to face unknown changes in our lives. I would like to say to you: don't be afraid of your future. Keep the faith that God will always send you butterflies to brighten your way through. And never forget that we are never alone. God bless you all."

The graduating students stood up at the end of her speech and applauded her with great enthusiasm for a long time.

Linda, Geraldine and Teresa watched the scene with great happiness, admiring that moment of bliss.

Nigel had been arrested a few years earlier. Having become a global organizer for illegal drug trading, he was caught and given a lengthy jail sentence. He ended up being killed some months later, the victim of a violent attack by another prisoner. His spirit went straight to the dark regions. Still very attached to his evil thoughts, Nigel joined a group of malicious spirits and began to torment Penelope. Once again caught in the same destructive circle, the two of them became involved in an obsessive and damaging relationship, still making the same mistakes. It was only after many years that Penelope began to understand how damaging her mistakes were, not only to those around her but particularly to herself. She prayed for the first time, asking for help, and in the same instant received a visit from enlightened spirits who advised her to continue praying and, most importantly, to change her ways. They told her that once she improved her thoughts and behaviour she would be rescued and taken to a spiritual colony. Penelope followed their advice, and eventually the day of her rescue arrived; the same day as Katie's graduation. Penelope was at last going to be rescued and taken to a spiritual colony where she would be able to attend school and return to her spiritual journey. Linda, Geraldine and Teresa sent vibrations of love to Katie and her family and left the Earth. Feeling very happy, they headed to the dark regions to rescue Penelope.

Meanwhile, Katie's colleagues were still applauding her beautiful speech. Katie walked down from the stage and joined her family. They all hugged each other, feeling overwhelmed with love and happiness. Katie then ran back to the stage, where all her class mates joined her. Together they all took off their hats and threw them high up into the skies to celebrate their graduation. They were all looking forward to their new life opportunities that lay ahead.

The end.

About the author

Valter Dos Santos was born in Sao Paulo, Brazil. He has been living in London, UK, for the past ten years.

At the age of eight, Dos Santos had to cope with the loss of his mother, Mariluci, who passed away suddenly, the victim of a brain aneurism when she was at the tender age of thirty. Since a very young age, he started to look for answers which could give him the comfort for such a dramatic loss in his life. He found in the

Spiritism doctrine all the comfort he needed to continue his life, knowing that the death of the human body doesn't mean the end but only the passage of our spirit from the material world to the spiritual world.

He felt - and even saw - many times the presence of his deceased mother throughout his life. The most memorable and special experience was when, after recovering from a coma, he saw the spirits of his mother and his grandfather Benedito (who had passed away before Valter had been born). Both spirits had been around him and looking after his soul while his corporeal body had spent three days in a coma. Since then Valter Dos Santos has dedicated his life to studying both the Spiritism doctrine and the work of Allan Kardec.

His first romance, *The Truth Never Dies*, released in Europe and the USA in August 2012, was written with the intention to share with the readers all the comfort and peace he learnt from Spiritism. The romance quickly reached the number one spot in the Amazon US and UK lists (spiritual category). The author felt immensely grateful for all the support and care from his readers around the world, and especially for all the messages of support and encouragement that motivated him to continue writing.

Having lived in the UK for over ten years, Valter Dos Santos is very thankful to the country that welcomed him with so much warmth and gave him so many opportunities. He remembers that at the beginning things were difficult, needing a lot of hard work and determination. "I worked very hard doing jobs such as cleaning for companies and washing plates in restaurants. It wasn't easy but I never thought of giving up on my dreams," he says.

Nowadays Valter Dos Santos is a regional manager for a multinational company. He remembers his past with great emotion and is very grateful for every opportunity received in his life.

The author sends a message to his readers: Never give up your dreams. Throughout my life I heard a lot people telling me things like "You will never make it." Many others even told me that I would never be able to write a book or get my manuscript published. I never paid attention to those people. I preferred to listen to my heart and to those who offered me words of support and motivation. Most importantly, I always kept my faith in God. I strongly believe that those who live with God within will never fail.

If you wish to get in touch with the author you can visit his Facebook page:

www.facebook.com/valterdossantos.autor

The Truth Never Dies

(by Valter Dos Santos) Published in August 2012

The Truth Never Dies is a story of love and spirituality. The book tells the story of Michael, a young journalist, who passes away leaving his wife, Gina, and his three children. At the moment of his human body death, Michael is greeted by his mother, Harriet, who had passed away a few years before, and he then discovers that we never die and that we are infinite. Michael is taken to a spiritual colony named The Towers and is then mentored by Harriet and her long-term spiritual partner, Mateo, on the mysteries of the spiritual world. Everything goes well until, during a visit to his family on Earth, he discovers that life has carried on for his family, and that his wife may have strong feelings for another man. Heartbroken, Michael faces the dilemma of continuing on his spiritual journey or going against everything he has learnt so far and fighting for the love of his life. Michael's spiritual journey takes us on a discovery about the secrets of the afterlife, the spiritual world, our past lives and how they affect our present lives and the meaning of real love. 'Try to imagine death not as the end but as the freedom of our spirits towards the way back home.'

www.ingramcontent.com/pod-product-compliance
Lightning Source LLC
Chambersburg PA
CBHW030026180626
46810CB00001B/227